Recipe for Mr Right

Anni Rose

Book 1 – Recipes for Life

Where heroes are like chocolate – irresistible!

Copyright © 2022 Anni Rose

Published 2022 by Choc Lit Limited
Penrose House, Crawley Drive, Camberley, Surrey GU15 2AB, UK
www.choc-lit.com

The right of Anni Rose to be identified as the Author of
this Work has been asserted by her in accordance with
the Copyright, Designs and Patents Act 1988

A CIP catalogue record for this book is available
from the British Library

ISBN 978-1-78189-513-9

Printed and bound in Great Britain by Clays Ltd, Elcograf S.p.A.

Carole Dean (1945–2015)

*For the many hours of dog walks,
kitchen advice, "common gossip"
and laughter.*

Acknowledgements

People say that writing is a solitary process, but there are many people who have encouraged every step of my writing journey, to whom I owe huge thanks. Too numerous to mention in person, but Clockhouse Writers, especially Xenia and Hilary, Dunford Novelists, Jill Sharp and the Tuesday morning writers, for all your lovely comments, please take a bow. Keith, Jane and Sarah, first readers, grammar checkers, bacon and banana sandwich providers, inner critic silencers, imposter syndrome slayers. Without you, I would never have got this far. Mandy and Pauline, always a source of inspiration! And of course, the dogs who have listened in silence (usually) to endless readings of this novel.

Last but not least I'd like to thank everyone at Choc Lit and Ruby Fiction for giving me the opportunity to share this story with you – particularly the Tasting Panel readers who passed the original manuscript and made publication possible (Ruth Nägele, Shona Nicolson, Helen Maddison, Luise Piri, Amy Nordon, Jo Osborne, Isabelle D, Fran Stevens, Joy Bleach, Sharon Walsh, Julie Lilly, Cordy Swinton, Carol Botting, Yvonne Greene and Gill Leivers), and my lovely editor – thank you for your patience and making the whole process so enjoyable.

Prologue

'Good morning Redford! It's eight o'clock. Welcome to a new year.'

Ruby Brooks winched one eye open and then the other. Both stung. She flung one arm out, but without exerting a lot more effort than she was prepared to apply, she couldn't reach the radio to switch off the incessantly happy presenter. She groaned.

'Our resident astronomer says for the Virgos among you, this year looks like being a fabulous one.'

Great. At that moment, instant death seemed a more attractive proposition. Her tongue felt as rough as sandpaper and the taste sensation she was experiencing suggested she'd been force-fed pickled eggs all night.

'But don't rely on others. You need to make your own luck. The only thing holding you back is you,' the presenter said, cheerfully. 'It is time to get off your backside and achieve your goals.'

Ruby threw back her blue floral duvet.

Tights under pyjamas. *No way.*

She sat bolt upright and clutched the duvet to her chest. Bile raced to her throat.

The empty, un-dented pillow next to her did nothing to quell her feeling of nausea, but she was relieved. Clearly whatever happened last night, she hadn't ended up in bed with a one-night stand or worse – her ex.

Her head hurt.

Why can you never remember how painful hangovers are going to be beforehand? And why do so-called friends think

1

it's a good idea to keep plying you with drink when they know the likely outcome?

She popped two Alka-Seltzers into the glass by her bed, waited until the fizz subsided, then necked them in one gulp before she found the note:

Resolutions:
1 – ten competitions a day

Redford Radio's astrologer should be pleased. If that wasn't making her own luck, she didn't know what was.

2 – kill kitchen fitter
3 – dream job
4 – visit Japan
5 – don't sleep with Daniel – ever, ever again

Actually, five wasn't so much of a resolution, more a statement of intent and shouldn't be difficult. She hadn't bought her flat through his estate agency. He had no idea where she was living. Her mother and brother, Ben, had been sworn to secrecy. She'd warned what would happen if either of them ever gave Daniel so much as a single syllable of her address.

Ben would be far too worried about his looks to take a chance she was joking and he had witnessed what she was capable of once before with his Action Man, or more accurately these days – Action torso.

Chapter One

Ruby's desk overlooked the main entrance to the Union House flats and the visitors' car park. She watched the postman arrive. It wasn't the handful of post he wielded, more the large square parcel he retrieved from the back of his van, before heading for the main doors to the building, that intrigued her. To the point that if she hadn't known the Post Office had a key for the main door, she would've been tempted to rush round and wrestle the parcel away from him in the porch.

Moments later when her doorbell rang, she was beyond excited. Her mind flicked back to last month's competition entries. There was a car or two among them, certainly half a dozen holidays, gym equipment and she seemed to remember a seventy-five-piece hand-tool set being in there; except the box the postman was carrying didn't look big enough to hold a cantilever toolbox or saw.

'Who's it from?' She smiled, happy to relieve him of it.

'Dunno. It's for number six anyway,' he said as he took a small book out of his pocket and made a note in it. 'I stuck a card through their letterbox already.'

There were no tell-tale senders' details on the package. Just stamps. The addressee was an "A Finder, 6 Union House, Redford". There was no subtle way in. Every edge of the brown paper had been sealed with clear sticky tape. Ruby pushed it against the wall under the coats hanging between the kitchen and the sitting room. It was hard, solid and heavy.

Flat 6, upstairs, belonged to Jason, but he'd been in Paris since Christmas.

Tea ceremony in Japan what absolute bliss ...

A Finder must be the friend Jason said would be house-sitting while he was away. Think. Had he said "he" or "she"?

Ignore it. She needed to concentrate on a Japanese slogan.

Easier said than done. She picked up a pair of scissors; common sense returning in the nick of time. The "I didn't realise it wasn't mine" line was unlikely to wash seeing as she'd signed for it. The postman had told her it wasn't hers. The "it could have been a bomb" would only work if the flats were evacuated and the parcel immersed in a bath of water or blown up and scattered across the car park.

She took a deep breath and returned to her desk. She had an entry to finish ... *With Pyramid's tea bags too good to miss.*

Ceremony or time?

Too many syllables in ceremony, time scanned better. She repeated the caption back to herself, pausing in different places. It didn't get any better. Nothing short of a miracle was going to turn those fifteen words into a prize-winning entry. Ruby sniffed. On the plus side, it rhymed. She typed the couplet onto the electronic form, flicked through the terms and conditions, entered the ceremony date on her phone calendar, and pressed send before embarrassment kicked in and she changed her mind.

She pushed back from her desk and stretched. Morning had already rolled into afternoon. It was February and cold, and despite warnings about global warming, the two cars, she could see from her window, that hadn't moved all day, were still covered in thick ice.

The one set of tyre marks from the gate to the middle of the frosty tarmac confirmed what she already knew, that even if she hadn't been sat there staring out, the postman had been the flats' only visitor that day. No sign of her missing kitchen fitter.

She'd waited long enough.

Ruby sighed, tapped the number she knew by heart into her mobile and held it to her ear. She checked her teeth in her phone's camera app, while she waited for Kevin to ignore her – again – and for his voicemail to kick in.

It would have been so much easier to dump a lot of vitriol on his Twitter account or Facebook page, but Kevin King appeared to have no social media presence at all. Instagramming a photo of the shell of her kitchen with #dodgykitchenfitter might provide a degree of satisfaction, but he hadn't even got an email address, let alone an Instagram account, or if he had, he hadn't shared that information with her.

'I can't come to the phone right now.'

'There's a difference between can't and won't,' Ruby muttered between gritted but nice-looking teeth.

Kevin's recorded message ran through her options. There was no point writing them down. Five weeks into her self-imposed daily routine, all his numbers were imprinted on her brain. His mobile was the only one that allowed any sort of message to be left.

'Wait for the tone, tell me your problem, best contact number, you know the sort of thing, and I'll get back to you as soon as I can.'

The shrill beep signified it was her turn to start talking. Time to be emotionally mature. Don't overreact, lose your temper or swear. Deep breath and go for it.

'This is Ruby Brooks. I will keep this short and speak slowly in case the reason for your silence is you haven't understood my previous messages.' The last three words, she stressed for dramatic effect. 'I expected you this morning, as I did yesterday, last week, last month – actually, even last year. I realise now that when you said at the beginning of last December, "Relax, it will be finished before Christmas" I should have asked you to be more specific about which

Christmas and not assume we were talking about the same one, but I have to warn you my patience is wearing thin.'

Another pause. Thin? It had flaming holes in.

She started tapping her fingers. How dare he keep ignoring her.

Bugger it.

'I'm not going to spout some cliché about becoming your biggest nightmare. By the time I've finished with you, you'll wish you lived on Elm Street because, compared to me, Freddy Krueger will seem like a simple, misunderstood individual.'

One of today's competitions had been to link film characters to addresses. She was pretty certain she'd got Freddy right. It was either Elm Street or Sesame Street and she already had Big Bird down for that one.

'If you think I'm joking, speak to my brother. He knows what I'm capable of. He's still traumatised by my last amputation. Get your arse round here now.'

Ruby put her mobile down and frowned. The outburst hadn't done her much good. She felt flat. Chewed up and spat out again flat and she still had one more competition to go.

An email flashed up on her computer screen which did nothing to improve her mood. *Subject: All we need from you, Ruby, is a number.*

She'd read copious terms and conditions over the last few weeks. She'd indemnified various promoters for any loss, damage, death etc. she might suffer as a result of winning a potential prize, but somewhere she'd missed a "don't-give-my-details to anyone who asks or fill my inbox with your daily diatribes" small print on one of the competitions.

And somebody had.

She wiggled the mouse until the cursor hovered over the unsubscribe button. She wanted a car or a holiday to Japan, not an email exchange with a complete stranger. She hadn't wanted a pen pal at the age of ten; twenty-two years later her views hadn't changed.

On the other hand, a competition was a competition. She opened the email.

"We asked 100 people their average, annual condom consumption, collated their results and have come up with a number. What we want to know Ruby is, is it the same as yours? You could win three years' worth of condoms and trouble-free sex. One number, any number between 1 and 996. Reply to this email, with your annual anticipated usage in the subject line and leave the rest to us."

No need to like a Facebook page.

Nothing she had to share with a handful of unsuspecting friends.

Just one number.

Ruby typed 182, expecting her nose to grow. For the last two years anything other than zero would have been a lie, but she pressed "send" anyway.

Ten competitions done and dusted. Today's efforts, even without the Japanese trip, meant she could become the owner of a garden trug, doorbell, annual cinema pass, birds of prey experience, torch, two feather pillows, a housekeeper for a day, a year's supply of dog food and now 546 condoms. But there was no point getting excited.

Five weeks, two days and three hundred and seventy competitions into her competition year, her prize haul so far amounted to a DIY guide to writing your own will and a pair of rubber gloves. She googled uses for unwanted condoms anyway, because if nothing else, in that time she'd mastered the art of procrastination.

After another five minutes spent reading some highly

dubious and disturbing results, the noises coming from her stomach reminded her, she'd missed lunch as well as breakfast. Time to raid the fridge, which sat in the opposite corner of her sitting room, doubling up as a TV stand. Sadly, it contained only half a pint of milk, a jar of juniper berries and a large pot of yoghurt.

The juniper berries smelt lemony with a hint of pine, in a disinfectant sort of way. She couldn't remember why she bought them or when, but as she hadn't been shopping, yoghurt and juniper berries were going to have to be lunch, probably supper too. She was about to mix them when the serving suggestion on the label caught her eye.

'I've waited in all day!' Ruby flung her front door open, drink in hand, and glared at the man on her doormat, dressed from head to toe in black.

Oops, not her kitchen fitter. She took a large swig of her drink and froze.

A beanie hat covered the top half of the stranger's face, a scarf hid his nose and mouth. All she could see were eyes surrounded by dark lashes. Definitely not Kevin. Even allowing for the fact this man had no toolbox and didn't reek of smoke. Of course, it had been over two months since she'd last seen her kitchen fitter. He could have given up smoking, lost some weight, become a goth or joined the SAS in that time – but unlikely.

She took a step back and leant against the wall for support. It had been a mistake to drink on an empty stomach.

The man took a step back.

Not Daniel. This man was taller and more athletic than her ex.

Perhaps he had a skin condition, which meant he had to stay covered up at all times.

She smiled as sympathetically as she could just in case.

'How can I help?' she asked and took another swig of gin and juniper berries.

'You shot my pa,' he mumbled.

She choked on her mouthful of firewater and dropped the smile. Great, she'd just opened the door to a psychopath. 'Prove it,' she choked.

Double oops, that wasn't a considered response.

Had she really just asked the Milk Tray terrorist to produce a dead body?

'I've never shot anyone,' she added, cautiously. 'I've never used a gun.'

'What?' said Darth Vader, and pulled off his hat to reveal a messy haircut, tapered at the sides. A pair of seriously gorgeous eyes stared back at her as a warmth flushed through her body that had nothing to do with her drink. Shame he was crazy or worse.

'I got a card.' He thrust a small red postcard at her.

She pushed her fringe out of her eyes and read it well enough to get the gist. 'It says I've got your parcel,' she said, more than a little relieved.

'That's what I said.' His face softened and Ruby's insides twisted themselves into an intricate knot.

'Are they juniper berries?' he asked. 'You should try them with venison.'

'This is gin.' Ruby hiccupped and eyed him suspiciously. 'Their bittersweet pine flavour with peppery aftertaste goes well with it – it says so on their label.'

'Your choice, but honestly they work as well with game.'

'I can't cook.'

Dreamy, expressive eyes fringed with indecently long lashes sent tingles to parts of her anatomy that hadn't tingled for a long time.

'I could show you,' he said.

'You can't.' She blinked.

'You're right.' The look was gone. 'Ridiculous idea.' He blushed, clearly annoyed with himself. 'Where's my parcel?'

'You don't understand.' Ruby fought back a tear that was pricking the back of her eye, threatening to make a break for freedom. She took another swig of her drink, just as something grey and fluffy, moving at floor level, caught her eye.

'Who do you belong to little one?' she said, bending down for a better look. Not that she was expecting the little grey ball of fluff to answer.

'Shit,' the stranger said. 'Is that mine?'

'Trick question, right?' Ruby had had a lot to drink, in a short space of time, on an empty stomach. She didn't feel sober, but she wasn't blackout drunk. She could probably account for everything she'd done that day, probably that week, if asked. She definitely hadn't acquired a dog in the last couple of hours. She squinted up at the man, expecting his face to suggest he was joking or being sarcastic, but he'd evidently been talking while staring over her head and focussing on the package at the end of her hall. His eyes were bulging and he was deathly white. 'Don't worry,' she said, trying to lighten the mood. 'It's not a bomb.'

'Of course it's not a bomb,' he growled, strode past her, picked up the parcel and left. He'd got to the stairs before he turned and shouted over his shoulder, 'Here.'

Ruby bit her lip as a tear hit her cheek. She knew the command was aimed at the dog rather than her. But the dog, flat on his back, legs in the air, was either very hard of hearing or doing his best to ignore his master.

'I think he's talking to you,' Ruby whispered as she tickled the dog's tummy. 'Best do as he says.'

She picked the creature up and followed her neighbour up the stairs he'd continued to climb.

'Sorry,' he said, putting his parcel down outside Flat 6. He threw her such a sudden and unexpected smile that Ruby's nerve endings twitched and more tears fell. He took the dog from her. His fingertips gently brushing her arm, and those endings went into full jangle mode. She'd forgotten she had so many. Ruby sucked in a breath and stared.

'For disturbing you,' he added, staring back.

'Nothing to disturb.' She shrugged when she managed to drag her gaze away. 'I was only calculating whether producing transplant organs, balloon animals or wetsuits for ferrets out of condoms would produce the best income.'

Chapter Two

She was seriously weird. That was all he needed.

'Don't look at me like that,' Adam said. He watched his neighbour walk back to the stairwell before kicking the parcel into his hallway. 'I didn't mean to make her cry.'

And of course it wasn't a bomb. Emily might be deranged but she wasn't a killer.

'I moved here for a quiet life,' he muttered to himself.

Jason had said the neighbours were considerate, would always help out if you needed them to, but left you alone the rest of the time. He failed to mention there was a mad woman with a drink problem living downstairs. He'd been about to mention her singing issue, until those incredible smoky eyes held his for a second. A second that seemed to stretch on forever as every inch of his body came alive.

It was only six o'clock in the evening, she was definitely tipsy and wearing a shapeless onesie with penguins all over it as if she was ready for bed. Not a look she rocked, yet there was such a vulnerability about her. He had the strangest sensation of wanting to wrap her in his arms and protect her. Her cheeks glowed, probably due to the drink and her eyes shone, until he'd offered to help her cook game.

And what was that all about?

It had sort of slipped out and had hardly been met with unqualified appreciation. Oh God, she was probably a vegan. He should have considered that. No wonder she'd looked on the verge of tears. But then there was her hair? It looked thick and glossy, but she'd dragged and twisted it into a topknot on her head with a severity normally reserved for middle-aged women in need of a facelift.

Adam shuddered as an image of his catering college tutor,

Mrs Winbourne, and her bun, sprung to mind. She was the one who, in his first week at college, had damned his onion-cutting ability. She told him he was too much of a liability with sharp implements to even think of becoming a kitchen hand, let alone a chef. According to her, he'd be lucky to finish his first year with all his fingers intact. Well he'd showed her. It had taken weeks of practice and many more cuts, but he'd made it and finished the course with both distinction and all his fingers. These days he considered his ability to slice and chop onions fast to be one of his greatest talents.

Adam put Brutus down. The dog immediately flopped onto the door mat and tipped his head in a questioning way, as if trying to understand this human's world and failing.

'Cut the expression. I'm not the one who got expelled from doggy day care because they shagged then ate his sitter's handbag. What on earth were you thinking?' Adam slipped off his outdoor jacket and boots and walked into the kitchen to think about supper.

Twenty minutes later a rap on the door lifted Adam's temper, even Brutus perked up. Perhaps she'd come back? His mood nose-dived seconds later when he found his boss, not his neighbour, outside the flat.

'One of your neighbours let me in,' Clive said, holding up a bottle of Barolo. A vintage he didn't advertise. This must be bad.

'We need to chat,' he said. 'Fancy a drink?'

They'd been friends too long for Adam to shut the door in his face, so he moved to one side of the hall and took the bottle. 'I'm making fish finger sandwiches. Want one?'

Clive stared at the box in the hall. 'You've only been here since the beginning of the month, don't tell me you're moving already?'

'No.'

'What's that then?'

'Dunno. It came today. Haven't had a chance—'

'You think it's from her, don't you?' Clive swung the parcel into his arms and carried it into the kitchen. 'Why don't I open it?'

The question was rhetorical and before Adam could stop him, Clive had grabbed one of his knives and sliced through half the Sellotape.

Adam turned on the cooker. The day just kept getting better. He'd already upset a neighbour, had a Border Terrier with a flaming ASBO and now a blunt paring knife. He added a knob of butter to the frying pan and began filleting a second piece of sole.

The parcel couldn't be anything gruesome – could it? Emily wasn't psychotic. Infatuated, delusional, but not dangerous. The police psychologist had stressed that. It was just the psychologist's last word that rocked his world. She'd added "Yet".

He sliced the fish into goujons and coated them with egg and breadcrumbs to which he'd added lemon zest.

'Cookery books,' Clive announced. 'There's a letter addressed to you, thanking you for your payment and apologising for the delay in sending them.'

Relief flooded through Adam's body. 'Glasses in the top cupboard,' he grunted as he took a warm baguette out of the oven and cut it into two.

Clive poured two glasses. They both took a sip and nodded at each other. 'Please don't tell our favourite sommelier we drank this with fish.' He shuddered. 'I'd never live it down.'

Adam smiled. He could picture the man huffing and flapping his hands. 'You haven't said what brings you to this part of town,' he said, buttering the baguette pieces and spreading a thick layer of tartar sauce over two of them.

Clive looked embarrassed.

'Don't do the, "Can't I visit a friend?" line. I've known you too bloody long. You said you wanted a chat.' Adam added the fish to the bread and when he was happy with the arrangement, pushed a plate across the worktop.

Clive took a bite of his sandwich. 'This is good,' he said.

'Thanks,' Adam mumbled. 'So is the wine. Now what's wrong?'

'The restaurant,' Clive said. 'Things aren't good. Don't pretend you haven't noticed.'

No, Adam had. Some evenings they didn't see a customer. 'So, what's this? Sorry, but you no longer need me?'

Clive took another sip of his wine. 'I have a proposition.'

'Proposition or ultimatum?'

'Look, things haven't been easy for you, what with the stalker business and all that. When I saw the box, I thought the worst too. I can't imagine how you must've felt.'

No, he couldn't, because Clive had never woken up to find declarations of love written in lipstick over his car. Clive didn't cringe every time his doorbell rang. Or worry about leaving his dustbin outside ready for collection in case Emily rifled through it and recycled anything she found into a grotesque greetings card. 'What's your proposition?'

'You're a far better chef than Jason or me,' Clive said.

Adam fiddled with the stem of his glass, unsure of where the conversation was heading.

Clive rolled his eyes. 'You could argue with that statement.'

'I ...'

'Only joking. I've watched you over the last couple of years ...' Clive paused. 'Look, you've lost weight and confidence. Your menus don't have your old flair. The food is as good as ever, but we're not attracting customers. And as your friend ...'

Great, this was about to get a whole lot more personal. Like the last time Adam's father had sat him down for a "personal" conversation. That time it had been to tell him he needed to start shaving and wearing deodorant. And if he wanted to know anything about the differences between men and women, he should talk to his mother. It had been excruciatingly embarrassing and the look on Clive's face, suggested their "And as your friend" conversation wasn't going to be any less so.

Clive swilled some wine around his glass. 'It hurts to see how unhappy you are. Jason is in France living your dream ...'

'He'll learn a lot.'

'I don't doubt it, but it's your dream, not his. You wanted to work alongside a French chef.'

'Only Xavier.'

'Who, by the way, rang me earlier. He still wants you out there and needs help. Three months' cover while his sous-chef's away, start beginning of March.'

Adam whistled. He'd always dreamt about spending time with the master. Xavier had held the prestigious three-starred Michelin rating for twenty plus years. Many top chefs had trained with him. The box of cookery books now stacked on his kitchen worktop were all Xavier's creations.

'Jason is rattling round in a three-bedroom apartment there – he'll be glad of the company.'

'And you? What's in it for you?'

Clive looked momentarily embarrassed. 'I'd save money by closing evenings. It would give me time to develop the lunchtime trade. When you come back, we could talk about re-launch evenings, with a new menu. Your menu maybe,' Clive said.

'What about Brutus? He's been the only thing keeping me sane over the last couple of years.'

'Take him with you. Look ...' Clive got up to go. 'You know my thoughts about Emily. One day you will have to stand up to her, tell her how you feel. You can't run away for the rest of your life.'

Do not *say "you need to be grown up about this"*. Adam narrowed his eyes.

'But three months away might give you breathing space.' Clive stopped, with one hand on the door handle. 'By the time you get back, there is every likelihood she'll have given up and found someone else to haunt, sorry stalk.'

'Yeah, right.'

Adam closed the door behind his boss. Drawing the bolt across, he leant back against the door. He was safe in Jason's first-floor flat, but deep down he knew it was only a matter of time before Emily tracked him down.

Whatever Clive said about facing up to her, he wouldn't. He couldn't. The woman had been the cause of his darkest nightmares for the last three years. The mere mention of her name gave him the jitters. Occasionally, he might smell a floral scent, like the one she used on her cards and he would sweat uncontrollably. Someone in the restaurant might laugh like she did, a high-pitched gurgle and he'd freeze, or get so flustered he'd start shaking and be incapable of rational thought or action. He winced. No – he would move if she ever found out where he was living.

His downstairs neighbour started her nightly bellow. 'Let's hope she's not in another of her bad moods tonight,' he said, scratching the back of Brutus's head. He ran a bath and grimaced as the refrain to "Drift Away" permeated through the floor. At least he thought that's what it was, except he couldn't remember a version that had been so completely mangled.

Brutus's head tilted questioningly at the floor.

Please. No. Not "Rubber Bullets". There was definitely something appealing about three months away.

Chapter Three

Eamon Dixon fidgeted with his purple silk tie. He'd drawn the line at wearing a jacket and, knowing how hot it got in the boardroom, he'd taken the added precaution of making sure each armpit had received an ample spray of antiperspirant. He pushed a small white tablet from its blister pack and swallowed it with a large gulp of cold coffee.

'Within me is a peacefulness that cannot be disturbed,' he said firmly. 'Within me is a peacefulness that cannot be disturbed,' he repeated, less firmly. 'Within me ...' *No there bloody wasn't.*

Colleagues, not usually seen anywhere near the television studios before two in the afternoon, hurried across the car park. Reporters, he thought away on foreign assignments, scuttled into the building. Some of them had been gone so long he struggled to recall their names.

At 8.45 he watched the producer of the lunchtime finance programme head through the doors. Eamon tightened his tie enough to hide the fact the top button on his shirt was undone, got up from his desk and walked over to the boardroom.

'What do we know about this new man?' he'd asked last week in the canteen queue when the appointment had been announced.

'Shoots from the hip, more likely to fire than hire,' one of the news team said.

Eamon took the news with a pinch of salt. After all it was the news team at Galaxy TV's "finger on the pulse, reporting on the edge, no story is too big or too small" attitude that meant they'd heard about the firing of their last director general three months ago – via a broadcast from a rival TV station. They'd watched the broadcast amazed as their DG was "escorted" out of their building by two mean-looking men, in black polo-necked jumpers and sunglasses, although on closer inspection, the thugs had turned out to be a Galaxy TV's cameraman and his assistant.

The same rival TV station, last week, was alleged to be behind the rumours Galaxy TV had appointed a new director general. They were right. Late Friday afternoon when office tensions had been wound tighter than Eamon's fake Rolex, senior staff received a generic email telling them to present themselves at a breakfast-without-breakfast meeting the following week to meet the new man.

The man's reputation entered the boardroom a full ten minutes before he did. Nervous anticipation stifled usual conversation about the weekend's activities, but when the door flew open with such an intake of breath, Eamon wouldn't have been at all surprised if the table they were sat round had disappeared into the vacuum they'd just created.

The director general sat down and flung a file across the table. Sheets of paper Eamon recognised as analysis of viewing figures spewed out. 'We need to raise our game,' he said.

No niceties.

'All of us. This station can't carry staff who aren't performing. I run a tight ship. There are storms ahead. This ain't going to be no cruise. It's your decision. Either get on or get off.'

Voluntary redundancy. Eamon wanted to write a book … Maybe with redundancy …

'Don't get complacent here.' There must have been thirty people in the room, but the man stared straight at him. 'I'm not talking redundancies. I don't reward incompetency. If you aren't up to the job, I'll hunt you down and have you out without so much as a reference.'

Galaxy's cookery expert caught Eamon's eye and theatrically blew the top of his first two fingers, before pointing them at Eamon and pretending to pull the trigger.

Eamon fixed him with his best drop-dead-and-die-bitch look.

'The public are sick of cookery competitions ...'

He wasn't looking so sure of himself.

'And with the country's housebuilding program the way it is these days, most of our audiences are lucky to have a car-parking space ...'

The Dream House team started to pale.

'Most people don't have a garden and never will. They're not interested in what you can do with fifty acres and frankly neither am I.'

The gardening team had begun to turn a less than healthy shade of green.

'We're in a recession. Money is short. People want to know how to make the most out of their money. How to feed a family for a week. Best deals and discounts. They don't want some banker telling them whether shares they can't afford to invest in are going up or down.'

If the financial woman hadn't been crushed between the drama and children's TV spokespeople, there was every chance she'd have fainted.

Eamon hoped he would run out of steam soon. Media was a young man's game, but it was all he understood. The prospect of looking for another position wasn't appealing. TV companies didn't take on sixty-three-year-old producers without references. It wasn't even as if he had a string of recent hit shows under his belt he could tempt prospective employers with. His last hit series had been three years ago. A dating programme designed to find true love for no-hopers.

The director general opened another folder which he briefly considered. He looked up. He seemed to be searching for something or someone in particular and his eyes settled on Eamon.

'Dixon, right?'

Eamon swallowed, but nodded very slowly.

'You can start. Why don't you tell us what you've got planned for this year?'

He was going to be out of a job by 9.15.

'I am working on a follow up to *Taking a Chance on Love*,' he said, cautiously, unable to judge the man's feelings about the subject. 'I want to revisit the characters from the last series. A sort of did the "datees" find the lasting romance they desired? Did they find happiness ever after? That sort of thing. Shows could be in the can by summer, ready for inclusion in autumn schedules.'

The man's eyes darkened and Eamon shut his own eyes, not wanting to see his colleagues' gloating expressions when he was fired.

'That might work.'

His eyes snapped open and he swung his head back round to the top of the table, cricking his neck in the process. In his line of vision he was pleased to see the cookery expert staring open-mouthed.

The director general smiled. 'I was a great fan of the original series.'

"Prepare to be amazed. Feel the rumble of a V8 from a Mustang, Corvette or a Dodge. This isn't a competition for the faint-hearted. When you win a day out in an American Muscle Car, all you have to do is choose which one. Choose any one of our twelve high-revving, exhaust-roaring vehicles. Then hit the gas and burn rubber as you go from zero to white smoke in seconds. Feel the thrust against your chest as you're pinned against your seat by the sheer power and force. Don't expect a comfortable ride: we're not talking automatic transmission or suspension. Hit a pothole – don't expect to hold on to your fillings. If you're looking for comfort and a

quiet day out, step away from your computer. Whatever you do, don't enter this competition."

Ruby's pocket vibrated as Nickelback started singing. She jumped. Her finger hit return and she submitted an entry. She stared at the computer screen as it changed back to the company's home page.

Shit. She'd entered. Maybe they'd let her change the prize. Perhaps a Morgan or Aston Martin instead.

She pulled her mobile out of a pocket too late to answer it. She should've been concentrating, not letting her mind wander off at a tangent to dream about the hunk upstairs. Something she'd done a lot of since yesterday. The parcel had been addressed to an A Finder at Flat 6, Union House. Clearly, he was Jason's flat sitter, but she had no clue what the A stood for. He didn't look like an Anthony, too young for an Albert. She'd been at school with an Adrian who had been an annoying little toad. The memory of being chased by him holding worms and spiders made her shudder.

She wondered if A Finder liked off-roading in a monster truck. She swallowed.

Nickelback started to sing again, Ruby looked down at her phone. She might as well answer; there were some people who just wouldn't give up. It would get it over and done with. 'Mum,' she said.

'Lily, darling,' her mother said sharply.

'Sorry.' Both Ben and Ruby had been told to use their mother's first name from an early age, and never call her Mother or Mum, both words she considered too ageing.

'And don't frown. The wind might change.'

How did she do that?

'What's new?' Lily Brooks had used the same voice for as long as Ruby could remember. A voice dripping with concern. Her sort of "poor you, but you brought this on yourself" voice.

Thank goodness it wasn't a FaceTime video call and she

didn't have to endure the angled sympathetic looks her mother specialised in.

'Nothing,' she said. 'Everything's great.' She tried to muster enough jollity to disguise her exasperation.

'There are a couple of adverts in this week's paper I think you should apply for.'

'I'm on garden leave, remember? I can't do anything until June.'

The conversation followed a distressingly similar pattern to the one they'd had every other day for the last five weeks. By the end of the month, they'd probably have had it at least another half a dozen times.

'Work no, but you could start looking. It's the beginning of February. You don't want people to think you're out of practice. Believe me I know what I am talking about. When I gave up work to raise you and your brother, I struggled to find a job afterwards. I don't want the same thing to happen to you.'

You were a Country and Western singer. I'm an Event Planner. You didn't want to sing any other type of music; I've been made redundant.

'What about the kitchen?'

Hit a girl when she's down, why don't you?

'No change.'

'Have you done anything about getting your money back?'

'My stars say not to sort financial problems out until March.'

'Don't be facetious. Ben's seen Daniel.'

Jackpot! Ruby looked at her watch. A record, even for her mother. In less than two minutes Lily had managed to get the conversation round to Ruby's ex. *End call*. Five more minutes and her mother would be listing the reasons Ruby should take him back.

'That's not unusual. They're friends and live in the same cul-de-sac.'

'He's upset.'

Remove battery. Destroy phone.

Ruby wouldn't normally wish harm on anyone or anything, but in Daniel's case, she made an exception.

'Ben is worried.'

'I don't care.'

'He's lost a lot of weight.'

'Still don't care.'

'He's sorry for what happened. He knows it was wrong. But I can't help thinking ...'

Not listening. Don't try and pin this on me.

'If you'd taken a bit more care with your appearance ...'

'Bye Mother.'

'Don't ...'

Ruby ended the call and threw the phone across the room with such force that the first time she heard the noise, she assumed it was her mobile objecting. There was no van, it wasn't Kevin. The postman had been and after yesterday's "parcel-gate" incident there really was no point getting excited.

But she was – a little bit.

It couldn't be her mother, she'd rung from her landline, so, unless broomsticks had become supersonic ...

She practised her smile all the way down her hallway and opened the door to find a Border Terrier, wagging his tail, and Mr Upstairs, with two cups of coffee, a smile and his big brown beautiful eyes, standing on her doorstep.

She sighed.

'I wanted to say sorry,' he said, struggling to control two cups and a dog who clearly didn't want to be held for a moment longer.

'What for?' she swallowed as Mr Upstairs put the dog down.

'For being a complete plonker and not saying thank you for looking after my parcel,' he said.

Chapter Four

She was wearing pyjamas – cracking outfit. 'Look I'm sorry. Yesterday wasn't a great start.' *Say something.* 'I'm Adam. And in case you're wondering, which you probably weren't, the package was books I'd ordered online.' *Don't look at me like that.* 'You were right. It wasn't a bomb, so thank you again.' He lifted the large white mugs he'd brought down from his flat. 'I come in peace, with coffee.'

She stared at him but held out a hand and he pressed a cup into it.

Today, her glossy chestnut brown hair bounced about her shoulders. It made her look younger than yesterday's topknot.

He waited until her fingers closed round the handle before he loosened his grip. When her fingers brushed his, Adam felt a sensation in his stomach he was pretty certain had nothing to do with his breakfast coffee, or the toast and marmalade he'd eaten earlier.

'Have I woken you up?' He regretted the words as soon as he said them, when she looked self-consciously down at her pyjamas.

She shook her head. 'I've been up for hours. I've let myself go – apparently.'

'Sorry, I didn't mean …' He tailed off. This wasn't going well.

'No need to apologise.' She grinned. 'However, if you ever mention I opened the door in this state to my mother, I will deny it and then have to kill you.'

He held out a hand. 'Deal. My lips are sealed.'

'I'm Ruby,' she said, shaking his hand.

The sensation was back, warm and tingling. It had been a long time since he'd felt anything like it, and it felt good.

'Do you want to come in?' She took a step backwards. 'You'll have to excuse the mess.' Brutus, sensing a new place to explore, shot forward, tail wagging and straight into a room on the left, which if the layout of her flat matched Jason's, meant he'd gone into her bedroom. Seconds later he reappeared, holding a pair of brief black lacy panties in his mouth, tail wagging, looking for someone to play tug with.

Adam winced. This really, really wasn't going well.

Ruby handed him back the mug and advanced on Brutus who instead of turning tail and running away, stopped dead.

'Dog, drop.'

Obediently, he relaxed his jaw.

'This way,' Ruby called over her shoulder as she removed the pants. 'Good drop,' she said and stroked Brutus's head. *Impressive!* He'd still be negotiating.

She shut every door she passed and lost the knickers behind one of them along the way. Brutus walked by her side, looking up intently.

Adam followed them down the hall and handed her back the coffee as soon as they reached what, in the flat above, would have been the lounge/diner. He stared, not able to think of anything to say. Jason's was decorated in a minimalist way while Ruby's had been crammed full, in a storage container rather than a room sort of way. He stayed in the doorway and stared, because to get much further would have required a degree of athletic ability he didn't possess.

'Ruby – nice name,' he said.

'Mum used to be a nightclub singer with a thing about Kenny Rogers. Apparently, my dad used to look a bit like him. They had a regular set at the working men's club in town.

'So, you're Ruby as in …'

'"Ruby, Don't Take Your Love To Town"'. She beamed, and Adam's heart did a flip thing.

'I've heard of it, although my parents were more the headbanging rocker types. They still are. I suppose I should be glad I was named after my grandfather, not a song, or one of my mother's rock heroes. They had some seriously weird names.'

This time she laughed, really laughed, a contagious sound and suddenly he was laughing too and flooded with a warm happy feeling.

'I like Ruby. It suits you.'

'Thank you.' She blushed. 'But in case you google the lyrics later and are worried, dad was just a guitarist, not a Vietnam veteran. Mum didn't leave him, he left her, for a Sade lookalike, just after I was born. I'm sure she used to piss him off, but I doubt he ever wanted to gun her down.'

'That's a relief.'

'And, for the record, I don't have a sister called Lucille. My brother's a geek, not a gambler and he's Ben not Tommy.'

'Does your mother still sing?'

'At home occasionally when she gets drunk. My father and his Sade friend took over the slot at the club. Mum couldn't get work, so she's nurtured a grudge against him for the last thirty-two years.' Ruby paused as she took another sip of her coffee. 'Sorry, bit of an information dump there. But that's basically everything you ever needed to know about Ruby Brooks.' She pretended a curtsey. 'You look better without the hat by the way.'

'Thanks.'

Her eyes looked as if a light was dancing behind them.

'I thought there must be something about your appearance you were embarrassed about.'

If only it was that simple.

'I like your dog.'

'Glad someone does,' he said, nursing his own steaming

cup of coffee and trying not to look horrified by the state of the room.

Boxes were stacked in tall towers. A big orange, squashy leather sofa, that had seen better days, took up most of one wall. Tucked between its arm rest and one corner of the room, her television appeared to be balanced on what looked like a fridge. Under the window, a computer sat on a small desk with papers spread all around it. The walls above were covered in small blue Post-it notes. A pile of plastic boxes and the coffee table jammed in the middle of the room ensured there wasn't much floor space to be seen.

The flats were a good size with two bedrooms. Jason used to use his second one as a study. He'd suggested Adam should use the larger main bedroom, after all it was likely he was going to be renting the flat for some time. 'Make yourself at home,' he'd said. 'Rearrange things if you want.' But Adam didn't want to get too comfortable. He hadn't rearranged any furniture; he didn't need to. He'd only brought two suitcases. There was no wardrobe in the office but having pushed Jason's computer into one corner of the desk, he tended to use it as a clothes rack.

Not ideal. Not home, but at the moment, the best he could do, even if it meant sleeping under an Arsenal Football Club duvet. That definitely wasn't perfect, but at least he could blame his sleepless nights on something.

At some point he would return home and face his demons. Just not yet.

'Have you lived here long?' Adam asked.

'End of November.'

He nodded, wisely. 'It takes a while to get sorted, doesn't it?'

'Sorry.' She collected the magazines, an atlas and a booklet about writing your own will from the sofa and shuffled them into a pile. 'Please sit down.'

The spot Ruby cleared was barely big enough for one buttock, but he perched anyway. 'Are you planning on taking a holiday?'

'What?' She looked surprised, but then saw the atlas. The penny seemed to drop. 'No, it's for ... work.'

'I've interrupted you. Sorry, I should've thought.'

'Really, it's fine,' she said, smiling at him. 'Nothing that can't wait.' She sat on the desk chair; one leg curled beneath her. Brutus settled next to her on a tiny bare patch of floor and she stroked him with a red-painted toe-nailed foot. He wagged his tail and Adam felt a stab of jealousy.

'So, you're above me in Flat 6. It must be awkward for him not having a garden?'

'Who? Jason?'

She giggled. 'No, Brutus.'

'At this moment, a garden's the least of his worries.'

'Don't tell me he's ill? The poor darling.'

Brutus allowed himself to be scooped up and cuddled. Both of them looked at Adam. Ruby's eyes were filled with concern. Brutus adopted a look of what could only be described as extreme smugness.

'Whatever's wrong?' she asked.

'Nothing physical, more an attitude problem. He's been excluded by his dog-sitter – permanently.'

'What? This little poppet?' Brutus licked her face.

'Poppet.' The word came out in a high-pitched tone, reminiscent of a Monty Python sketch.

Ruby stared at Adam. Brutus closed his eyes and snuggled into his new best friend's arms as if they were the safest place in the whole world. She stroked him and Brutus sighed happily.

'He made the poor woman's life a misery – apparently.'

'You?' Ruby tilted Brutus's face up and looked into his eyes.

'Don't be fooled by his butter wouldn't melt look. The incident with her handbag was the final straw. Doctors can't say with any certainty she'll ever return to normal.'

Ruby giggled and Brutus wagged his tail some more.

Adam barely knew his new neighbour, but he felt comfortable and started to relax in the companionable silence that ensued.

'I can't remember when I last had proper coffee,' Ruby said as she sipped her drink. 'Are we going to be neighbours for a while?'

'Would that be okay?'

Her eyes were bright, 'Yes, lovely.'

Was she blushing? Adam, in danger of staring at her, picked up the atlas. 'You're going to Japan?'

Ruby nodded towards the map. 'I'm hoping to soon. Number one destination on my bucket list.'

Move over Poirot. Unusual working hours, maps and computer printouts all over the place, elementary my dear Hastings.

'I guess you're an air hostess.' Adam was lost in the catering trade; he should've been a detective. 'Long flights don't worry you?' He drained his drink and went to get up. Easier said than done. The sofa was wide, the cushions deep.

'No.' Her eyes were alight. 'I want to see cherry blossom, snow monkeys and bullet trains.' She hugged her knees and looked as if she'd lost herself somewhere far away. 'I want to wear kimonos, drink Saki and eat sushi.'

'Have you ever tried Japanese food? It's not all cold rice and raw fish. They do have many amazing flavours.'

She shook her head. 'Indian or Chinese is usually as adventurous as I get.'

Watching her, lost in her own thoughts and stroking his dog, Adam wished he could show her how beautiful food could be. How it should taste without the endless spices and seasoning of the nation's favourite curry or a sweet and sour sauce. He wanted her to close her eyes and give him the look she'd given him when she tasted his coffee and to laugh with eyes that sparkled and lit up the room. He could hear music, happy sounding music.

Ruby crossed the room between them.

Adam closed his eyes and waited for some form of contact. His skin tingled with anticipation.

'Hello.'

He opened his eyes. She'd pulled a mobile from behind one of the sofa cushions.

Time to go before he made a fool of himself. He gathered up the coffee cups, mouthed "Thanks", scooped Brutus up and left.

Ruby hoped it was a wrong number. She wanted to hang up and get to the door before Adam got outside.

'Ms Brooks?'

She nodded. He thought she was an air hostess. She ought to put him right.

'Ms Brooks are you there?'

The front door closed with a click. He'd gone.

She exhaled.

'Hello. Can you hear me?'

'I don't want windows, a conservatory or insurance.'

'I'm not selling.'

'Life insurance or a funeral plan.'

'Really not selling.'

'You're not from a call centre in Asia?'

'I'm Clive Ford from Bootles.'

'The restaurant on the high street?'

'Bistro. You visited us recently.'

A month ago, she'd met up with a couple of old colleagues for lunch. They'd all been made redundant and were in similar boats, except they had their lives mapped out. They knew what they were going to do.

Beth had been trying for a family for some time. Armed with a large redundancy cheque, she'd made an appointment at a London fertility clinic.

Rachel had planned a holiday round Europe with the possibility of looking to buy a property in France.

Ruby listened to both of them and made approving noises from time to time. But when she mentioned starting her own event management business, they laughed, told her they were *sooo* glad they were out of it and changed the subject.

It had been a nice lunch and mid obligatory air-kisses afterwards they'd promised to keep in contact, but they wouldn't.

'I remember,' she said, quietly into the phone.

'Well congratulations, you've won the perfect Valentine's evening from Bootles' Bistro. Our chef will cook you a romantic meal and serve it in your home. He will even wash up. You won't need to do a thing apart from relax with the love of your life while our special blend of Bootles' Bistro romance ensures you have the best Valentine's night ever.'

Chapter Five

'Kevin. Lovely to see you.' Putting on a forced smile, and trying to sound bright, not homicidal, Ruby leant against the wall, glad of the support. Definitely don't sound homicidal. 'It's been so long.'

'Sorry, haven't been in touch, slipped over in the snow, put my back out.' He had the grace to look embarrassed. Shifty, but unquestionably embarrassed.

Yeah right.

'Snow, you say?' Keep smiling. 'Poor you.'

The sarcasm appeared to be lost on him. He'd clearly forgotten Redford had just experienced one of the warmest winters on record. Ruby hadn't.

Do not antagonise him. Don't say you don't believe him. Okay, you don't believe him, just don't say it.

'You're here, that's all that matters,' she said. 'And fully recovered? Not coming back to work too soon?' An Oscar-winning performance. A tad overdone perhaps, but entirely lost on Kevin.

'Still feeling rough,' he said, and coughed.

You look it. She'd forgotten how scruffy and unkempt he was. 'Oh dear.'

'Been on painkillers for the last six weeks.'

You can't seriously be expecting sympathy. Ruby strained to maintain her fixed smile.

'Haven't worked since before Christmas.'

'What a shame,' she said, her lips stretched across gritted teeth.

Seemingly convinced she wasn't about to rip his head off, his face morphed into a grin. 'I hope those cupboards are clear?'

And have been since before Christmas. She gritted harder to prevent herself saying something she might regret and nodded.

Kevin winked at her. 'That's my girl.'

Was he flirting? Ruby's stomach hit the floor. Ten weeks of worry and unanswered phone calls rose like burning bile. Not the tiniest acknowledgement. Nothing. Not even a single phone call. Suddenly there he was, stood on her doorstep radiating stale cigarette smoke and even staler BO and bloody flirting as if he was the answer to all her prayers.

He wasn't the only one feeling rough. She'd had weeks of sleepless nights. Every time she looked in the mirror, she saw darkening circles around her eyes.

Her heart hadn't leapt when she'd seen his red transit pull into the car park. She'd pinched herself, to make sure she wasn't dreaming, while she'd watched him struggle across the grass dragging his toolbox and yanking his jogging bottoms up as he walked.

'We'd better get those units ripped out then. Kitchen's this way, isn't it?'

Kevin didn't wait for an answer, he'd already thrust his toolbox through the door and dragged it down the hall.

'I had a phone call from the suppliers,' he called over his shoulder. 'New units should be here in'—he looked at his watch—'about an hour.'

'Give me a call, gorgeous girl. We need to get moving on this. Ciao.' It was the sixth message, in as many days, that Eamon had left on Emily Watkins' answering machine. She hadn't bothered to ring back on any of the previous occasions. He had no reason to think this time would be any different.

He made a note of the date and time of call and looked at the website of an agency offering employment opportunities for TV professionals. There was a vacancy for an associate producer on a new comedy show on one of the mainstream channels. He frowned; it was a temporary position. The only other job advertised was for a producer on a Welsh radio station. He might be desperate, but Wales ... Too far away to even contemplate. He heard a noise and spun round to find the cameraman looking over his shoulder. He wondered how long he'd been standing there.

'She won't ring back. You know that, don't you?'

Eamon put the phone back on its cradle and tried to think of something more reassuring to say than "She will".

'Accept it old man, she's not interested in another fifteen minutes of fame. The researchers have tried to reach both of them without any luck.'

'She'll do it.'

'You'll have to own up at some point – tell him upstairs you have no idea what's happened to her. He won't be happy. I can't see him agreeing to do the series. He said her episode made the last series.'

'She'll do it,' Eamon snarled. He'd spent all weekend updating his CV in case. He'd stressed words like "positive" and "flexible". The abilities to meet tight deadlines and to manage and reconcile budgets were mentioned as some of his core skills. But the last few years had hardly thrown up a wealth of original or creative programme ideas he could boast about or ones anyone would remember. The remake of *Taking a Chance on Love* had to work, and he would do whatever he had to do to make sure it did.

'You haven't found the waiter – the one you dragged in when the other bloke didn't turn up? Have you spoken to him?'

'You mean the chef?'

'He didn't want to do the original programme. I can't see him wanting to get involved again. If I was him, I'd tell you where to stick your follow-up.'

'According to Emily's Christmas card, they are still together and very happy.'

'And I'm Elvis.'

'He's dead.' Which, frankly, was what Eamon would like the cameraman to have been, but the very much alive, annoying little git chuckled and shook his head.

'Not as dead as you're about to become, old-timer.'

Eamon narrowed his eyes and cursed him under his breath.

'Although, I understand we're looking for a new local news presenter.'

'What happened to …?'

The cameraman drew his finger across his throat. 'Gone. Mind you, it wouldn't be any good for you. Because you're such a people person. Interact well with people, always enjoy working with a wide range of lifestyle genres. Whatever that means.'

Eamon recognised the line from his CV and threw a notepad at the cameraman who stepped neatly out of the way. The pad landed the other side of the office partition with a thud and someone shouted, 'Oi, Pea-Brain, what do you think you're doing?'

'Haven't you got a lens to clean, or an electrician to wind up?' Eamon growled and went to retrieve the offending pad.

'Kiss goodbye to your desk and your pension, old man.' The cameraman walked away, laughing. 'If I were you, I'd pack before you tell the DG you've screwed up,' he shouted from halfway down the office, which caused everyone else to turn and stare.

Eamon rubbed his temples with his knuckles. He hated Mondays.

Chapter Six

Adam watched a skip being unloaded in the front car park as he listened to Clive's message. 'Details for this evening. Woman's name is Ruby Brooks.'

No way. He pressed rewind and played the message again.

'Flat 4, Union House. That's your block. It makes sense for you to do it.'

It must be her.

'Ring Brian with your wine list and any ingredients you'll need. He'll have them ready for you to pick up by lunchtime. And Adam – a photo or quote would be good. Something we can use for the local paper. We need some publicity out of this.'

Adam listened to the message another three times and then still rang the restaurant back just to make sure.

He was relieved Clive answered the phone. 'Definitely Flat 4, Union House – Ruby Brooks. I rang earlier to remind her,' Clive said.

'She's my neighbour.'

'You got a problem with that? It's either her or …' Clive put the phone down while he shuffled through what sounded like a large pile of papers. 'Emily Watkins. They were the only two entrants.'

Adam froze. 'I thought there were loads of entries,' he said.

'There were. Only 278 of them were Emily's. We were going to give it to her for sheer persistence, but she's your "stalker" isn't she?'

Adam let out a long sigh. He knew this was a bad idea when Clive originally voiced the romantic meal suggestion. 'What did you tell her?'

'Multiple entries made her entry invalid.'

'Not Emily – Ruby.'

'I didn't speak to her. Some guy answered.'

'Who?' It took seconds for the words to filter through to Adam's brain, but when they did, it felt as if he'd taken a right hook. He rubbed his neck in a bid to get rid of the confusion.

'I didn't ask. Presumably her date. Anyway, he said he'd tell her we would provide a three-course meal, freshly prepared, together with an appropriate wine selection from our extensive cellars for the perfect night in.'

'Does she know it's me?'

Clive laughed. 'Don't tell me, you've upset another woman.'

'Get lost.' Adam put the phone down and made himself a coffee while he considered what to do.

If it had been anyone else, he'd have happily chosen any of the items from Bootles' menu to cook. That had been the idea – to promote the restaurant. Whatever his boss said, it was a good menu. Customers loved it, but this was personal.

He tapped his pen against the piece of paper on his table.

Clive would probably throw a tantrum at the cost. Sod it. Hang the expense. It would serve him right.

Ten minutes later, the words on the page even made his mouth water. If he could pull that meal off, it would be amazing.

He rang Jason, in Paris, for reassurance. Jason suggested one or two small changes to the menu. 'Promise me if I ever find the girl of my dreams'—he chuckled—'you'll cook it for me?'

'Every girl you meet, is the girl of your dreams. That would bankrupt me. How about for the first relationship that lasts more than six months?'

'Six months – that's a frigging lifetime,' Jason said. 'You'll be using the dreaded "C" word next.'

'What, coriander?'

'Commitment. I come out in a rash just saying it.'

Adam laughed. There was about as much chance of Jason committing to anyone as Clive deciding Bootles should be a kick-boxing venue. He looked at his watch. Eight hours to get everything done. Plenty of time – except he had to get to London for some ingredients. It would be cutting it fine, but no point assuming any of Clive's regular suppliers would be able to come up with white truffles at short notice. And he had to have white truffles.

'I hope she's worth it,' Jason said. 'But if she is, plate up the smoked mushroom and white truffle terrine, cover it with a glass dome, then whip off the dome as you serve. It should give out a lovely aroma of maple chip and rosemary as the smoke wafts gently around the table.'

Adam traced his finger over the words written on the pad in front of him and smiled. Ambitious, but sensational. He finished his coffee, grabbed Brutus, his keys and imagined Ruby's face alight with amazement at the spectacle.

Valentine's Day sucked. Every competition had been themed around "Love". Ruby studiously avoided anything mentioning cute memories, Mr Right or relationships. Ones that offered heart-shaped chocolates or Prosecco as prizes were deleted without a second glance. She ignored the "Tell us about your most romantic Valentine's Day ever" competition. Not hard; Daniel wasn't one of life's romantics. Last year, for the first time ever, he'd bought a gift because he'd forgotten to book a restaurant. A token of his affection, he'd said, handing over a box of ankle weights and a celebrity keep-fit DVD. The writing had been on the wall then; she should've read between the lines.

Submitting her details for a tenth time with a feeling of achievement, Ruby walked into her kitchen. It had been completely stripped, not in a tidy minimalist way, and was now completely and utterly vacant.

A kitchen no more.

Just a shell.

Two capped off copper pipes stood proud of the floor where the sink used to be. The grey plastic waste jutted out of the wall between them, but the sink, like the units it had once been perched on, had disappeared. They were in the skip outside, along with a bike she'd never seen before and three sacks of garden rubbish, which, considering she didn't have a garden, was impressive. The only thing still attached to the wall was her boiler.

The old cooker and freezer had been forced into her bedroom to be surrounded by a pile of saucepans, bread bin and a chocolate fondue set she didn't remember she owned. With the narrowest of walkways to and from her bed, she couldn't afford to put on any weight. As it was, she had to turn sideways and shuffle to get there and if she wanted clean knickers anytime soon, she was completely buggered.

She tracked the washing machine down to the spare bedroom by following the odd-coloured wet drips down the hall. The microwave was perched on her bedside table, underneath a pile of boxes. Many other huge brown boxes turned the rest of her apartment into an assault course. Ruby picked up the delivery note from the windowsill. Everything on it had been ticked off. She tried to understand the shorthand description of each item.

'Could I see the plans?' she asked. 'I'd like to check ...'

'Ruby, Ruby, Ruby – trust me.' Kevin turned around and snatched the delivery note back. 'You've got everything we've talked about.'

'You're sure they'll fit?'

He put a hand on his heart. 'Who's the kitchen fitter here, darling?'

Darling! 'That says there's only one drawer unit.'

He tilted his head.

'I asked for two.'

'Trust me. One will look better.'

'You quoted for two.'

'You need more cupboard space.'

'What about the fridge/freezer?'

'Coming from another supplier. I'll pick it up when we're ready.' Kevin stood, hands on hips, legs akimbo. 'You really do have to trust me.'

Luckily for him, that hammer resting on his toolbox was well out of her way. Had it been within reach ...

'By the way, some restaurant rang to say your grub will be delivered at 6.30 tonight.'

Shit. She'd forgotten. 'Tonight?' *Shit, double shit.* On the plus side, it meant she would eat.

'Something about a meal for two.'

Ruby could see the plates, cutlery and glasses. They were probably less than six foot away – on top of a wardrobe. Who, in their right mind, thought that a sensible place to store them? Daft question. The same person who seemed hell-bent on single-handedly demolishing her flat.

She flopped down on her bed, then sat straight back up pulling the kitchen knives and their rack from beneath the quilt. *Wanker!*

'Whatever possessed you to put it there?' she hissed in a tone reminiscent of her mother as an idea popped into her head.

The man upstairs – Adam.

She couldn't – could she?

Okay, he seemed to think a beanie hat appropriate indoor headgear, but he had gorgeous brown eyes and made great coffee. The food had been good in the bistro. She didn't know what their takeaway menu was like, but he looked like he could do with feeding up. She was pretty certain he was single. She didn't remember seeing a girlfriend coming or going.

Ruby shot out of the flat before she had a chance to change her mind. She practised her best, "Hi there, you'll never guess what I've done? Only gone and won a competition for a takeaway for two. Long story. I'll tell you about it later. Anyway, there's going to be way too much food for me. Especially as I've spent the day eating my own body weight in chocolate. So, if you're not doing anything tonight, fancy coming over? You can bring your dog", as she ran all the way upstairs.

She wouldn't mention Valentine's Day. That could send out the wrong signals and cause all sorts of problems further down the line. She stopped outside number six and breathed deeply. The smell was divine. Someone was cooking, and judging by the smells coming from his flat, he was cooking for someone pretty special.

Clearly Adam was busy. Of course, he was. It was Valentine's Day. Everybody was busy apart from her.

It felt as if someone had pulled out a valve and she was deflating fast as she walked back to her flat. She rang her mother.

'Lily, why don't you come over tonight?'

Her mother laughed.

'I've got a meal on its way and thought it would be nice to spend the evening together. I could show you the plans for the kitchen.'

She fiddled with a pound coin in her pocket while her mother muttered something about having plans for a yoga session.

'It's Valentine's night,' Ruby argued, as she reached her flat.

'All the more reason for me to rid myself of negative energy,' Lily said.

'I'll join you. I could do with relaxing too, then we can eat.'

'You – yoga! Don't be ridiculous,' Lily said. 'Must be going.' She sounded shifty; something was going on. Another time Ruby would have pressed for more details, but today she had more urgent things on her mind and there was only one person she knew who might be free at short notice. Heads she rang Daniel. Tails she didn't.

'Got a date yet, darling?' Kevin asked as she passed the kitchen.

Ruby checked her watch – 6.30. She hadn't put the television on, but it definitely was. For a second, she understood what it must feel like to return home and discover you had squatters. Except Kevin was there at her invitation.

With any luck, he'd be gone within the hour and she could curl up alone and watch *Schitt's Creek*.

At least he had the grace to look surprised by the suggestion. At first, she thought he would turn her down. Then suddenly as if his lemons had rolled into line and he was assured a jackpot win, he turned rather too enthusiastically for Ruby's liking and smirked at her.

'You want me to be your Valentine?'

'No!' *I want the guy upstairs to be my Valentine, but he's busy.* 'Nothing like that, it's a meal and as you're here ...'

'What time's the grub coming?'

Ruby suppressed a shudder. 'The restaurant said 6.30, didn't they?'

'There's not much point me going home. I might as well stay,' he said.

And he had. On her sofa, in jeans and a dust-covered T-shirt. The only concession he made was to take off his boots, which were on the sofa beside him, while his socked feet rested on the coffee table and her business plans.

'Any chance of a tea, darling?'

Ruby wrinkled her nose and scooped up the boots. She opened her front door. Had it not been for the man on her doorstep, she would have launched them down the hallway in the direction of the front door.

'Adam. Saved by the bell,' she said, dropping the boots.

'From what?' Adam asked. He was dressed from head-to-toe in white.

'Tea-making duties.' Ruby looked him up and down. 'Go on then, what are you going as?'

He stared at her. 'You're not expecting me?'

'Trick question, right?' She spoke slowly. 'I'm having a takeaway at home and you look like you're off to a ghostbuster's convention.'

'I'm your chef.'

'Yeah right.'

'I work for Bootles.'

Her forehead creased into a frown.

'The bistro in town?' Ruby's mouth opened and closed. 'You mean you've brought my takeaway?' She followed his eyes down to the two large, insulated boxes on either side of him.

'Not exactly.' An expression she couldn't put her finger on clouded his brown eyes.

The silence between them seemed to stretch on forever, but when it became clear he wasn't going anywhere, she said, 'You better come in then.'

Adam stood in her kitchen and stared open-mouthed. 'It's all gone.'

'No shit, Sherlock! Crikey, how did that happen?'

He put the two boxes on the floor and looked at her with not the friendliest expression in the world. Ruby bit her lip.

'What exactly are you expecting from this evening?' he asked.

She shrugged. 'Something to eat. Hot bath. Double episode of *Schitt's Creek*. Early night, that sort of thing,' she said, her voice breaking.

'What did the restaurant tell you about the meal?'

The tone of his voice stung her. 'Just that someone would bring round three courses and some wine,' she whispered.

'You entered a competition to have a chef cook and serve you a romantic meal for two.' He sounded exasperated. 'A competition you won. Please tell me you're not expecting me to drop off a takeaway curry.'

'Bootles isn't an Indian,' Ruby said, her eyes burning.

Maybe pommes frites.

'Is that the food, darling? I'm starving.' The theme music played in the sitting room to signal the end of *Eggheads*. 'The clever bastards won again.'

Adam took a deep breath. 'I've spent all afternoon preparing your meal. I am not going to serve it here.' He exhaled loudly. 'Give me ten minutes, then bring Romeo upstairs.'

Chapter Seven

What had he been thinking?

Adam checked the food. He ignored Brutus who slunk off to find his bed and bone the minute his master started slamming doors.

He should've said no as soon as he realised it was her. There were other chefs at Bootles who could have prepared a passable meal and welcomed the overtime.

He cleared the table and laid it. Jason didn't run to matching plates, cutlery and glasses, but everything was clean.

Be professional. Treat them as you would any other diner. Make them feel special. The doorbell rang as he uncorked the champagne.

Smile. Professional. Okay. 'Hi,' he said, opening the door. 'Come in.'

In the intervening minutes since he'd flounced out of her flat, Ruby had put her hair up and applied some lipgloss. It was difficult to say whether the Neanderthal who trailed after her had made any effort apart from putting on the boots Ruby had dropped outside her flat.

'Straight through.' He pointed to the sitting room, but Ruby ignored him and handed him a bottle of wine. 'I thought …'

Good label. Not cheap. Brutus appeared, his tail wagging and produced an enormous toy rabbit. Ruby laughed and scooped both dog and rabbit into her arms.

'Thanks,' Adam said. 'There was no need.'

She shrugged. 'Can I help?'

He should have said 'No, make yourself comfortable'. But he wanted her close. Closer to him than to the lout in the front room. 'Perhaps a hand with the champagne?'

'Champagne?'

'You don't like champagne?'

'I love it.' Ruby nodded with such force that Brutus cradled in her arms appeared to nod too. 'I can't remember the last time I had any.'

'How about a drink, squire?' The goon stuck his head round the door and Adam fought back a scowl.

'I should introduce you,' Ruby said. 'Adam, this is Kevin. He's fitting my kitchen. Kevin, this is Adam, my neighbour obviously and our chef for the evening.'

Their acknowledging nods were perfunctory, invisible to the naked eye. Adam filled up two glasses. Kevin took his and disappeared into the sitting room to watch another quiz programme.

'I didn't realise your boyfriend was your kitchen fitter,' Adam said.

She took a sip. 'God, no. You can't think ...' she spluttered. 'He's not my boyfriend. I didn't know you were cooking. Or that you'd go to this much trouble. I thought ...'

Ruby put down her drink. Her eyes glistened. Adam hoped she wasn't about to cry. She turned a deep pink colour and buried her face into Brutus's fur. He wagged his tail and tried to turn upside down to lick her.

'Any chance of a top-up?' Kevin appeared, wiggling an empty glass.

'Here, take the bottle,' Adam said and thrust it at him in his eagerness to get him out of the kitchen. 'The glasses are ridiculously small,' he added, when Ruby looked up with a raised eyebrow.

Kevin took the bottle but not the hint. 'You thought about having this kitchen remodelled?' he asked, opening and closing a cupboard door.

'Adam's house-sitting for a friend,' Ruby said. 'It's not his apartment.'

'Shame. This space could be used much better.'

Any publicity is supposed to be good publicity, but Clive might object if all the national papers covered the fatal stabbing by Bootles' chef of a really annoying customer.

'I wouldn't be a good kitchen fitter if I didn't point that out to you,' Kevin said after a while. 'Why don't you give your mate my card? Very competitive pricing.'

'Look, I need to plate up the starters and check the mains,' Adam said, conscious he was fighting a losing battle to keep his temper.

'Why don't we sit down?' Ruby said, widening her eyes as she steered Kevin out of the kitchen. 'It smells like supper won't be long.'

'Where do you want us?' Kevin asked, over his shoulder.

Please don't bloody tempt me.

Adam made sure they were both seated, and each had a full glass of wine.

'I'm more a beer man, but if this is all you've got, I'll cope,' Kevin said and drained his glass immediately.

'Your starter,' Adam said, ignoring him. He produced two individual plates, each covered with a glass dome. He put a plate in front of Ruby and one in front of Kevin and then whipped off both domes, watching Ruby's face as he did.

Smoke rose gently.

'It's a smoked wild mushroom and white truffle terrine,' he said.

She breathed deeply and smiled. 'I can smell rosemary. I love the smell of rosemary.'

'You've burnt it, haven't you mate?'

'What?' Adam spun around.

'Well, I'm not Egon Ronay, but ...'

Adam hated people who emphasised speech with imaginary quote marks and this guy was up there with the best of them. Actually, even without the finger gestures, this guy had surpassed them.

'This is smoking, and you've tried to disguise the smell with a pretty heavy air-freshener.' Kevin pushed his plate to one side. He ignored the glass he'd been drinking out of, pulled a bigger one across the table and filled that from the bottle of wine. Ruby stared at him open-mouthed. 'Maybe you'll have more luck with the main course,' he added.

'Please, enjoy your starters.' Adam backed out of the room, before he lost the ability to control the urge to bring one or both of the glass domes down on Kevin's head.

Ruby brought the plates out to the kitchen as Adam put the finishing touches to the main course.

'I'm sorry,' she said, quietly. 'It was either him or my ex. I thought no one could be as bad as Daniel.'

'I think you're wrong.' Adam looked at her on the other side of the kitchen, tendrils of hair escaping from her hair clip.

Adam closed the door to the sitting room. 'Are you okay?' he asked, turning towards her.

'Just thinking.'

'Penny for them.'

Ruby twisted her hands together and looked as if she was wrestling with the decision whether to tell him or not.

'At school, there was this horrid girl. Everywhere I went, she followed me. She always wanted to know where I was going, what I was doing. In the end I reacted badly.'

Adam stopped stirring the jus and looked up. 'What did you do?'

'I said, "Fuck off, Lucy".'

Adam fought an urge to laugh.

'She ran to the teachers. The headmistress called Mum in, I was grounded and had to write 500 lines about not swearing. Mum said it was okay to think it but not say it.'

'You never said it again?'

'I have thought it from time to time.' Ruby looked at her hands. 'But thinking it is nowhere near as satisfying.' She shook her head. 'I worked with a Fuck-off Charlotte once. Awful woman. Never listened to the clients, so when they turned down her proposals, which they did all the time, it was never her fault. Nothing ever was.'

She paused and Adam watched her, but she didn't look up.

'Then there was Fuck-off Daniel – my ex.'

'And he did?'

'No. I left him. Now there's Fuck-off Kevin and I'd really love to say it to him, but can't afford to, in case he does, and I don't get my kitchen fitted.'

She looked unhappy.

'It's okay,' Adam said, quietly. She looked so vulnerable, he just wanted to take her in his arms, hold her tightly and kiss her hard.

'No, it's not,' she said, closing her eyes for a moment. 'I wish I'd never entered the bloody competition. He's getting horribly drunk.'

'I'm glad you did.'

She took a deep breath before she looked at him again. 'Thank you.'

'Now I have a pretty decent Chablis to accompany the main dish, maybe you could pour Kevin a glass.' Adam took the bottle from the fridge, uncorked it and pushed it across the worktop. 'I'll dish up.'

He stared at her and she stared right back at him with melting chocolate eyes and he gripped the worktop to stop himself reaching out and touching her.

'Okay,' she said and walked back to the table.

Adam shook his head to clear his mind of all inappropriate thoughts. It was hardly professional to lust after customers, and he needed to concentrate. He served up, taking extra care to ensure the presentation was perfect before carrying the two plates through to the table.

'Your main course tonight is a seafood broth, turbot, mussels, scallops and oysters served with saffron and salsify,' Adam said, putting Ruby's dish down first.

'Fish?' Kevin stared at the bowl Adam placed in front of him.

'Turbot. A highly prized flat fish noted for its delicate flavour. More wine, sir?'

Kevin nodded. 'So where are the chips?'

'I can't wake him, so I phoned for an ambulance,' Adam said. 'Just precautionary.'

Ruby's eyes widened. 'You don't think we've killed him?'

'He's breathing. But he has guzzled the best part of three bottles of booze.'

'Did he hit his head when he fell?'

'I don't think so.'

'What if he's allergic to fish? He could be unconscious and unable to tell us about his allergy.'

'He looks normal. A little pale maybe, but he doesn't appear to be reacting to anything.'

'Are you sure?'

'We had a customer once in the restaurant who had a nut allergy. He went red in the face and passed out just like that. The first we knew anything was wrong was when his girlfriend straddled him and stabbed his leg with a pen contraption. Kevin looks nothing like him.'

Ruby smiled. 'Presumably he hadn't spent half an hour proclaiming the Flying Fish sold the best chips in the world and the girl on the counter could batter his—'

A long buzz of the main door intercom signalled the paramedics had arrived.

Adam gave them directions to his flat and waited for them

in the corridor. He came back moments later with two men in green uniforms who strode purposefully down the hall, weighed down with all sorts of equipment. They fussed around Kevin, asking questions about his health and history neither Ruby nor Adam could answer. Kevin lay motionless throughout, to the point Adam started to worry he had misjudged the situation and the man was genuinely ill.

After a few more attempts, the paramedics, seemingly bored with shouting at Kevin and shining lights in his eyes, loaded him onto a stretcher and carted him off to the Redford Emergency Department.

Adam watched until the ambulance turned the corner of the road before he returned to the flat to find Ruby flopped down on the sofa; Brutus flopped down next to her.

'I am so sorry,' she said, stroking the dog's head.

Adam handed her a glass of wine, poured another, and sat down at the table. 'It's certainly been eventful,' he said. 'Are you all right?'

She nodded; a tear glistened under the lights as it started down her cheek. 'Don't say anything nice. I might cry. You seem to have that effect on me.'

'Should I sing to you about brown paper packages?'

'You went to so much trouble.'

'Or snowflakes playing on your nose and eyelashes.' Adam didn't want her to cry, and if he had to channel his inner Julie Andrews to cheer her up, something he hadn't done since his balls dropped and his voice broke, he was prepared to give it a go.

'Definitely not.' Her eyes smiled, even if the rest of her face didn't share the same emotion.

'That's a relief.' He picked up the bottle and offered her a refill, but she shook her head.

'I've had too much already.' Her voice was only a minuscule degree louder than a whisper.

He filled another glass and sipped at the wine, enjoying the refreshing acidity of the Chablis as it hit his taste buds.

'Any more and there's every danger I might break into song, even if you don't.'

He put the bottle down between them. 'Should I worry?'

'Definitely. Another drink and I'd probably find it easier to sing from the top of the table.'

'The table is clear and the ceiling's high enough. In some modern flats that might be a problem, but you should be fine. Be my guest.'

'It's not a pleasant experience for anyone but me. My mother's the singer. I was thrown out of the choir at eight, when they realised where the bum notes and dodgy tunes came from.'

'Your teachers sound so cruel.'

'The choir mistress wasn't as bad as the recorder tutor. I forgot my instrument one day; she couldn't disguise her relief. She gave me a ruler and told me to pretend to blow and practise my finger positions. When I said I wouldn't forget the recorder again, she smiled sweetly and said it might be better for everyone if I did.'

'Brutal! You must have hated school.'

'It wasn't that bad.' Ruby smiled. 'I was primary school chess champion for six months.'

'So, if you start looking like table surfing, I could get a chess set out?'

'That should do it.' She blinked at him. 'I think you're lovely. That was the most amazing meal I have ever tasted.'

Adam stared at his drink, the carpet and the table. He gave the room more attention than he'd given it in the whole two weeks since he'd moved in. He looked everywhere except at the woman sitting opposite him. The first few bars of "Drift Away" snapped him back to reality. She was humming.

'Sorry, you don't like it?'

'I didn't say that.' It wasn't a song he remembered hearing a great deal of before he moved into the flat above her. 'You sing a lot.'

She frowned and grabbed the arm of the chair. 'Oh God, I'm sorry, you can hear me in here? Jason always used to have his radio on when he was at home. I never thought …'

Adam ran a hand through his hair and shrugged. 'It's not an issue. I only ever hear snippets when the windows are open.' It was still February and he didn't think he'd opened a window since he'd moved in, but she didn't argue.

'Sorry.' She grimaced. 'If I bother you, you would say, wouldn't you? When I'm happy – I remember I can't sing, but when I'm stressed, I start with Dobie Gray and if that doesn't calm me down, I move on to Meatloaf. When it really can't get any worse, I hit 10cc.'

'That means something's really wrong?'

She nodded. '"Drift Away" – things are bad, stressed girl in need of chocolate. "Rubber Bullets" – the girl's gone wild. Send alcohol and reinforcements. What about you?'

I run away. Adam stared at his empty glass rather than meet Ruby's eye. She was probably watching him; he didn't look up. It wasn't a conversation he wanted to have just then. It would need too much explanation. He heard her shift in her seat.

'I should be going. I am dangerously close to the tabletop thing,' she said, and stood up. 'Do you really know all the words to that *The Sound of Music* song?'

Don't go. 'Absolutely not.'

'I bet you sing along every Christmas.'

'I can't.'

She stopped, her face creased with concern. 'Why?'

'I forget what comes after Doorbells and Sleigh bells.'

'Schnitzel and noodles. I knew it.'

'I haven't sung it all the way through since I was about

twelve.' Adam stood up and puffed out his chest. 'It used to be my party piece at family gatherings. My mother would let me have a sip of her sherry if I sang it. Obviously, child exploitation, but for the most part I think I'm over it.'

'And these days?' Ruby giggled. 'What do you do to relax and calm down?'

'I cook. It's all I've ever wanted to do.' Adam smiled. She was gorgeous. 'In principle, I have my dream job. I'm a chef. And ...' He rubbed his nails against his shirt, 'a bloody good one.'

'I wouldn't argue with that. The food tonight was delicious.'

'The night isn't over yet.'

She gave him a sidelong look. 'I really have to go.'

She had every right to look concerned; the line sounded like it came from a bad horror movie. 'I didn't mean ... I wasn't trying ...'

Ruby wiggled forward on the sofa.

'Please. Stay until you've tasted my chocolate fondant with white chocolate and caramel surprise, accompanied by burnt cream?'

She stopped wiggling and sat back. 'That sounds lovely, Julie, although if you could set it to music ...' She held the cushion he threw at her against her face. He hoped the shaking meant she was laughing not crying.

'Just a moment.'

She didn't wait, she followed him into the kitchen and sat on the worktop watching as he slipped a sharp knife round each of the pudding moulds to release their contents. She bit her bottom lip and concentrated hard. 'You said in principle, what did you mean?'

'One day I'd like my own restaurant.' He hoped the fondant would come out whole. It looked okay, but only time would tell. He covered the mould with a plate, inverted it and shook the whole thing before turning the plate back over and lifting the mould away to reveal deep brown steaming puddings. And breathe.

Ruby's eyes got wider by the minute.

'Taste this.' Adam dipped a spoon into the pudding, then the cream and passed it to her.

She made no attempt to take the spoon but closed her eyes as it came closer and let Adam feed her chocolate pudding.

'That's bloody awesome,' she said. He fed her a second mouthful, then another. For those brief minutes, the look on her face and the evident delight she experienced was worth all the effort and stress of the last few hours. He'd wanted her to taste his cooking. She had, and she liked it.

'So,' he asked, quietly. 'Still want to sing on my table?'

Ruby had just had the most incredible evening, despite how it had started. She felt alive. It hadn't been lovely; it had been amazing. It no longer mattered her flat was a mess and she had to share her bed with a mixer and various bowls; she'd had an outstanding time. Okay, it wasn't a real date, but it felt every bit as special as any date she'd ever been on. Adam walked her home – accompanying her down the flight of stairs and short corridor. She'd turned to give him a peck on the cheek to say thank you, but he turned to say something, so her air-kiss landed firmly on his lips. He hadn't recoiled, hadn't pushed her away. He'd kissed her back.

'Goodnight,' she'd said. 'Thank you.'

'Goodnight,' he replied. 'My pleasure. Maybe you'd like to do it again sometime.'

She nodded enthusiastically. 'Shall I speak to Kevin in the morning, see when he's free?' She tried to keep a straight face but couldn't. He laughed and pulled her into a hug. Then he dropped another kiss on her forehead and walked away.

She waited until she heard his flat door shut, before she

closed her own. Now, the boiler had been disconnected, the flat wasn't any warmer inside than out, but with all the feelings dancing throughout her body Ruby didn't notice the cold. The way she felt at the moment had nothing to do with anything she'd eaten or drunk. It was a nice feeling, new, exciting and she liked it.

With so much electrical activity pulsing round her body she wasn't ready for a night spooning with her mixer. Balancing the kettle on the coffee table, she made a hot chocolate, changed into her pyjamas and carried the drink back to her desk.

Moving the mouse brought her computer back to life. She sighed at the sight of her inbox. In excess of a hundred emails, despite the fact she always ticked the "Don't Contact Me" box. Her nightly ritual was to delete everything. The only way to avoid drowning under a tsunami of junk offers. She skimmed quickly through them. There were no congratulatory ones, but in the middle, she found one from Daniel. She recoiled in horror at the name. In the subject line he'd written "Valentine, we need to talk."

Ruby rubbed her cheek. She needed to wash her face. She needed to clean her teeth. She was desperate for biscuits and fluffy slippers without holes in, but she definitely didn't need to talk to Daniel.

Remember resolution number five – her self-conscience mocked. She stuck out her tongue at the computer. Daniel wasn't happy, that much she gathered from his first line. 'Not my problem,' she said, deleted the email and switched off the computer with a degree of satisfaction. She'd had an amazing evening with an amazing man. Not even Daniel could spoil her mood.

Chapter Eight

Under the banner headline *"Valentine Meal Winner"* there she was, on the front page of *The Chronicle*, staring slightly, okay *very*, drunkenly back at herself. Adam had asked if she minded having her picture taken. His boss had asked for pictures of the couple and food, for publicity. Both of them had agreed a comatose Kevin probably wouldn't be a good advert.

"Ruby and her companion experienced a three-course meal in the luxury of their own home," she read, *"cooked and served by Bootles' head chef. 'It was amazing,' Ruby said."* And it had been.

There was another image of Adam's fabulous pudding. The grainy black and white photograph didn't do it justice but made her mouth water at the thought. She quickly turned the top few papers face down on the stack by the till and concentrated on arranging her shopping on the conveyor belt, desperately trying not to catch anyone's eye.

With it being February and cold, she'd dressed up for her shopping trip, padded jacket with fur-trimmed hood. She hadn't expected to be front-page news though, so pulled her hood as far forward as possible. So far so good. She hadn't been recognised, or if she had everyone was too polite to mention it. It was early and the supermarket wasn't too busy. She'd buy the few items in her basket and then stay indoors all day. Tomorrow, she'd be old news.

Ruby opened the three packets of cupcake mix as soon as the cashier scanned them, before adding them to her carrier bag. "Congratulations – Winner!" All the flaps screamed. "Have a party on us."

'They all say I've won ten packets,' she said, tearing the

flaps off and handing them to the checkout girl. 'That's another thirty boxes.'

Baking for Ruby was something of a spectator sport. She was a *Great British Bake Off* superfan, but that hardly made her a "star baker", and with her kitchen completely missing, now probably wasn't the right time to start, but the "every one's a winner" sign had taunted her from the other side of the store. *"Win anything from a recipe card, 10p money off vouchers to a trip to the home of the cupcake."*

'Another thirty boxes?' the woman behind the till repeated. Ruby nodded and the cashier rang her bell to highlight she had a problem. The queue behind Ruby who had clearly thought three packets of cupcake mix and six bottles of "three for £10" wine shouldn't take long, tutted – loudly.

'What is it Zara?' an older woman turned up. She had a bunch of keys in one hand and a supervisor badge pinned to her chest. 'She's old enough for alcohol.'

'Nah,' the cashier said, as she waved the flaps. 'She's opened the boxes and wants another thirty packets of cupcake mix.'

'Thirty?' The supervisor said and took her time reading the vouchers, clearly hoping the small print would give her some sort of get-out clause. 'Okay,' she said, finally. 'That's quite a lot of cupcakes. Have you paid for the rest of your shopping?'

'Yes,' both Ruby and the cashier said at the same time.

'Customer services then.'

There came a collective sigh of relief from the queue building behind.

'We need to take some details,' the supervisor said.

'You'll send them to me?' Ruby asked.

'No, you can take what we've got. I'll get someone to clear the shelves.' The woman looked at her bag. 'Plastic bags will be 5p each.'

Shouldn't winning prizes feel amazing? She should be on

cloud nine, but following the woman down the store, with everyone staring, Ruby felt like a criminal. *Did they suspect she'd been shoplifting or recognise her from the paper?*

'You're not going to open any more boxes in here, are you?' The supervisor frowned as a young shop assistant packed six bottles of wine, her three packets of cupcake mix and a further twenty-seven into a large trolley – along with a Cornish pasty, a packet of hot cross buns and a TV guide.

'You haven't got any more,' Ruby said.

The last three items the supermarket had given her in exchange for three packets of cupcake mix. They'd run out and couldn't be sure when they'd get another delivery. They didn't even charge her for the eight plastic bags that were full to bursting.

'You'll have to come back if you win with that lot. Probably best to ring first and check we've got enough,' the supervisor said.

The young assistant was on his way out of the shop with the impressive tower before she could stop him. 'Where's your car,' he asked, standing looking at the car park.

She blushed, suddenly consumed by an embarrassed heat. She'd walked this morning.

'Ruby?' a blonde woman said. 'Is that you?'

She looked around. Normally she had a good memory for faces. This woman didn't register on her radar. Not an ex-colleague. *Someone she'd done an event for?* She didn't think so. One of Daniel's colleagues' wives – perhaps. 'Yes,' she said cautiously.

'I thought it was. Hi, Emily – Emily Watkins.' The woman stuck out a hand.

'Where's your car, madam?' the shop assistant asked again.

'At home,' she said. 'Sorry. I didn't bring it this morning. Could you look after those for me? I only live ten minutes away. I'll be back within half an hour.'

'Why don't I give you a lift,' Emily said and before Ruby had a chance to argue, the woman directed the assistant to her car. 'You live in Redford, don't you?'

Kevin King Kitchen's van was still in the car park when they pulled up at Union House. The morning's ice had started to melt on his windscreen, but it obviously hadn't been moved. Ruby phoned the hospital first thing, only to discover he'd been discharged in the early hours of the morning. The nurse who answered the phone couldn't tell her anything else. He'd have to come back to the flats even if only to collect his transit.

'Where do you want these?'

Ruby indicated the sofa and the lounge table. It took them three trips to get everything out of the car and then turn boxes of cupcake mix into some weird art installation.

'You had a romantic meal in this.' Emily's voice rang with rich, thick sarcasm. Her bright pink mouth pursed tight; she sounded as if she barely managed to hold back ill-disguised disgust. 'Adam cooked in here?'

Whoa, where did that come from? 'Look lady. It might not look much to you, but this is my home.'

Emily looked embarrassed. 'I'm sorry, I didn't mean ...' she stuttered.

'No, he didn't cook here. It may have escaped your notice, but the television over there is balanced on my fridge. The kitchen units are in my spare bedroom. The cooker and freezer share my bedroom. He's a great cook, but he's not a flaming gymnast. He cooked upstairs.'

'Upstairs?'

Okay this was getting weirder by the second. 'Remind me, how do we know one another?' Ruby put her hands on her hips and frowned. Something wasn't right here. 'Who exactly are you?' Thirty years ago, she would have sat on her brother until he surrendered and told her everything she wanted to know. Ruby considered that option. Build-wise, Emily Watkins shouldn't be too much of a problem, even if she was sheathed in layers of scarves and shawls in varying colours. Maybe in her spare time she performed the dance of the seven pashminas. But … if Ruby took a running jump from the top of the sofa, she ought to be able to bring her down.

'We don't actually know each other. We haven't met before.'

Ruby wasn't going completely mad then.

'I recognised you in the supermarket from this morning's paper.'

'Are you a nutter?' *Good question, Ruby Brooks. Direct, no beating about the bush.* Emily looked mortified, but worryingly didn't deny it.

'And Adam?' Hands still on hips, Ruby stood facing the woman in her best "don't mess with me, or I might have to draw my gun" pose – as borrowed from any American Western.

Emily coloured, flopped down on the arm of the sofa and burst into tears. 'He's my boyfriend,' she mumbled through the tissue she was using to wipe her eyes.

Ouch. Didn't see that coming. It was like being knocked over with a sledgehammer. Then, while you were lying on the road, getting driven over by the heaviest steamroller in the world. 'You're his girlfriend?' Ruby said, as the breath fled from her flattened body.

'I'm sorry. I wanted to meet the woman he spent Valentine's night with. I wanted you to be old, married, devoted to your husband. Then I wouldn't have felt so bad about being stood up, but you're not. You're lovely and I'm jealous.'

Even completely flattened, Ruby should have thrown her out, but when someone tells you you're lovely, even if they're probably crazy, you sort of warm to them.

'Do you think I could have a drink,' Emily sobbed. She was looking at the bottles of wine.

'Tea,' Ruby said, firmly. 'I could probably run to a cold cross bun.'

It would have been easier to give Emily a glass of bloody wine. It took her ten minutes and by the time she got back with two mugs of tea and a plate of buns, Emily had composed herself, taken off her coat, re-applied her make-up and was fiddling with her handbag.

Ruby handed her a mug.

'Could I ask a huge favour?' Emily stressed the "huge".

Say no. Not difficult. One little word.

'Would you give this to Adam, next time you see him? I don't want to leave it outside his flat. I'd planned on taking it to Bootles after I'd been to the supermarket, but what with helping you, I'm running a bit behind.' Emily didn't wait for an answer. She pulled a folded orange shopping bag advertising their local supermarket out of her handbag and pushed it towards Ruby. 'Do you have any plans for the kitchen?'

Oh, usual thing, put everything back in. 'Sore point,' Ruby said, watching over the top of her mug. 'How long have you and Adam been an item?'

'About three years. He's my soulmate.' Emily smiled. 'Has he told you how we met?'

Ruby felt she was being flattened and fast. Steamrollered flat. Adam hadn't mentioned a girlfriend. Not when he fed her chocolate pudding, teased her with spoonfuls of burnt cream or kissed her outside the flat.

'I don't know him well,' she said.

'I thought it was a fix,' Emily said. 'You winning the competition.'

'Someone had to.'

'Yes, but rather convenient don't you think, with you living so close.'

Ruby didn't like the way the conversation was going. She took a mouthful of bun and studied Emily.

'We met in Bootles,' she said. 'It was like a blind date. His boss cooked for us. It was incredibly romantic. We were right for each other. Adam was so lovely.'

He still is.

Emily put her cup down. 'We really ought to go and have another meal there. Only Adam says it would be too much like a busman's holiday.'

'Couldn't you go somewhere else?'

'I thought it would be more romantic to go back to the place it all started three years on, to celebrate our anniversary,' Emily said. 'I don't think he realises how much I want to do it.' She paused. 'Perhaps, if you were to explain how important it is to me ...'

'I don't know,' Ruby said, miserably. Last night had been brilliant. She'd been happy. Dazzled by the food and Adam's smile, but today reality had returned, like some sort of bad joke. 'We're not that close.'

Emily made a show of looking at her watch. 'Look, I've got to go,' she said. 'My shop opens at eleven on Tuesdays.' She stood up and was back in her coat, in a movement Wonder Woman would have been proud of. 'Please try,' she added. 'You know what men are like.'

Clearly not. Otherwise Ruby would have guessed Adam was involved with someone else and wouldn't have wasted last night dreaming about him. The female intuition gene had either bypassed her completely or been hijacked by life. She'd got it badly wrong three times now: first with Daniel, then her kitchen fitter and now Adam.

'You've got someone, haven't you?' Emily asked, as she strode down the hall.

'What makes you think that?'

'Ruby and her companion, the paper said. Are you telling

me there was no companion?' Her eyes narrowed and her cheeks puffed in a puce sort of way. She looked scary.

'Oh him,' Ruby said. 'He's just someone I know. That's his van in the car park.'

Emily looked out of the window. Some of her colour dissipated; she was still flushed, but no longer looked like she was about to explode. 'Not your romantic ideal?'

'I'm not looking for romance,' Ruby said. 'Too much on my plate.'

'That's a shame,' Emily said. 'I hope you change your mind soon and when you do find someone, hold on to them. Life's so much better when there are two of you.'

Would opening another seven packets of cupcake mix constitute the requisite competition entries for the day?

Ruby looked at the cupcake mix boxes piled up on her desk while the computer booted up. The thought of winning the wherewithal to potentially feed a small town was more than she could stomach. She searched for less fattening prizes – an axe-throwing experience, weekend in the Yorkshire Dales, theatre tickets, lashings of gin, a personalised baked beans can, a car and a funeral plan.

Emily was wrong. Ruby was free of Daniel and life was better on her own. She'd stayed with him far too long. Initially, she'd tried to work at the relationship. Humour him. Let him be in control. That didn't work and staying didn't make her a better person; it just made them both miserable.

Their relationship never made her feel dizzy or as alive as Adam had made her feel last night. She understood now what people meant when they said sparks flew or the earth moved. No fireworks or bulldozers had ever been operated where Daniel was concerned. Her heart had never missed a beat when someone mentioned his name. Yet, when Emily mentioned Adam's name, her insides felt as though they were dancing.

She used to envy her brother, Ben, and his fiancée, Belinda, their closeness. Ben never suggested ways for Belinda to correct her imperfections. Or made her feel so guilty going out with her friends that eventually she cut them off. They hung on one another's words, laughed together, held hands and gazed at each other adoringly.

They were made for each other. She and Daniel weren't. Still, her mother liked him. Ben and Belinda loved him, but then they had every reason to. Daniel had helped them find and buy their home.

In private, his criticisms about her clothes, her make-up, her friends, her cooking and practically everything she did or said, wore Ruby down. Most of the previous four years, when she thought about it, had been spent walking on eggshells.

Her job had given her a purpose; she'd given it everything she'd got and had been rewarded well. Her annual bonus allowed Daniel to buy the latest gadgets he craved.

Last year the company didn't pay a bonus. The directors said it was a hiccup and no reflection on the amount of effort anyone had put in over the year. Daniel didn't believe her at first and then blamed her for not working hard enough. He walked out to drown his sorrows and she walked out with the imprint of his hand on her left cheek. She never went back and six weeks later she moved into Union House.

A month later, just before Christmas, "the hiccup" her company was experiencing had grown into a full-scale burp. A slimline version merged with a London firm wanting to expand its operations further afield, and in the resulting right-sizing, Ruby's department was given redundancy and put on garden leave.

Crazy times, but her flat had felt like home from the minute she moved in, in a way the house she'd shared with Daniel never had. It felt right. Her own space. She could decorate it any way she wanted. She could shut the door and be her own person. It needed updating, that was part of the attraction. It meant she could put her own stamp on it, paint the ceilings red and the skirting boards purple if she wanted. Okay, she didn't: pale matt walls and white ceilings and gloss work were more her bag, but if she wanted to introduce splashes of colour then she could without having to explain her choices to anyone.

She hung pictures on the walls, wore the clothes she liked and enjoyed the freedom of eating what she wanted and visiting places and people without repercussions.

No, Emily was definitely wrong. She decided she was far happier on her own as she answered her phone the second it started to ring.

'Ola,' she said, in the best foreign accent she could muster. 'Zees is Ruby's phone. Please, I help you.' She sounded like goodness knows what crossed with a woman on helium. She waited. Nothing. Nada. Silence.

'You no want my help. Okay. Bye.' Now she sounded like Inspector Clouseau crossed with something out of *Finding Nemo*.

'Excuse me, I need to speak to Miss Ruby.' A deep male voice said in a foreign accent, far more convincing than anything she could conjure up. Someone was taking the piss. Odds on it was her brother, Ben.

'Why is your number hidden?' she asked in her normal voice. 'Don't muck about, I'm not in the mood.'

'Miss Ruby, is that you?'

Ruby stayed silent.

'This is Mr Tahsin. I have your carpet. Your prize-winning, beautiful carpet.'

She had no idea which competition he was talking about, but with over six hundred entries under her belt, she couldn't remember every one she'd entered.

'I am serious, Miss Ruby, you have beautiful Egyptian carpet. I deliver – now.'

'No.'

'Tomorrow, I come tomorrow. You see it and you will be happy.'

'Look, I'm sure the carpet is divine, but I have no space at the moment for a bath mat let alone a carpet.'

'Everyone, Miss Ruby, has space for a carpet. I come tomorrow.'

'Here let me help you,' Adam said. 'If I take the boxes, you open the door. I don't know the code.

'It's the devil's number – 666,' Ruby said as she typed the number into the keypad and pushed the door open. 'Jason told me that, the first time I met him.' She smiled at the memory. She'd met Jason in almost the same place, just outside the bin cupboard, the week she moved in. She'd been halfway through the chorus of "Drift Away" while trying to remember the code.

'Great choice of song,' he'd said.

'You recognise it?'

'Words, yes. Tune, no.' He'd laughed and she'd stuck out her tongue.

'So, what's the problem today Miss Songstress?'

'The code.'

Jason had punched in the number 6 three times and the door clicked open. 'Which makes 25.803 the root of all evil,' he'd said and laughed again.

They'd arrived home at the same time a few days later, just before Christmas, to find the Rotary Club ensconced on the front lawn singing carols for all they were worth. He'd turned to her with a raised eyebrow. 'Do you want to get lost in their rock and roll? Or do you fancy a curry?'

A sort of hello and goodbye meal, he'd called it.

'You look like you're having a clear out,' Adam said.

'Packaging,' Ruby said, bluntly, then added, because she didn't want to sound rude, 'I've unpacked my kitchen units.'

'I see Kevin's van's still here. Is he suffering badly?'

'Don't know.' She shrugged. 'Haven't seen him. I bloody hope so.'

'You don't think we killed him?'

'No, more's the pity. I've spoken to him.' Her head hated Adam, it just hadn't communicated the fact to her heart, which performed a most unnatural dance the minute she spotted him.

'But ...'

'He's not going to be here again, until I cough up another £400 because he hadn't calculated the granite for the worktops correctly.'

'He can't do that,' Adam said. 'I hope you told him.'

'I did and firmly.' Ruby rubbed her neck. *What was it with today? Was she walking around with a bloody sign on her head – "Doormat, please walk all over me"?* 'I said he quoted a price and had to stick to it.'

'And?'

'He laughed and said, "No way. If you're not prepared to cough up, there's no point me coming back." I said, "What about my money?" and he said, "You've seen the last of that".'

'Bastard.' Adam's eyes were wide with compassion he had no right to show. 'Is there anything I can do to help?'

Yes, leave that woman, take me away from here and next time make sure the kitchen fitter doesn't live. She shook her head. 'Thanks for asking.' They walked back to the flats together and were at Ruby's door before Adam spoke.

'I was just coming down to see you,' he said. 'I wanted to make sure you hadn't died of food poisoning.'

'It was a lovely meal,' she said. 'Hold on a second, I have something for you. I was going to bring it up. You've beaten me to it.'

She could have invited him in, it wasn't as if he was holding her up. Different emotions welled up and she wasn't sure how they were going to manifest themselves. Part of her wanted to slap him. Part of her wanted to burst into tears and another part wanted him to wrap his arms around her and look at her like he did last night. That part she thought she could control.

Ruby picked up one of the bottles of wine she'd bought earlier. It wasn't the one she'd intended to give him, but Emily's visit put paid to gifting the "nice" wine. The thought of him and Emily sharing a bottle she'd taken from Daniel's wine rack when she moved out was too much to bear.

Ruby thrust the bottle of wine into his hand. 'This is to say thanks for last night.'

'Lovely,' Adam replied and hesitated. 'Would you like a coffee?' he added after an uncomfortable silence.

'Sorry.' She shrugged. 'Lots to do, so little time ...'

'You've got to get to work – of course, I should've thought.'

Was that disappointment she could see in his face? For a moment, she even considered taking him up on his offer. No, that would be a big mistake, so she nodded. The orange bag she'd promised to deliver rustled behind the door, reminding her of its presence.

'Emily asked me to give you this,' she said, pushing the bag at him. 'She said you were expecting it.'

Adam's head jerked up and backwards as if she'd given him an electric shock.

His eyes widened. He stared at Ruby, then the bag and

even though he didn't reach for it, she still let it go. They watched it fall between them. As in the best movies, it took forever to hit the ground. When it did, it didn't sound like it had broken.

'Emily,' he said, huskily. 'You spoke to Emily.'

'You two need to talk,' Ruby said quietly and closed the door.

Chapter Nine

The man in the brown leather jacket who stood on Ruby's doorstep at nine o'clock in the morning was handsome in a dark, swarthy sort of way. And he had a killer smile.

There couldn't be a girl in the world who wouldn't have wanted him to lift her up on to his white charger and carry her off into the sunset, unless they were allergic to horses.

'Miss Ruby?' he said in a deliciously exotic accent.

There should be music.

'It is me, Mr Tahsin. We speak yesterday.'

Mr Carpet. Like a scene from Aladdin, except if they were to fly off on a magic rug, she hoped he didn't think she would wear anything as skimpy as Princess Jasmine, it was winter after all.

'I have carpet.'

Ruby frowned. It wasn't clear where he'd left it. When she imagined a carpet, she assumed it would need, at least, a small van to transport it and there wasn't one in the car park. She peered round him to take another look for good measure.

Bloody hell.

There was no van in the car park.

Kevin's had gone too. He must have collected it overnight. Not good; well he could whistle for his toolbox. That was still in her flat. She would hold it to ransom. *Return my money or finish my kitchen if you ever want to see your precious tape measure again. Any delay, I'll remove your screwdrivers one by one and use your chisels to remove tiles.* That should have him worried.

'Where is it?' she said. 'The carpet?' Because Mr Carpet

stood there with the smallest of briefcases even if he did have a smile to die for.

'Yes.' He smiled back. 'I have carpet.' Yesterday, she'd won a bag of frozen chips – the company emailed her a voucher. Maybe he'd present her with a voucher she could take to her nearest rug store and choose her own carpet. 'And forms to fill,' he added.

Ruby led the way to the kitchen.

'Uh-oh,' Mr Carpet said, his eyebrows having risen up his forehead.

She couldn't have put it better. In two syllables he'd summed up the state of her kitchen. She'd spent the previous night dragging units into the kitchen. Partly because she needed to do something to relieve her anger and partly because having found Kevin's toolbox, there were some plans inside which might or might not have had something to do with her dream installation. They were on a sheet of lined paper, the only straight lines on the page, so it was difficult to tell. Still, Ruby had a few GCSEs under her belt. She'd organised corporate events for the last twelve years. She regularly did Sudoku puzzles and had once discovered enough clues to get out of an escape room party, with very little help from anyone else. How tricky could deciphering kitchen plans be?

'Where is kitchen man?' Mr Tahsin asked, standing between two cupboard units and shaking his head.

'There's not one.'

Ruby felt a spurt of irritation as tiredness kicked in.

There had been no two ways about it, the plans didn't make sense. The units didn't fit, but in the cold light of morning, she needed to be sure. She picked up a tape measure.

'Hold that,' she said and handed Mr Tahsin one end of the measuring tape.

'Please Miss Ruby, I do carpets not kitchens.'

'You've said. Stand there and hold that.'

She squinted at her end of the tape and wrote down the measurements in both centimetres and inches to be on the safe side and compared them to the marks on the page. 'Shit, they're all different,' she said, staring at the plans. 'Now what do we do?'

'What we do?'

What is it with men? When they are surprised, they don't bother to hide the fact. His question ended with the same upward inflection her mother used when Ruby announced she'd left Daniel. Although to be fair to Mr Tahsin, he didn't look like he'd sucked on something unpleasant.

He tutted loudly and shook his head.

'Thank you.' Her irritation grew. 'I know, you do carpets not kitchens. But do you need this?' She rolled the tape measure back up. 'Shouldn't you measure the room the carpet is going in?' She waved a hand at the door to the living room. He might be good-looking, but he got on her nerves.

'You want big carpet? I take you to factory, you buy big carpet.'

'No way.'

'Your husband help with kitchen?'

'I don't have a husband.' The flash of gold when he grinned suggested some of his teeth were capped. Not a good look.

'No husband?'

'Not yet,' she said, uncomfortable with the direction his questions had taken. Yesterday the only thing the chip company wanted to know was "Is your printer connected?"

'My son does kitchens. He does whole houses. Very clever boy. He's at the factory. We go there and you meet my son. He is not married. You will like him.'

She'd rarely been so relieved to hear the sound of the front doorbell. Mr Tahsin looked down the hall. An expression she couldn't fathom clouded his face. Ruby legged it down the hall and threw the door open.

Brutus charged through.

Adam stood on the doorstep holding yesterday's orange bag. He looked uncomfortable. 'Please allow me to explain,' he said.

'Darling,' she said, loudly. 'Come in. Mr Tahsin is here with our carpet.' She put an arm through Adam's and dragged him down the hall ignoring his look, which if looks had speech bubbles would probably have said, "Fuck!"

'This is Adam, my fiancé.'

'Very good,' Mr Tahsin said, picking up his briefcase. 'I hope you marry happy and have many children.' It didn't escape Ruby's notice he'd lost his smile. Without it, he looked frankly shifty. On top of one of the units was a small, strangely coloured piece of material which hadn't been there minutes earlier, but then again it was so small she might've missed it.

She assumed it must be a sample until he waved a hand at it and said, 'Thank you, Miss Ruby. Be happy with your carpet.'

And he had gone.

Ruby pounced on the square of rug. Picking it up, she examined it carefully. 'This isn't even big enough to be a table mat,' she said, flinging it against the wall. 'I've won a bloody coaster.'

Brutus, clearly sensing some sport to be had, charged behind the units and appeared moments later holding it.

'What the hell just happened?' Adam, a faraway look in his eye, appeared to be focussing at a spot on the wall.

Ruby squinted at the wall. 'I took the tiles off. I have new ones.' She'd lost a bit of plaster in places but nothing serious; surely the gaps could be filled easily enough.

Adam continued to stare at the wall. He held the orange bag to his chest. She began to understand what people meant when they talked about silence being deafening.

'You called me, darling,' he said. He removed the carpet from Brutus' mouth, handed it to Ruby and left.

'What is it about me that attracts wankers?' Ruby recoiled as the door slammed. 'It's not like I bloody advertise. I should've realised something was wrong when your master came to pick up his parcel wearing a beanie hat, even if his coffee and cooking are to die for.'

Brutus wagged his tail by way of response, clearly not concerned about being dumped in a flat with a strange woman.

When she'd opened the door to find Adam there, she'd been relieved.

'Let me explain,' he'd said, clutching Emily's orange bag.

She hadn't given him a chance. Not that she needed to hear the "my girlfriend doesn't understand me" line.

She sat down at her desk and wiggled her mouse to get her screen back to life. An early start this morning meant she was already nine competitions down and today's prize haul could include a casino experience, an outdoor shower attachment for a caravan she didn't own, waterproof trousers, inch loss treatment, an electric chainsaw, an eco-friendly frying pan, a three-day residential course at the Exmoor Yoga fest, a suitcase with wheels, and a flower pressing kit.

'He'll have to come back for you?' Ruby said, staring at Brutus.

When he did, she would apologise for the fiancé stunt. It wasn't as if she didn't know about Emily. She'd explain she'd only done it to get rid of Mr Tahsin and he presented an option cleaner and simpler than murder. He'd understand, wouldn't he?

Chapter Ten

Adam stopped at the side of the road and said 'Sit' before he realised, he wasn't being followed by a Border Terrier. *Shit.* He'd have to face her again, sooner than he hoped. His heart pounded. Not yet. His head throbbed. He needed to calm down.

It was okay to say think rationally. He had. It had all been so clear in his mind this morning. He'd take the bag down to Ruby, show her the card. She seemed a reasonable woman, she'd understand. He'd explain about Emily. They'd laugh, have a cup of coffee and things could go back to normal. Or they would as soon as he could seek out and destroy the bloody Meatloaf CD that had kept him awake half the night.

He took the footpath to the high street.

Normal. A nice word, but what was normal these days? Living on his own in a friend's flat, too terrified to go home? Cooking mediocre food in a mediocre bistro in town because he didn't have the get-up-and-go to do something about getting a place of his own?

He didn't want normal. He wanted a life. He wanted to cook food, amazing food for people who appreciated it. For a woman who sometimes sat on his worktop and smiled heart-stopping smiles at him.

Not a normal life, but a normal woman would be good.

Not someone certifiably nuts. Not again. What on earth had Ruby been playing at, introducing him as her fiancé? She hadn't minded upsetting the man she was talking to. Adam had been so shocked he'd forgotten the guy's name or what he'd been doing there.

What next? Hearts or kisses in lipstick on his front door.

She wasn't Emily.

Nothing like.

She'd called him darling. Clive did it all the time in the bistro. "Can I take your coat, darling?", "How was that for you, darling?" None of the women he addressed like that turned and rushed out.

She'd intimated there was something going on between them. That they were getting married. Then she'd lost her shit over a carpet tile.

Okay – he'd overacted. Acted like an arse and now she had his dog.

Adam's step faltered.

She must know Emily, how else would she have got the bag? She'd told him he should speak to her. Who was she? The only things he knew about Ruby Brooks were that she was an air hostess, had strange taste in music, was a lousy judge of character when it came to choosing kitchen fitters and, judging by the bottle of wine she'd given him yesterday, wine. He could help her with the latter. He smiled, a picture of her with her eyes shut savouring the taste popped into his head.

What if Emily had put her up to entering the competition? What if they were friends?

He was surprised by how much he hated the idea. He shivered and zipped his jacket up against the weather and the chill taking hold of his heart.

He had to sort the Emily situation out, once and for all.

Adam pressed the button at the traffic-lights and waited for the flashing green man to tell him it was safe to cross.

He'd spent most of the night worrying what to do, although the reason for his sleeplessness probably owed a lot to "Bat out of Hell" thumping out downstairs.

Up until eleven o'clock last night, Meatloaf had been one of his favourite musicians. By 2.30 in the morning, he'd dropped from that lofty position. By 6.00, he was down with

Brotherhood of Man and the Smurfs – music he hoped never to have to endure again.

And then when he finally managed to drop off, Ruby appeared in his dreams, standing, hands on her hips, just as she had yesterday, while she fought back emotions he couldn't fathom. He'd woken convinced she felt something for him. He hadn't expected it to be quite so full on. One frustrated stalker was enough for any man to have to cope with in a lifetime. He thought with Emily he'd reached rock bottom; that he couldn't get any lower. Wrong. This morning, the bottom of his world had dropped several more fathoms.

Adam carried the orange bag into the police station, holding it carefully in his handkerchief, between two fingers. As soon as he was through the doors, he dropped it onto the desk and sank into one of the visitors' chairs.

Not again. It couldn't be starting again. He'd started to relax. How on earth had Emily managed to track him down this quickly? What on earth had Ruby told her?

Inspector Lenham came out of a door to the left of the reception desk and smiled at him. 'More trouble?'

He felt like a child again waiting outside the head teacher's office. He resisted the urge to pout and look away – but only just.

At thirty-five, he'd never been in trouble with the police. Not so much as a parking fine. He'd only ever been in Redford police station once before this kicked off because he'd found some money on his way into work. Now, he felt like he was making up for all the years in-between.

The inspector signalled to another door. 'Let's talk in there – we won't be disturbed.' She picked up the bag from the reception desk and held the door open for Adam. 'How are you?' she asked, with genuine concern in her voice as he walked into the room. He collapsed into the chair she indicated and dropped his head into his hands. 'I was doing okay,' he said.

She put the bag on the table. 'Anything unpleasant?'

Adam shook his head. 'Another card.'

Inspector Lenham picked at the bag with suspicion as if any sudden movement might blow them both to kingdom come. Emily wasn't dangerous. Weird perhaps, but as far as he knew they were still two very different things. Peeling the carrier bag down, the inspector revealed a very large and very pink card.

'Wow, it must've taken her hours,' she said, poking it with a pen. 'Look on the bright side though.'

'There is one?'

'It's in better taste than her last Christmas card.'

He groaned, as he remembered the three wise men who all had faces glued over Eastern-looking robes, which may or may not have been cut from underwear. Somebody, one of the women PCs, had said the robes looked and felt like silk. Adam couldn't face touching any of it. The faces appeared to have been cut from old *Dad's Army* pictures; Jesus, in his crib, bore more than a passing resemblance to Pike. But more worryingly, the picture Emily had used for Joseph was a slightly out-of-focus image of him.

Adam hadn't believed it at first. He'd squinted at it several times, hoping he was wrong, except he recognised the shirt. Next to him, standing in what looked like a school uniform, a girl, presumably Emily, half a lifetime ago.

The police asked him to try and work out when the picture could have been taken. He'd bought the shirt in early November. The lightweight jacket he was wearing suggested one of the warmer winter days.

The Valentine's card on the table didn't have faces, just two hearts. Adam shuddered and Inspector Lenham pulled a face. One, a glittery foam heart had "Adam" written over it, in what could possibly be lipstick. The other appeared to be cut from a medical magazine. That heart looked like the real thing. "Emily" had been written above that one and she'd drawn arrows stuck in it from every direction. The card had a strange aroma.

'She's perfumed it.' The inspector bent down and sniffed it.

'That's perfume?' Adam asked.

'Can't imagine it was one of the supermarket's most popular scents.'

He smiled.

'I'm going to have to ask. Have you done anything to encourage her?'

'No.' He sat up straighter in his chair.

'It's okay. I believe you. What about any other contact?'

Adam told her about Bootles' competition entries.

'278. Wow, one determined lady. I bet she didn't take losing well. That could have prompted this. Anything else?'

'Nothing since the Christmas card, but I've moved into a friend's flat. I haven't been back to the house to check, but my boss is keeping an eye on things.'

The police psychologist had taken one look at the Christmas card and diagnosed Emily as infatuated rather than delusional. He'd said that, as if it should be good news and Adam should be pleased.

Until he changed his number, there had been phone calls, ten to twenty a day, leaving messages when he didn't pick up. Changing his address hadn't been so easy and over the years there had been a number of love letters and cards that he hadn't felt the need to read. Gifts, he hadn't opened. Flowers posted through his letterbox.

Things escalated last year when Emily rang Bootles and booked a table for a Saturday evening. They'd taken her booking. They had no reason not to. Adam was visiting his family at the time and only heard about it later. She'd sat in the restaurant alone and eaten her meal. She told the waiter she'd been stood up. She told other diners her other half wasn't able to be with her because he was working in the kitchen that evening. She even told them he'd recommended the sea bass. Jason asked her to leave and Clive barred her for life.

Adam found a rose tucked under the windscreen wipers of his car when he got home, with a note that said, "Sorry to have missed you" and lots of kisses. He still thought he could handle it and hadn't bothered the police until the card arrived and she'd drawn lipstick hearts all over his car.

'She's getting braver,' the police psychologist had said. The picture of Adam as Joseph, he seemed to think, had most likely been taken when Adam arrived or left work.

The police weren't hopeful of a conviction. It wasn't as if Emily ever threatened him in any way. There was, they assured him, very little risk of danger.

'What do I do?' Adam asked.

'The best thing,' Inspector Lenham said, 'is to try and play a low profile for the time being.' She sighed. 'It's not what you want to hear. I'm sorry.'

Adam had shrugged.

She'd leaned forward and tapped the card. 'I probably wouldn't consider another romantic entanglement at the moment either if I was you.'

'After this?' He'd laughed cynically. 'Do you think I'm stupid?'

When Jason moved to Paris and rang to say he was considering letting his flat, Adam practically bit his hand off.

He moved into Jason's flat hopeful the bad times were over. He had a new place to live; surely things could only get better.

For a while they did. Clive checked his house for him at least once a week. So far, there had been nothing other than the usual pile of utility bills and junk mail. But yesterday, it felt as if someone had pulled the rug out from under his feet.

'Tell me it's not always going to be like this,' he said, looking down.

'I can't do that,' the inspector said.

He reached across the table for a polystyrene cup of water and she put her hand on his arm.

'I won't lie to you,' she said. 'I've known cases like this that have gone on for years. Some victims have given up jobs, even moved to new areas.' Shaking her head, she added, 'Some think they can brave it out, but some end up resorting to alcohol or drugs to cope with the stress.'

'You think that will happen to me?'

'I didn't say that.'

Adam shook his head. *Where would he even go?* It wasn't as if he had endless friends he could move in with.

'Look,' Inspector Lenham said, sympathetically. 'We'll have a word, maybe threaten her with an injunction. Hopefully that will stop her.' She said it in the sort of voice that left him in little doubt there was more chance of David Beckham winning Wimbledon.

"I need a climbing helmet because ... Finish the slogan in fifteen words or less."

Tricky – at that moment it didn't matter if Ruby had fifteen or a hundred words to play with. Her mind wasn't on slogans. 'Can you think of something pithy and amusing to say?' she asked, stroking Brutus. 'About anything, preferably using words such as well-ventilated, multi-strapped and mountaineering. No? I thought not.' She shut the page. 'But look, a football shirt for your pet, in your team's colours?' She scanned the list. 'How would you like a Brentford shirt?'

Brutus licked her face.

'I'll take that as a yes.'

The entry confirmation email popped into her inbox as soon as she pressed enter only to be deleted along with the "must-have-compost" and the "You don't want to die before …" ones from earlier. Her phone started to ring.

'I haven't forgotten, Lily,' Ruby said. 'Dinner at six and don't be late because Ben and Belinda will be there.'

'Don't use that tone of voice, darling,' her mother said. 'I wanted to make sure you're coming alone.'

Ruby hadn't got to thirty-two without recognising a loaded question. 'Not exactly.'

'Daniel's right. You did leave him for another man.'

'That's what he told you?'

'Are we going to meet the "companion" you spent Valentine's night with?'

'What?'

'We read the papers, darling. We all do. But next time, go for a smile rather than a leer and you could have made more of an effort with your make-up.'

'I'm not going to dignify that with a reply.' *But next time you see Daniel, please sit on his head and fart in his face.*

'So, you are bringing someone?'

'Brutus possibly.'

'A dog?'

No, a Roman centurion. 'Yes, a dog.'

Lily sounded relieved. She was plotting something.

'Will you be drinking?'

In case I get drunk and feel the need to mention to Belinda red and yellow haven't been used as an effective fashion combination since Noddy's demise?

'You know me, I'll probably manage a glass or two just to be sociable.'

Ruby made a face at Brutus who tilted his head in a quizzical fashion in answer and wagged his tail. 'Mother,' she mouthed and covered the mouthpiece. 'You won't be wagging later. If your dad doesn't pick you up soon, you're coming too,' she whispered, stroking his head. 'Once you've met my mother, you'll never want to see me again.'

'Your brother has an announcement he wants to make.'

'He's running off to join a Taiwanese commune?'

'Don't be ridiculous. He's brought his wedding forward.'

That had been the purpose of the phone call. There was no way Lily Brooks was ever going to let her beloved son deprive her of making that announcement.

'He's been promoted. He's going to America for two years. They want to get married before they go. Belinda worried she'd have to find a different venue, but it's okay, the hotel has a vacancy in June.'

'That's only four months away.'

'Three and a half, so we need to arrange a shopping trip for your dress.'

'Sorry, I'm busy.' Ruby pulled at her fringe. It had got long. She stared at the ends and scowled. Maybe she should take a leaf out of Nickelback's book – cut her hair and change her name.

Silence again, except this time it felt armed and dangerous. 'We'll set a date to suit everybody, but seeing as you're not working at the moment ... Belinda would welcome help with planning the wedding, you know. She's got so much to do before they go.'

'Mum, I'm an event planner. Corporate events not weddings.'

'Not at the moment, darling, and what's a wedding, if not an event?'

In Ben and Belinda's case that wasn't an exaggeration. The planning for this had been going on for many years.

'How different can it be?'

You have seriously no idea.

'I'm on garden leave. I can't work without permission

or else my old company can demand repayment of my redundancy. I can't afford that, so as much as I'd like to ...'
Actually, I'd rather pull out my toenails without anaesthetic.
'I can't.'

'Who'd know? We're family. Everyone expects family to muck in and help arrange things. If it was the other way around, Belinda wouldn't hesitate.'

'I can't afford to take the chance. Obviously the original date of October wouldn't have been a problem, I'd have been happy to help.'

'They're leaving at the end of September.'

'Damn. That's unfortunate.'

The deep intake of breath on the other end of the phone told Ruby the silence that followed had teeth. 'Six,' Lily Brooks said as she hung up.

Glad to be free of the police station, Adam walked home across the playing fields. Lent was just around the corner. If the Christmas and Valentine's Day cards he'd received were anything to go by, he could be reasonably certain whatever the inspector said, Easter would mean a card covered with yellow pom-poms, cotton wool or worse. He shuddered.

From the top of the high street he made out the doors to Bootles' Bistro. The lunchtime sitting would be over. Tonight was his night off. He should go home, apologise to Ruby and collect his dog.

Adam crossed the road to the empty playground. He ignored the sign on the gate which warned of an unnatural end to anyone over twelve found in the play area and sat on the green swing.

He held the chains and let his legs rock backwards and forwards, rocking his upper body in time with the movement. Very soon he built up speed, rhythm and height. He could see the whole of Bootles' Bistro door and the board advertising afternoon tea and muffins, with free refills until 4.30.

He swung and wondered about Jason working in Paris. Was he missing home?

Clive's suggestion had been something he'd kept coming back to over the last few days. Three months – spring in Paris would be lovely and it sounded as if the writing was on the wall for his job, whatever Clive said. Adam couldn't afford to lose any hours. He had started looking at adverts for chefs. There were some interesting vacancies out there, both locally and further afield. But his heart wasn't in it. When it came down to it, he didn't want to work for anyone again.

Three months wasn't long.

Could it be my chance for a fresh start?

Paris would certainly put distance between him and Emily. He just needed her to get fed up waiting for a response and find someone else to stalk.

Could he afford not to take it?

It would give him time to clear his head and learn from a master. "French-trained chef" had a nice ring to it.

He was hardly in a great place at the moment. What did he have to lose?

Adam pulled his phone from his pocket and scrolled through his contacts.

'Jason. How are you? No, nothing's wrong with the flat. Everything's fine. How's Paris?'

He'd opened the flood gates. Jason was young, excited and clearly loving the Parisian experience.

Adam listened while Jason extolled the virtues of Paris, the menus and Xavier. He barely drew breath. But Adam was okay with that. As each minute ticked by, he became surer about what he needed to do.

Chapter Eleven

The faceless man on the other end of the legal helpline did nothing to comfort Ruby or alleviate her distress.

'You paid everything?' he said. 'You shouldn't have given him anything more than a small deposit. Haven't you watched any of the rogue trader or cowboy builder programmes that television companies love to run?'

Ruby was tempted to ask if he was related to her mother. 'Okay, I've been naïve. Now what?'

'Well ...' No doubt the man was sitting in a huge office, smugly rubbing his chin. 'You've tried contacting him?'

'He seems to have blocked my number.' She'd started the daily calls again but wasn't even being offered the chance to leave a voicemail now.

'You need to write to him. Tell him he's left you no option: if he doesn't recommence work immediately, you will take him to court.'

'You think that will work.'

'No.'

The day was getting better and better. Ruby stroked Brutus. At the moment, it felt as if he was the only creature in the world who hadn't tried to shaft her or run off when she needed help.

'From what you've told me, this man hasn't acted professionally, potentially even fraudulently. I have no doubt you would win the case. The judgement would be in your favour and Kevin King will be ordered to pay you back in full.'

A glimmer of hope. Light at the end of the tunnel. About bloody time.

'That sounds promising.'

'Don't get excited. I imagine he'll give the judge a sob story. Say he can't afford to pay you immediately, but as an offer of goodwill, he'll pay £1 a week until things improve and then he'll settle.'

Nope. Light firmly extinguished. 'You can't be serious. That would take nearly 200 years for me to get my money back?'

'Approximately, assuming the secret of eternal life is discovered before either one of you shuffles off this mortal coil. Or he doesn't default.'

From the other end of the phone it sounded like the man was typing.

'What did you say his name and company was?'

'Kevin King Kitchens.' The words stuck in Ruby's throat.

'Hang on.'

Brutus gave her a lick.

'Oh dear. Not good news I'm afraid. It seems his company folded seven years ago. Oh dear, oh dear.'

'What?'

'It gets worse. It appears he's in the middle of bankruptcy proceedings. Sounds like you're not the only one he owes money to. Didn't you check?'

'No,' Ruby mumbled. When she'd first seen the flat, it didn't have the kitchen of her dreams, but she could see beyond the tired, carved wooden cabinet doors. It had potential. Her redundancy cheque gave her the opportunity to not only follow the dream, but to make it fly.

Kevin King had said all the right things. He'd convinced her that her dream could be achieved. An ex-colleague recommended him; she hadn't mentioned any problems with bankruptcy.

Kevin told her he'd done a lot of work for a local hardware store. She'd asked them for a reference, but only this morning. Stable doors and missing horses came to mind.

They had no idea who she was talking about. 'Not one of ours,' the manager told her cheerfully, 'but we could give you a quote if you like.'

Plague victims had red crosses painted on their doors to minimise the risk to others. Surely people purporting to be professionals who were undischarged bankrupts should have similar marks on their business cards if not tattooed across their foreheads. Ruby pulled her desk drawer open in search of a red pen and found a pair of scissors. Not sharp. She hacked his business card into tiny pieces and found it strangely satisfying.

'The undischarged insolvency register gives the last known addresses for insolvents.'

Ruby stopped hacking.

'There is one for a Kevin King, kitchen fitter.'

'Where is he?'

'According to the register – Essex.'

Ruby sighed. 'He moved into Redford about five years ago.'

'Sorry, then. What about his office stationery? Do you have a letterhead or business card?'

Ruby put the pieces of his card back together, but already knew the answer. 'Just a mobile number.'

'Social media details, Facebook page or a Twitter handle,' the man asked.

'No handles at all, a bit like my kitchen,' Ruby said.

The man tutted. Clearly, he felt she had no one else to blame. He was right, if she hadn't been so eager to get on with the kitchen, of course she would have done some checks – wouldn't she?

Kevin had said he could visualise exactly the kitchen she was talking about. He had showered her with endless catalogues and told her about a supplier who would be happy to supply yellow gloss fronts for her cabinets. He'd even showed her pictures. However, it seemed he hadn't bothered to order them. On closer inspection of the delivered boxes, the doors and drawer fronts appeared to be a very washed-out colour; so washed out they were almost white.

'Anything else I can do for you today?' the man on the end of the phone asked.

Not unless you can recommend a good hitman. Ruby chopped angrily up into her fringe.

A lump of hair joined the massacred business card. Squinting at her reflection in the computer screen, even without her glasses, she could tell it wasn't good, more scarecrow than supermodel.

Ten minutes later, she'd created a pelmet rather than a fringe. She pulled the edges down either side of her face and tipped her head. At an angle of about thirty degrees it was almost straight.

Brutus angled his head too, presumably in sympathy. Ruby put down the scissors and sighed. 'It doesn't look as if your master is coming back anytime soon. We seem to be stuck with each other. Are you okay for a walk? I need to pay a quick visit to the supermarket before we go to mother's.'

Brutus wagged his tail and picked up a shoe. A gesture she took to mean "Yes".

'Only trouble is, your dad didn't leave a lead.' A rummage through Kevin's toolbox produced a length of thin cord with a weight on the end. 'This'll have to do.'

She picked up the scissors again and chopped off the weight.

'You've been reported,' Inspector Lenham said. 'A woman rang the station. She was worried and demanded to know exactly how many serial sex offenders have been released recently into the community in and around Redford. I said none. She refused to believe me, accused me of a cover-up, because she'd seen this dodgy-looking character hanging about in the kids' playground. I promised to check it out.'

'Dodgy?' Adam slowed his swing, relieved to see the inspector was on her own. She wasn't wearing riot gear, brandishing a truncheon or handcuffs. 'I'm only having a swing.'

'Yep, I can see that, and the sign by the gate, thanks to our own local graffiti artist, says this area is suitable for anyone under seventy-two years of age, but it should say twelve and technically you are breaking the law.'

Adam looked at where she was pointing. He could see what it said. 'You're going to arrest me?' he asked.

'God, no. Think of the paperwork. I've got delusional stalkers to track down and take out. I haven't got time to arrest you.' She smiled. 'But if you could leave the kids' playground quietly, so I don't need to use my taser or police-issue revolver, I would be most grateful. Actually, on second thoughts, it would give the locals something to talk about. Show we're taking our policing in the community work seriously and are not prepared to let anything get in the way of our wish to make Redford a safer place to be.'

Adam nodded. 'Sorry.'

'No need to apologise.' She held the gate open for him and walked with him across the park. 'You going back to your friend's flat? Want a lift?'

Having not decided where he wanted to go, that seemed like the best option.

'Thanks,' he said, climbing into her car. He could have a bath, collect Brutus, apologise to Ruby and let Clive know his decision about Paris.

Ruby. He came over all clammy. If he hadn't already been strapped in, he'd have changed his mind about the lift.

It took fifteen minutes to get through the rush hour traffic.

'Look.' Adam gasped, as the inspector indicated to turn

into the car park. He tried to flatten himself against the seat and hide below the dashboard.

'What?' The inspector peered through the windscreen.

'Emily. By the front door.'

'She looks so normal doesn't she?' The inspector got out her phone.

'Are you calling for backup?'

'No, taking a picture.'

'What should I do?' Adam's head ached.

She looked down at him, tucked into the footwell of her car. 'I'll deal with her.'

'What about me?'

'Stay there. If she looks like she's going to pull a gun, ring the police.'

The conversation, from a distance, seemed to be animated. Emily had her back to the car, so it was difficult to tell what her reaction to the confrontation was, although there was a lot of arm waving.

The inspector got a pad out and made some notes. She stayed put until Emily had left the front door. 'She's leaving. You should be safe,' she said, slipping back into the driver's seat.

Adam sat up straighter. 'What did you say?'

'Some of the residents had reported seeing a stranger hanging around outside and called the police.'

Adam watched his stalker get into a small car.

'She told me, there was nothing for me to worry about. She was waiting for her boyfriend and her friend, who were both out. I asked her to ring them, so I could have a word. As soon as I could confirm with one or the other that they were expecting her, I could leave her to wait.'

'She didn't ring.'

'It seems she doesn't have either number – someone called Ruby.'

'She didn't have Ruby's number. Are you sure?'

The inspector looked at him, closely. 'Ruby? Didn't you say she was the one you dumped the dog on?'

Adam blushed.

'She maintained the numbers must've slipped her mind because I had upset her.'

'You believed her?'

'I wasn't born yesterday. These days, everybody has everyone's contact details on their phone. She said she cleared her list down regularly, but there were pages of calls to one Redford number over the last few weeks and a few others.' The inspector showed him the numbers she'd written on her pad. 'Any of them mean anything?'

'That's Bootles' number,' Adam said, pointing one out.

'Your work?'

He nodded.

'Do you recognise any of the others?'

He shook his head.

'There are a couple she calls a lot. I'll have them checked out when I get back to the station. Just to make sure it's only you she's pestering.'

It hadn't occurred to Adam someone else might be experiencing the same problems.

'I carried out a stop and search. No weapons, but she was brandishing a lemon drizzle cake. Judging by its weight, you should be thanking me for saving you from a serious calorie overload.'

'You think I overreacted about the card, don't you?'

She smiled. 'No, I don't. And I told her that if there were any further complaints from residents or if her name came to our notice, in any other connection in the next six months, I would be speaking to her again and may consider bringing charges. She pulled the "Do I look like a criminal?" line.'

Struggling up onto his seat, Adam watched Emily do up her seatbelt. When she looked out of her window, he turned away and tried to shield his face, taking an unhealthy interest in the inspector's car's audio.

'She's gone,' the inspector said, quietly. 'Why don't I wait until you let yourself in?' She looked at her watch. 'I can spare a couple of minutes and I'll get the night team to add Union House to their patrol route over the next few days. If she's left anything in the porch, come straight back.'

Adam wished he was army trained. He could've rolled out of the car, run crouched and hidden from view until he reached the grass area. There, he could check the coast was clear from behind the bins and make a dash to the door. A rifle would be useful, just in case. He wouldn't kill anyone, but would randomly shoot into the air, so they knew not to mess with him. 'Thanks,' he said.

He paused at the main entrance, turned and waved. Inspector Lenham wound down her window.

'You leave those kiddy playgrounds alone, you hear.'

He responded with an improper gesture.

She laughed and drove off.

He watched until she was out of sight before he went in. She'd driven off the same way as Emily. Towards the town. He was alone.

As soon as his door shut behind him, Adam held his breath and listened; the silence unnerved him. Nothing, not even Meatloaf. He exhaled and went to find some aspirin, before he noticed the postcard on the doormat.

Ruby's mother opened the door and paled.

'Good God girl, what have you done to your hair?' Lily screeched.

The outburst had Brutus cowering in Ruby's arms.

'Belinda!'

Belinda came running. She did a double take when she saw Ruby.

'Please tell me you can do something with that.' Lily pointed at Ruby's head and closed her eyes. Her mum was dressed in her Sunday best, with a flowery apron protecting her outfit. Her nails were done, her hair set, and she was wearing make-up. She looked as if she was on the way to an evening out rather than cooking a family dinner.

'You should've rung, I'd have cut your fringe,' Belinda said, smiling. 'Just pop into the salon next time. If I'm busy, one of the other girls will do it. We never charge for a fringe trim between appointments.'

'She looks ridiculous,' Lily screamed. 'She did it on purpose, so she doesn't have to be a bridesmaid.'

'It's not a problem,' Belinda said quietly. 'It needs a bit of a tidy up, but I've got my scissors in my bag. I'll have a go after supper. It will look lush by the time I've finished. You'll still be able to be my maid of honour.' Before Ruby could run screaming from the house, she and Brutus were swept into a rib-crushing embrace. 'I don't want anyone else to do it,' Belinda added and disappeared back into the kitchen.

Ruby would've agreed to anything if it would stop her mother screaming. 'I've brought you some chips,' she said, handing over a winning bag of partially defrosted potatoes. 'I was going to bring wine, but you never approve of my choice.'

Lily took the bag, her face a picture, before she adjusted it accordingly to stare at Brutus as if he was the spawn of Satan. He sank as far as he could into Ruby's arms, his tail clamped between his legs.

'At least you're on time,' she said. 'That's something.' She pushed a cheek forward for a kiss. Ruby obliged. Brutus shook some more. 'Your brother and Belinda have been here for ages and they've made somewhat ...' Lily looked Ruby up and down. She should have been on stage. She was wasted tucked away in Redford. 'More of an effort.'

Purple sweater, jeans and clean underwear was an effort whatever the rest of the world thought.

There were sounds of laughter coming from the kitchen. Ruby could hear Ben laughing and Belinda screaming like a choirboy on speed. She took a deep breath and with Brutus firmly nestled under one arm she pushed open the door with her free hand and walked straight into her mother's beautifully fitted, Shaker-style kitchen and her ex.

'Hello, Ruby,' Daniel said. 'We need to talk.'

'You didn't think to mention he'd be here,' Ruby hissed at her mother behind her. Lily had effectively blocked her exit, while trying her damnedest to look every inch a domestic goddess.

This had to be someone's idea of a joke. Ruby shook her head waiting for the punchline. There had to be a punchline.

'Don't make a fuss,' her mother hissed back, without moving her lips. 'If I'd told you, you wouldn't have come. I'm not stupid and he is going to be Ben's best man.'

Ben held up a bottle of wine and offered her a drink.

Ruby felt her throat tighten and her eyes prickle with angry tears. She'd been set up.

'Conference in the closet,' she said and snatched the large glass from him. It was their code for a private conversation.

Ben nodded, sheepishly and led the way to the conservatory, because the downstairs toilet was barely big enough for one, let alone two people, a glass of wine and a dog. Ben made sure the doors were shut behind them.

'I'm sorry,' he said, the corners of his mouth turned downward, and he threw her his sad look. His "You're my sister but" look. 'I asked him last year when things were good between you. You know I did. I couldn't *unask* him.'

'I'm your sister. You're supposed to have my back. That's what siblings do.'

Ben looked down. He was about to deliver one of his killer sentences. Nobody knew her brother as well as she did.

'It's not like there's anyone else I could ask.'

'Bollocks,' she said.

She felt a low rumble against her chest, clearly Brutus felt the same. It was a comfort to have someone in your corner, even if it was only a dog. She rubbed his ears and he licked her face.

'Please, Ruby, be reasonable. Daniel's already sorted the stag weekend and we've been measured for our suits. He was devastated when you left. Really devastated. I'm concerned for his mental health. If I tell him I've changed my mind, it might push him over the edge. How would you feel then?'

'Okay,' Ruby said.

'Thank you.'

'No. I'm okay about you pushing him over the edge. Preferably a long and painful death. Could he potentially lose a limb or two on the way?'

'You don't mean that, and let's face it, you left him, not the other way around. Frankly, I don't understand what your new "man" has that Daniel hasn't, but …'

'Get this straight. There is no new man,' Ruby said, loudly and Brutus snarled. 'I don't know what he bloody told you. Do you want to know why I flaming left him?'

Ben held up his hands in mock surrender. 'None of my business.'

Brutus growled again, this time louder and he curled his lip back for an added threat. God, she loved that dog.

'Belinda's made him a special gift. I don't want to upset her. She's been amazing about the change of date and is working so hard to sort everything. It's only one day. Please Ruby.'

'You promise I don't have to talk to him, or sit with him?'

'Done,' he smiled, and Ruby knew she had been. What the hell had she just agreed to? She swallowed the rest of her wine and put the glass on the conservatory table.

'We should get back,' Ben said. 'Mother and Belinda have worked all afternoon on the meal.

'You get back,' Ruby said and let herself out of the conservatory doors. The very last thing she heard as she set off down the path was Ben saying something about Daniel still loving her.

Chapter Twelve

'Before you start, I am sorry about the stunt with the carpet guy,' Ruby said.

Adam stood outside her flat watching her intently, it made her flustered, but her heart raced.

'I thought I was in danger and that if he thought I was spoken for ...' She trailed off becoming tongue-tied and inarticulate. 'Look I don't want to buy a carpet or get married. In fact I can't think of anything worse.'

'Can't you?' He raised an eyebrow.

He was laughing at her. Ruby caught her breath. 'Well, someone might force-feed me mashed potatoes.'

'Mashed potatoes?'

'They're the worst.' She grimaced and shook her head. 'Did you get the postcard?'

He smiled. 'I was very glad Brutus felt the need to tell me where he was, or I would have worried.'

'I thought you'd be at work until late,' she said, feeling flustered under his gaze. He looked like he was calm.

'My night off. Are you okay?' He leant against the door frame still watching her.

'Yes.'

They stared at each other; Ruby was the first to look away. 'No.'

'I'm sorry I dumped Brutus on you. He can be a pain.'

'He's gorgeous and has been a perfect poppet. The one bright spot in an otherwise dreadful day.'

'And now?'

'I'm going to get drunk.' She waved the bottle of Daniel's Margaux at him. Want a mug?'

'Hold that thought.' And he was gone.

'What did I say this time?' she asked, scratching Brutus's chin as she topped up her mug. She'd been about to close the front door when Adam reappeared with two large glasses.

'We can't possibly drink that wine out of a mug,' he said.

Warmth flooded Ruby's body, her heart hammered against her chest and incapable of forming a rational sentence, she managed a "thanks" and passed him her mug.

He poured the contents into one of the glasses and handed it to her, his fingers accidently brushed hers as she took the glass. An electrical jolt shot up her arm and she shivered with pleasure.

'Where have you been?' he asked.

'Walk and we popped in to see my mother. I got away as soon as I could. My ex was there.'

'That must have been ...' He paused.

Ruby tried to work out the expression on Adam's face. 'Bloody awful,' she said and shuddered. 'Daniel has told my family I left him because I met someone else, but he's prepared to forgive me. Draw a line under the matter. And according to my brother, he still loves me and will try and live with my hormone issues.' She gulped her wine. She wanted to eradicate the image of her ex from her brain. Destroy it permanently.

'Why did you go?' Adam asked, topping up her glass. 'If you didn't want to see him.'

'I didn't know he'd be there. We were supposed to be having a family meal to discuss my brother's wedding plans.'

'Wedding plans, I am reliably informed,' Adam said, 'are only marginally better than mashed potatoes.' He was beaming at her, his cheeks glowing.

'Exactly.'

He really was a good-looking man and his eyes sparkled when he smiled.

'My brother's brought his wedding forward. He asked

Daniel to be his best man ages ago, and now he says he can't unask him. I'm the matron of honour, only I'm not married, so that makes me maid of honour or chief bridesmaid, depending on who you talk to. Apparently one of the jobs of the best man is to look after the bridesmaids.'

Her glass was empty.

'Can I ask you something?' Ruby mumbled.

Adam sipped his wine and wrinkled his forehead.

'Can I look after Brutus again sometime? Maybe when you're at work?'

'You're joking, right?' Clearly, he hadn't been expecting that.

'You said the dog sitter had given up on him.' She couldn't read Adam's expression. 'Sorry, I expect you've made other arrangements. Okay, forget I said anything.'

'No,' he said sharply. 'I haven't made any arrangements, but I need to. I'm going away for a while. I was going to speak to my parents. See if they can help out.'

'No need. I could have him.'

'For three months?'

'Three months?'

'I'm going to Paris, same place as Jason. I am going to work with Xavier too.'

'The chef that Jason raved about?'

'Everyone raves about him. That man is the most amazing chef and I've been given this wonderful chance to learn from a true master. It's too good an opportunity to turn down. The only fly in the ointment is this little man.'

'I could have him for three months.'

'I couldn't …'

Ruby gave him her best pleading look. 'I've always wanted a dog.'

'Are you sure?'

Ruby was, at least about the dog. In the twelve hours

Brutus had been with her, she'd enjoyed his company and hated the thought of giving him back.

Adam looked at Brutus. 'Too right, I'm laughing. She thinks you're gorgeous. How wrong can one person be? And don't think you're sleeping on my bed when I get back.'

He shut the door behind him still smiling and not just because she liked his dog. There was something about that woman that did it to him every time. Something had happened to her hair. It looked like she'd had a fight with a pair of scissors and lost, but somehow it made her look younger and more vulnerable. He walked into Jason's kitchen and trailed a dishcloth over an already spotless worktop. He wanted to be the one to protect her.

He'd been amazed when she opened the door waving an expensive bottle of decent wine and wearing the most interestingly angled fringe he'd ever seen.

He intended telling her about the police and his stalking problem, but Inspector Lenham seemed to think she'd persuaded Emily to leave him alone – perhaps there was no point. Ruby hadn't mentioned Emily. And he couldn't think of a good way of just dropping the question "and how do you know my crazed stalker" into the conversation. Yeah not really a good chat-up line.

She clearly had issues with her ex. He should have told her about Emily. He wanted to tell her about Emily, but it sounded like she'd had a miserable evening with her family and the last thing he wanted to do was dump his problems on her as well. There was a pain behind her smile when she discussed Daniel that Adam hadn't noticed before. *What on earth had the bastard done?*

There had been a second when it looked as if she was about to cry. He always seemed to have that effect on her. He didn't want to upset her; it was the last thing he wanted to do. But looking at her eyes glistening, tears threatening, he just wanted to pull her into his arms, kiss her and somehow make her pain better.

Three months away. It wasn't as if anything was going on with Ruby and he really wasn't in the right place to get involved with anyone at the moment. The inspector had practically said the same. He rubbed his temples and sighed. It had been the right decision to take the job, he was sure of it. It would be good to throw himself into Xavier's kitchen and spend the time learning the finest French cooking. Ruby had been excited for him. She brought out his protective side. He thought occasionally from the way she looked at him, she might be starting to feel things for him. Might they have a future when he got back? Thirteen weeks wasn't forever. And career and Emily wise it was a no-brainer.

Chapter Thirteen

Belinda stood behind Ruby, holding a small hand mirror, so she could see the back of her head in the big salon mirror in front of her, and smiled. 'There I told you, an asymmetrical bob would look amazing,' she said.

'You've made a feature of my fringe.'

'It was either that or cut everything very short to even things off. You don't like it?'

'Actually, I love it. You're a genius.' Ruby tossed her head as the salon door tinkled to indicate a new customer. 'It's just not what I understood by a quick fringe trim.'

'Next time could we chat about the style you have in mind before you start cutting chunks out.' Belinda squeezed her shoulders and untied the gown she'd insisted Ruby put on over her clothes. 'Here's Lily.'

'Oh God.'

'Relax, it's going to be all right. She's promised not to mention Daniel, best men or spending all day cooking for an ungrateful daughter. It's okay, don't look like that, I'm joking.'

'Was she really angry?'

'Ben said you were worried Brutus wasn't right and wanted to get him to the vet before they shut.'

Belinda spun Ruby round. 'What do you think Lily?'

Her mother walked across the salon. Ruby froze waiting for some pointed remark, but her mother nodded and smiled. 'You look lovely,' she said.

Belinda grinned. 'Let's go hunt down my wedding dress. I thought we'd start with the bridal shop round the corner.'

Start and with any luck finish too. A day shopping with her mother was at the very top of Ruby's list of absolute never – not even if your life depended on it – to do days. The one and only time they'd been clothes shopping together was for her first bra twenty years ago. Throw Belinda into the mix and 'shoot me now' came to mind. Add wedding dresses, and suicide seemed the sensible option.

'Belinda's got pictures of the dress she's set her heart on,' Lily said while Belinda went off to get her handbag. She produced a page, ripped from a magazine. The sheer quantity of gauze-like material and train made the dress look like a cloud.

'Don't you think it's beautiful?' asked Belinda as Ruby felt a pain in her shin that made her scream.

'It's certainly big,' she said, glaring at her mother's shoes and this time prepared to fend off a kick.

'My only concern,' Belinda said, 'is whether it will make my hips look enormous.'

'Nonsense,' Ruby said.

'It would make everyone's hips look enormous,' Lily muttered as they left the salon. 'It's lovely, but I'd rather see you in something more fitting. With a corset maybe?'

'What do you think?' Belinda asked, slipping her arm through Ruby's.

'Don't ask her,' Lily said. 'She's jealous of your curves, Belinda. Never having had them. Did she tell you about the lady in the dress shop when we went to buy her first bra? She told her a whopping lie and Ruby's never forgiven her.'

'Really?'

'No, not really,' Ruby said.

'She told her it was good the double AA fitting was too big because it meant she could grow into it – only she never did.'

Both women laughed. A passer-by turned and stared at Ruby, then laughed too.

This was the second and bloody last time she would ever go shopping with her mother.

'Daniel said she was hard to buy for. She never liked anything he bought,' Belinda said.

His name alone made the hairs on the back of Ruby's neck stand up. 'He once bought me a Celine Dion CD for my birthday. Do you blame me?' She could at least defend herself on that score.

Lily Brooks sniffed as they turned into Church Street.

Ruby raised her head and locked eyes with her mother, challenging her to argue.

There was another sniff, but Lily had clearly decided it wasn't the right time to list Daniel's virtues. 'Did you speak to the hotel?' she asked.

Belinda nodded and pulled a length of baby-pink voile from her bag. 'They've let me borrow one of the chair ribbons, so we should be able to match the maid of honour's dress to this.'

Shit! How much worse could this week get? Now she was going to be dressed as camouflage for a chair.

Lily Brooks stopped in front of a large window covered with a frosted privacy film. 'Here we are.' She pushed open the door of The Little Shop of Dresses.

'I'm dying to see you in your dress,' Ruby said, trying to sound enthusiastic.

'I really hope they have one like it.' Belinda smiled.

'You mean you haven't checked they have one in stock?'

Belinda shook her head. 'I thought it would be unlucky to do it too early. A bit like buying a pram before the baby's born.'

The shop assistant shook her head when Belinda showed her the picture. 'We've got nothing like that,' she said, and promptly produced a ballroom gown-style dress. 'We can probably get one of these in your size,' she added. 'But you've left it a bit late.'

'See, I told you,' Lily butted in. 'It's karma. What about a mermaid style?' she asked the assistant. 'Something with a corset that would show off her curves.'

'Where's your picture?' Ruby said. Belinda's lower lip had started to tremble. Ruby wrapped her arms round her sister-in-law-to-be. 'It's going to be all right,' she whispered. 'Leave it with me.' She sat in the corner of the boutique while the proprietor tried to make encouraging comments about the amount of weight Belinda could lose in two months if she dropped her calorie intake to less than one hundred a day.

It took half an hour to track down the designer of Belinda's favoured dress. Ruby explained the problem with the timescale and answered the woman's questions regarding sizes and budgets. She was scheduled to be in London that afternoon and would be happy to see Belinda, she said, as she gave Ruby directions to the gallery she was showcasing her work at.

Ruby slipped her notebook back into her handbag. 'I'm sorry,' she said. 'Belinda, we need to go.'

Lily stared at her, daggers drawn. But Ruby wasn't in the mood for one of her mother's rants and glared back. 'We're going to London.' She smiled at the assistant. 'Maybe you could find something for the mother of the groom. She pulled the pink net out of Belinda's bag. 'She's partial to this colour.'

Chapter Fourteen

Ruby worked out where the top of the base units should be and marked the kitchen wall accordingly. They had each come with a sheet of drawings. There were numbers, arrows and a lot of words, but not in a language she recognised. She didn't have time to learn German or possibly Russian and when Google Translate came up with some ridiculous suggestions, she searched for do-it-yourself videos on YouTube.

She was a good student. And she had a toolbox.

Okay technically it was Kevin's toolbox, but possession being nine tenths of the law, meant it was mostly hers. He owed her nearly £10,000, he could hardly object to her borrowing a few tools.

In one afternoon, she learned to work from the corner outwards. She made sure there was enough space for the washing machine and cooker. It looked like she could use the existing pipe work and electrics for both.

When she was sure she'd got the positions of the units right, she pushed the first one into place, laid a spirit level on top and then extended the legs on each corner until the bubble settled in the middle.

She balanced a tray on one of the units as a temporary worktop. On top of that, she arranged her mug and kettle. There, it was starting to look like a kitchen already. She could live without the sink, but a cup of tea never.

She made a cup of tea and carried it back to the sitting room, dropping the spoon off in a washing-up bowl in the bathroom en route.

Under her desk, Brutus lay in his basket. As Ruby sat down, he looked up and thumped his tail excitedly against the toaster and saucepans piled up around him. She stroked his head until he settled again.

"*Win a plastering course*", she read on the screen over the top of her mug.

She sighed. Ten competitions a day had become a bit of a slog. What was the point? Sitting on the floor was a netball and a family pass to a Lawnmower museum.

Her phone sounded. Since the wedding dress shopping trip, Belinda had taken to ringing daily to discuss minor details. And despite her refusal to be the wedding planner, Ruby enjoyed helping with the arrangements. Belinda had even gone along with her suggestions about bridesmaids' dresses. The youngest flower girls would be dressed in sugar pink while the colour of the older girls' dresses would intensify with their ages. By the time it got to the maid of honour's dress that was a deep raspberry creation – chosen to match the colour of the men's ties, but Belinda had agreed she only had to wear it until the photos had been taken. After that Ruby had a long dark green designer dress in mind for the evening reception. A crepe satin body-sculpting number that she'd never been brave enough to wear before. Daniel had declared it far too provocative; the sort of thing hookers would wear and hidden it away at the back of their airing cupboard. If he thought it was still there, he was going to be in for a shock.

Ruby tucked the phone between her shoulder and ear as she listened to Belinda wittering on about Daniel and the plans for Ben's stag do. She stuck the postcard of the Eiffel Tower she'd received that morning on the wall above her desk. The back of the card read, "Arrived safely, tower still here. Jason sends his love. Give Ruby a kiss from both of us." It had been addressed to Master Brutus Finder at her address, and she smiled every time she saw it.

'Would it be all right for me to bring someone to the

wedding?' she asked as soon as Belinda paused to take breath.

'You've met someone? Does Lily know?'

'No one knows.' Ruby could imagine her mother's expression when Belinda broke the news. Belinda or Lily keeping a secret was less likely than Daniel finding religion and running off to join a cult somewhere in Outer Mongolia.

'Of course, that's brilliant news.' Belinda sounded genuinely excited. 'You must bring him.'

Or would it be taking their relationship to a whole new level? She was in deep. It didn't feel one-sided, but she knew very little about Adam other than the fact he was a chef, had the cutest dog in the world and was a friend of Jason's. She wanted to know more. Spend longer with him. Make him laugh.

If she took him to the wedding, she'd have to introduce him to her family and Daniel. She shuddered. There would be all sorts of embarrassing questions. It could kill anything before it started. If he had any sense, he'd run a mile. Suddenly an invitation didn't seem like such a good idea.

'Of course he might not be able to make it,' Ruby added, trying to concentrate on answering the plastering questions on her screen.

'Tell him he has to. When are you seeing him next?'

'Not for a while. He's in France.'

'Ooh La La,' Belinda said. 'Do I know him?'

'No.' Ruby selected the (b) answer and pressed enter.

'Have I met his dog?' Belinda chuckled.

'Yup. Do you know anything about plastering?'

'What?'

'Another name for plasterboard is: a. dry as a bone, b. dry wine, c. drywall or d. dry ice.'

'Drywall. How long?'

There was no putting off this girl.

111

'He's due back at the beginning of June.' Ruby typed her name and address into the computer-generated form as she'd done so often recently.

'You're a dark horse. Is that why …?'

'No. No. No. I met him last month. He lives above me. I didn't leave Daniel for him. I left Daniel because Daniel is a complete …'

'I think the word you're looking for is wanker.' Belinda giggled.

Ruby stared at the phone. Surely Belinda was one of Daniel's greatest fans. 'I thought you liked him.'

Belinda hesitated. 'Ben likes him. He makes me feel … I know it's silly, but …'

'But what?'

'Sometimes he makes me feel inadequate. Like he's poking fun at me. Ben says he's just teasing, but it doesn't feel like that.'

'You're not inadequate,' Ruby said, quietly. 'I think you're amazing.'

Belinda blew her a kiss or that was what it sounded like. 'Thanks lovely, but I really should go and get your brother his tea.'

They said their goodbyes and Ruby walked back to the kitchen. She felt positive, but it was a short-lived feeling. The fridge/freezer unit was missing, and she had no idea where it was supposed to be coming from. And the gap she'd allocated it lacked any form of electrical wiring. She remembered changing a plug once, but she wasn't entirely sure she could remember how and rewiring the kitchen was probably a step too far.

She took a deep breath. 'It's no good,' she told Brutus, who had joined her in the kitchen. 'Why did I ever think I could do this?'

She wasn't sure what constituted a sympathetic look in a Border Terrier, but she was pretty sure he was doing his best.

The light faded as they walked to the park and back. Normally, the walk would have cleared her head but today the fresh air wasn't cutting it. There were too many thoughts running around her mind. By the time she put a bowl of dog food down for Brutus and made another cup of tea, it was too late to think about shopping for food, so she changed into a pair of pyjamas and curled up in the armchair, letting Brutus climb onto her lap. She put her head back, rubbed her temples and closed her eyes.

Adam was beside her. They were talking, and he took her hand. It felt good. There was a strange noise. She looked up. He said something, smiled and moved towards her. Ruby waited, expecting to be kissed, it didn't happen. There was that noise again. Brutus started barking. She opened her eyes.

It was pitch black outside. In early March that meant it could be any time between six in the evening and six in the morning. She couldn't have been asleep for that long – could she? It was difficult with a Border Terrier licking her face to focus on the clock.

There was that noise again; someone was knocking on her door and clearly, they weren't going away.

Flat 1 stood on her mat with a man a step behind him who looked vaguely familiar. 'I let him in,' Flat 1 said. 'He was buzzing your intercom. I knew you were in. I saw you come back with the dog earlier. You might want to check your batteries.'

'Thanks,' she said, looking over his shoulder at the younger man.

'I am Malik Tahsin,' he said.

That answered that question then. Ruby kept staring at him. Why was he here? She thought his father had bought the idea she was engaged to someone else. Maybe he hadn't.

'You know my father.'

She nodded cautiously.

'He brought winning carpet.'

'I don't want to buy a bloody carpet. I am not going to any warehouse and I should tell you, I have a dog.' Although Brutus was nowhere to be seen. Not even barking. 'And I know all about sword fighting.' Just for good measure she lunged at him with one of the smaller kitchen boxes.

Malik moved forwards, a smile had crept up on his face. 'You have nice tap?' he said.

Chapter Fifteen

April Flowers was squashed between two charity shops on Templeton High Street. Ruby could see through the window that Belinda was already there. She waved her arms around as she talked to a woman with her back to the window.

They'd said 9.30. It was only 9.15. There was a lot of head nodding and hand waving. Ruby hoped she was in time to stop Belinda making impulse purchases or being talked into a completely new scheme.

'Wedding flowers, not Chelsea Flower Show,' she muttered.

Daniel once said Belinda was so impressionable her face wore the imprint of the last arse who sat on it. It was an unkind thing to say, but Daniel's remarks were frequently cruel.

Ruby tucked Brutus under one arm, ignored the guide dogs only sign and marched in. 'Belinda,' she said. 'You're here.' She braced herself for the sort of bone-crushing hug her sister-in-law-to-be specialised in. Today's didn't disappoint.

'Sorry,' Ruby gasped as her breath was squeezed from her lungs. 'You should've said you wanted to meet earlier. I've just dropped my dress off at the dry cleaners down the road, but I could have done that later.'

Belinda finally released her. 'You're not late. I got here outrageously early. Now you're here, explain to Emily what we need?'

Emily?

'I hope you haven't blown the budget …' The words dried in Ruby's mouth as the woman turned around. It was her.

The look on Emily's face probably reflected Ruby's own. Ruby's mouth opened. Nothing came out.

'I tried to describe the centrepieces and the bouquets

and think I've confused her.' Belinda turned back to the shop assistant. 'Ruby has the most amazing green dress. It's gorgeous. She's going to wear it for the evening do.'

Emily recovered, quickest. By the time she spoke, her face was swathed in smiles. 'Hi Ruby,' she said. 'How are you? Lovely to see you again.'

'Hi,' Ruby said, cautiously.

'You know each other?' Belinda said, clapping her hands. 'That's cool. Ruby is my wedding planner, only she doesn't like to be called that.'

'Why ever not?' Emily gushed. 'It sounds like the most romantic job in the world. If I wasn't a florist, that's a job I'd love.'

'Coordinator not planner,' Ruby said, pulling her folder out of her bag. 'Planners help from the outset. Coordinators pull everything together to make the day run smoothly.' She had to be pedantic. She didn't want anyone thinking she had anything to do with the invitations or the cake.

'Do you supply flowers for Ruby's events? Is that how you know her?'

Ruby stared at Belinda hard in a bid to try to telepathically shut her up.

God love her, Belinda ignored the daggers look and wittered on, seemingly unaware of the tension between the two women. 'She does big events usually. Corporate parties, that sort of thing.'

'She lives in the same block of flats as my boyfriend,' Emily said. 'I helped her with her shopping a few weeks ago. She was supposed to deliver a Valentine's Day card for me.'

'I did,' Ruby said, quietly.

For a second Emily looked about to argue, but then the smile returned and she turned to Belinda. 'Why don't we have a cup of tea and you can tell me your ideas. I'm sure we'll be able to help.'

'We're only getting quotes at this stage,' Ruby said.

'Don't worry about the money,' Emily said, pointedly ignoring Ruby. 'I'll happily match any quote and it's always nice to keep things local, don't you think?'

'Absolutely.' Belinda grinned. 'I think we're going to get on fabulously.'

Ruby stiffened.

'How's your kitchen?' Emily asked, setting down a tray.

'Getting there,' Ruby said.

'Is it?' Belinda stopped flicking through a photo book of wreaths and looked up. 'You never said.'

Emily handed her a cup and saucer. 'I'm sorry I can't run to *cupcakes*. Would you like a biscuit instead?'

'Cupcakes?' mouthed Belinda.

'Long story,' Ruby muttered.

'Oops, sorry.' Emily smiled. 'Was it supposed to be a surprise? Are you making Belinda's wedding cake? It's trendy these days to have tiers of cupcakes, isn't it?'

'No,' Belinda and Ruby shrieked together.

'Did your kitchen fitter come back?'

'Uh-huh,' Ruby said as non-committally as she could. She pursed her lips and fought the urge to say, 'Fuck off, Emily', which was on the tip of her tongue. No doubt Belinda would quiz her on the subject of her kitchen later, but she didn't want her private affairs discussed. It was touch and go for a moment; no one said a word.

Ruby took a deep breath. 'Could we talk flowers?' she said, in a bid to get the conversation back on track. She produced the mood board she'd put together with more detailed illustrations that showed the colour scheme and flower arrangements agreed with Belinda.

Emily looked at the designs, made notes and asked questions about the numbers of buttonholes, bouquets and table decorations. Ruby showed her pictures of the flowers

Belinda would be wearing in her hair and the cascade that would fall from the top of the cake. Emily was very complimentary about everything. Ruby sat back in her chair and started to relax.

'Very contemporary,' Emily said. 'I like the simplicity of the arrangements. You've certainly put a lot of thought into this. She let a silence hang between them for what felt like forever. Ruby was just about to gather everything up when she announced, 'I'd be happy to work with you.'

'Hang on ...'

'Great, that's fabulous news.' Belinda grinned.

Emily grinned back. 'That's all set then. Obviously, I will be there on the day to make sure everything is set up properly and you're happy with all aspects of the floristry. I'm happy to help with buttonholes and sort out the flower girls if you like.'

'There's no need ...' Ruby said, quickly.

'Of course, there is. It's all part of the service.' Emily, hands on hips, glared at her. 'We pride ourselves on our exceptionally high levels of customer service at April Flowers.' The words were sharp and clipped which made them sound less like a company strategy than a thinly disguised threat. Ruby was left feeling more a knife thrower's target than a client.

Eamon flicked the balls on his management stress toy and entered his expenses to date on a spreadsheet. He was glad he'd arranged an appointment with his therapist that afternoon. He needed reassurance.

The budget he'd been allocated was a fraction of the previous series and he'd be lucky to stay within it. There was no money this time around for psychologists, wardrobe advisers or make-up. He'd had to fight to be able to offer each contestant a meal. If finance had their way, it would have been coffee and a quick interview, probably done remotely to avoid travelling expenses of those taking part.

His budget certainly didn't run to hotel rooms or overnight stops. There wasn't the usual camaraderie. He was lumbered with one cameraman who had to arrange his own lighting. Both of them had spent most of the last month crowded, with various equipment, into the smallest car in the world between venues.

They'd filmed and edited most of the episodes. There were just the voice-overs to do. The actor chap they'd used before was considered an unnecessary expense. 'You can do it,' the director general had said.

Eamon hated the sound of his own voice. When he got excited, it got higher and faster. Maybe his therapist could recommend something to help.

The episodes looked good. There was genuine emotion in most of them. He'd gone through hours of footage with the cameraman. Sometimes they'd cut new and old footage together. Eamon needed to pull a clip from each episode for the trailers. He was pleased with the way it was going. Galaxy TV should be pleased. So far only one of the original couples had said a definite "no".

Emily Watkins hadn't said no; she hadn't said anything. The researchers might have given up on her, but he hadn't. He couldn't afford to. The director general had told him that in their last monthly meeting. 'She's the one the viewers care about. They are waiting to see what happened to her. They want to know she found happiness.'

A fourteen-week slot starting in the middle of August had been agreed with one of the major networks. The plan was to re-run the whole of the first series and then show the new programmes.

He'd end each episode with an update on black screens with white writing, music playing like in the silent films:

"*Eamon is still employed by Galaxy TV as their star producer. There is a rumour his name will appear on next year's Honours list*". That sort of thing.

He might not be here next year. He'd been warned. He needed viewer ratings, great feedback and another idea for his next show, or he was out. No pressure then? Bollocks. It felt like the sword of Damocles was hanging over him. One false move and he'd be gone.

Deep breaths. Remember anxiety can be overwhelming. What was it his therapist banged on about? You shouldn't try and second-guess what is going to happen, predicting the future is your mind's way of preparing you, but it's not always a positive thing. Just because something bad might happen, doesn't mean it will. Think of good things. Focus on them and on what you need to do to make sure they happen instead.

Flowers ordered, customer service levels agreed upon, daggers safely sheathed, Belinda and Emily were discussing hairstyles.

'You should've seen what she did to her fringe,' Belinda joked. 'I thought her mother was going to have a coronary.'

'I wanted an edgier style.'

'Next time don't design it using an Etch A Sketch,' Belinda said. She and Emily roared with laughter.

'She's so lucky you're such a brilliant hairdresser,' Emily said. 'Could you do something with my hair? I want a trendier look.'

Ruby got out while the going was good. Belinda's eyes had got that faraway look in them. Once you got her on her specialist subject, she would talk for ages and refuse to be derailed. Emily hadn't mentioned Adam or the card again. She hadn't questioned why Ruby was looking after Brutus. In fact, she'd hardly taken any notice of the dog at all, or him her, although he had been delighted to see Belinda.

There was no need to rush home, but the flower shop had become claustrophobic; she needed to get away and her kitchen was taking shape and she was looking forward to helping Malik.

In three weeks, they'd chased out walls, fitted sockets and base units. They'd dragged the free-standing appliances into their proper places. The flat looked less like a warehouse and Ruby enjoyed his company. His English was improving. He already knew all the words to "Holding out for a Hero" and she was proud of what they'd achieved together. Her dream kitchen was starting to take shape and she was helping to make it happen.

'Good day, Miss Ruby. How are you?' Malik asked, slowly, concentrating over every word, when she arrived home.

She smiled. 'I'm fine. And you?'

His face lit up. 'Outstanding. Thank you for asking.'

'Has something happened?' She felt a sharp pain in her chest. What if he said he was going home? He couldn't leave yet.

He pulled his phone out of his pocket, tapped a few times and held it out. She could see an email that looked a bit as if someone had had an accident with a keyboard and hit the letter "A" a few too many times.

'An email?' she said.

'From Jamila.' His smile was infectious.

'Is she okay?'

'Very, very okay.'

From previous conversations and Google Translate, Jamila, Ruby had worked out, was Malik's girlfriend. They were childhood sweethearts from the same town somewhere unpronounceable south of Cairo.

'What does she say?'

He looked at the screen. 'She is unhappy.'

'That doesn't sound okay to me.'

'She liked my English and says she miss me. So that is very okay, isn't it? She says my English is good and I will soon be home.'

Malik had asked Ruby for help with the first sentence of his last email. The one that read, "Thank you for your email, England is very nice". He'd wanted to write it in English, so Jamila could see he was progressing.

'I will soon be tour guide.' He put his mobile back in his pocket and smiled. 'We write back this afternoon.' Their arrangement meant they spent mornings working on the kitchen and afternoons on English lessons.

Ruby nodded and wished she shared his confidence.

'It is only job I want,' he told her in broken English. 'I cannot marry Jamila until I work as guide. I not make her happy as builder.'

That was Malik's ultimate dream. He'd told Ruby as much on many occasions. It was good he had goals, knew what he wanted from life.

Everyone needed goals.

Being her own boss was hers. Having her own corporate event business had been her dream for as long as she could remember.

The only difference between them was Malik had got off his arse and done something about achieving his ambitions. He'd travelled halfway round the world to learn English.

Ruby wandered back into the lounge. What had she done? Stuck Post-it notes over her desk. Ideas, nothing concrete. She needed to stop prevaricating and start planning. She needed stationery, a social media presence and a business plan. She needed to think who her potential clients were and the best way of advertising to them. She needed to look at suppliers and contractors. Work out her competition. What were they doing that she could improve on? She sat down at her desk, pulled a pad of paper across it and started making notes. An hour later, she looked at the scrawl and smiled. Her dream was on.

Malik's dream started badly. Arriving in England, he found the school that had taken his money for his English course, shut and boarded up.

He hadn't given up at the first hurdle and returned home, dreams in shreds to rethink his future. He'd kept going. He'd never spoken a word of English in his life, whereas she had twelve years' work experience to fall back on.

Okay, so possibly he should have gone home or at least told the Home Office about his course. His student visa wasn't valid if he wasn't studying, but he'd stayed and helped his father sell carpets.

Three weeks ago when he'd stood on her doorstep and said, 'Father send me to do kitchen', Ruby had run her hands through her hair and exhaled with exasperation. 'I told your father, I have no money. Not for carpet. Not for kitchen. Nothing.'

He'd smiled throughout her rant. 'I mend kitchen, Miss Ruby. You teach me England.'

'England?'

'Yes, yes.'

She'd continued to say "no" for a number of reasons, but he wasn't put off easily and turned up the following morning insisting "he no understands".

Malik told her through broken English and a series of hand gestures and movements that he didn't want to sell carpets any more than he wanted to be a builder, but he saw both jobs as stepping stones along a river to his future.

The last bit was Ruby's interpretation, not his. It made more sense than hopscotch or a neurological disorder.

He'd ignored all the obstacles she put up as to why he couldn't work on her kitchen. He'd laughed when she finally made him understand she had no intention of marrying him, so if his father's plan all along was for him to get an English wife to get a visa, it was a non-starter. He accepted she had no money to pay him, had nowhere for him to live. And she finally accepted that he just wanted to learn English and needed help with his application not to have his student visa terminated. He didn't want to stay in England forever, just long enough to learn English.

He was proving a good student. His vocabulary was coming on, even if from time to time they had to go through a bizarre game of charades to make one another understand. Malik tried to make her understand she needed to put a fused spur where she could get to it easily. Ruby tried to make him understand she didn't want a socket where he suggested. It had been a long and painful affair. Finally, he drew a picture of what was needed. The electrical suppliers explained it to her and supplied everything.

Today's challenge was wall units. Space in the kitchen was limited and she had no ladder. By exercising all her acting skills, Ruby tried to explain the difficulties they faced getting high enough to fit the cupboards.

Malik laughed a lot. It was infectious and she laughed too, even if she wasn't fully convinced he'd grasped what was actually needed here wasn't an upside-down washing-up bowl and a swivel chair.

Chapter Sixteen

Adam walked through Paris and smiled. He felt free. He wasn't looking over his shoulder in case Emily bloody Watkins was waiting around the next corner. He'd been there nearly two months and life felt worth living again.

He chose a large café, a block and a half away from the restaurant, with a dozen tables outside and sat down. The morning was warm, and he turned his chair round slightly, the sun on his face.

When a waitress came to take his order he asked for a ham omelette. It was brunch. He would eat properly later before the restaurant opened up for service and all the preparation had been done. The staff sat down together every night. More often than not Xavier would cook for them, either that day's special or a recipe he was thinking of introducing. The food was always amazing. He would ask about seasoning, but the man had been cooking so long, he knew instinctively what a dish needed. The only time Adam had ever seen him angry was when a customer asked for salt and pepper.

Adam put today's postcard on the table and pulled a pen out of his jacket pocket. He'd written Brutus a postcard every week. Ruby said she enjoyed them. She was the only thing he missed about Redford.

They'd had a few telephone calls, but it was difficult with the long hours he was working. The only long-term relationship he'd ever had ended when his girlfriend at the time eventually lost patience with his working schedules and told him to make a decision. The fact he even had to think about it told her all she needed to know. I've been dumped for a steak Diane she'd say repeatedly when asked. He heard she'd married an insurance broker who worked regular nine-to-five, with half-day closing on Wednesdays.

Calls to Ruby could be justified on the grounds of "Brutus care". He'd rung her when he'd forgotten to book the annual check-up at the vets. And she'd rung him to check the exact percentage of the dog's bodyweight that he could be given in treats on a daily basis. He was clearly being treated like royalty. It would take ages to get him back into a normal routine when he returned to the UK. Not that he minded. Brutus had pulled him through some pretty rough times in the past. The dog deserved to be pampered for a short time. They'd talked about a variety of things, laughed a lot and on one occasion she'd quizzed him about food. He even had the date in his diary for her brother's wedding except he wasn't sure if she'd actually asked him to be her plus-one or if he'd invited himself and she'd been too polite to refuse him.

He remembered the Valentine's Day kiss. They hadn't talked about it, he wasn't even sure if she remembered it, she'd had a lot to drink, but he did. He hadn't moved to Union House to get involved in a relationship. He'd moved there to get away from Emily and yet in less than two weeks she had tracked him down and he'd done what he always did and run away, but this time, Emily or no Emily, he had a reason to go back. Somehow Ruby had got under his skin and he was happy that she had.

He'd sat down with Jason and Xavier yesterday, and over a bottle of very decent wine and a lunch he'd cooked, they'd talked about his plans for the future. Suddenly, they didn't seem so outlandish; he had rediscovered his love of food and had some great ideas for menus.

'So where will you cook this marvellous food?' Xavier asked. 'I hope you go home to do it. I don't want such competition here.'

They'd laughed and drank some more. This morning he'd

googled estate agents in Redford and rang most of them to find out what premises were available. He was supposed to be the chef in charge at Bootles when he returned. Clive had said he could run the evening sessions, but Adam wanted his own place where he could be in complete charge.

He loved Bootles. The restaurant he described to estate agents, trying to make them understand what he wanted, was more or less the same sort of thing. Okay, in all honesty, it was exactly the same. He needed to have a chat to Clive, too. The man had been a good friend over the years; he owed it to him to be honest about his plans, and that would also be easier face to face. They'd talked occasionally too since he'd been in Paris. Bootles only opened lunchtimes at the moment. Clive said it wasn't a great money-spinner. Most lunch customers wanted a quick meal before they went back to work. He'd developed a sandwich and light snack menu. 'Fish finger baguettes are still the most popular item.' He laughed.

A couple, hand in hand, stopped to look at the menu board outside the café. Adam couldn't make out what they were saying. His schoolboy French had improved since he'd arrived, but he struggled to pick up every word. The man said something, the woman smiled. She put a hand up, stroked his face, then kissed him and shook her head. They both laughed and turned away. Adam envied them their closeness and evident happiness. Xavier and Jason were great sounding boards for his plans, but he wanted someone to share his excitement with. Not anyone. He wanted Ruby. He could picture her face. He could see her expression when he'd told her about Paris. Her expression when he'd sat her on the worktop and fed her chocolate fondant pudding and when he'd said she could look after his dog. He missed her and although he would never admit it to anyone, he'd even started to miss Dobie Gray.

*

'You'll never guess what,' Ruby screamed. 'The flaming dry cleaners have only gone and lost my dress!'

Belinda's hair salon wasn't busy. A young girl, behind the reception desk, stared at a computer screen, while another appeared to be trying to curl hair on a plastic head.

'Are you sure?' Belinda asked.

'Of course, I'm sure. I've been all the way to Templeton and sat in the shop for nearly an hour while they searched for it. They definitely haven't got it.'

Belinda who had been standing with her back to the door, a client in her chair, now swung round. Her eyes travelled down to look at Brutus. If she intended to mention dogs weren't allowed in the salon, she clearly thought better of it. 'Not your Amanda Wakeley?'

'Uh huh, the one I was going to wear to the evening do,' Ruby said. 'Now, what am I going to wear?'

The salon was small, immaculately painted in yellow. It looked fresher and friendlier than the others in town that were finished in blacks and chrome. There weren't pictures of hairstyles all over the place for a start. No teenage models stared down from huge black and white canvases. Belinda preferred landscapes and modern pictures to give splashes of colour to walls. Ruby liked them. Normally they felt relaxing. Today they didn't.

'Hi.'

Ruby did a double take at the seated woman whose head was half-covered in foil. 'Emily?'

Emily waved a hand at her reflection in the mirror and smiled. 'Belinda is giving me a new look. I've been going through her magazines to find a hairstyle.' She looked up at Ruby. 'What kind of cut do you think I should go for?'

Power cut. 'No good asking me,' Ruby said.

'Not only a hair re-style,' Belinda said, concentrating on brushing the next section of hair. 'Emily is having the full experience – our top to toe day. What did the dry cleaners say about your dress?'

'Someone must have collected it. First, they said it must have been me, but I still have the ticket, so clearly it wasn't. They're going to get their manager to ring me.'

'It'll be an honest mistake,' Belinda said. 'Someone will get home and realise they've got the wrong dress and take it straight back. You'll have it in a day or two.'

'I hope you're right.'

Belinda was such a lovely person. She always thought the best of everyone. Ruby wished she had her conviction, but she didn't.

'What about this one?' Emily held up the magazine. Ruby squinted at it and was saved from answering by Belinda.

'That one won't suit you. You need a sharper cut. I'm going to lighten your colour with some ash blonde highlights through your T-section.' She pointed at another picture in a magazine.

Emily nodded and grinned. 'It's going to be expensive. It will be worth it.'

Ruby flopped down in the chair next to Emily. 'It's all right for Belinda,' she said. 'She has the most amazing dress ever to wear to the wedding.'

'That's because I'm the bride,' Belinda said, focussing on wrapping more of Emily's hair in silver foil.

One of the juniors came racing over and offered Ruby a cup of coffee.

'She's not staying,' Belinda said.

'I'm not staying,' Ruby repeated. 'Come on Brutus we know when we're not wanted.'

'Good.' Belinda grinned. 'And don't forget the bridesmaid dress fitting and practice a week on Saturday.'

Ruby stuck out her tongue.

Chapter Seventeen

Emily held up two dresses. 'What do you think?

Her new hairstyle looked great. Belinda had done a wonderful job.

'You look fabulous, but what are you doing here? What are they?' Ruby's first thought was fancy dress.

'The problem with the dry cleaners,' Emily said. 'I know you're trying to sort it out. But in case you can't, borrow these. We're almost the same size.'

'Thank you,' Ruby said. 'They look ...'

'I designed them,' Emily said. 'I love making clothes. If you like them, but they don't quite fit, I could adjust them. Why don't you try them on?' She pushed the dresses at Ruby.

'Thanks,' Ruby said. *What else could she say?* She took the two coat hangers through to her bedroom and hung them on her wardrobe. 'But I don't have time at the moment.'

'Do you like them?' Emily asked, as she followed Ruby down the hall.

'They're certainly original.'

Emily smiled, clearly she considered that a compliment. 'You'll look good in them. Yellow is such a forgiving colour.'

Perhaps if you had jaundice. Ruby shuddered. The dry cleaners had better find her dress. The manager had said he would do his best and be in touch. She'd showed him the receipt and the sheer expense seemed to concentrate his mind.

'I adapted two patterns.' Emily stood millimetres away from her, clearly having no concerns about invading personal space.

'Great shoulder pads and frills,' Ruby added and stepped back to put a comfortable distance and a bedside table between them. 'Very eighties.'

'Go on, try them, then I can make any adjustments while I'm here,' Emily said.

'Really not a good time,' Ruby said. 'I'm on my way out.' It was stretching the truth. She'd found a company outside town who could supply and fit granite worktops. She needed to visit them, but she also needed to buckle down and get on with her business plan. Emily's visit might be well-intentioned, but she resented being disturbed.

Malik's father had taken him off to visit some relatives in Manchester and Ruby had hoped for three uninterrupted days on her own to catch up. She had no intention of spending them modelling clothes that looked like they'd been created for a TV costume drama or a bad taste party.

'I will try them later.' She sighed, trying not to let exasperation creep into her voice.

'If you're just being kind and really don't like them,' Emily said, 'we could go shopping and see if we can find something more suitable.'

'Not now. I have an appointment. I have to go out – alone,' Ruby said, hoping God was too busy to notice such a blatant lie and she wouldn't be struck down. She walked back to the sitting room, Emily hot on her heels.

'It wouldn't take long,' Emily said. She moved a pile of clothes off the sofa and sat down. 'Belinda's worried about your outfit. Wouldn't it be good to be able to tell her you're sorted?'

Had the woman taken lessons in "management by guilt" from Lily?

'By the way.' She dug around in her handbag. 'I met the postman on the way in and he gave me your post.'

Ruby flicked through the pile. She opened the one white envelope that looked least like junk: an appeal from a celebrity astrologer, surprised that Ruby hadn't been in touch for a personal horoscope or biorhythm chart.

The company were so sure it was an oversight, they were prepared to offer her a once in a lifetime deal. Ruby was entitled to a £25 discount providing she signed and returned the form within seven days. The annual price quoted was only marginally less than the latest kitchen increase Kevin had tried to charge her.

Why did everyone on the planet imagine she had spare cash? With all the kitchen bits she had to buy, she was barely able to afford necessities at the moment. Surely any celebrity astrologer, who had as much second sight as this one claimed, should have known that.

Ruby screwed up the letter and threw it at the waste basket. It arced, peaked and started to descend into the bin. There was no way it could miss, until Emily, in a manoeuvre any premiership football club manager would have approved of, swerved in and scooped it up.

'Can I have this?' she asked, straightening out the crumpled piece of paper. And before Ruby could answer, pocketed it.

Shit, she's weird.

Ruby stopped mid envelope opening and decided to wait until she was on her own before she read the rest. She put the pile on the desk, kicking a netball out of the way in the process.

'Is that a netball?'

'Yep,' Ruby said.

Emily bent down and studied it. 'There are names all over it?'

'It's been signed by the England women's team.'

'Why?'

'You know what sportswomen are like. A bit of adrenaline and a felt-tip pen, they'll sign anything.' Ruby kicked it back under her desk.

'I mean, why have you got it?'

'Ben and Belinda's wedding present.'

'Are you sure you read their list correctly?'

'It's an investment,' Ruby said. 'In years to come, they'll thank me. Look, thank you for the dresses, only I do need to get on.'

'You want me to go?'

Got it in one. 'I'm sure you must be busy.'

'Not today.' Emily flashed her the widest of smiles.

That went well. Ruby felt the tune to "Bat out of Hell" running round and round in her head. Her stress levels were seriously overloaded. Any minute now she was likely to break into song.

'Belinda's lovely, isn't she?' Emily said. 'Has she told you she's invited me to the wedding?'

No, she didn't.

'I see your kitchen's been started,' Emily added. 'I didn't think you could afford to get anyone in.'

Ruby was certain she'd never discussed her finances with the woman. Belinda must have said something while she was doing Emily's hair. Her problems with Kevin were hardly secret and as far as she was concerned, the more people who knew he was a total wanker, the better. 'I can't,' she said. 'I'm doing it with help from a friend.'

'You are so clever. I wouldn't know where to start.'

Why wouldn't the woman take a hint and go?

'You hear of all sorts of horror stories about rogue traders, don't you?'

Ruby froze. Emily was smiling but her words sounded like a thinly veiled threat.

'One badly wired plug and the whole block of flats could go up.'

The woman gave her the creeps. Still, Ruby made a mental note to get the electrics checked.

Malik had an Egyptian history degree. She had no idea what other qualifications he held, or in what capacity Jamila's father employed him before he came to England.

'Adam is pleased with the way it's going.'

'Is he?' Ruby said, suddenly feeling cold.

'He's so particular. Everything has to be perfect.'

Ruby narrowed her eyes. Her anger started to surface, and her face burned.

'He was so upset about you being let down, just like him to step in and help. He's so capable, isn't he?'

Keep calm. Deep breaths. She's Adam's friend.

'Did he tell you that?' Ruby asked, impressed by how calm she managed to sound. It was only a matter of time before she lost it completely.

'We talk all the time,' Emily said. 'We have so much in common. I guess he'll be down later?'

'You guess wrong.' Ruby felt ridiculously calm. Emily seemed to have inside information on her kitchen saga, either that or a rare psychic gift that was wasted in Redford, except she hadn't picked up Ruby's current line of thought – *Get stuffed, bitch* – and she didn't know Adam was away.

'Is he working then?'

'Look, thank you for the dresses, but I am busy and ...'

'Why don't you get on with whatever you need to do? I could make us a nice drink?'

'I want you to go,' Ruby said, firmly. 'Now.'

Emily adopted the sort of open-mouthed stare Ruby's grandfather's old wooden soldier nutcracker achieved when the handle on its back was wrenched up as far as it would go. If Ruby had had some walnuts to hand, Emily could have made herself really useful.

'There's no need to be like that,' Emily said. 'I was only trying to help.'

Ruby's blood pressure soared to megalithic proportions as she watched Emily walk across the car park. *Shit, the woman was scary*. There was no way she could relax. Ruby hummed the opening bars to "Rubber Bullets", picked Brutus up and rang the first number on her list of granite suppliers.

Chapter Eighteen

'Okay, okay, I've missed her.' Adam threw his hands up in the air and Jason smiled triumphantly.

'So, ring her.'

'And tell her what?'

'That you're coming home.'

'It's only for the weekend.'

The estate agent's particulars sat on Adam's iPad screen. He had an appointment to view the property on Saturday. Xavier had agreed to a weekend off. Part of him was excited to be going home. Part of him was excited he'd taken the first step in a new life; a restaurant of his own. A huge part of him was excited by the thought he would soon see Ruby again. He missed her more each day he was in France. It must be true what they say about absence making the heart grow fonder unless homesickness had kicked in.

His excitement was tempered by the details of the leasehold property he stared at. Not quite what he wanted. For one thing, it was in the arse-end of town. 'High Street footage comes at a premium,' the estate agent stated, implying it to be way beyond his means. 'Besides people drive ridiculous distances these days for a decent meal.' He then went on to expound the virtues of the *Le Manoir aux Quat'Saisons*. 'My wife and I frequently pop over for a special meal.'

The property hadn't been used as a restaurant for over two years. The previous tenants had done a bunk and the owner hadn't been keen to go down the rental route again, but eighteen months of trying to sell it had proved fruitless and seemed to convince him another tenant would be his best chance of an income. It needed work. The last tenants left in a hurry and the pictures Adam scrolled through suggested the owner hadn't bothered to do anything since. Tables and chairs were dotted around the main dining room. There were pots and pans hung in the kitchen and a note in the particulars suggested all equipment could be negotiated into the lease if the new tenant required. Adam shuddered. Even on a ten-inch screen, the place looked like it needed a deep clean.

'Does she know you're coming home?' Jason asked, peering over his shoulder.

'Who?' Adam knew exactly who he meant, and Jason fixed him with a look that suggested he knew Adam knew.

'Ring her.'

'And say what?'

Jason clutched his chest. 'Darling, life without you has been unbearable, so I am coming home,' he said, in a falsetto voice.

'My balls dropped before you were born. And I'm back for Sunday night service.'

'Are you going to ask her to view it with you?' Jason gestured at the screen.

'I might.' Adam shut down the iPad.

'Good, because you need someone to talk some sense into you.'

'I want to be my own boss. Cook my own food.'

'Great, but Larkhill? Are you sure? Surely you want somewhere a bit more upmarket. Somewhere with windows perhaps?' He laughed.

'Leases aren't cheap,' Adam said. There was a bit of a snap to his voice and Jason turned and stared.

'Just remember mate, no one found happiness settling for second best.' He didn't wait for a reply, rather he waltzed off humming "Simply the Best".

Life was so easy for Jason. He sailed through it untouched by disaster. Girls came and went. He'd never had problems like Emily. There was no elephant in the room he had to deal with. If Adam wanted any sort of relationship with Ruby, he needed to tell her about Emily. Not a conversation he looked forward to having. The longer he left it the more difficult it would become. He should have told her straight off.

Adam practised what he wanted to say the minute he was on the Eurostar train in Paris.

'I owe you an explanation.' He watched the French countryside rush past, then the tunnel, the oast houses and more familiar Kentish scenery.

By the time he reached London, his monologue had become second nature like breathing, but he had butterflies in his stomach as the train drew into London. People gathered their possessions. Adam waited for most of them to alight before he slung his overnight bag over his shoulder and headed for the Redford train.

Ruby would be sympathetic, look at him with concern in her eyes. It would be okay. Or else she'd laugh. That would hurt. People reacted to stress in different ways. He would be patient; make sure she understood.

'I don't care if Emily is your friend, I need you to listen to me.'

The guard who took his ticket looked up. 'Okay,' he said, warily.

By the time Adam got to Redford, he'd even rehearsed Ruby's responses.

Being pursued sounded a bit lightweight but he couldn't bring himself to say stalked. He'd tried to come to terms with the word over the last three years. He couldn't. This sort of thing didn't happen to people like him. Celebrities had stalkers, not ordinary people. He'd play it down; he didn't want to frighten her off. Emily wasn't a mad axe-woman. She'd never threatened him. There was no reason why she should. They'd never had a relationship. He'd never done anything to offend or upset her. In fact, the opposite: that's what hurt. He'd been kind, when she most needed it. So why she'd felt the need to persecute him, he had no idea.

His colleagues teased him, but then he'd never actually told them how terrified he was. Or how his health had been affected. The only people who knew how difficult he found things were Clive and Jason.

He'd steered away from relationships because of Emily. He didn't feel he could enter into a new one with her hanging around. Added to which, he distrusted practically everybody he met.

Until Ruby.

He hated Emily, but Paris had convinced him he had to do something. If necessary, he'd tell her to her face to get lost; he couldn't run away any more. He had to get his life back under control, and soon. Emily had stolen far too much from him already; she wasn't going to steal Ruby.

His mouth twitched just thinking about the woman. Ruby made him smile even when she was miles away. Smiling – something he hadn't done a great deal of in the last few years.

Spending so much time with Jason, he'd even bought into the guy's favourite mantra of "Better to jump, however badly you land, than never to take off in the first place".

Finally, he was ready to jump, well take a step in the right direction at least. He would ask her out for a meal. Tell her about Emily.

If it went well, he might mention he didn't think she'd completely cracked the tune or the words to "Drift Away".

Adam stood in front of Flat 4, Union House and took a deep breath, then sweated a bit and knocked. No going back now.

'It's your lucky day. I come bearing gifts, news and the post,' he said as Ruby's door started to open. 'Put on your best dress Cinderella ...'

And there stood a man.

The smile on Adam's face died faster than a Lewis Hamilton pit stop. 'I was expecting to see Ruby.'

'Miss Ruby out.'

Adam hesitated, unsure what to do, but his mind was made up by Brutus charging down the hall, his tail spinning like the rotors on a helicopter. He threw himself at Adam's knees.

'You come in.' The man seemed to consider being recognised by a Border Terrier a good character reference. 'I'm Malik.' He held out a hand. 'I hope your family is well.'

'Adam.' Adam shook the offered hand and shut the door behind him. 'Will she be long?'

'She has gone to be fitted for a maid. She not happy.'

Picking up his dog, Adam followed Malik down the narrow hallway. Stepping over a small pile of coving, he followed a trail of dust to the kitchen.

It had changed. *Boy had it changed.*

At some point in the last two months, base units had been installed and granite worktops fitted. There was a sink. He leant against the counter. 'You're Ruby's kitchen fitter?' he said, noticing the wires hanging from the ceiling; what was left of it. Some of the coving was missing, presumably the missing bits were the lengths lying in the hall. The worktops were covered with pale grey plaster dust.

'No.' Malik stamped a foot and looked affronted. 'Kitchen fitter is a wanker.'

'You've met him too?' Adam laughed.

'No. He is a bad, bad man, but I am good. I am Miss Ruby's friend.'

Adam nodded. 'So am I.' At least, he hoped he still was.

'Good. We finish the ceiling before Miss Ruby comes back.'

Ruby was tired and hungry. The entire afternoon had been

spent having the final fitting for her dress while trying to control a mob of bridesmaids.

'Can't you contain that lot?' Lily asked as soon as Ruby's own torture session finished. It hadn't been great as ego trips went, despite the woman telling her how marvellous she was going to look. She had more puncture marks than a serial drug user and now knew her shoulders weren't level and she needed to make more of an effort to keep her bottom in when she walked.

'I'm sure it's the maid of honour's job to keep them calm and under control.'

'Have you got taser guns and handcuffs, because I haven't,' she said as two of the youngest chased each other into a rack of dresses. 'Could we lock them up?'

'Mmm, not a bad idea.' Her mother smiled. 'There must be a cupboard, a changing room, or something.'

'You've done the mothering bit, what do they need?' Ruby said.

Lily shrugged. 'You and Ben used to let off steam in the garden.'

'No garden.'

'Probably a good thing. It usually ended up as a mudbath and a fight, because you'd bitten the legs off his action man.'

'I did that once. And only one of them.'

'You'd already tattooed his arms.'

'Soldiers always have tattoos. Ben said he was going to join the army.'

'You cut them off at the elbow to do it.'

'I stuck them back on.'

'Not the right way around. The poor boy was traumatised.'

'Have you got any sweets to bribe them with?'

Lily raised her eyes. 'No sugar or E-numbers.'

'Why did Belinda decide she needed so many bridesmaids and flower girls?'

'She didn't want to upset anyone.'

'Tell me about it,' Ruby said. 'You know she's added another ten to the guest list, including the girl doing the flowers?'

'Your friend.'

'She's not my friend. I met the woman once. She helped me get some cupcakes home.'

One of the children charged up to them with what looked like a dummy's leg. 'It fell off,' she protested when challenged.

'How's your yoga?' Ruby asked.

'Coming along nicely,' Lily said, her face breaking into a serene smile. She had a faraway look in her eyes. 'Very relaxing. You ought to try it.'

'Right.' Ruby stood up. 'You lot, over here. Lily is going to show you some yoga poses.'

'What,' her mother said. 'Don't be silly.'

'You keep them quiet. I'll refit the leg,' Ruby said. 'Then I'll see if I can find sugar-free tranquillisers.'

There was no post on her mat when she pushed open the door, but Ruby could hear voices. Brutus rushed down the hallway and she bent down to say hello, noticing mid-bend the coving had disappeared. She scooped him into her arms and dropped her handbag onto her bed.

A smell, Ruby couldn't place, floated through her flat. A good smell that heightened her feeling of hunger. There were two men in her kitchen, stood with their backs to her. Both with grey hair, they appeared to be staring at the cooker. Without moving closer, she couldn't hear what they were saying. She moonwalked backwards silently.

The way she saw it, she had three choices. One – take them out with a well-aimed blow, except she could only do that one at a time and with what? There wasn't even a piece of coving to hand. Two – run for it. Or three, she could yell "What do you think you're doing in my bloody flat? Please leave or I'll call the police!" – from the locked bathroom.

She opted for number three.

Closing the seat on the toilet, she sat down to wait until the intruders had seen the error of their ways, preferably leaving whatever was smelling delicious, and disappeared. Then, as an afterthought, she opened the door and shouted, 'I'm armed.'

Not technically true but she had bleach and bathroom cleaner in handy trigger operating bottles. Both of which had dire warnings about the dangers of accidentally getting them on the skin. Accidentally, my arse, if push came to shove, she was prepared to squeeze both triggers with venom.

Ruby wasn't sure quite how long burglars needed to leave a property, so she did what she always did in times of stress and tidied manically. The bathroom had never looked so good; then the bathroom cupboard. She refolded all the towels. For good measure, once everything else had been tidied away, she trimmed her toenails and plucked her eyebrows, which took her way past Brutus's teatime; something he appeared to have noticed. To start, he'd looked as if being locked in the bathroom with Ruby was all a dog could wish for. Ten minutes ago, he prostrated himself on the floor, staring up at her, as if too weak from hunger to move. His eyes followed her round the room imploring her to feed him. Ruby hadn't heard anything for a while. Actually, she hadn't heard anything since she'd locked herself in.

Brutus started to whine. She knew how he felt. Hell, it was past her teatime, but having left her handbag, with her phone and cards, on the bed she had no way of contacting anyone. Her stomach rumbled as if in confirmation. She could imagine the red-top newspaper headlines: "Girl found in bathroom, half-eaten by Border Terrier".

Ruby opened the door quietly until the space was wide enough for her to squeeze through and with her back flat to the wall, she inched her away along it. Just before the sitting room door, she ducked down on to hands and knees and crawled along until she had a clear view of the kitchen door.

Shit, they were still there. She wished whatever it was that they were staring at on the cooker didn't smell so enticing.

Something brushed against Ruby's leg and she screamed.

Brutus!

'Hello to you, too.' A very grey Adam was looking down at her.

For a split second, she was glad to be on her hands and knees. If she'd been standing, the shock would probably have floored her. For a longer second, she was glad her eyebrows were plucked, her toenails short. If she'd known he was here, she would have applied some make-up.

'Bloody hell,' she said. 'You look ill.'

In the few weeks since she'd seen him, he'd aged. Could people really turn grey overnight? In Adam's case, it seemed they could, and completely.

'Thanks.' He grinned and held out a hand. She took hold of it. He pulled her up and kissed her forehead.

'Hello,' she said, reaching up and meaning to kiss him on the cheek, but somehow her mouth slid across his cheek to his mouth, then she felt his arms around her waist, and she leaned into him and kissed him harder.

When she pulled away she noticed an equally grey man stood just inside the kitchen.

'Malik, whatever's wrong?'

'Plaster dust,' Adam said.

'I've made food.' Malik grinned wildly.

'You can't cook.'

'Your friend teach me. Now you're here, I cook rice.' He put two packets in the microwave and set the timer.

143

The kitchen was much tidier than she'd left it before she went out and it had never smelt so good.

The ceiling was no longer covered with patterned Artex but the smooth dark pink of newly applied plaster. The granite worktops glistened. The floor looked clean. She could even see out of the window. For the first time in ages, Ruby looked around the kitchen and liked what she saw. Okay, there were wires everywhere and marks on the wall where some wall units needed to be fixed, but it was starting to come together, starting to look like a kitchen.

On the cooker stood a covered pan. Ruby lifted the lid. The contents were green, dark green, but any worry she had about the colour was soon displaced by the smell. She closed her eyes and breathed through her nose, enjoying the sensation as spices she couldn't begin to comprehend assaulted her nostrils.

'Green coriander curry, Adam said.

'I cooked it,' said Malik.

Ruby laid the table, Adam popped upstairs for a bottle of wine while Malik stirred the pot on the cooker.

'You not touch the ceiling, Miss Ruby, you promise?' he said, waving his spatula around. 'You paint it when it's dry and ring me.'

'You not touch sink until tomorrow, Miss Ruby.' Adam laughed. She hadn't heard him come back. She spun round. He was smiling.

'What's wrong with the sink.'

'Nothing's wrong with the sink, but we'll wash up later.'

Ruby sighed. 'It should have been a Belfast sink, but it's a Butler sink. The granite man put some off-cuts of granite under it to bring it up to the right height.'

Adam nodded. 'He's made a good job of it, but are you sure Kevin King is a proper kitchen fitter? Malik told me about some of the problems you had with the base units.

Didn't the fact the man arrived on a horse suggest all was not what it seemed.'

'Believe me, Billy the Kid, or John Wayne would never have caused as many problems as he did.'

'Ye ha!'

'Malik's been brilliant. It was his father with the carpet the day I said you were my fiancé and you ran away. At least he sent his son.'

'I come,' Malik said. 'Because father is no kitchen fitter.' He folded his arms. 'If one door closes ...' he hesitated as if waiting for a reaction, then slapped his head. 'I remember now, another door opens.' He laughed. 'Joke,' he added. 'Adam teach me joke.'

Adam shrugged. 'It's lost a bit in the translation.' He grinned. 'Malik tells me he's going to be a tour guide and you're helping him with his English.'

'That surprises you?'

'Some of the things he's come out with surprise me.'

'Like?'

'How about, "It may sound trite, but it's love at first bite".'

'Bananas, I think. I can't remember where from. I didn't win anyway.'

'Nearly as impressive as "responsive to life and stains of today, it's ecologically sound in every way". Not quotes usually found on any Level 1 English as a Foreign Language course.' Adam's eyes were bright.

Ruby sighed, overcome with warmth and happiness. 'He knows the words to "Rubber Bullets" too,' she said.

'Please, God, tell me you haven't tried to teach him the tune.'

'You've been avoiding me, you naughty girl.' Eamon filled Emily's glass with wine. No time for half measures. He had a programme to put to bed, a filming schedule to screw down.

He had to get her agreement to film the sequel, whatever it took.

Waiters laid their napkins across their laps and hovered anxiously waiting for a decision on food.

'I have only been in Bootles once since the filming,' Emily said. She looked around. 'Adam always said it felt like a busman's holiday coming back when he wasn't working.'

'You didn't mention he's working at Xavier's in Paris at the moment.'

'Didn't I?' She coloured. Spots of red appeared on each cheek.

'No,' Eamon said, watching her warily. 'The waiter told me. Is there anything else I should know?'

There followed a lengthy silence. She took a long sip of her drink. Eamon waited.

'No, nothing,' she said, eventually. 'I thought I'd mentioned it. Must have slipped my mind, but we are both so excited about the idea of being filmed again. Must be something to do with my hair colour or age.'

'Really?' Eamon said, quietly, a feeling of unease started in the pit of his stomach.

'Really,' she repeated. 'Do you like my hair colour? I have a friend who's a hairdresser. She's going to do my hair for the television episode. I mean I liked what your make-up team did for me last time, but Belinda understands my features and what makes me look good. I have a lovely dress for the occasion, too.'

Eamon gripped the menu, his knuckles white. He didn't give a toss. She could use a top London hairdresser for all he cared. He wasn't paying and he didn't care if she shaved her bloody head as long as she signed his paperwork.

Emily studied the menu with exaggerated interest. She read out every dish, its name, its contents and then asked his opinion. By the time she had got through the starters, he reached out and took her menu. He tried to make it look casual and not to show his irritation. He flashed a smile. 'Why don't you let me choose for you,' he said, through gritted teeth. 'I think I can guess what you'd like.'

She smiled coyly and batted her bloody eyelashes. Eamon patted her hand reassuringly and tried to disguise the shudder he felt about to erupt. He fiddled under the table and twiddled the positive mantra bracelet tied around his wrist, the one his counsellor suggested he wear at all times. He muttered under his breath, 'I am a superhero. I am happy. Today is going to be a good day.' He wondered how many more times he'd need to tell himself the same thing before he started to believe it.

He reached into his jacket pocket, pulled out the sheaf of papers he needed her to sign and placed them on the table. 'The thing is Emily, I need you to read through these and sign them,' he said, pushing them across to her.

Her face lit up. 'Wouldn't it be the best episode ever, if we went to Paris and filmed in the restaurant there? You could arrange it to look like a repeat of last time, he comes out of the kitchen and is transformed into my date.'

'Sorry,' Eamon said. 'Budget restrictions.' He tapped the pile with his pen before laying it on top.

'Oh well, just an idea.'

'The thing is,' he said, as their starters arrived, 'your episode is important. The one the series hinges on. People care about you. Even my director general is looking forward to seeing it. Do I have your word you have spoken to Adam about this and he is happy to go ahead with the filming? I can't afford for this to go wrong.'

'Don't look so worried.' Emily picked up the biro and added a flamboyant signature to the end of the document. 'There. Happy now? You really need to take a chill pill.' She speared a length of asparagus, while he glared at her. 'This is very good. You should try it. I am sure more green vegetables in your diet would help. And there's no problem with Adam, trust me. We're both going to a wedding together soon.'

Eamon folded the papers back into his pocket and breathed a sigh of relief. Everything would be all right. 'I have to tell you, flower, that's music to my ears,' he said, following her lead with the asparagus.

Maybe the bracelet had worked. Today would be a good day. Such a good day, he didn't mind offering Emily a pudding and a glass of dessert wine to go with it.

Chapter Nineteen

Adam flicked through the plans the estate agent had given him. The photo on the front of the leaflet showed the same restaurant door, but not the boarded-up window, or the other one, covered in what looked like white paint, apart from the word "help" that had been rubbed out. He checked his watch. They were definitely in the right place, but the estate agent wasn't.

'Remind me of your surname,' Ruby said.

'What?'

'Your surname.'

'Finder.' He stole a look at her. She was writing something on what looked like a postcard. 'Why?'

'No reason,' she said. 'Have you ever been to see Templeton Rovers play?'

'No.'

She stopped writing and put the postcard into her bag. 'For goodness' sake, relax,' she said. 'You're making me nervous.' She laughed when he started to apologise. 'Tell me why you think this is your perfect restaurant.'

'I can afford it.' He shrugged. 'It's far enough away from Bootles not to be a problem with competition. There's parking outside.'

'It's not in the town centre – you won't get passing trade. How many meals do you think you need to serve each day to make it financially viable?'

Adam turned around and gave her his best smile. 'I've based my calculations on an average sixteen covers a night.'

Ruby nodded. 'So that's a minimum of eight tables. I guess you're thinking about one sitting. And this place is what you are looking for?'

He had no idea. On paper it looked a possibility, but sitting outside the rundown restaurant, he felt flat, even with a gorgeous woman by his side.

He checked his watch again. Ruby reached out and squeezed his hand. 'He'll be here.'

Ten minutes later, she started to hum "Give me the beat boys" and Adam's blood pressure started to rise. Suddenly, a black sports car drove up and skidded to a halt at an angle across two of the disabled parking spaces.

'Ain't it a shame,' she sang.

They were milliseconds away from the chorus; he'd never been happier to see anybody.

'Sorry. Sorry. Sorry.' A well-dressed man in a suit and tie, jumped out, looking anything but.

Adam shrugged. There was no point in starting off being negative.

'Shouldn't take us long. It's not huge,' the estate agent said, taking a large bunch of keys out of his pocket. Selecting the right one, he opened the door. 'Ladies first, Mrs Finder,' he said and threw in a mock bow for effect.

Adam was about to put him right, but Ruby just smiled and walked through the door, so he shrugged and followed her in.

'What are your first impressions?' she asked, looking around a small room.

'Dated, dark.'

'You need to look beyond that.' Once in a while, she would write something in her notebook. Adam couldn't imagine what.

The agent was right, it wasn't huge, but it had a decent-sized kitchen. Not exactly what Adam wanted, but he needed to start small and gain a reputation for good food. No point in going too big to start. He could always expand later.

He wanted somewhere cosy, not a formal restaurant. That wasn't his style.

Ruby took her time in the kitchen, making copious notes and checking out every cupboard.

On the wall above a small serving hatch, the "Specials" board had Egg Mayonnaise, Coq au Vin and Black Forest Gateau listed as the Chef's choice. It had probably been the same specials board every day of the last thirty years, but that didn't bother Adam. He was going to create his own menus.

'How negotiable is the price?' Ruby asked, looking at her list. 'Obviously you need to do quite a lot of work before you could open to the public.'

Adam nodded. Nothing about her expression gave away what she was thinking.

'We'd be looking at a rent-free period of at least six months to give us time to get things up and running,' she said to the estate agent.

'We would?' Adam whispered under his breath.

'Shouldn't be too much of a problem,' the agent said. 'Depending on the length of lease.'

Ruby looked at Adam. He smiled. A feeling of warmth rushed through him.

'You like what you see?' the estate agent asked.

'It's given us something to talk about,' Ruby said. 'We do have a number of other properties to look at. We will let you know our decision on Monday.'

The estate agent looked crestfallen. 'There's been a lot of interest.'

'I'm sure there has,' Ruby said. 'We'll speak on Monday.'

Adam said goodbye and they walked back to the car. He took one last look at the property.

The level of investment meant he'd have to sell his house, but as Jason had no plans to return to the UK, apart from the odd weekend visit as guest chef, he'd already said Adam could carry on using the flat while he was away, until he sorted himself out.

'What did you think?' he asked.

'It's got potential.' Ruby looked down at her list. 'I think it could be done up, to be quite nice. The plasticised menus and fluorescent cocktail pictures need ditching. The pine cladding needs to go. Unless the new lessee is planning on turning the place into a sauna.'

'You mean me?'

'No, I don't mean you. It's okay, but it's not what you want. Your heart wouldn't be in it.'

Adam frowned.

'Okay,' she said firmly. 'I'm going to channel my inner Kirstie Allsopp here. It's a bit like buying a house,' she said. 'You know the minute you walk into the right place you've found your home. I did with my flat. It's a feeling, you can't explain it, but you'd know if you'd had it. You didn't get it. You couldn't wait to get out.'

She was right, even if it pained him to say it.

'There's no point doing this, unless you're one hundred per cent committed,' she said. 'It will take a lot of money, time and energy. You have to be sure. At the moment, you're looking at places and asking whether the level of compromise is reasonable or not.'

'I'm not.' He pouted, knowing she was right.

'This is your opportunity to achieve your dream,' she said. 'Don't settle for second best.'

Clive wrapped Adam in a bear hug before they took seats at a table in Bootles' window, overlooking the high street. 'Good to see you,' he said. 'You're looking great.'

Xavier had sent a very decent bottle of wine back from France with him. Clive poured, they swirled their glasses, smelt it, then took a sip. Both nodded with satisfaction at the same time.

The rest of the bottle went down as easily as their

conversation. It was good to see him again and Adam relaxed as they laughed a lot.

'You look good,' Clive said as coffee was served. 'Happy even. Do I detect the presence of a woman?'

'No,' Adam said. The expression on Clive's face suggested his response had been too quick to be entirely convincing.

Clive laughed. 'Good for you,' he said. 'The same woman who's looking after your mutt?'

Adam nodded. 'It's not what you think,' he said and straightened in his chair.

'Never is.' Clive grinned over the top of his liqueur glass. 'You're going to have to take a chance on women again sometime. I've heard they're not all unhinged psychopaths, although having been married for thirty odd years, I'm still on the fence on that. Talking of which, Emily Watkins was here yesterday.'

'She's banned.'

'The television producer booked lunch and the waiter didn't realise.'

Adam put down his cup. Even hearing the name unnerved him. Pull yourself together, he told himself.

'I understand she's doing the sequel of *Taking a Chance on Love*. They're filming it here.'

'She can.' Adam swallowed the last of his coffee and looked at his boss. 'I'm not.'

'The TV company has booked the restaurant out for a lunchtime the week after next. They must be going ahead with just her if you don't know anything about it. Sounds like she's finally realised there is no happy ever after as far as you're concerned. That must be good news. More coffee?' A rhetorical question as Clive was already topping his cup up from a cafetière. 'How long are you home for?'

'Just the weekend, but I do need to talk to you about coming back.'

Clive concentrated on stirring cream into his coffee. 'I don't think I can afford to open evenings yet,' he said, without looking up. 'And it's probably best you're out of the way until the filming's finished. I don't suppose Xavier could use you until September?'

'Probably, but I'm starting to feel homesick.'

'Oh.' Clive swilled the last dregs round in his glass.

Outside cars and buses rumbled past. People would walk by, occasionally slowing down and looking in.

Adam finally broke the silence. 'I've had a look at a place in Larkhill,' he said. 'I think it's time I opened my own restaurant.'

'You've decided to take the premises?'

'Not yet.'

Clive took another sip of his coffee and sucked the cream from his upper lip. 'What's wrong with them?'

Adam had brought the estate agent's plans with him. He handed them over. Clive carried on drinking as he read. Occasionally, he would nod or screw up his face. Adam watched him, trying to judge from his expression what he was thinking, but didn't interrupt. The older man had finished his drink before he put down the plans and smiled. 'Looks okay.'

'Has potential.'

'Can see why you were interested. I'd have thought it a bit small though?'

'Smaller than I'd like, but cosy.'

Clive sighed. 'So, what's wrong with it?'

Now or never. Adam took a deep breath. 'It's not this place,' he said. 'When I think of my own place and picture me working in the kitchen, it's this place I imagine.'

'I thought that once,' Clive said, refolding his serviette. 'These days it feels more like a noose round my neck.'

'Might you consider selling or be prepared to talk about a partnership?'

Clive looked up at him. Adam couldn't gauge his expression. *Shit, had he completely fucked up their relationship and any chance of returning to work here?* 'I know you have put everything into this business, and I can understand that you wouldn't want to ...'

'I would to you,' Clive said, quietly. 'Well maybe not sell all of it. I'm not ready to hang up my apron completely, but I'd like to take a back seat, take the pot off the boil. Maybe become a sleeping partner.'

'Are you serious?' Adam managed to squeeze out in an unnaturally high-pitched voice as soon as he'd stopped opening and closing his mouth like some demented ghoul. Clive was saved from answering by the front door opening.

A smartly dressed man entered. 'Thank God, you're open,' he said. 'There's been a bit of a balls-up. I've got a minibus of senior citizens outside. Can you do twelve of us for a meal?'

'What do you think, partner?' Clive grinned. 'You up for a spot of cooking?'

Chapter Twenty

Ruby started in horror at the life-size picture of her brother as a baby, taped to the back of the door. 'What's that doing there?'

'Pin the bollocks on Ben,' Belinda said matter-of-factly. 'Your mother's idea. She's organising the games.'

'Talking of Ben. What's he doing this evening?'

'Daniel's arranged for them to go to London. Dinner in a Japanese celebrity chef's restaurant and then onto a club.'

Ruby grunted. Trust bloody Daniel; it sounded like it would cost a fortune. She had no money, so not an option she'd considered. 'Would you rather have gone out somewhere?' she asked. 'I mean this can't compare to a Japanese chef.'

'I wanted a bridal shower, not a hen night.' Belinda hugged her. 'It sounds more grown up; more glamorous and intimate, don't you think?'

'Apart from semi-naked pictures of my brother.'

There was a large amount of giggling from the kitchen. Lily and Belinda's mother were in charge of the food. Ruby hated to think what was so funny about tonight's menu.

'This is brilliant. Crowds and sushi aren't for me. I'd far rather have a girlie night with all my friends. This is the best thing – really!'

Ruby looked at the half-full glass of wine in Belinda's hand. There was nothing in her expression to suggest she wasn't being sincere. Slightly drunk maybe, but still sincere. Belinda wasn't known for her ability to hold drink and the canapés hadn't materialised so far.

Ruby topped up Belinda's glass from the bottle on the table. 'Emily says you've invited her to the wedding.'

The decorated veil Belinda insisted on wearing already

showed signs of coming off, along with the L-plates and other bits she'd stapled to it. If she turned her head too fast, she was likely to kill someone with the wooden spoon. 'She's being so kind and with the two of you being such good friends,' she said.

'I'm guessing she told you that,' Ruby said.

Belinda took another sip of her drink. 'She said she'd dropped two dresses off for you so you have something to wear to the wedding. That you don't have time to go shopping for new ones now you and Adam are spending so much time remodelling your kitchen.'

'She said that?' The mention of his name made Ruby sit up and her heart miss a beat.

'Yes, I think so.' Belinda's voice was becoming slightly slurred. 'So sweet of her. I know how upset you were when the dry cleaners lost your dress. Any use?'

'Can you see me wearing floral patterns and ruffles?'

Belinda frowned, clearly concentrating hard. 'No ...'

'And you never bloody will. I half expected them to have matching knickers.'

Belinda's cheeks had already reached sugar pink colour and she had a grin fixed to her face. 'Your mother said you used to hate it when she made knickers to match your dresses.'

'I did. Those knickers scarred me for life.'

'Is it true you once took a pair off and threw them into a waste bin on the way home from school?' She hiccupped.

'Lily told you.'

'Weren't you embarrassed?'

'There was no one there,' Ruby said. 'But that's not the point. I am not wearing Emily's bloody dresses.'

Belinda blinked. 'You'd look fabulous in anything. Try them.'

'Shan't.'

'What does Adam think of them?'

'Adam?' Ruby asked, stunned. She was pretty certain she'd never told Belinda his name.

'Emily's told me all about your plus-one for the wedding. I can't wait to meet this man. She said he's really gorgeous.'

Shit. 'You haven't invited her tonight?' Ruby asked.

Belinda shook her head. 'Did you know she had a date yesterday with a television producer? I'm cross.' She pouted. 'She promised to ring and tell me how it went.' But at that minute, Belinda's attention was diverted by the arrival of the girls from the hair salon, who'd arrived and seemed intent on tying helium-filled condoms to Belinda's veil.

Ruby left them to it and took the half-empty wine bottle into the kitchen. If she thought Belinda was worse for wear, the sight of Lily and Belinda's mother giggling over the cheddar beignets and smoked salmon roulades told her they were already streets ahead.

'Have some wine, darling,' Lily said, waving a half-empty glass. The oven timer pinged. 'That'll be the Parma ham tarts and the prawn crostini.' She tried to get up.

'Stay where you are. I'll do it,' Ruby said, as the noise coming from the front room escalated.

'Sounds like the stripper's arrived,' Belinda's mum said.

'You knew about this?' Ruby stared at them both.

'Her idea. Don't blame me,' Belinda's mum said, as she stood up and grabbed Lily's arm. 'He's her yoga master. Come on! Let's go and see his downward Ashtanga or whatever you call it.'

'Well, you weren't going to organise anything, were you?' Lily took the bottle from Ruby and lurched unsteadily after the other woman.

'I'll take care of the food then,' Ruby called after them.

Ruby, loaded up with uneaten canapés, took the long walk

back from her mother's, along the high street and round the park. It wasn't late and it was still light. She was glad of the fresh air and time to think.

She'd known Emily would be doing the flowers, but thought she'd be gone before the actual ceremony bit. Once the buttonholes were installed there was surely no reason to hang around, even if she was looking to get some sort of customer service excellence award. And then Belinda had gone and invited her to the whole darn shooting match. Emily was going to be there for the duration.

Ruby wondered whether she could tell Adam she'd made a mistake? That his girlfriend, his ex, or whatever she was, would be there. She loved the thought that he'd agreed to go with her. But the thought of the two of them in the same room together bothered her more than it should have.

She needed to speak to him sensibly, ask him about Emily. The girl was starting to freak her out. He hadn't mentioned Emily when she'd kissed him last night or when he kissed her back. He hadn't held her off and said, 'Sorry I'm already spoken for.'

She stood outside number six for a few seconds. They needed to sit down and talk. Like the two adults they were. He knew everything there was to know about Ruby Brooks – didn't he? But all she really knew about him was that he desperately wanted his own restaurant. He loved cooking.

He knew about Daniel, but every time they got close to discussing his past relationships he skirted round the issue or something had come up. He still hadn't explained the problem with Emily's card, or where he'd rushed off to. Yes, she would tell him they needed to sit down and talk. She would listen to what he had to say. She was good at listening, that was why she was so good at her job. She wouldn't be judgemental. Her judgement when it came to men hadn't been great in the past. If she'd spent a little longer getting to know Daniel then maybe, just maybe they could have avoided a lot of unhappiness later down the line.

Then the door opened. Adam stood there in his bare feet. God every inch of him was gorgeous. His smile lit up his hallway and Brutus bounded out, wagging his tail and carrying a sock.

'Hi,' Adam said. 'I hoped you'd call. I wanted to tell you about my lunch with Clive.'

'Hi yourself,' she said, grinning back as her brain fogged up, her legs weakened, and she conveniently forgot about the whole grown-up conversation thing.

She put down the boxes and walked forward into his arms. He hugged her and she felt safe. He kissed her and when they finally pulled apart: 'How was the hen?' he asked, smiling widely

'Bridal shower,' she said. 'Not good. I have just watched twenty drunken and blindfolded women trying to guess where my brother's genitals were. And a seventy-year-old ex-bodybuilder in a fluorescent mankini demonstrating yoga poses and trying to make out with my mother while I played pass the parcel and handed out drinks and canapés.'

'You're home early.'

'Mother found her singalong version of *Grease*.' Ruby frowned. 'By the end of the first song, Belinda was already snoring. It was definitely time to go.' She looked down at her feet. 'Let's just say, I've had better times.'

'Come here.' He held her against his chest. She relaxed into him.

'What's in the boxes?'

'I bought some beetroot and goat's cheese blinis back with me.'

'Sounds good. Is there enough for two? It's probably a bit late to start on a bottle of wine ...'

'Oh God, I'm sorry. I forgot you're going back to France first thing tomorrow. Look I'll take Brutus and go.'

He reached for her hand and stroked her wrist. 'I was going to say, I make a mean hot chocolate and I want to tell you about a chat I had with Clive, my boss and …' He hesitated. 'There's something I need to ask you.'

Ruby pulled back slightly and took a deep breath.

Here it came. The "Dear Jane" speech.

Adam froze. 'Look, I know you invited me to your brother's wedding …'

She tensed too and shut her eyes. She even debated turning around and walking away. Here it came – the "there's someone else" line.

'Is this goodbye?'

'No way.' He looked surprised by her outburst.

'Because if it is, just say it.'

'Really, that's the last thing …'

'Are you telling me to go and boil my head?'

'No,' he said. 'I just need to stay in Paris for a couple more weeks. There's something I need out of the way before I come back.'

'Like my brother's wedding?'

Adam dropped a kiss on the end of her nose. 'Not at all, I wish I could be here for that.' He wound a loose tendril of her hair back behind her ear. 'And it's only another two weeks.'

Ruby humphed with an overwhelming feeling of relief and smiled. 'Probably a wise decision. Mother has written out a protocol list for guests, what to wear, how to behave, you know the sort of thing. No, you probably don't, but her family has always been a source of embarrassment ever since my cousin's wedding. They wanted a black-tie do. The bride's family came in full evening dress, tuxedos, floor-length dresses. They looked amazing, but mum's family looked as if they'd come straight from a funeral. She's not taking any chances this time around.'

'When I do come back, I'd love to meet your family.' Ruby looked up and he kissed her again, hard and urgent.

A warmth crept over her body. She liked this man – a lot. She wanted to tell him she would always be there for him; however crazy her family were.

Chapter Twenty-One

Greytowers Hotel had a timeless elegance that Ruby had always loved. The sweep of the tree-lined drive up to the front door. The imposing building. The Georgian furniture. The clock that struck every quarter of an hour. Even the signs for the Brooks' Wedding had been placed in gold-edged frames. A few wedding guests had already arrived; the women in long dresses and the men looking suitably formal. She smiled at them all.

Belinda was right. The raspberry pink bridesmaid's dress suited her. It wasn't as nice as her green number, but the silk hung beautifully and swung with her every move. Ruby felt good.

She checked her notes and did a final circuit of the rooms to make sure everything was in place.

Emily had delivered and set up floral displays. They were amazing; their contemporary feel complimented the period features of the hotel. Belinda would be blown away. The balloon arch had been erected at the front of the ceremony room where Belinda had determined it should be.

The seats were decorated with pink voile bows. There was an order of service on each along with a box of confetti and a bottle of bubble mixture. Ruby winced. That combination had disaster written all over it, but Belinda wanted to walk in on a carpet of flower petals and out through a cloud of bubbles, with confetti thrown as the newlyweds walked out into the garden – and nothing could persuade her otherwise. Everything was in the right place, but add people and alcohol and anything could happen. Still, it wasn't her problem. Once she'd checked everything one last time that would be her wedding coordinator role over.

Ruby checked her timetable. Mothers – tick. Maid of honour – tick. Bridesmaids – done. She looked at her watch; the flower girls should be having their plaits sorted. Then just the bride left.

The dining room had been set. The table plans placed beside the door. Ruby checked the top table and was surprised to find her place setting had been moved next to Daniel's. In somebody else's dreams, maybe, but not hers. She checked the table plan and swapped her card with Emily's, which oddly enough, despite the plan, had been placed next to Ruby's plus-one on the Aunts' table. *Shit, she'd forgotten to tell Belinda Adam wouldn't be coming.*

The cake had been delivered and took pride of place by the fireplace. When the bride and groom cut it, the staff would spirit it away, and serve slices with coffee, before the speeches.

Once the wedding breakfast was cleared away, the dining room would be laid out ready for the evening's entertainment. The band was due at six. Ruby spoke to the lead singer yesterday and he assured her they would arrive in plenty of time.

Emily had left the bouquets and buttonholes with Lily who, thankfully, was sober. The photographer was taking pictures of the bride getting ready.

Ruby watched a red sports car race up the drive and skid to a halt at the bottom of the steps. Ben climbed out of the passenger seat. Daniel climbed out of the driver's side and she retreated behind one of the doors. A waitress floated around, offering glasses of champagne. Daniel said something to her as he helped himself to a glass. When the waitress turned away, she was blushing. Ruby raised her eyes and ticked off the final item on her list. "Bridegroom".

She could do no more. She checked her watch; time to finish getting ready.

The girls from the hair salon pulled her hair away from her face, twisting and plaiting it into a complicated roll on the back of her head, before finally threading some rosebuds into the creation. It took a full couple of seconds before she realised the face looking back at her from the mirror, fully made-up and with the sculptured hairdo, was hers.

The hairdresser carefully teased and curled a few wisps of hair around her face to soften the look.

Putting a hand up to check everything was still in place, Ruby felt feminine and gorgeous. She wished Adam was there to see her.

'For God's sake, you are not five years old any more.' Lily frowned at her daughter. Even Botox could not disguise the annoyance lines etched into her face. 'Eat the sandwich.'

Lily had been in her element all morning. She'd passed through rooms so fast Ruby had only been conscious she'd been there by the slight floral scent she'd left in her wake. Until she'd stopped directly in front of her, holding out a plate of sandwiches. She was cross, every inch of her posture said as much. 'Eat,' she said.

'The hotel provided these?' Ruby looked at her, feeling not for the first time in her life that there must have been some sort of weird mix-up in the maternity unit. Surely, she couldn't be related to this woman, could she? Was it too late to go back and ask? They'd be all right, she wouldn't sue, so long as they told her the truth.

'What's wrong with them?'

'They are marmite, and ...' Ruby opened the sandwich, 'green stuff.'

'What's wrong with watercress?'

'This isn't down to the hotel, is it? You manufactured these.'

Lily stared at her with undisguised infuriation. 'I

suppose you're going to tell me you don't like marmite and watercress.'

The accusation was punctuated with such ferocity that people turned around. They were staring.

Not when it looks like Uncle Norman has already chewed it.

'No ...' Ruby whispered. Up until that moment, even dressed in raspberry silk, she had been enjoying the noise and the bustle as everyone got ready, grateful she could soon merge into the background.

'Well, someone had to do something. Belinda's sister's children are all vegans.'

'You thought marmite and watercress sandwiches were the answer?'

'Yeast extract is perfectly suitable for vegans.' Lily sniffed.

'Why haven't they eaten them?' Ruby asked. 'Don't tell me you buttered the bread.'

Her mother coloured.

'You did, didn't you?'

'Oh grow up,' Lily hissed, and snatched the sandwiches back. 'I don't know why you're looking so smug seeing as you've been stood up.'

'I haven't.'

'So, where is he then? This man you told Belinda you were bringing. Because unless you're hiding him somewhere, he's not here.'

She should've been on *Mastermind*. Lily Brooks, specialist subject – *The Bleeding Obvious*. She was quite right – he wasn't here.

The sneer reappeared. 'Did he find something or someone more interesting to do?' She stomped off holding the sandwiches, looking for another unsuspecting person to foist them on.

Belinda, smiling widely at everyone, came across. 'It's

okay.' Belinda reached out and squeezed her arm. 'Adam will come.'

Ruby tried to smile. Now wasn't the right time to tell her he was still in France. 'Are you sure you want to join this family?' she asked. 'It's not too late you know. Make a run for it. I'll cover, then meet you outside.'

'Actually, it is – too late.'

Whoa, that hadn't been what she expected. 'Nonsense, if you have any doubts at all, you shouldn't get married,' Ruby said, slowly trying to figure out the best way of telling her brother and the rest of the party that the wedding was cancelled.

'It's okay,' Belinda said. 'I don't have any doubts.'

'Are you sure?'

'I knew I'd found my Mr Right within a month of meeting Ben.'

'And he felt the same?'

Belinda grinned. 'It took him a bit longer to come to the same conclusion, but we're both on the same page now. And I'm looking forward to meeting your Adam, the man who changed your resolution about not going anywhere near men ever again, even with a ten-foot barge pole.'

'I'm sure I'd have made it longer than that,' Ruby said, and in a desperate bid to change the subject added, 'How can you be so sure about Ben?' She didn't believe for one minute that her brother and love should ever be used in the same room let alone sentence.

'My heart still skips when I see him, or I hear his voice. If I think we're going to meet, I get butterflies – hours before sometimes,' Belinda said.

Ruby tried to work out whether she was joking.

'I look into his eyes and it's like looking into his soul.'

Yeah right.

'I don't feel happy when he's sad, tired or ill.'

This is my brother we're talking about. As children, the only time I was happy was when he was sad, tired or ill.

'I see him smile and I want to smile.'

I see him smile and I think he's been drinking.

'He laughs.'

In that case he has. Probably taking drugs as well.

'And I laugh. I don't feel complete when we're apart.'

Hold the wedding! The bride needs to be sectioned.

'The only time I'm whole is when he's with me.'

'Sounds like you've got it bad.' *Someone help! Woman in need of a straitjacket.* 'What did you mean about it being too late to leave then?'

'I'm pregnant.'

Ruby said, 'Oh my God.' She must have. She felt her mouth open and close, but she didn't hear any words come out. 'Does Lily know?' she mouthed.

Belinda shook her head. 'Do you have to ask that? If she even as much as thought I was, everyone would know.'

'That's true.' The sheer enormity of the situation suddenly dawned on Ruby. 'That means I'm going to be an aunt ...'

There were tears in Belinda's eyes. 'I hope you're pleased?'

'Pleased. I feel like all my Sundays have come at once. It's brilliant news! You'll make a fantastic mother.'

'You won't be such a bad aunt.'

'Look who I've found.'

Ruby spun round to see her mother, her arm through Malik's, advancing on her with the speed of a formula one car, but the grace of a small herd of white rhinoceros. Her heart sank. Chairs were flung out of the way as Lily escorted him across the room to her daughter's side.

'I found Adam,' she said. A smile was pasted on her face, as false as her natural-looking nails. 'Boy, you have excelled this time. You must be old enough to be his bloody mother,' she hissed into Ruby's ear. 'And he's brought his ruddy dog.'

'Adam. Darling, thank goodness you're here.' Ruby kissed Malik on both cheeks, amused to see how much he blushed. 'And you brought Brutus. I'm sorry, I haven't introduced you two properly. This is my mother, Lily Brooks. Mother, this is …' She hesitated. Every bone in her body told her to tell the truth. 'Adam,' she added.

'I hope you are well, Mother,' Malik said, sticking out a hand. 'And thank you, so am I.'

Lily stared hard and gave his hand the briefest of shakes, before pointing at Brutus lying in Malik's arms. 'And the dog?'

'Brutus likes weddings.' Malik smiled. 'So quiet, you will not know he's here.' Brutus tilted his head and looked at Lily.

She narrowed her eyes and sniffed. 'Has anyone seen Daniel?' she asked eventually. 'He's supposed to be on the top table.'

'Is he the wanker …?'

'Not since the service,' Ruby butted in. She didn't feel the need to say she'd been deliberately avoiding him.

'He's had too much to drink.'

Maintain dignified silence. Do not say he's not my problem. 'Oh dear,' Ruby said politely. 'Darling, why don't I show you to our seats. Come and meet Granny Ealing and Uncle Norman.'

Ruby spent much of the meal being glared at by Emily and Daniel. Lily was right. Daniel had clearly had way too much to drink. He'd reached the stage when he thought everything he said was funny, even if he was the only person laughing, although Emily did seem to hang on his every word, leaning in very close, stroking his arm and gazing into his eyes with an intimacy more appropriate for reunited lovers than a dinner date you'd just been lumbered with.

Bloody hell, she wasn't just flirting, she was going for full on seduction.

Ben stood up and thanked everyone for coming. Then came Daniel's turn.

Not easy listening. His "When we met Belinda in the pub" joke reduced Belinda to tears and made Ruby so dammed mad, if it hadn't been for the four tables between them, she'd have run him through with the wooden skewers she'd found on the chocolate fountain table, as soon as she'd stripped enough of them of their strawberries and marshmallows.

'We tossed for her,' he went on, despite her best telepathic efforts to get him to wind his neck in, but then he'd never known when to stop. 'And the reason you're all here is because Ben lost.'

Belinda started to colour again, a prelude to more tears, but Daniel waited until the audience had laughed embarrassedly before he apologised to her. Ruby hated him even more. She pulled another chocolate covered marshmallow from its stick and chewed hard.

'Belinda dresses to kill,' laughed Daniel and the guests laughed too. 'Unfortunately, she cooks the same way.'

The guests were up and down at appropriate points, making toasts to the happy couple, the bridesmaids, the catering staff and God knows who else. So fast at times, it looked as if they were playing some elaborate variation of musical chairs.

It all became too much for Uncle Norman, and Granny Ealing signalled to two waitresses, who pushed him out of the room in a wheelchair. Ruby couldn't see what had happened but wouldn't have been surprised if he'd died of excitement. Granny Ealing, on the other hand, remained in her seat and continued to knit.

When Daniel finally sat down, he appeared to be waiting for a round of applause.

None came. Some of the guests started talking again, clearly believing the speeches to be over.

They weren't.

Ruby stood up.

Ben turned towards her and mouthed something that could have been "For God's sake sit down" or it could have been a smile of encouragement. Okay, no it couldn't. And it would have been so easy to sit down; Ruby didn't do speeches.

She tapped the side of her glass. 'If you'll excuse me, for another minute, I think as maid of honour it's my turn.' She smiled at the guests who'd turned to see what was going on. 'I will try and make my speech much shorter and less painful than the best man's.'

Thankfully someone did laugh.

'I've never had a sister.' She looked at Belinda who was blushing and looked nervous. 'I have, however, spent most of my life with my brother Ben. After the first ten years, I would rather have had a pet. After the second ten, I'd have settled for a Tamagotchi.

'Belinda, I don't understand what you see in Ben. I am sure you've already discovered he has some weird friends, some even weirder habits, but I hope the rose tint never falls from your spectacles and that he will always make you happy.'

Ben's colleagues cheered. They were probably being rude, but Ruby didn't care. She went on. 'I don't know what girls are supposed to do with sisters, but I look forward to finding out.'

The table in front of her clapped and Ruby saw Belinda smile.

'Belinda said to me earlier today,' said Ruby, 'that she knew instantly she'd met Mr Right when she met my brother Ben. Unfortunately, she didn't realise at the time his first name was Always.' There was another rumble of laughter. 'The old ones are the best.'

She was relieved Belinda was still smiling and blew her a kiss.

'I have no idea how Ben ever persuaded this lovely lady to marry him, I'm just glad he did. This woman is the kindest, most generous person I have ever met, and I speak for both Lily and me, when I say we are delighted she's joining our family. So, will you please raise your glasses and drink a toast to – new relations.'

There were tears in Belinda's eyes as she mouthed "Thank You".

'It's traditional in this country for the bride and groom to have the first dance. They usually choose a song that means something special to them,' Ruby explained, as the DJ announced the first record would be an Ed Sheeran number.

Malik nodded. 'We listen to this, then we dance. That is good, but I think this is not your choice.'

'You think right,' Ruby said.

'You and Adam will dance to the song about bats perhaps?'

'Shhh,' she whispered. 'You are Adam today, remember. We're not getting married. I'm only looking after his dog.'

'He likes you very much. He looks at you like man in love.'

Ruby felt a wash of warmth rush through her that had nothing do with alcohol consumption. Her stomach did a weird gymnastic manoeuvre and she felt light.

She would have liked to question him more, but Malik was up on the dance floor. He marched across to the bridal couple, ignoring the fact they were still mid-kiss. Ruby threw Brutus at Granny Ealing, kicked off her shoes and ran after him.

'May we dance?' he said.

Belinda turned and smiled. 'Of course.'

'Thank you, ma'am,' Malik said. Swerving past Belinda, he took Ben's arm. 'In Egypt men dance together.'

Belinda grinned and threaded her arm through Ruby's. 'Good, that gives us a chance to sit down.'

'Okay.' Ben loosened his cravat and undid the buttons on his jacket. 'Come on then mate, let's hit the floor and throw some shapes.'

'I hope he knows what he's doing.' Ruby winced as Ben performed a star jump. She poured Belinda a glass of champagne and they sat and nattered happily as they watched Belinda's sister's children try to teach Brutus the Hokey Cokey. 'For later,' the girl explained. 'Mummy says everyone will have to do it.'

'I'm sorry,' Ruby said, as the fourth record came on and Malik and Ben were still gyrating, having been joined by other men. 'Shall I rein him in and get your husband back?'

'No need. I think Adam's lovely, and Ben's not drinking while he's dancing. I couldn't bear him to get into the same state as Daniel. Oh, speak of the devil.'

'Why are you sitting here?' Daniel asked, leering at Ruby. 'What's up, your younger boyfriend got too much energy for you? That's the trouble when you cradle-snatch. I hope he's good in the sack, because it doesn't look like he has anything else going for him.'

'What do you want Daniel?' Belinda asked. 'We're talking.'

'I'm going to ask my girlfriend if she wants to dance with a proper man. You up for it doll?'

'Ex,' Ruby hissed, as she felt Belinda's hand tighten around her wrist. 'It's okay. I wouldn't waste good champagne.'

'There's Emily,' Belinda said and waved her over.

'Where's Adam?' Emily asked. 'Is he here?'

'Yes.' Belinda smiled.

'Where?' Emily started revolving, her eyes wide as she searched the guests like a heat-seeking missile. At one point, she spotted Uncle Norman's empty chair and Ruby thought she was about to vault onto the table for a better look.

173

Belinda smiled at a few people then tugged Emily's sleeve to get her attention. 'Do Daniel a favour,' she said. 'He's looking for a dance partner and we're too exhausted. Would you dance with him?'

Emily didn't need to be asked twice. Her arms were round him and they were heading for the dance floor before he had time for any sort of response.

'Thank you, sister,' Ruby whispered as the couple walked away.

'My pleasure,' Belinda said as they clinked glasses. 'For what it's worth, whatever Lily says, he's definitely not the right one for you. If you even think about taking him back, I will have to kill you.'

Adam's heart skipped a beat, and he had a sudden urge to grin as he accepted the FaceTime call. 'Hi,' he said, and rubbed his eyes.

Ruby sat on her kitchen worktop in a long, pink dress clutching Brutus. It couldn't be a dream. He hadn't been asleep that long.

'Pistachio or lemon?' she asked.

She looked gorgeous, dressed in the most amazing number. Her hair was pinned up, despite its best efforts to be loose. 'Look Brutus, there's your dad. Say hello,' she said and wiggled the dog's paw.

Brutus looked like he was in heaven. Lucky devil.

'You look lovely,' Adam said.

'Say thank you, Daddy,' Ruby said, holding the screen closer to Brutus's face.

'Not him.'

'Thank you,' she said, staring hard at the screen. 'Which one? Lemon or Pistachio?'

'What are you trying to cook?'

'Are you in bed?'

'Yup. It's one o'clock in the morning here.' Adam sat up, grateful most of his nakedness was covered by the duvet.

'Shit, I forgot about the time difference. Sorry, I'll go. Forget I rang. We can talk another time.'

'Never.' Adam smiled. 'Don't worry. I'm happy to discuss recipes with you whatever the time.' Tiredness had deserted him the moment he'd seen her face. He would suffer for lack of sleep tomorrow, but tonight he had no intention of letting her go.

'I'm painting, not cooking,' she said with a sort of strange gurgle. 'Kitchen colours.' She pointed to two squares on the wall behind her.

'My mistake.' Adam grinned. 'Only you're not dressed for decorating.'

'I don't know. This is my maid of honour dress. I'm never going to wear it again. It's long and covers more than overalls – I think it's perfect to paint in.' She pouted as if challenging him to argue. 'So, what's your favourite colour?'

'Blue, but kitchen-wise, you can't go far wrong with white.'

'That's so boring.' She raised her eyes and made him grin more. 'I think I like the lemon best. I've always wanted a yellow kitchen. What do you think?'

'Yellow would be perfect and you look seriously gorgeous.' *So gorgeous, I wish I wasn't five hundred miles away. If I was The Proclaimers, I'd run the whole bloody way, let alone walk. Apart obviously from the bit I'd have to swim.*

'How was the wedding?' Adam sat up straighter. He needed to change the subject; below the duvet he was getting aroused.

She frowned. 'They're married. Belinda's pregnant and my brother Ben is worried about moving to the States. Malik danced with him. Brutus danced with the younger bridesmaids. Granny Ealing knitted two dishcloths which turned out to be her wedding present for the happy couple and told everyone who'd listen marriage wasn't a word it was a sentence. Oh and Mother's yoga master led the way in the Macarena.'

Ruby tilted her head to one side and looked at her phone with what could be a concerned expression. 'You look tired,' she said.

'I'm fine.'

Her eyes were wide, her hair starting to collapse, but to Adam she'd never looked more beautiful.

'Did you say Malik danced with Ben? Malik as in your kitchen fitter? He was invited?'

'Not exactly, you were, only I forgot to tell Belinda you weren't coming. When everyone started to ask where you were, I asked him to come, mainly to stop my mother telling everyone you'd dumped me. Only then everyone thought he was you.'

'Because he was young and good-looking. An easy mistake to make.'

She giggled. 'No, because Emily told Belinda my kitchen fitter's name was Adam, so when Malik said he was fitting my kitchen, Lily put two and two together and assumed he was you.'

'Emily,' Adam said.

'Uh huh.'

'As in Emily Watkins?'

Ruby nodded. 'Can I ask you a personal question?' she asked. 'I mean you can tell me to mind my own business. I won't be offended.'

'Really?'

'Well, I might be, but I promise I won't tell you if I am.' She smiled at him in a sort of a lopsided way. She was biting her lip. 'You and Emily ...'

Adam felt the temperature in the room drop. He narrowed his eyes. 'There is no me and Emily.' That came out harsher than he intended.

Ruby's eyes widened.

Adam's chest tightened. 'I'm sorry, I know she's a friend of yours.'

Ruby snorted. 'God no. She's no friend of mine. The woman gives me the creeps.' She paused and looked at her hands. 'I only met her recently and then again when she did the flowers for Belinda's wedding. I mean you can go out with who you like, it's none of my concern.'

There was so much wrong with that sentence. He needed to sit down with Ruby and explain the situation, but not over the phone. He should have told her already. But not at one o'clock in the morning.

'I wish you weren't in France.' Ruby looked straight at him. Her eyes sparkled. Was she crying?

He wanted to hold her tight and never let her go. 'Why?'

She looked so vulnerable sitting on the worktop.

'Because I really like you and ...'

'Yes?'

'Your dog.' Ruby tucked her fringe behind her ear.

If he could have found a way to teletransport, he would have gone back there and then. He wanted to be the one tucking her fringe behind her ear. 'I really like you too,' he said.

'But on the bright side, at least in France you didn't have to endure mother's marmite and watercress sandwiches.'

'I love marmite and watercress. The woman's clearly a culinary genius. Maybe I should consult her about menus for my new restaurant.'

Ruby squealed. 'That's fabulous, does that mean it's all going through?'

'The bank agreed a bridging loan while I try to sell my house.'

'That's fantastic news.' Ruby's smile was infectious. It seemed to take all her effort not to get up and dance. 'Okay, we need to start planning the launch. It's essential. A well-executed event with the right guests is much better than any other form of advertising. It gives people the chance to taste your food. I'll have a think about who you should invite and what's needed.'

Her enthusiasm was infectious, and Adam felt a lightness in his chest. 'But, could we do it when we've both had a little more sleep?'

Ruby blew him a kiss and they said their goodbyes.

He slipped down in the bed, closed his eyes and grinned. She liked him.

Chapter Twenty-Two

Eamon watched the cameraman taking some background shots of Bootles restaurant. 'Cut and for God's sake tell me that's in the bag.'

The cameraman whistled. 'Not exactly the episode we had in mind.'

Eamon looked through the front door to where a waiter was helping Emily's date into a taxi. 'He did sign the release contract, didn't he?'

'Some people will do anything for a free meal. Don't they always say, the way to a man's heart is through his stomach?'

'Yes, but everyone knows the best way is straight through the ribs with a sharp knife. Or in his case, a round of drinks.'

Eamon had a faint stir of anxiety. 'We do have some footage we can use, don't we? It's not all about him and his bloody job.'

'Relax.' The cameraman wound up an electrical flex and put it into one of the bags. 'We'll go soft focus and moody if necessary. I've got some nice pictures of the restaurant. Slow down the greeting kiss and with some judicial editing they'll look like the dream couple. Although when we get to the bit where she said "We clicked the first time we saw each other. It was like one of the old romantic movies" we'll have to cut the bit where I'm choking.'

'Remind me why I do this bloody job,' Eamon said.

'Galaxy TV pay you shedloads of money and you're too old to do anything else.' The cameraman swung the camera from door to Eamon and held it there.

The red light suggested he was still recording.

Eamon's face flashed with annoyance, but ever the professional he didn't react, waiting for the camera to be lowered and the light to go out before he answered. 'I am so not,' he said, at length. 'I could get any job with any TV company I wanted. Daytime TV keep ringing.'

'Yeah and I'm a bloody womble. Where's Emily?'

'Reapplying her make-up. She'll be out in a minute. We'll do the interview out here.' He looked around and sniffed. 'Did she mention why Adam wasn't here?'

'Something about him getting stuck in France.'

'He used to be a chef here, didn't he?'

'A nice guy,' Eamon said. 'Shame he's not here. Stepped into the brink last time when her date didn't show. I didn't think there was any chemistry, but the following Christmas they sent me a Christmas card, thanking me for helping them find each other.'

'How come you didn't realise they weren't together? You know the researchers recommended to the director general this episode should be pulled, but you went ahead.'

'I've had cards every year. I even had lunch with her ten days ago and she promised me there wasn't a problem and that they were both looking forward to it.'

'You might need to work on your line of questioning for in-depth interviews if you're serious about moving into mainstream television.'

'Get stuffed, pointy-nosed furry creature.'

The click of heels on the tiled floor heralded Emily's arrival back at the table. 'Where is he?'

'I'm sorry darling, I sent him home,' Eamon said.

She stared at him as if he was Cruella de Vil and had just slaughtered and skinned the first hundred Dalmatians.

'We need a chat and you know how long these things can take.'

'But I thought ...' Emily looked miserable.

'He said to tell you he'd had a lovely evening and he'd see you soon.'

'He did?'

Relieved she was smiling, Eamon tried to ignore the cameraman mouthing "Oh no he didn't" directly behind her and hoped he wasn't sitting in front of a mirror.

'Darling, believe me.' *Why? No one else would.* He reached inside his pocket and pulled out one of the restaurant's business cards with a telephone number scrawled on it. 'He gave me his number and made me promise I would pass it on.' Eamon handed over the card. Emily's eyes lit up and she wrapped her fingers around the card.

'Okay,' she said, flashing a megawatt smile at the camera. 'I'm ready. What do you want me to tell you?'

'You ready Orinoco?' Eamon asked the cameraman.

'We're bringing forward the screening of *Another Chance on Love*, the director general said, taking his usual seat at the top of the table and dispensing with any pleasantries. 'Any problems with that?'

Eamon choked on his tea.

One of the secretaries followed the director in, carrying a cup of steaming coffee and a large cookie, which she ceremoniously placed in front of him, making sure the handle was facing in the right direction.

This was the moment any sane man would have said, 'Yes, quite a few.' This was the point he should have mentioned the editing wasn't finished.

'There's a problem with the schedules and with no local cricket clubs in the quarter finals of the National Championship, we're only going to show highlights of the rest of the games, not whole matches. Starting this Friday, we'll show an episode of the first series every night for a week and then straight into A.C.O.L Thursday nights for the next eight weeks.'

Eamon mouthed "A.C.O.L" at the cameraman, who simply shrugged.

'We'll kick off with the Redford girl. The one in the trailers. My personal favourite. Is that a problem for you, Eamon?'

Eamon shook his head and said, 'No, it's cool.'

'We're too late to get the change into this week's TV guides, but we're going to plug it every opportunity we get, and I've spoken to a couple of the radio producers. They're going to remind their presenters to mention it.'

The director general looked at him, over the rim of his glasses. 'Good,' he said, slowly and nodded, as if talking to a very small child. 'I'm glad you're happy. We're expecting great viewing figures.'

Eamon nodded. It would have looked rude not to.

'I've been told you have ideas for another programme. What is it?'

Eamon kept nodding because someone seemed to have control of his head. 'Early days,' he said. 'Still embryonic.'

So embryonic it hadn't been conceived yet.

'In fact, I should be going. There's a line of enquiry I'm following up. I'm afraid you'll have to excuse me.' He gathered up his notebooks and left before anyone could stop him. He wouldn't go back to the studios today. He needed space to clear his head. His counsellor told him about the importance of distancing himself from stressful situations. She should be proud; he'd done that.

Chapter Twenty-Three

'This isn't quite what I meant when I asked if there was somewhere we could talk,' Adam said. The sports hall was packed with leotarded women.

'You didn't exactly give me much notice.' Ruby smiled. 'Forty-five minutes, then I am all yours.' She handed over a piece of paper to the woman on the desk.

'You're our winner. Oh congratulations.' The woman smiled. 'And this must be your partner?' She wrote down their names on a long piece of paper, then stood up and shook Adam's hand. 'Welcome to our Zumba course. We hope you enjoy every moment. Go in and take your places.'

Women appeared to be stripping off along the walls, even Ruby had shed her top layer.

'What did she mean our winner? And what exactly is Zumba?' A woman in front of him started to go through a strange assortment of movements that made him wince.

'I won a local radio competition and the prize is a ten-week course for me and a friend.'

'Didn't they specify the sex?'

'No.' She looked around the room. 'I see what you mean.'

'What's Malik doing?'

'Writing an email to Jamila, his girlfriend back home. He's writing in English. I've promised him I will check it tomorrow. Why?' She looked at him and then smiled. 'Oh, you think I should have asked him instead. If you hadn't been so specific about the timing of our conversation, I'd have come on my own. You said you needed to talk to me before eight o'clock. What's going to happen then? Are you going to turn into a werewolf?'

'What?' Adam was distracted by the amount of warm-up exercises going on around him. It had been a ridiculous idea. He winced as someone attempted the splits. Flying home for twenty-four hours. He could have rung Ruby, except he didn't want to tell her over the phone, or for her to find out before he'd told her. He should have told her months ago. He owed it to her to tell her face to face. Bollocks, he'd wanted to see her. Wanted to hear her laugh, even listen to her singing about freeing her soul.

'You rock up at 6.30 and tell me we need to talk ...'

'Yes.'

'Why?' Ruby's warm-up routine seemed to involve hands on hips and a lot of staring but very little other movement.

Adam was saved from answering by a woman in a leotard with a microphone walking to the front of the room. 'Familiarise yourselves with the space around you. Make sure you are aware of everyone else. We have a full class tonight.' The women around him giggled, but the microphoned woman looked deadly serious. He'd left it too late to run; he was surrounded on all sides. But he stayed because of the woman on his left-hand side. She turned and smiled again. His heart melted. He hoped she'd see the funny side later.

Leotard woman stood in front of the class and told them to move to the left. Ruby mirrored her and collided with her next-door neighbour, who very pointedly told her she'd shuffled to the right.

Ruby mouthed an apology and saw Adam grinning.

'Are you all giving the boy the come-on today?' Leotard woman focussed on Adam.

'Does she seriously want me to answer that?' Adam asked, sweating.

'Come to me, boy,' laughed Ruby, before flinging her arms in the air and shaking her wrists to the chorus of "Livin' La Vida Loca".

'Cha, cha ladies to your right into your karate kid pose and hold it.'

Or in Ruby's case straight into Adam who grimaced as she made contact.

'Scream as you kick and punch forward,' the leotard shouted above the music, punching the air in front of her and marching forwards.

Adam didn't hear whether Ruby screamed. There was every danger if he didn't move, he was going to be trampled underfoot by a fast advancing Zumba mistress. He didn't care whether or not she screamed. He did.

Why had he ever thought asking Ruby to watch the television programme with him would be a good idea? The theme music alone brought him out in a cold sweat. He'd regretted every day for the last three years that he had allowed himself to be press ganged into taking part. He pressed a glass of red wine into Ruby's hand.

She looked worried. The Zumba class had been fun. She'd been happy. The last thing he wanted to do was upset her, but the sparkle in her eyes had started to fade.

'There's a programme on TV tonight,' he'd said as they walked back from the gym. 'A series, no hopers meet and go on a date together. It's a repeat.'

Ruby blinked at him. 'I thought you wanted to talk about Emily?' she said. 'Is there something going on between the two of you?' she added quietly when he didn't say anything.

'No,' he said.

'So, let me get this straight,' she said. 'You two were an item, but you're not now.'

Adam flinched. His head snapped up, his eyes flashed, and he turned and looked at her as if she was a sandwich short of a picnic, a cushion short of a suite, a floor short of a bungalow. 'We were never an item,' he said, in a voice marginally softer than a bellow. 'You have to believe that.'

'It's okay,' she said slowly. 'We both have pasts. I'm not judging you.'

'There's nothing to judge.'

'But you both like this programme and you think I should see it.'

'No. We were both in it.'

'Right.' she said, stopping in her tracks. Her eyes drilled into him, clearly trying to make sense of his reaction.

'I was a last-minute stand in as Emily's blind date. That's the only time I "dated" her if you could call it that. Her date didn't show,' Adam explained, starting to shiver. Perhaps he was coming down with pneumonia or worse. 'Emily sat in the middle of the restaurant, sobbing her heart out. The producer panicked. The programme was the last in the series and scheduled to be shown a month later. The television company couldn't afford the delay. There were three chefs working that night, which was unusual, but everyone in Redford seemed to know there was a television crew in town and Bootles was full, despite it being a Wednesday.'

'So, girl in distress. Time to call for a superhero.'

'Hardly.' Adam watched Ruby, unsure whether she was being sarcastic or joking. He felt clammy. 'I was the closest in age.'

He thought she might sound off. He thought she might ask a lot of questions, but the one he hadn't expected her to ask was, 'What time is it on?'

'Eight o'clock.'

She looked at her watch, threw her sports bag into the spare bedroom and said, 'Come in then, we can watch it together although I expect you've seen it a thousand times before.'

No, he bloody hadn't. He'd never watched it. He couldn't bring himself to, not even when it first came out.

'Sorry,' she said. 'I haven't got much food in, but if you're hungry, we can send out for a takeaway.'

'I'm not,' he said.

'You might not be,' she said. 'I am. I need to eat.' She flung open the fridge.

'Wow, that doesn't look good,' he said, staring at two lemon-flavoured mousses and some chilli jam. If this had been *Ready Steady Cook* even Antony Worrall Thompson would have found it a challenge to come up with something mouth-wateringly delicious from that. 'Give me fifteen minutes.'

'The programme starts in twenty.'

He raced upstairs, heated up some chicken soup he'd frozen before he went back to France and warmed some bread. Chicken soup and hot bread were the perfect answer to everything. Comfort food and boy, did he need comforting now.

'That was delicious.' Ruby said, putting her spoon down as the titles started to roll.

They sat on the sofa and watched as Emily entered a nightclub with the woman who had been Emily's life coach and adviser for the last six weeks. They were seen at a table having a drink, talking about what sort of man Emily was attracted to. There was a blurred back view of some men standing at the bar. The woman suggested Emily should ask someone to dance. She approached the group and one of them followed her to the dance floor. There were some shots of the nightclub and people dancing, but no close-ups of Emily and her partner. At one point, Adam thought he could make her out but wasn't sure. The woman Emily had been with was doing a voice-over, explaining things looked like they were going well.

Next to him, Ruby moved and Adam jumped.

'Are you okay?' she asked and put a hand on his leg. 'We don't need to watch it, if it makes you uncomfortable.'

'I'm fine,' he said, feeling anything but.

The dance finished and Emily could be seen talking to someone in the shadows then she walked back to the presenter and gave her the thumbs up.

'I'm supposed to have given her my phone number,' Adam said. 'Then a couple of days later she phoned to ask for a date. That's what happened with her proper date.'

'Except he then had the sense not to show up.'

Adam recognised Bootles' familiar interior as the camera panned around. The television crew had taken most of the day to set up. The restaurant was packed. The TV crew had arranged the tables and told the restaurant staff where to seat the paying customers, so they had a clear, uninterrupted view of Emily and Adam's table.

'Is that your boss?' Ruby asked as Clive, dressed in a dark suit and tie, came on to the screen.'

Adam nodded. Clive had assumed the maître d's role for the evening. The bistro had been promised shedloads of cash if everything went smoothly and Clive had promised a healthy bonus for everyone involved.

The camera cut to the door as Emily arrived. Clive showed her to the table where Adam was reading the menu, a jacket draped over the back of his chair. He couldn't have worn it if he'd wanted to as it didn't fit. He wore a tie one of the waiting staff had lent him.

'I thought you said she cried her eyes out in the middle of the restaurant.' Ruby stared intently at the television. 'She looks okay to me.'

'They had a whole make-up team on-site who tidied her up and then filmed her coming back in.'

The camera closed in on Adam's table. He stood up and handed Emily a single flower. She giggled shyly. He complimented her on her outfit and waited until Clive seated her before sitting down, too. He made it look natural but had followed the television crew's instructions to the letter.

He made conversation about her day and listened patiently while she went on at length about the highs and lows of floristry.

'She did an amazing job of the flowers at Ben and Belinda's wedding,' Ruby said.

They watched as Adam asked Emily what she would like to eat. When Clive came over, Adam ordered for her, checking he'd got it right. She giggled, watching him the whole time, seemingly oblivious to anything else happening around them. Clive poured wine and waited for Adam to taste it. He raised his eyes when Clive presented the bottle. It was a good vintage, but then the TV company was paying.

Adam nodded and let him fill their glasses. They could have been any one of the hundreds of young couples who'd dined in the restaurant over the years.

Ruby's brow furrowed. She wasn't smiling. Adam had no idea what she was thinking. He wanted to turn off the television.

On screen, Emily destroyed a breadstick while telling him about the intricacies of decoupage.

Ruby grinned.

'What?' Adam frowned. He was glad she was finding this funny.

'That girl can take decoupage and collage to a whole new level.' Ruby smiled. 'She's great with flowers but give her a magazine, a pair of scissors, glue and glitter-encrusted decorations and she has a complete taste bypass. You should have seen the home-made card she produced for Belinda and Ben. It looked as if a five-year-old had had an accident with net curtains, feathers and confetti.' She stopped as she saw Adam's face. 'Sorry, I'd forgotten about your card.'

Ruby turned her attention back to the television. By the end of the starters, Adam had discovered Emily liked boy bands, brightly coloured flowers and jigsaw puzzles. By the end of the main course, he and the rest of the programme's viewers knew all about her dreams of a happy-ever-after ending, a house in the country, three children, the last book she'd read, the last film she'd seen and her feelings about frozen curries.

'Good questions,' Ruby said when an advert break interrupted the programme. 'You come across well. Sounds like you're really interested. I'd have liked it on a first date if my companion had been that interested in me. Although, I probably couldn't have nailed the long looks and flirting quite as well.'

Adam flushed.

Then came the after-meal interviews with both of them filmed separately and he cringed as the camera zoomed in on him.

'Are you in the men's loos?' Ruby asked.

Adam looked through the fingers of his hand. 'This bit is the worst. I'd forgotten about the interviews.' He gave monosyllabic answers to the questions put to him by someone not in shot. And he didn't remember saying "Yes" all those times.

'I didn't say I wanted to see her again,' he said. 'Definitely not.'

'Was much of that down to careful editing?'

Adam looked down at his hands. 'I probably said she was a nice girl and had faultless table manners.'

'And that she had a nice smile.'

'There were a lot of questions. Did I think she was pretty? Did I like what she was wearing? Was the food good? Was the wine good? Would I see her again? In case you're wondering, I definitely said "No", because she wasn't my type.'

'Not according to this,' Ruby said.

'My words were taken out of context.'

Ruby turned back and gave the television her full attention.

Then came Emily's interview. 'He's lovely,' she said. 'A few rough edges, but I like a challenge and he really likes me. At one point, we were playing footsie under the table.'

'We weren't,' Adam said.

'It's okay,' Ruby stroked his cheek and snuggled back into his side.

'You wouldn't do that if you didn't like someone, would you?' Emily looked happy.

'Join us next week,' the presenter said as the camera followed them leaving the restaurant, 'to find out three years on, whether Adam and Emily are still together and whether they both got what they wanted out of the relationship.'

'Did you see her again after the programme?' Ruby didn't take her eyes off the television.

'No. Yes. Not as a date,' Adam said, and ran his hands through his hair. 'It's not what you think. I can't talk about it. I thought I could, but I can't. It's complicated.'

Ruby didn't move.

'I'm sorry,' Adam said, standing up shakily. 'This was a shit idea. We shouldn't have done this. I've got to go.'

Chapter Twenty-Four

'When someone says they shouldn't have done something, it's usually something horrific, not watch a television programme,' Ruby said, taking a large bite of toast and marmalade. 'Take films, it's usually a murder at least.' She waved her grilled bread to stress the point.

Brutus's eyes followed it.

'Are you listening to me?'

Another bite of her breakfast and Brutus was focussed back in on her face again.

'A body is lying in a street, bleeding from a gunshot wound. He's trying to get his last words out. The assassin blows the end of his gun, puts it back in his pocket, shakes his head, looks at him and says, "I'm sorry I shouldn't have done that". No, don't dribble poppet.'

Brutus tilted his head as if trying to digest the problem if not the toast.

'The injured party dies, obviously. It wouldn't be much of a murder if he didn't. But do you think the corpse feels any better about his last moments on earth, knowing his assassin feels remorseful about the whole state of affairs?

'It's not like I'm a prude. We've both had relationships before. I mean take Daniel.' Ruby picked up the second half of her toast and, ignoring Brutus's whine, turned back to her computer. She bit through the bread and licked a lump of marmalade that looked about to fall off. 'I wouldn't judge Adam. I thought we were getting on okay. We laugh a lot. I enjoy being with him. He makes me feel smiley inside. I guess he used to make Emily feel the same. You've known him a lot longer than me – did she hurt him? Don't stare. I'm comfort eating.'

Brutus sniffed and started chewing his leg.

By eleven o'clock and another two pieces of toast later, her heart might be broken, but she'd stopped feeling hungry. She wiggled the mouse and the screen sprung into life. A short movie of a speedboat flying across the water started playing. When the boat disappeared, a question appeared.

The Power Boat engine was a Yamaha, wasn't it? Ruby selected option B and hit send.

'Five,' she stroked Brutus' head. 'Five more to go.' Although she didn't have time today because she had more pressing matters on her plate. Along with two chocolate digestives, there was a small matter of the pelmet for the cupboards.

She'd been going to have a quiet morning, until Malik had asked, 'Where is the pelmet?' Actually, he hadn't. He'd drawn her a picture of the missing bit, but they'd got there after a visit to the local DIY shop. He pointed out the bit they needed to the shop assistant.

'He means a pelmet,' the middle-aged assistant said slowly, clearly and loudly. 'How many lengths does he need?'

'How many lengths do we need?' Ruby asked Malik equally slowly, clearly and loudly.

He held up four fingers.

'Four,' she told the assistant.

'Four?' repeated the woman and told her the cost.

'It'll have to wait,' Ruby said. 'I'm sorry.'

'What do you need, Miss Ruby?' he asked when they got back, and she'd checked her bank balance. No way could she afford to spend that amount of money; she only had one more month's salary due and then she was on her own.

'Someone to kidnap Kevin bloody King and hold him ransom until he gives me back my money,' she said. 'Alternatively, a rich husband.'

She had to speak to Kevin. She'd tried tracing him through electoral rolls, telephone directories, even her ex-colleague. She had his bank details and telephone number, but nothing with an address on. As far as the world was concerned, Kevin was a non-person, something, if he hadn't stolen such a large chunk of her money, Ruby would have been more than happy to go along with.

'Shall we sing about Cilla Black fans on bike?' Malik asked and went into an impressive Meatloaf impersonation.

'Silver black phantom bike,' she corrected and left him in the kitchen fitting handles to the doors while she entered competitions for an omega food balancer for horses and body armour with detachable shoulder protectors, something she wouldn't normally consider to be a great look, but by the time Malik came in holding a panel, she was long past rational thought.

'No handle,' he said.

The final straw.

The kitchen company were singularly unhelpful. They needed to speak to Kevin before they could send out another. They needed him to report it missing, after all he'd signed to say the order had been delivered complete.

'But it's my kitchen,' Ruby had pleaded. 'I can send you a flaming picture.'

'There's no need to be rude,' the man on the other end of the phone said and hung up.

She picked up the phone and dialled again. 'Don't hang up,' she said. 'I'm sorry I lost my temper.'

Silence.

'I shouldn't have. It's not your fault.'

At least Brutus wagged his tail, when she talked to him.

'But you see my problem is I don't know what was on the original order. I can't get hold of Kevin to find out.' *And as he's already conned me out of my life savings, why should he worry about a dishwasher panel handle?* 'I don't suppose there is any way you could email me a copy of the order.'

'We supplied everything he ordered.'

Apart from the dishwasher panel handle.

'I'm sure you did.' Ruby straightened in her chair. 'If I could check it against the units I've got ...'

'We're professionals.'

She guessed he didn't mean in a sort of Bodie and Doyle, Ford Capri, 1970s way. 'It would mean I would be able to see if he's forgotten to order anything else.'

The silence stretched into minutes.

'If I can prove it is Kevin's fault not yours, I could take the problems up with him and leave you in peace.'

Three metric dog-bone-wrenches sounded exactly what she needed; she entered her details.

'Okay,' he said, 'Deal.' And hung up.

'Hi.' Ruby sounded wary.'

'Look, I'm sorry for running out on you,' Adam said. 'I would understand if you never wanted to see or hear from me again. But before you put the phone down or tell me to sod off, please listen to what I have to say.'

There was silence at the end of the phone. He checked his signal. 'Are you still there?'

'Yes,' she said after a second's pause.

He breathed a sigh of relief. 'I wanted to tell you this face to face, but I chickened out. I thought I'd put it behind me but clearly I haven't. I thought distancing myself from everything would help.'

'Slow down,' she said, quietly. 'You're not making much sense. What did you want to tell me? If you're going to give me the "it's not you, it's me" lecture, or tell me you want your dog back, you should know I'm having a bad day and I can't guarantee I will react in a grown-up or ladylike fashion.'

'Promise you won't sing?' The woman opposite him was staring, making no attempt to read the paper resting on the table in front of her.

'You have five minutes Buster, then I am putting the phone down. Things to do, people to kill.'

Adam wanted to be with her, to be able to pull her into his arms and hold her tight, instead of on a packed train to France. He had to do this before he lost his nerve. He took a deep breath. 'For the last three years, Emily has not been my girlfriend. She's been stalking me.' It sounded pathetic.

'What?'

'You probably think it's a huge joke and I'm being ridiculous not being able to stand up to her. Go on laugh. You wouldn't be the first.'

'I'm not laughing.'

He couldn't see her expression, but if she was laughing then she was doing it silently.

'She's taken me to hell and back.'

'You're telling me Emily's a certifiable nutter?'

'Your words, not mine.'

'Crikey. I mean she gives me the creeps, but I didn't think she was – well, dangerous.'

'Apparently, even the quietest, sweetest people can be stalkers or serial killers.'

'What happened?'

'At first, I thought it was a coincidence that I kept bumping into her everywhere. I suppose I thought I'd probably seen her before, but until the programme I didn't know who she was, so I hadn't taken any notice. You know what it's like when you're introduced to someone and then realise they live and work quite close to you.'

'She lives and works in Templeton, not Redford.'

Adam nodded. 'I can't remember when it didn't feel as if we were just passing in the street. When I noticed her hanging around outside work and then my house. When I kept feeling as if I was being followed.'

'How did she find out where you live?'

'The police told me stalkers can be like detectives. Once they fixate on someone, they try to find out as much information as possible and that can include following them or their friends. One morning I came out to find lipstick hearts all over my car.'

'You went to the police?'

'There was little they could do. Until the lipstick heart business there was no physical proof.'

'Oh my God!'

'What?' Adam panicked. He briefly thought about pulling the communication cord and telling the guard he had to return to London. 'Ruby are you okay?'

'It's my fault, isn't it? Emily approached me in the supermarket. She said she recognised my picture from the paper. She offered to help me with my shopping. I brought her back to the flats.'

Adam nodded. 'Probably. Up until then, I'm pretty sure she had no idea where I'd moved to. When you gave me the card, I realised the game was up. That's one reason I took the French job. I had to get away.'

'From me?'

'No.'

'I'd only met her for the first time the day of the card. She made out the two of you were practically engaged.'

'She's delusional. Look, I know it's hard to believe, but she's not and has never been my girlfriend. I really did say I didn't want to see her again, whatever the TV programme showed. For the last three years, it's been, well, difficult. Always feeling you're being followed. Not wanting to open post in case it's something inappropriate or unpleasant. Then I met you. Even when I thought she was a friend of yours and common sense told me I should run for the hills and forget you both, I couldn't. I didn't. I can't. I don't want to.'

'Say that last bit again, I didn't quite hear what you said.' Ruby had heard perfectly well, the lightness in her voice told him as much.

Chapter Twenty-Five

When the documents arrived from the kitchen company, Ruby grinned. Finally, she had Kevin's address. It was written at the top of his order.

The missing piece in the jigsaw puzzle.

'No time like the present,' she said as she picked up her car keys. 'Just off out,' she told Malik.

'You find handle?'

'I'm going to bloody try,' she said.

Kevin's house was in the middle of a terrace. A row made up of similar-looking three-bedroomed houses, whose owners had all tried to make their own look unique. Except for number 37 Fairgrove Road. Number 36 had stone clad their walls. 38 had put a small white fence round their garden.

Ruby parked outside and checked the number on the paperwork the kitchen manufacturers had emailed through. Although if she'd been asked to guess which number the Kings lived at, she'd have plumped for 37.

Kevin didn't dress like a man who took pride in his own appearance; his house reflected that. If she had any doubt, his van parked in the drive was the proof she needed. At some point, the garage door must have broken. Bits of it were padlocked to the woodwork that surrounded it. The small window in the side wall of the garage had been boarded up, sometime ago, if the mildew on the frame was anything to go by.

Ruby shuddered. Next time she needed a craftsman, she'd ask to see pictures of their property first. It would be nice to get confirmation that they were, well, tradesmen. *Next time. Who was she kidding?* She was through with home improvements forever after this.

The curtains were closed, despite it being nearly midday and sunny. The front garden was a small square of mud, on which stood a dodgy-looking car. As garden features went, this one sucked even if it didn't smell as bad as the row of wheelie bins she had to squeeze past to get to the front door.

A light was on inside the house. It shone through the gap in the top of the grey-looking curtain linings and somewhere inside she could hear a radio or television. She knocked.

No one answered. But the ghostly listeners turned the television down and the light off.

Like the traveller, she smote upon the door a second time.

There was someone in and she had a pretty good idea who. Either that or she'd fused the electrics by knocking.

She knocked again.

Mid knock, 36 came out and looked at her through narrowed eyes and put something into one of his bins.

Still no answer.

When he appeared for a second time, putting another equally minute piece of rubbish into the same bin and making no attempt to disguise the fact he was staring at her, she gave up.

For the neighbour's benefit she lifted the letter box and shouted, 'I'll be back! Don't think this is the last you've heard from me.'

Number 36 was still fiddling with his dustbin trying not to look interested as Ruby walked to her car. She burrowed in her handbag, found her mobile and stopped at the end of the drive. Looking back at the house, she phoned her own number.

'Hello, this is me,' she said, loudly, when her answering machine invited her to leave a message or leave her alone. 'You're quite right. The whole terrace is showing preliminary signs of subsidence, but I have been unable to gain access to number 37. No … He's in, I heard him turn off the television and someone's turned off the lights ... Don't forget he knows why I am here ... Of course, I'll try again ... It's probably too early to get the courts involved ... You know how awkward Health and Safety can be. Yes ... They'd want us to evacuate the whole road before we can start checking the foundations.'

Number 36 had paled considerably by the time she drove away.

She wanted chocolate.

By the time she got to the top of the high street, the want had become an urgent need. By the time she got to the supermarket, it was fast becoming a matter of life and death.

She pulled in, parked and switched off the engine before she recognised Emily. Great! Some days just got better and better. She pulled on her new "Films are Fabulous" hat and sunglasses, heaved her bag out of the car and strode towards the door.

Shit. Emily had spotted her too and at an exaggerated fast walk made it to the automatic door before her, leaving Ruby no choice, but to force a smile. 'Emily, how are you?' she said as they entered the store.

Emily smiled. 'I'm good. Great even. How are you?'

'Definitely great, too. Nice to see you, but don't let me keep you.' Ruby selected a trolley, in the same way warriors used to select weapons, convinced she'd be safe as soon as she'd passed the vegetable aisle. Emily was already carrying a bagful of shopping. Surely she was finished. Wrong.

'You're not keeping me. I wanted to see you anyway. I wondered if it would be okay to pop over and pick up my dresses. Perhaps when you've finished your shopping. I could give you a hand carrying it back in case you wanted to clear them out of cupcakes again.' She giggled. 'Belinda thought that was very funny when I told her.'

I bet she did. 'Not great timing at the moment,' Ruby said.

'I'm not going home. There's someone I need to see. I'll drop them into the shop next time I'm passing.'

'When will that be?' Emily asked. 'Only I have a date next week.'

Adam was away until the middle of the month, so it definitely couldn't be him.

'I thought the red would be perfect. I've some flat shoes that are an exact match.'

Do psychos dress in red floral print?

'I'm sorry, I should have dropped them in sooner.'

Emily waved her apology away. 'Has Belinda told you I've a new boyfriend?'

'Belinda and Ben are still away on honeymoon.'

'She hasn't messaged you?' Emily looked surprised.

'I think she's got more important things to do, or I hope she has.'

'How's your Adam?'

'Good,' Ruby said, unsure whether she meant Malik, whom she'd left trying to work out how many of Henry VIII's wives were executed while she went in search of handles, or the real one, speeding towards Paris on the Eurostar.

'Is he Mr Right?'

What was this girl on? 'Look I'm in—'

'I mean it's early days, but it feels like we've known each other forever. He's very different to Adam, so kind and generous. We're going to the Badger and Oak Tree next week. I expect you've been there? Do you think the red dress will be suitable?'

'I'm sure the red dress will be perfect.' The Badger and Oak Tree used to be one of Daniel's favourite haunts. The up and coming place in Redford for trendy estate agents to be seen in. 'I'm sure your new guy will love the dress. You've made it beautifully. I wish I could sew as well as you.'

'I could show you.'

'That's sweet of you, but I am busy. I have quite a lot of other things on my plate, talking of which I best get on.' Confectionery was the other end of the shop. Ruby carried on down the World Food and Pasta aisle.

'I think the two of you make a lovely couple.' Emily practically ran to keep up. 'I know some people say you're far too old for him. A bit of a cougar ...'

'*What?*' Ruby screeched to a halt, spun her trolley round and managed to floor a woman bending down to look at the macaroni in the process. 'Are you for real?' she asked, helping the woman up and putting a large bag of macaroni into her own shopping trolley.

Emily's smile wavered. 'I thought ...'

'Well stop thinking.' Ruby turned and sprinted down the Home Baking aisle. By the self-raising flour, there was no sign of Emily, but she took advantage of the blockage in the dairy aisle and abandoned her trolley by the double cream. The desire for chocolate had gone.

A short, blonde middle-aged woman, who looked as if mud-wrestling crocodiles was second nature to her, opened the door of number 37 Fairgrove Road, when Ruby returned half an hour later.

'You again,' the woman spat, legs apart, arms folded and glaring. 'What do you want?'

'Me again.' Ruby smiled. Normally introductions were made by shaking hands as she'd taught Malik. But with the stance this woman adopted, Ruby was loathed to extend anything in case it got ripped off or the woman had her on her back before she'd figured out what was happening. 'Kevin. Is he in?'

'Why?'

What was it with people today? Some questions only need a yes, or no. 'I'll take that as a yes.' *Stay calm.* 'He'll know what it's about.' Ruby mirrored the woman's position. 'Tell him Ruby's back.' Arms crossed, legs apart. 'Of course, if he'd prefer, I can stand on the doorstep and shout. I'm sure next door'—she nodded at 36—'would be interested in what I have to say.'

The minute Ruby pulled up, 36 had shot out of his front door and started ferreting round the bins, which appeared to have moved closer to 37's since she was last here.

The woman looked set to argue but caught sight of her neighbour. The look she shot him suggested there wasn't a great deal of love lost between them. She moved to one side and flicked her head towards the door. 'He's in the kitchen.'

The smell of cigarette smoke and old fried food hung heavy in the dingy interior. Ruby wished she'd mentioned to someone else where she was going. Hell, Emily would have probably jumped at the chance of coming with her.

The kitchen resembled her own in an unfinished sort of way. It must be a design idea Kevin had come up with. She was relieved to find the deep fat fryer on the worktop wasn't industrial-sized, although by the smell and the greasy feel to the atmosphere, they used it on a regular basis. Still, if they had any intention of doing away with her and disposing of the evidence by frying her, they'd have to cut her up into very small pieces.

'Hello Kevin.'

He looked shaken and tried to flatten himself against the kitchen wall.

'I've come back, like I said I would.'

'You've been here before?' Crocodile Dundee had clearly left her post at the front door.

'No, she hasn't,' Kevin said, a shake to his voice. 'What do you want?'

'That's what I asked,' the woman behind her said.

'You run off with my money and you want to know what

I want?' Ruby stood up straight and narrowed her eyes. She was pissed off.

'I don't owe you nothing,' Kevin shouted.

'My point precisely.'

'You can take me to court.' His eyes darted all over the kitchen. He was frightened.

Ruby wasn't usually a confrontational person. Her brother Ben brought out the worst in her, but she didn't like shouting. As a child when her parents argued, she'd go away and ignore them. When Daniel shouted, she'd cry.

This was different. These were evil people. Her blood pressure rose, but thankfully her tears did not. Anger replaced her fear. 'You took money for a kitchen you had no intention of fitting,' she said. 'You owe me. There's not a court in the land which wouldn't agree with me.'

'He's going to fit your kitchen,' Kevin said without moving his lips. Something which seemed to surprise him as much as Ruby.

This wasn't the time or place to mention her kitchen was fitted, almost. Ruby spun round to face the woman.

'You have no idea how delighted I am to hear that. When exactly?'

Kevin's face turned completely white and he muttered something about being busy for the next three months.

'And in the meantime ...' Ruby laid the copy of the order on the worktop. 'Perhaps you could explain where my pelmets and door handles are?'

'You've got everything,' the woman said, scowling from the middle of the kitchen.

'Butt out Boadicea.' Ruby kept staring at Kevin. 'According to the paperwork, both were delivered here.' She and her brother used to have staring competitions. The first one to break the stare lost – it was always Ben, and Kevin didn't have his skill.

'Think about it. If I had them, would I be round here asking for them?'

'You've got my toolbox,' he said. 'I can't work.'

'You've got my money, neither can I.'

'Just give her the parts.' The woman adopted an expression that suggested she thought Ruby's antenna wasn't picking up all channels.

'And money?'

'I haven't got it.'

'In that case, I'm calling the police.'

'No,' Kevin said. 'Please. I'll give you your money back.'

'You will?' said Ruby and the crocodile wrestler in unison. Kevin nodded.

Result. 'All of it?'

Kevin nodded.

Back of the net. 'I'll take the parts and you've got a week to pay the money back'.

'Okay.'

'Don't forget, she'—Ruby jerked a thumb at the woman—'is a witness. Whoever she is.'

'I'm his wife,' the woman said.

Ruby started to laugh but stopped mid-guffaw when she saw the look on the woman's face. 'Oh my God,' she said. 'You're serious.'

Chapter Twenty-Six

April Flowers embraced summer in a big way. Sunflowers and big colourful dahlias covered every surface. Very contemporary and modern. Ruby pushed open the door. Emily concentrated on tying a large bunch of flowers together with a ribbon and didn't look up.

Ruby put a shopping bag on the counter. 'Your dresses,' she said, her other hand on her pocket mace spray, in case. The encounter in the supermarket had unnerved her. A dodgy line in greeting cards and fashion sense didn't necessarily mean danger, but with what Adam had told her she wasn't prepared to take a chance. She'd seen *Single White Female*. One could never be too careful when dealing with a deranged lunatic. Watch any psychological thriller. Ask Bridget Fonda.

'I'm sorry it took me so long to return them.'

Emily stared. 'You didn't have to bring them. I could've popped in and picked them up when I was in Redford.'

'I didn't want to put you to any trouble.' Ruby turned back to the door. 'I hope your date goes well.'

'I'm ready for a cup of tea,' Emily said, moving between Ruby and the door. 'Stay. It would be nice to have a chat,' she added, in a sweet, homely sort of way.

'What about?' There was something about the woman that freaked Ruby out. She looked normal. Attractive and ordinary looking. Not someone you'd look twice at in the street. Nothing about her screamed delusional disorder. God, she'd make a lousy policewoman. 'I can't,' Ruby said. 'Things to do ...'

'Have I upset you?'

She stopped. It had been thrown out as a challenge. 'No.' She watched Emily, smiling back at her, her face, a picture of innocence.

'Are things not going well with Adam?' Emily picked up and trimmed the stalk on a white flower. 'Maybe you're not getting enough sleep?'

'I get plenty of sleep.'

'That's good.' Emily picked up another flower and sniffed it. 'Women need a lot of sleep. Especially pregnant women.'

'I'm not pregnant.'

'Not you,' Emily said. 'I am.'

'What?' Ruby should've said congratulations, jumped up and down for joy, her brain was telling her so, but the words got stuck in her throat and her feet felt as if they had been glued to the floor. Deep breaths. She needed to be calm. The calmest woman in the world. 'Wow,' she added, because some sort of reaction was called for.

'It's not Adam's,' Emily said, as she picked a few more flowers from the vases around the shop and started to trim leaves from some of the stems. 'We split up. Has he told you?'

'Not said a word.'

Emily laid all her selected flowers in a line along the counter, arranged them into different heights then deftly stuck them into green oasis until the foam block was completely covered. Ruby wanted to go, this was getting seriously weird, but she wanted to see the end result as well. The combination worked well.

'What do you think?' Emily asked, standing back.

'I'm gobsmacked,' Ruby said, contemplating a run for the door. 'What about morning sickness?'

'No, silly.' Emily looked at her. 'I meant the flowers, not the pregnancy.' There was something about her look that scared Ruby. 'That's early days. I shouldn't have said anything. We agreed to keep it quiet until we've had the scan. But you are practically family.' She added some gypsophila to the arrangement and stood back to admire her handiwork. 'Do you think a pink ribbon would work?'

Chapter Twenty-Seven

The theme music to the new series of *Another Chance on Love* played, over photos of Emily three years ago and Adam. 'Oh my God,' Ruby shouted at the television.

Brutus looked in the direction she was pointing, in case there was food or a ball that needed retrieving. But realising there wasn't, he took the opportunity to make himself more comfortable and sank back onto her lap.

She couldn't sit there alone. Adam should know. He was home, she'd seen a taxi arrive ten minutes earlier. He'd said he'd call as soon as he'd sorted himself out, but she couldn't wait.

The presenter explained how three years ago, Emily thought she'd found love, but it wasn't to be. A computer graphic showed a picture of Adam and Emily side by side, both staring at the camera. Adam, pale and clearly upset, while Emily looked blissfully happy. A digital eraser then rubbed Adam out and Emily's picture filled the screen.

Adam would never believe her, unless he saw it. Ruby charged out of the flat, clutching Brutus and the remote control. She raced up the stairs and knocked feverishly on his door. The noise brought not only Adam to his door, but his neighbours on either side, too.

'Emily is on television,' she screamed. 'You've got to watch it, come on.' She was into his flat closely followed by his neighbours before he'd said a word.

Pointing her remote control at his television, only to be frustrated when nothing happened, Ruby was vaguely aware the whole room seemed to be covered with A4 sheets of paper. Adam took her remote away, cleared a space on the sofa and turned on his television.

'*Once again, we are delighted to be back in Redford at Bootles,*' the narrator intoned as Adam scooped up another pile of papers from the armchair before Flat 7 flattened them.

'*Those of you familiar with our programmes will remember Emily.*' Emily's face flashed up on the screen. '*A young woman who we hoped had found true love at the end of our last series. Have you, like me, spent the last three years with your fingers tightly crossed?*' The presenter waved a hand at the camera. '*Were you hoping she'd got the ending she deserved?*'

On screen, Adam sat at a table in the restaurant, fiddling with the cutlery.

'Is that you?' Flat 5 asked getting closer to the television. 'I live next door to a TV star and never knew.'

'Hardly,' Adam sighed. 'Yes, it's me.' He nodded and cleared a chair for her. 'Drinks anyone?' he asked.

The camera caught Emily coming into the restaurant. She looked around nervously until she caught sight of Adam and walked over.

Ruby looked up at the genuine Adam, thinking he was much better looking in real life and smiled. 'Have we interrupted something?' she asked, when the piles of paper caught her eye again.

He shook his head, intent on watching as his younger self continued to stand until the waiter pulled up Emily's chair and smoothed a pressed serviette into her lap. While the waiter took her coat away to hang up, Adam on the television looked at Emily and said, 'You look nice tonight.'

'What a lovely thing to say,' said 7 and 5 simultaneously, each taking a glass of wine offered by Adam.

'Saw this bit last week,' Adam said.

'I expect they're scene-setting,' 7 said. 'All the follow-up programmes do it.'

The waiter came back and lit the tea light in the middle

of the table and poured some water into two large glasses and asked what they'd like to drink. Emily asked for a sweet sherry and Adam asked for a glass of wine, similar to the one his guests were enjoying. He caught Ruby's eye. She smiled and moved over so he could sit down. 'Sorry,' she whispered.

He shrugged. 'Have you eaten?'

'Don't worry about me,' 7 said. Having finished her wine, she handed the glass back to Adam. 'I wouldn't have thought she was your sort at all,' she said.

'She's not,' he grunted. He filled up the glass and handed it back.

'*What has happened in the last three years?*' the narrator said. '*Did Emily find the happiness she longed for? Was Adam her Mr. Right? Let's return once more to Bootles' Bistro and find out.*'

The restaurant hadn't changed a great deal in the last three years, but the shot was of Emily, her hair arranged, her face made-up and wearing – *no, she couldn't be!*

'That's my bloody dress!' Ruby screamed. 'She's wearing my bloody dress!'

'Shh!' said the neighbours simultaneously.

'She's stolen my dress!'

'*Emily,*' the narrator said. '*Here we are again.*'

Emily smiled.

'*You're not with Adam any longer I understand.*'

Emily shook her head and fiddled with her napkin. She'd clearly been there a while. She'd already completely rearranged the table's centrepiece.

'*Are you able to tell us what happened?*'

'*He cheated on me,*' Emily said, a theatrical moment later. Her eyes glistened. Tears were clearly not far away. '*With my best friend.*' She looked down at her hands.

'Oh, that's awful,' said 5, looking pointedly at Adam who was staring at the television open-mouthed.

'*You must've been devastated.*' The narrator placed unnecessary stress on the last word.

'You shouldn't have done that,' said Flat 7.

'You cad.' Ruby smiled at him.

Everyone watched as Emily nodded, still staring at her hands.

'*How did you find out?*' asked the narrator.

'*A friend. She's my hairdresser. She did my hair tonight. Do you like it?*'

'She's talking about Belinda,' Ruby said. 'This must have been filmed straight after the wedding but before she went on honeymoon cos she's only back today.'

'*It's lovely,*' the narrator said. '*And this friend? She told you?*'

'*She was getting married and my best friend was her maid of honour,*' Emily said.

'Is she talking about you?' Adam whispered.

'*Adam was supposed to be my friend's plus-one for the wedding.*'

Ruby spluttered a mouthful of wine. 7 and 5 tutted and looked at her in disgust.

'*But all was not lost, I understand,*' the narrator said. '*You met someone else at that same wedding.*'

'Please don't tell me she's going to rock up with Uncle Norman,' Ruby said. Adam's neighbours tutted again and turned their attention back to the television.

'*Yes.*' Emily looked straight at the camera and smiled. '*But the funny thing was, we met three years ago. We didn't know we were both going to be at Belinda's wedding. But as fate would have it someone changed the seating arrangements and I ended up sitting next to him at the top table.*'

Ruby snorted. 'She sat next to Daniel at the wedding.'

'Shh!' said 7.

'*This time you think he's the one?*' the unseen narrator asked and the Emily on screen nodded and smiled widely.

'*This time I'm sure he is,*' she said. 'He's the nicest, most genuine person in the world.'

'*He's here, Emily. Enjoy your meal and we'll talk later.*' The camera pulled back to take a wider shot of the restaurant as a man in jeans walked towards the table.

'Shit,' said Ruby. 'Double shit. It is Daniel!'

'Daniel?' Adam asked.

'My ex.'

'Is there more wine?' asked 5.

'*Daniel,*' Emily gushed and stood up. '*Lovely to see you.*' She leant towards him and there was a lengthy awkward kissing moment.

'*Hello doll, looking good,*' he said. '*Nice dress.*'

Ruby squirmed. 'He hated that dress, said it made me look cheap. He'd never let me wear it.'

'*Do you come here often?*' Emily asked and then giggled. '*I'm sorry that sounds so clichéd, what must you make of me?*' She held his gaze until he laughed and picked up his glass. He waved it and a waiter appeared.

'How rude,' said 7.

For the next thirty minutes Ruby watched as Daniel ate a substantial three course meal and drank his way steadily through a bottle of wine. Emily checked the calorie content of each individual dish, then picked at her meal, and sipped her original glass of wine, as slowly as possible.

Daniel talked about iPads, 3D TVs and all the other gadgets he'd love to own. Emily talked about crafting kits. He talked about his last relationship. How misunderstood he was and how unhappy the woman had made him. Emily was unbearably sympathetic, even Flat 7 cringed. Daniel talked about his job, how hard he worked. How they failed to appreciate exactly how much he did for them. Emily commiserated with him. When he was quiet, she reached out, fluttered her eyelashes and squeezed his arm reassuringly, while the narrator talked over them, about how in a bizarre twist of fate, Daniel's ex was also the woman who stole Emily's love away from her.

'That's bollocks,' Ruby said. 'I'm going to prosecute.'

'Sue,' said Flat 5. 'Slander's a civil, not a criminal offence.'

The programme ended with Daniel winking at the camera and saying, *'I think I'm on a promise tonight.'*

The four people in Adam's flat stared at the television until the credits had rolled. Then Flats 7 and 5 stood up, thanked Adam for his hospitality and left.

'If you'd like to appear on our next series to be filmed this summer, please contact us by the end of the month,' the narrator said, as the screen went blank and filled with a Freephone number that Ruby copied down on the back of some of Adam's papers while he saw his neighbours out.

'Thinking of applying?' he asked, coming back into the room.

'No. I'm going to complain. Genuine, my arse,' Ruby said, indignantly, still unable to believe what she'd just heard.

Adam grinned and walked into the kitchen.

'What's so funny?' Following him, she suddenly realised how hungry she was.

'Relief I guess. If she's involved with someone else then she's not going to bother me again.' He smiled. 'And I've spent most of the day trying to figure out the best way to ask you to come over, so I could cook supper.'

'And I turn up anyway?'

'With my neighbours. Neighbours, whom I should mention, I've never met before. I thought we were in for an unreal evening, but even I couldn't have thought it would be this bizarre. But not in a bad way. Now would you like something to eat, or do you share Emily's views on calories?'

'I don't share her flaming views about anything. But if you

214

don't stop laughing this second, I might feel the need to go and fetch my new housey-mousey decoupage set.'

'You are joking?' Adam held up a spoon.

'Oh shit, I can't.' Ruby froze.

'It's okay, I don't know you well, but I'm pretty certain there's no way you'd be seen dead buying a decoupage set.'

'I won one.' Ruby shook her head. 'It's not that. I've forgotten my key. I was in such a hurry to come and see you I didn't pick it up. I'm locked out.'

'I guess I should be flattered. Any windows open?'

She shook her head.

'Keys within easy hooking distance from the letterbox with a bent coat hanger?'

'Nope.'

'Does the door open with a credit card being slipped down the side?'

She stopped shaking her head and stared at him. 'I bloody hope not.'

'Is it likely to collapse with one well aimed kick?'

'You're planning on breaking in? Forget it Buster. You are not kicking my door down. The neighbours have already got you down as a cad.'

'Says the strumpet,' Adam said in a voice that sounded very much like Flat 5 and Ruby giggled, despite her predicament.

'Anyone else have a spare key?'

'Malik, but he's away with his father this weekend.'

'Are you likely to be seeing him anytime soon?'

'Monday, I think.'

'Okay, worst case – Monday you should be back in your flat. That's only two days away.'

'That's if he comes back after the weekend.'

'He will.'

'I hope so.'

'Hoping is good. Knowing is better. Has something happened?'

'I upset him today. He broke a whole box of tiles. And I might have mentioned I was a tiny little bit pissed off.'

'He wouldn't have done it deliberately.'

'I still can't afford to replace them.'

'Anyone else?'

'Belinda.'

'Your new sister-in-law. Can she bring it over?'

Ruby frowned. 'They only got back from their honeymoon this morning.'

'Send her a text. We can pick it up tomorrow. Don't pull faces like that. What's wrong?'

'My mobile's in the flat too. Could I use your phone? I'll ring mother. I can't remember Belinda's number. She'll have to pass the message on.'

Lily Brooks picked up the phone after the third ring. 'You've done what?' she grumbled, when she realised it was her daughter. 'How old are you for heaven's sake?'

'A neighbour said I could stay the night.' Okay he hadn't actually said as much, but that was what she inferred from his suggestion about popping over to Belinda's tomorrow. 'Could you let Belinda know …?'

'Oh, for God's sake.'

Ruby smiled, trying not to let Adam guess her mother had already put the phone down. 'Okay, thank you. Love you, too. Bye.'

'She'll speak to Belinda in the morning,' she said.

'How hungry are you?' he asked. 'On a scale of 1 to 10? Where one is sending out for a home delivery pizza and ten is home-made ham and leek pudding with parsley sauce.' That explained the smell pervading the flat since she'd waltzed in with half the neighbourhood.

'Oh, you know,' Ruby said, pretending to think about the question. 'About three and a half.'

Adam's face fell as her stomach, not wanting to be left out, rumbled.

'Only joking.' She giggled.

Adam asked her to wash and chop the parsley while he prepared some vegetables and they worked in companionable silence. After ten minutes he took the knife away from her and deftly turned her pile of mangled leaves into a mound of finely chopped parsley that he swept into the milky sauce he was stirring on the cooker. A car pulling into the car park caught Ruby's eye.

A silver-coloured Ford.

She froze. She only knew one person who drove one of those. That wasn't entirely true. Probably loads of her friends and acquaintances did, but there was only one she hoped she'd never see again. The silver Ford owner, she had never given or had any intention of giving her address to, got out of his car and looked up at the block of flats. She shrunk back from the window into Adam who put out a hand to steady her. 'Are you okay?' he said. 'Have you burnt yourself?'

Ruby shook her head and pointed.

Adam looked over the windowsill. 'Hang on a minute. That's the guy on the television?'

'Daniel,' she whispered. 'That's Daniel. Everyone was under pain of death not to tell him where I live.'

'Looks like he knows now.' Adam continued to watch. 'He's throwing something into the air. Looks like keys.'

'Shit. That means he can get in.'

'I'll head him off at the pass,' Adam said, kissing her forehead. 'Keep stirring the sauce while I go and get rid of what's his name.'

'Daniel,' Ruby said weakly.

Chapter Twenty-Eight

'You must be Daniel.' Adam opened the front door to the block of flats. 'Ruby's mother said you were on your way with her keys.'

'She did?'

A pungent smell of undoubtedly expensive aftershave threatened to overwhelm him. Daniel stood, studying the front door and tried to juggle keys with a bunch of pink roses and a bottle of cheap champagne.

Adam was tempted to cover his nose with his handkerchief. 'If you let me have the key, I'll look after it until Ruby gets back from work.'

'She's working? Her mother didn't say.'

'Yes.' *No, and you've got to hand over the key and disappear because I don't trust her with my suet pudding.*

'Where is she?'

Adam squared up and crossed his arms to block entrance to the flats. 'Manchester, I think. She's short haul at the moment.'

'She's an air hostess?'

'Look I don't mean to be rude, but I'm in the middle of cooking.'

'Her car's in the car park. The bright red estate.'

'That belongs to Robert.'

'I recognise her number plate.'

'She sold it to him when she bought her new one.'

'Well, I'm not in a hurry. I'll sit and wait. Don't worry about me.' Daniel held up the key. 'I can let myself in. I'm sure she's probably got some milk in the fridge.'

Adam hated Daniel. He hated the way his smile crooked up one side of his mouth. He hated the smell of aftershave that he must've drunk rather than sprayed. He hated the man because he clearly thought Ruby could be bought with pink roses and fizzy wine. But most of all he hated him because he just wanted to thump him, and he hadn't felt that way about anyone since David Carter stole his favourite pencil back in junior school and chewed it to a stub within seconds.

Brutus picked up one of Adam's shoes and stopped just out of Ruby's reach. He wagged his tail and then backed off, so she had to chase him. A signal he needed a walk. She was concerned there was no sign of anyone in the car park although Daniel's car was still there and parked at a strange angle. Where was he? And more to the point, where was Adam? Adam had left his keys by the door. Making sure she turned the cooker off and locked the door, she took Brutus across the road to the small grass wilderness sporting a sign which read "Site of New Country Park" and which someone had crossed out the "New" from.

They walked back to the flats. Ruby skirted around the car park in case Daniel was lurking in his car. There was a light on in her flat. Of course, Adam couldn't get back into his own flat, he must have let himself in to hers to wait. She'd barely got to her front door before Adam flung it open.

'Darling,' he said. 'You're home. How was Manchester? Did you have a good flight home?' He wrapped her into a tight embrace and kissed her hard. 'Tell me you turned off the oven,' he whispered in her ear.

Adam slid his hand round her back and pulled her towards him. She'd imagined they would eat first, but blow it, food could wait. She reached up and put her hands round his neck and kissed him back. She felt warm, safe and alive from the passion in that kiss. She groaned as if she had been plugged into the mains.

More electrical charge ran through her extremities and she

groaned again. She looked up at Adam, looking down at her, and judging by the intensity in those dark gorgeous eyes, he was feeling the same.

She kissed him again and started to move towards the bedroom. She'd left the flat in a bit of a hurry earlier, but she had made the bed.

Brutus's growl from the direction of the lounge made her stop. Over Adam's shoulder Ruby caught sight of her worst nightmare sat on her sofa and staring at her.

Talk about passion killer.

'Daniel?' she whispered against Adam's cheek.

He nodded. 'He insisted on waiting.' His hand slid down her back to her waist. 'I tried to get rid of him. I told him you'd be late.'

'Bryan and I have been talking.' Her nemesis got up and came to the door with a bunch of roses and a bottle. 'These are for you,' he said.

'From who?'

'Me.' Irritation punctuated Daniel's words. 'Who else?'

'Good,' said Ruby. 'In that case I'm not going to offend anyone else when I ask you to take them and go. Thanks for the keys, but I don't want your flowers or wine.'

'It's champagne, sweetheart. The sort you like.' Displeasure narrowed Daniel's eyes and he scowled.

'No, it's flaming not,' Adam said. He dropped his arm and Ruby immediately missed its warmth and security.

'Butt out Bryan. We've been together for nearly five years. I know my girlfriend better than you.'

'Bryan?' Ruby mouthed. She could feel Adam tense up; she wasn't letting go. She kept her arms wound tightly around him. 'I am not your girlfriend, Daniel. That ship not only sailed, it bloody sank.'

'Now doll, I was an arsehole, but we were meant to be together. Surely you can forgive me.'

'Of course I can.'

'Hallelujah! Does that mean we can go home?'

'You can. I'm not going anywhere.' Ruby didn't move from Adam's side. 'This is my home.'

'But you said …'

'I can forgive you for being an arsehole. That doesn't mean you're not one. Thank you for bringing my key, but I've had a tiring day and Bryan and I have plans.' Adam put his arm around her again and she looked up and smiled.

'I think what you're trying to say, darling, is get lost, aren't you?' Adam said.

Ruby grinned. 'Couldn't have put it better myself.' Actually she could have done, but her version might have included a number of expletives.

'No need to be like that, doll. Does Bryan know you've been playing the field while he's been away?'

'What?'

Daniel laughed. 'The guy you brought to Ben and Belinda's wedding. Can't think what you're playing at. It was embarrassing. Half your age and after you'd stolen Emily's boyfriend, too. Talk about rubbing her face in it. She was upset. Lucky I was around to comfort her.'

'Indeed,' Ruby said. 'One lucky lady. Now, if you don't mind, give me my key and get out.'

Standing with Adam's arms around her waist, they watched until Daniel's car had pulled out of the car park. 'Run the Bryan thing past me,' she said, turning to face him. Only he didn't. He kissed her and she kissed him back, her tongue exploring his mouth. He let out a low groan. When they pulled apart, he was smiling down at her, his eyes heavy with lust.

'Can you wait for supper?' he asked.

She nodded. 'But there is one thing you should know,' she murmured breathlessly. 'I am not, and never have been, an air hostess.'

'Really? But when I first met you, weren't you on your way to Japan? I'm sorry, I sort of made an assumption that you worked for an airline.'

'I've never been to Japan. I enter competitions, it was a New Year's resolution to turn my life around and I'd just entered a competition to win a VIP holiday to Japan with a presentation to prize winners at The Ritz.'

'Nice, Michelin starred restaurant, great chef, amazing menus,' Adam murmured.

'Talking of which, what are you doing this weekend?'

'You want to take me to The Ritz?' Adam's breathing was laboured.

'No,' she said. 'But I do have tickets for Templeton FC's charity game on Saturday.' He kissed her neck and she breathed in the scent of him, every nerve ending screaming with pleasure. She closed her eyes and exhaled. She felt alive. She leant back against the wall. He slipped a finger between the buttons on her shirt and she tugged his T-shirt over his head.

'I don't suppose you have any condoms?' he said.

'Uh-huh. 546,' she said as she trailed a hand across his chest.

Chapter Twenty-Nine

Eamon grinned, not only because he was wearing his best waistcoat, although it always made him happy, particularly the fact he could still get into it and do all the buttons up, but because Emily's episode had received great reviews. The public loved a happy ever after story. He'd checked his Twitter feed and Facebook pages over the weekend. The director general had to be impressed.

He'd bought all the papers on Saturday morning and couldn't wait for the press office to send the clippings through. It always took them a few days to catch up. He read each, with his morning cup of tea, grimacing at some of the more lurid headlines. The most glowing articles he cut out and laid in a pile on his desk. He made sure the pile was fanned out so anyone walking past could see. The less complimentary ones, he binned.

Sometime over the weekend Radio Four's *Woman's Hour* had been in touch wanting him to talk about Emily in a programme they were calling "Rebound or Real Love". He checked in his diary and asked one of the secretaries to confirm Thursday with them. It meant having to cancel his appointment with his counsellor, but at the moment he was on top of the world. He didn't need some psychotherapist preaching about emotions, coping skills or facing your fears. He would stick all the reviews in his "happy" book; that would impress her next time he saw her.

He decided on a cravat for *Woman's Hour* in case they filmed the episode to air on their website later and flicked through the latest Facebook posts. He liked a few, thanked others for their kind words and one he even added an emoji to. The office administrator handed him three sheets of paper listing all the calls received about the programme. A recorded message told anyone who wanted to be considered for the new series to apply online. A few had ignored the request and left a message anyway, all with their own reasons for wanting to find love. He'd ask the administrator to contact them with the link to the website and the form they had to complete in order to be considered. There was no hurry. The director general had hinted if the reviews were good enough, they would schedule the filming of a new series in the spring. The reviews were better than good. So far, they had been bloody fantastic.

Two messages stood out. A woman who recognised the dress Emily was wearing as the one she'd had stolen from a dry cleaners. Eamon had been about to scribble through the message with a thick black pen, until he saw the administrator's note about another three things the TV station should know, too. She hadn't run off with Emily's Adam, although he was her neighbour and a dear friend – and had been stalked by Emily for three years. Two, she wanted to talk to someone about Adam's new restaurant and wondered if Galaxy would be interested in covering its launch. And lastly, three, if they were planning on producing a show about cowboy builders, she could give them chapter and verse on a dodgy kitchen fitter.

Eamon made a note of her name and number on the top of his jotting pad. There was one other call of interest; a rival television company asking him to give them a call. That number he wrote down too. He tore the sheet of paper off and put it in his wallet, and then obliterated that line too on the administrator's pages.

People arriving for work dropped by his office to tell him how much they enjoyed the programme and asking if he'd seen one of the tabloids was running a feature on blind dates.

The cameraman walked across the office and perched on

Eamon's desk. Annoyingly, he sat on top of the clippings pile. 'I found the old outtakes from the last series,' he said. 'Do you remember we cut most of the footage of the nightclub scene and her meeting with lover boy out of the episode at the time in case anyone realised he wasn't Adam?'

'And this Daniel, was he really the one who stood her up?'

'I'd say so. A bit older. He's put on a bit of weight, but clothes are similar.'

'Why didn't he say something?'

'Looking at the old recording, by the way he was eyeing her up throughout their conversation, I'd say he was very drunk at the time.' The cameraman shrugged. 'It's possible he didn't remember.'

'He must have given her his number.'

'That's the odd thing. After the dance he went back to his friends. We've got footage of the whole evening. At no point did they exchange numbers.'

'She said they'd talked on the phone for hours and he was coming.'

'Yes, you said.'

'Be serious. I wouldn't have set the whole bloody meal thing up unless I thought it would happen.'

The cameraman shrugged. 'It's irrelevant. This time, he seemed happy enough. His only concern seemed to be how much it was going to cost him. When he found out the TV company were picking up the bill, he went for the most expensive wine on the list and the chateaubriand.'

'I like a man with a good appetite,' Eamon said in a high-pitched voice. His best imitation of Emily, only it appeared to be lost on the cameraman who looked nervous.

'You said they signed the necessary paperwork,' the cameraman said.

'It's all in order.'

'The legal department are okay then?'

'They're going through everything at the moment.'

'I understand there are concerns about some derogatory remarks Emily made about her best friend. They're considering damage limitation.'

Eamon smiled and tapped his wallet. Maybe he would give Miss Brooks a call.

Chapter Thirty

Ruby hadn't dressed up to the nines; she'd gone well into double figures with a dress, a padded bra, high-heeled shoes. Her face sported the brand-new cosmetics she'd plundered her local department store for. She'd even let the sales assistant advise her. Together, they'd chosen foundation, blusher and mascara to complement her skin tones, hair and eye colour. She no longer looked like Ruby Brooks – kitchen fitter. Hell, she had cheekbones.

She'd gone for professional; businesswoman oozing confidence. Power dressing finished with Eau de Cologne, and Border Terrier. She would have to take him, she didn't know how long this would take.

One last look in the mirror. She was looking as good as she could as she scooped Brutus into her new dog carrying bag. Throwing in her keys, she nearly did her back in trying to lift everything. Okay, the carry bag might be able to accommodate "six and a half kilos" of dog and Brutus looked happy enough, but she needed to develop muscles before she carried him for any length of time.

'You're walking until we get close.' Unzipping the bag, she ignored the doleful stare. 'Come on matey. I'm not a flaming powerlifter.' Brutus flopped down on the mat and stared as if to cajole her into staying put and cuddling up on the settee.

'We can't,' she said, clipping on a lead. 'Not today, I need to stand up to bullies. I'm not going to let them win and you have to come with me, because your dad's got an appointment with some potential suppliers in London and won't be back until later.'

She started to hum "Drift Away" and kept humming for the next twenty minutes until Brutus was back in his bag and she'd been ejected into the plush offices of Events 2 Go by the revolving door.

The soft furnishings and newly decorated reception area didn't suggest the company had just been through its worst year ever, although the enormous desk was only manned by one girl, and not someone Ruby recognised.

She had to wait nearly an hour. Her fault for turning up without an appointment. However, she made it clear she would wait all day if necessary.

The phone rang. The receptionist looked at her but turned away as she spoke. It was clear from the odd word Ruby did hear that she was the subject of the call. 'Yes, I'm still here,' she wanted to say.

Fifteen minutes later, the lift doors opened and a woman, barely old enough to be out without her parents let alone in charge of a department, emerged. She stuck her nose in the air and made a beeline for Ruby. Thanks to her ridiculously high heels, her progress across the plush carpet was painfully slow. Probably not a good time to mention sensible shoes might make more sense.

The woman's left boob was labelled Team Manager. Russian dolls weren't the only things full of themselves.

Time to turn on the charm offensive.

'Hello. Thanks for seeing me.' Ruby smiled and stood up. 'I appreciate you're busy, but there's clearly been a mistake and I'm sure you want to get it sorted out straight away.'

'Your handbag is moving,' the woman said stiffly. She sat down, crossed her legs, arranged her clothing and placed a large file face down on her lap.

Ruby sat down, too. She wasn't going to be allowed past the security doors, not even to one of the private interview rooms off reception. Maybe they thought she was working for the opposition and was there in a counter-intelligence capacity to spy on them, or else anything she wanted to say wasn't important enough to be done in private. 'I couldn't leave Brutus at home on his own.'

'We don't allow dogs in the office. You should know that.'

'Oh, I am sorry,' Ruby said. 'Clearly, I was so stressed about your recent missive that your rules must've slipped my mind.' She faked a smile. 'At my age what do you expect? If my memory gets any worse, I will be able to organise my own surprise party, but I didn't come to discuss pets.' She tried to hand over the letter the firm had sent by recorded post. The woman wasn't paying attention, with her arms folded in a non-friendly way, she studied her watch.

Ruby sat quietly. Her best serene look fixed in place. She had all day and was quite prepared to wait for as long as it took until she had recaptured the woman's attention.

'What is it you want?' the woman said, turning eventually to face her.

Ruby fought the urge to shout "I win" and run a lap of honour. 'Just to understand what you mean, when you say I've broken the terms of my termination contract?' she said, calmly.

The woman's lips twitched and tapped on the file that rested on her knees. 'We know you've worked since you left the company.'

Ruby's inner pedant wanted to point out she hadn't actually left, not of her own accord, she'd been ousted. 'News to me,' she said, biting her tongue.

The woman opened the folder, so only she could see the contents and squinted at it. 'I understand you are a flight attendant.'

'You understand wrong.' Ruby laughed.

The woman didn't.

'Oh, please. Even you must realise that's ridiculous. If I'm too old to be an event planner, I am certainly way too old to be an air hostess.'

There was no indication the woman found this anywhere near as amusing as Ruby. 'The information came from a reliable source, someone, I understand, who knows you well. We have no reason to believe it's not true and I should warn you, we are prepared to pursue this through legal channels if necessary, so if you hand over a copy of your flight plans for the last six months, our legal team will write to you in due course advising you of the amount you need to return. You will be given fourteen days from the date of their letter to make full restitution.' She hesitated over the last word. 'Your last month's money, obviously, will be forfeited. Anything else?'

'Flight plans. Is that your idea of a joke?'

'This is not a laughing matter,' the woman scoffed. 'The company does not find it funny and nor does your boyfriend. He was concerned you were doing something illegal and as it transpires you were.'

'Boyfriend?' Ruby struggled to keep her voice neutral. She was upset. She was angry.

She moved; her handbag moved, too. The woman looked at it nervously.

Adam had called her an air hostess, but he couldn't really think that, could he? They'd never discussed her job. The woman said boyfriend, so it couldn't be Emily.

Then came her Jessica Fletcher light-bulb moment. The one when everything becomes clear, the mist lifts and scales, or whatever they are, fall from her eyes.

Manchester.

'Look, I don't know who you spoke to.'

Actually, I do.

'I have not broken the terms of any agreement. In the last six months, I've almost rebuilt my kitchen and been bridesmaid at my brother's wedding, but I haven't flown anywhere. I have not left the county let alone the country.

I suggest you go back to your informant. Tell him he's lying and ask him to prove his allegations or retract them. Do you have his number, or should I give it to you?'

The woman looked down at the folder full of papers. She didn't confirm or deny anything, but Ruby could see a line of numbers at the end of the page. She got up. 'I expect to receive a letter rescinding your accusations and apologising for any upset caused, by post tomorrow, together with confirmation that my final month's salary will be paid on time, otherwise your managing director will be hearing directly from my solicitor.'

There was a flicker of concern in the woman's face although there was no need to be worried – could you win a solicitor for a day? She might check later when she got home. 'Furthermore, I expect to be compensated for any charges I incur as a result of your incompetence.'

The woman looked about to argue.

'Save it,' Ruby said. 'Put your apology in writing. In the meantime, the only thing I want to hear from you is confirmation I am out of contract. My garden leave has ended.'

The woman opened the folder again, this time making no effort to hide the telephone message sheet on the top. She turned it over and read through the document underneath. 'It ended at the end of last month.'

The woman shuffled the file about in an embarrassed sort of way. She was flustered. 'You're out of contract and free to work for anyone.' The words seemed to stick in her throat.

'Thank you.' Ruby fought the urge to punch the air. *Remain dignified.* She lifted Brutus's carrying bag onto her shoulder with as much grace as she could muster, put on her sunglasses and strode out of the office. For the first time in ages, she felt free. She never wanted to work for anyone again.

She had Adam's restaurant launch to plan and now it was all systems go. It would be the best restaurant launch in the history of the world. She'd show Events 2 Go exactly what they'd lost.

A lot of her old clients were still out there. She would target those she knew wanted seminars, conferences and balls. They should be easy enough to find. This time, she would be her own boss. While she waited for the contracts to come flooding in, she should even have time to think up a long and painful death for Daniel which would give her a use for the large bagful of chopsticks that had arrived in the morning's post.

Ruby popped into the off-licence and let the guy behind the counter patronise her for a bit. She chose two bottles of the "manager's special" which meant Brutus had to walk. She hoisted the wine and bag back onto her shoulder, glad the bottles weighed considerably less than a Border Terrier and took a short detour to see her mother. Best strike while the iron's hot and before she lost her nerve.

Ruby let herself in. She called 'Hello' as she checked Brutus's feet and took her own shoes off. Certain things had been instilled into her at an early age. No outdoor footwear in Indian temples or Lily Brooks' home.

Ruby put her own shoes on the rack between a strappy pair of gold sandals, a pair of black suede ankle boots she stroked lovingly and considered trying on, a pair of trainers and a large pair of Doc Martens.

To the best of her knowledge her mother had size six feet and had never worn Doc Martens of any size. Lily was more country and western than punk; more woman about town than environmental change activist.

Ruby froze. Something was wrong.

The house was in silence. That wasn't right either, not if the alarm wasn't set. Lily never went out without setting it ever since the neighbours had been burgled.

In the garden?

Ruby walked into the kitchen and peered out of the window. Lily wasn't there either.

The back door wasn't even locked. Ben wouldn't be happy. He'd installed a state-of-the-art system to protect their mother. The doorbell even sent a message to Lily's phone whenever the button was pressed, along with a live view of the visitor. Lily could watch and talk to the person ringing the bell and respond from anywhere in the world. Ruby considered it a gadget too far. One of the reasons she never rang the bell, but maybe today she should have.

Her sense of panic rose. The kettle had been boiled recently. Today's post had been put on the table.

'Darling, nice to see you.' The voice was flat and low. No warmth. The words were there, the sentiment wasn't.

Shit. The hair stood up on the back of Brutus's neck and he wasn't the only one to be worried.

Ruby spun around imagining Lily's expression, to be greeted by a face, clean and totally devoid of make-up. Ruby couldn't remember the last time she'd seen her mother barefaced ... or wearing a shell suit.

Surely not.

Yep. Shiny, pale-pink silk effect but probably nylon and finished off with bare feet. Even more surprising, Lily's hair had been scraped back off her face with what looked like a red plastic Alice band.

'Have I woken you?' Ruby asked in a quiet voice.

'No, of course not. It's mid-afternoon. What do you take me for?' There was an edge to her mother's voice.

'Do you want to talk me through the outfit then?'

'Don't be ridiculous. Have I missed a call? Did you ring to say you were coming?' Lily's expression didn't change. Normally, her mother was elegance personified. Next to her, Ruby looked awkward and ungainly, but in such a shapeless outfit Lily looked vulnerable and old. Something was definitely wrong.

'Are you ill?'

'I'll call you later?' Lily said. 'Thank you for your concern, but this is not a good time. You need to go.'

'No. I'm here and what I have to say can't wait.'

Ruby hadn't walked halfway across Redford in a dress and ridiculously uncomfortable shoes to be turned away.

'Well, go on,' Lily challenged. 'Say it and then go. I'm busy. What do you want to talk about?'

'Daniel. Don't pretend you don't know what I'm talking about. My ex. Ex – as in no more. As in ex-tra, as in ex-cess, as in wasted, pointless, purposeless, redundant ...'

Lily was staring at her nails in a contemplating her next manicure rather than listening to her daughter's rage sort of way.

'I know you think he's some sort of demigod.' Ruby's voice rose. 'And you think I should be lucky someone like that is the slightest bit interested in me. But do you know what he's done this time? This time, he's rung my old company and told them I have been working as a bloody flight attendant. They want me to pay back my garden leave.'

Lily started to look uncomfortable. 'There must be a mistake. Daniel wouldn't ...'

'Daniel bloody did.'

'Why don't you come in and sit down, dear.'

Lily's lips were far too tightly pursed to emit anything other than a high-pitched whistle. She'd either mastered ventriloquism or ... Ruby turned as the sitting room door opened.

'You seem to have a blocked Qi flow. What's wrong?' A man in an equally shiny shell suit appeared and grabbed Ruby's left wrist with surprising strength. Before she had a chance to argue, he'd wrenched her into the sitting room past her mother. 'Come and join us.'

Ruby sat on the barstool by Adam's worktop and watched him chop vegetables. Even his back was sexy. She moved and gasped.

Adam stopped mid-chop and turned round. Concern etched on his face. 'You okay?'

He put down the knife and lifted her leg very gently. 'Stay there, I'll get some ice for that ankle. It's quite swollen.' He laid a tea towel out on the surface of the kitchen units. Taking an ice tray from the freezer, he ran it under the tap until some cubes dislodged themselves then wrapped them in the tea towel.

'Let me get this straight. You descended on your mother in the middle of a yoga session.'

'I just wanted to clarify the situation about Daniel and me.'

Adam raised an eyebrow.

'I didn't know she's having private lessons. It was Jeffrey's idea I join in. He said I looked like I needed to release my stresses.' Ruby winced as the cold tea towel and its contents made contact with her skin.

'Your foot's quite swollen.' Adam tied the tea towel around her ankle and secured the ends.

'According to Jeffrey I need to be more aware of my feet position if I'm to attempt'—Ruby waved a hand—'Big Foot Eagle Pose or something like that in future.'

'Did you ask your mum about the key?'

'I asked her a lot of things, but she lay down on a rubber mat and played dead.'

'You mean she was relaxing.'

'Jeffrey called it the Corpse Pose. Did I tell you he's the same guy she invited to Belinda's hen party and wedding. Something's going on. They sent me out to hug a tree.'

'You did what?'

'Okay Jeffrey told me to take Brutus and wait in his car while they arranged their next session. I didn't think she'd looked at another guy since Dad left.'

'For all you know she could be regularly scanning all the never-too-old singles websites and hooking up with "good-looking man, own car and doc martens".'

'They kept smiling at each other when they thought I wasn't looking. And shell suits ... Jeffrey is supposed to be helping her regulate her stress levels, connect her mind and body and promote serenity.' Ruby demonstrated a gentle stretching movement and grimaced.

'Careful,' Adam said, massaging her calf.

'I'm not a prude and if she wants to have mind-blowing orgasms to help unblock her energy channels, I'm not going to stand in her way. I just wish she'd told me.'

Adam shot her one of his irresistible smiles and Ruby flushed with desire.

'Mum was looking after my key and all Belinda and Ben's keys while they were on honeymoon. She's promised to give them back the key in the morning. I want her to be happy, honestly, I do. Daniel mentioned you to Mum by the way. Well he told her about Bryan. She's worried I've started chasing unsuitable men, blames it on my hormones.'

'Me – unsuitable. She said that?' Adam moved his hand slowly up her leg.

Ruby grinned at his attempt to look hurt – and what his hand was doing. He was sporting a five o'clock shadow which highlighted his cheekbones.

Adam lifted her chin and kissed her. A kiss that cleared her head quicker than any of the afternoon's inverted Asanas or forward bends.

'I think I should meet this woman,' he said. 'I need to put her right on a few things. But talking about mind-blowing orgasms ...'

Chapter Thirty-One

Ruby drummed her fingers on the tablecloth, her notepad open in front of her and sucked her pencil. She'd been surprised to get the phone call from Galaxy TV midway between entries for eyelash extensions, pole-dancing experiences and a collection of beautiful, bespoke, vintage-style, wooden signs.

It had been her idea they met at Bootles. Having seen Adam's plans she wanted to check the place out properly.

She arrived fifteen minutes early and looked around with a critical eye. The decor was dated, the upholstery faded, and many of the dining chairs didn't match. She made copious notes.

'Would you like some breadsticks?' A waiter appeared by her side. He wore black trousers and a polo shirt, clearly washed to within an inch of its life.

She took the pencil out of her mouth to say no, but she hadn't eaten breakfast and was starving. 'Thanks.'

The restaurant walls were plain and where pictures had been moved, there was discolouration. Pictures – she made more notes. Okay, so technically fully rebranding went beyond the remit of an event planner, and she hoped Adam wouldn't feel she was overstepping the mark by making some suggestions, but she knew how important it was to him.

The waiter produced her pot of breadsticks as the front door opened, and a man in a waistcoat entered. Eamon Dixon, it had to be.

He wasn't carrying a white carnation. He didn't need to; every step this man took oozed television and extrovert. His shiny electric-blue waistcoat stood out from the subdued decor like a beacon. Below a slicked back, centre parting she noticed his eyes. They matched the waistcoat. They couldn't be natural, surely. He looked around and headed towards her.

'You must be Ruby.' He stretched out a hand. 'Ruby Brooks?'

She was the only diner. It didn't take a nuclear scientist to deduce that.

He slipped into a seat opposite her and spread a napkin across his lap. She guessed that meant they would be eating.

In a previous life she would have slid a business card across the table under an elegantly manicured hand and in age-old tradition, he would have returned the favour. Collecting business cards to professional adults was as much of a pastime as collecting promotional toy cards was to junior school children. Only adults didn't have the luxury of coloured albums to store them in or a queue of acquaintances willing to swap duplicates.

'Ruby Brooks from Dream On.' She smiled. It had a ring to it, sounded good. 'Sorry no cards at the moment.' She took his hand and had her arm pumped enthusiastically.

'Sorry I'm late,' he said in a tone that suggested a greeting rather than a serious statement, so Ruby didn't bother with an answer. 'Got caught up in a meeting to discuss ways forward after this series.'

'What are you thinking of doing next?'

'Galaxy want me to produce another series of *Taking a Chance on Love*. I'm keen to expand into other areas, but they insist.' He sniffed and buffed his nails on his jacket lapel. 'More low key than last time. This time we're going to let everyone wear what they like.'

'Best warn the police,' Ruby said. 'In case they all decide they need new outfits and raid the local dry cleaners.'

'Ah yes. The message you left on the answerphone suggested you believed Emily was wearing your dress?'

'She *was* wearing my dress.'

'You don't think it could be a simple coincidence? Similar ages, similar tastes, especially when it comes to men it seems.' He sniggered and Ruby considered stabbing him to death with a sharpened breadstick.

'No, I don't,' she said, pointedly. 'It was a designer sample dress. Only the one has ever been made. The police have the CCTV from the dry cleaners. They're investigating, so I guess it's *sub judice* and we shouldn't talk about it. Mum's the word and all that.'

'Really?' Eamon said, warily.

'I'm sure they'll speak to you soon.' Ruby snapped a bread stick.

He swallowed hard. His Adam's apple bobbed nervously in his thick neck. 'Well, the public response to the programme has been amazing,' he said, with a smile and changing the subject. 'We've had hundreds of calls saying how much people enjoyed it. "Reality TV at its best" according to one of the TV critics. Emily was "raw", that's why they liked her. Even the nationals have picked it up. "No self-respecting dating show would ever have put those two together", one of the tabloids said. But Galaxy did and it worked.' He smiled. 'Have you eaten?'

'Just these.' Ruby took another breadstick from the pot and pushed the rest towards him. She'd been anxious about the meeting. It would have been a comfort to dull her neuroses with a glass of wine while she waited, but she wanted Eamon to see her as a professional, level-headed businesswoman. Efficient to the core. *And I have no idea who's paying for this.*

Eamon signalled to the waiter hovering anxiously by the bar. 'They do a very good value lunch menu.'

They were the only two in the restaurant. From the limited conversations she'd had with Adam, she understood lunchtime trade could be slow. Today wasn't slow, it was dead. Definitely something he needed to develop.

Eamon was intent on studying the menu. 'I think,' he said, after a long pause, 'I'll have the squid for starters followed by the pork belly.' He looked up and winked. 'Galaxy TV's treat, least we can do.'

'In that case, so will I.' Ruby winked back.

He flicked through the wine list and ordered a bottle of the house white. 'Your telephone call said Adam was about to launch his own restaurant,' Eamon said. 'I expect they'll miss him here. I was speaking to some of the staff when we filmed the last episode. Trade has been slow since he's been away. France wasn't it?'

'He's not leaving,' Ruby said. 'He's taking over this place. And he has some interesting ideas.'

The waiter poured their drinks and they made small talk about Adam's plans for the restaurant until their starters arrived.

'Your telephone call ...' Eamon said. 'Well, let's just say you raised some interesting issues.'

'Good, although I was surprised you suggested lunch.'

'I was glad of the distraction. Things are a little strained in the office what with budget and staff cuts, stationery lockdown that sort of thing.'

'After all the rave reviews you've received, you can't be worried.' Ruby speared a piece of fried calamari and took a sip of her wine.

'Television is so insincere,' Eamon said. 'Today you're golden boy but you could be out on your arse tomorrow. You're only as good as your last review. That's why I need to come up with an idea for a new reality show. Show that I'm not a one-hit wonder.'

'What ideas have you come up with so far?'

Eamon shrugged. 'Nothing that hasn't been done before.'

'The dating thing was hardly original, but by going back

and checking how the couples were getting along three years on. You managed to give it a new spin.'

'More by luck than judgement.' Eamon fiddled with his place setting. 'The biggest lucky stroke being Emily, for some reason the audience loved her. Seriously, is Daniel really your ex?'

Ruby nodded.

Eamon moved his knife and fork slowly and carefully until they were square on to the edge of the table. 'I wonder ...' he said, once he seemed happy they were straight. 'If we were to run a season finale. Could I interview you? Ask you how you felt, seeing Daniel on television. It would give you a chance to set the record straight.'

'No point,' Ruby said. 'I don't care. He can date who he likes as long as he leaves me alone.'

'Did you know he was the man who stood Emily up for the original programme?'

'He couldn't have been.'

'Why? Because you were together at the time? Life spoiler alert, sweetie. Sorry to have to be the one to tell you but he wouldn't be the first man to cheat on his partner and he's unlikely to be the last.'

If this had been a date, Ruby would have probably poured her drink over Eamon's head and marched out. 'No,' she said, 'because Daniel would never have turned down a free meal.'

'Bit of a sponger?' Eamon laughed. 'I have to admit we were surprised when she rocked up with him. We didn't recognise him until she told us. We had to go back and check our original footage. The funny thing is I'm not entirely convinced he recognised her either, but I suppose she looks very different from three years ago. Very "trendy".' He wiggled his fingers in an annoying air-quote way. 'Your sister-in-law – Belinda, isn't it? – did great things with her hair and make-up. A number of the girls in the office asked me for the salon details when they heard I was meeting you. And that dress – sorry *your* dress – was a real stunner.'

He didn't need to tell Ruby. She bloody knew it.

The waiter set two plates of food down and explained what they were about to eat. He poured them glasses of water and topped up their wine.

'We'd thought she was still with Adam. When I had lunch with her a month or so ago, she assured me he was looking forward to the programme.' He shook his head. 'Then here we were again, camera rolling. She was here, we were just waiting for him to arrive when suddenly she looked up and said, "By the way, Eamon. Did I tell you my date tonight is Daniel?" That's when she made the allegation about her best friend stealing Adam away from her. I assume that's you from your outrage on the message.'

'I assume so, too.'

'Was it, handbags at dawn?'

'Nothing like that.'

Eamon looked round the restaurant. 'Apparently she's barred from this place? The owner wasn't happy about us filming this series' episode here. Cost a pretty penny, but I generally find money can get around most problems, don't you?'

'You know why she was barred?'

'Ordered the wrong colour wine with her fish, I expect.' Another shrug. 'Prosecco with her cheeseboard?'

'She stalked Adam for three years following your programme. All he ever did was help you out of a tricky situation. He had to move because of her. Thanks to me, she knows where he's living now. She even tried to get me to talk him into bringing her back here for an anniversary meal. I didn't steal him away from her. He was never hers in the first place.'

Eamon watched her. His Adam's apple danced again. 'Those are pretty serious allegations.'

'And Emily going on television, wearing my dress, and accusing me of being some sort of boyfriend stealer isn't?'

He refolded his serviette. 'She rang this morning by the way to say how much she and Daniel had both enjoyed the programme. Apparently, her friends have been most complimentary.' The waiter topped up their wine glasses at Eamon's signal and he took a sip.

'Did she tell you she was pregnant?'

Eamon went puce and spat his drink out. 'No way. Who's the father?'

'Daniel, I guess. Although it's early days and they're keeping it quiet until they've had the scan.'

Eamon mopped his chin with his napkin. 'Are you sure?'

'I have an idea,' Ruby said. 'For your series finale.'

Something flickered in Eamon's eyes.

'You could film Adam's restaurant launch. You could invite some of the subjects of *Another Chance on Love*? Even run it as a trailer for the next series.'

'And if all the episodes for the next series were filmed here'— Eamon stirred his coffee slowly—'it would be great publicity for him, but Emily and Daniel – they'd have to be invited.'

'I'd have to talk to Adam about that.'

Eamon nodded. He looked like his brain was trying to make sense of the idea.

'And if he agreed,' Ruby said. 'You'd have to be responsible for Emily.'

'Do you think Adam would do an interview?'

'Absolutely not and you'd need to set the record straight, explain he and Emily were never proper dates. Explain how he'd stood in at the last minute three years ago when her real date, Daniel, let her down. That was what happened, wasn't it?'

Eamon nodded. 'You know, I think that could work.'

Ruby's mind had gone into overdrive. She was back in business. A press release headline was forming in her head. *Tables of the Unexpected.* In her notebook, she scribbled the initial letters to jog her memory later.

Eamon smiled.

The waiter cleared their plates. Ruby looked up to find Eamon grinning at her over the top of his glass.

'That embryo might have legs,' he said. 'I need to run it past a few people. Let me have your contact details.'

Ruby pulled one of Kevin King's flyers from her bag and wrote down her email address and phone number on the back.

Eamon turned it over. 'Kevin King Kitchens.'

'My dodgy kitchen fitter. Although technically he didn't fit my kitchen, he ran off with a large chunk of my money. You wouldn't want to touch him unless … Unless you were planning on doing a reality programme about cowboy builders.'

Eamon looked up, his eyes widened, and he smiled.

Chapter Thirty-Two

'These are for you,' Ruby said. 'I made them.'

Adam, standing in his doorway, smiled and came towards her. 'Er thanks.'

'They're muffins, not cupcakes,' Ruby started to say as he kissed her, a slow gentle kiss that built quickly into something more urgent. 'Banana and chocolate,' she whispered against his lips, stepping backwards. 'I made them from scratch. No packet mixes were harmed in the making of those', she added. 'I thought you might be hungry.'

'They look wet?'

'Blame it on the American hurricane or storm Brendan or something. I put them on the windowsill to cool down and it started to rain.'

'Okay,' Adam said, a little cautiously, taking the plate from her. 'How's your ankle?'

Ruby stared at him, unblinking, thinking how difficult it was to focus clearly on anything when he was watching her like that. 'Fine now.' She skipped from foot to foot to make a point. 'I followed the TV chef's instructions to the letter, never having made muffins before. You use oil not butter – did you know that?'

'I did.' Was he laughing at her?

'I've got a fan oven, so turned the heat down by ten degrees and made sure it reached its full temperature before I put them in.'

He nodded again.

'I googled buttermilk. I didn't have any, but you can use yoghurt thinned with milk and a little vinegar.'

'I could have let you have some.'

'They're a bit darker than the ones on the television but taste all right.'

They'd been in the oven for longer than they should have been, because she'd forgotten to set the timer and it had taken her ages to enter the competition for the roof-mounted bike carrier for her car, the limited-edition scented candle and a zoo-keeping experience.

Adam continued to look at the plate. 'They look lovely.' He said with considerably less enthusiasm than the celebrity chef's television audience. 'Are you coming in? We should try one.' There was a glint in his eyes that made Ruby feel alive and she nodded enthusiastically, not mentioning she'd already eaten two or three.

'Then can we sit down?' she asked. 'I've some ideas for the restaurant launch I want to talk through.'

'Okay,' he said, letting her pass him into the flat.

By the time he'd got back from the kitchen with two mugs of coffee and some plates, Ruby had spread a pile of papers out on the coffee table and was curled up in the corner of the sofa, with her legs tucked under her.

'TOTU?' Adam stared at her notebook.

'Tables of the Unexpected. My idea of shorthand. Press release heading, something to grab the attention.'

'I like it.'

'Good.'

'No, I mean I really like it.'

'Really good.'

'As a name for the restaurant. Short, catchy, sounds modern. If someone asks, we can tell them what it's short for. *We. He said "we".*

'What about Bootles? Won't you keep the name?' Ruby met his eyes; she didn't think he was being sarcastic.

'No, fresh start and all that. Besides, the name was only ever a mistake. The sign writer got it wrong. It should have read "Bottles and Bistro". By the time he agreed it was his error, we were used to the name, so it stayed.'

He raised his cup. 'TOTU it is, and God bless all who eat in her.'

'The restaurant looks a bit dated and needs a good clean but doesn't look like it needs a huge amount of work.'

'You've been to the restaurant?'

'Lunchtime …' Ruby hesitated, suddenly worried she might have overstepped the mark. 'Was that all right?'

His face broke into a smile. 'Of course, you know I value your opinion.'

'I had lunch with Eamon Dixon, the television producer.'

'Did you ask about your dress?'

'Yes.'

'And complain about the suggestion you stole me away from Emily.'

'Uh-huh.'

'And something else?'

'We talked about him televising your launch and he's talking about setting the next series of *Taking a Chance on Love* in the restaurant. Have a muffin.'

Adam took one cautiously and carefully unwrapped it.

'What do you think?'

'It stinks.'

'I thought it smelt of banana. Don't eat it, if you don't want to.'

'Not the muffin.' He grinned and pulled her into his side. 'The launch idea.'

'It would be great publicity. Give a far greater audience a chance to see your new modern look and menu. Adam Finder, chef extraordinaire has arrived with a bang. No interviews about anything but food. Kitchen out of bounds to everyone. He promised me they won't get in your way and thinks they could offer a pretty substantial fee. Eamon said all the right things. There are some phone calls he needs to make, but he thinks as long as it happens in the next couple

247

of months, it could be shown as a series finale and trailer for the next series of *Taking a Chance on Love*. And if you're in agreement, he is proposing using your restaurant exclusively for the next series.'

Eamon had talked about needing to talk to Adam and schedule the episode quickly before the TV listing magazines went to print, but he couldn't see it would be a problem. He'd paid for lunch, promised Ruby he'd call and left her with air-kissed cheeks.

'Clive said he thought it would be great publicity for the restaurant. Last time, just the one episode attracted a lot more diners than usual for a few weeks, so an eight-week series would be great. Clive said you would have to insist that certain precautions were in place and some mention given on each episode to the menu and the food chosen. He'd be happy to talk to you about the contract.'

'You met Clive.'

She nodded and gave him her most dazzling smile, the one she hoped said *Trust Me*. 'What do you think?' Ruby shut her eyes and took a deep breath in and held it. She needed him to like her ideas. This felt like the most important job she had ever worked on. Everything was riding on this one.

'Okay.'

She exhaled and opened her eyes. Adam was folding the muffin wrapper into tiny little quarters.

'Damned with faint praise. You sound like my headmaster. "Ruby needs to apply herself more fully to cooking to achieve more edible results."'

'He actually wrote that on your report?'

'My mother was mortified.'

Adam laughed and reached for her hand. 'I meant the restaurant,' he said, taking another muffin. 'These aren't bad at all, and you're right about the place looking dated,' he added after swallowing a mouthful.

'It wouldn't cost a fortune to smarten the place up.'

'You'll help?'

'You bet,' Ruby said happily. 'And if we think we're likely to have problems, Malik will too. It'll be fine. We'll be ready to launch TOTU to the world in no time.'

The director general looked at Eamon from the other side of his enormous desk. 'I'm impressed,' he said. But clearly not enough for his eyes to reflect that. The words were there but the emotions weren't. This could go either way. 'Reviews are great. You've breathed new life into the programme. And the idea of bringing them all together for a final meal, a stroke of brilliance.' He turned and stared at Eamon. 'I have to admit, I didn't think you had it in you.'

Eamon felt warm.

'The finale sounds good. I understand this is going to be filmed in the restaurant Emily's previous date is taking over. Nice touch.'

Eamon pulled down his cuffs and smiled. 'And we've been given exclusive rights to film the launch night of the restaurant. I thought it would be a nice touch to end on a high. New beginnings for everyone. I don't want to say any more yet'—he tapped his nose with his finger—'but you can expect a couple of exciting announcements.'

'Emily's first date.' The director general flicked through some papers. 'Adam. Is he okay with all this?'

'We've come to an arrangement.'

'What about the allegations Emily made about his new girlfriend. I understand the legal department had some concerns.'

'I've spoken to the new girlfriend – Ruby. She has been very reasonable. In fact'—Eamon coughed—'Some of this was her idea. We're going to explain what happened the first time around, show footage of Emily meeting Daniel in the nightclub, that sort of thing. Set the record straight.'

The director general nodded. 'Good. So, there's nothing else you feel I should know?'

'Like what?'

The big man sighed. 'Members of staff have suggested you might not be up to the job.'

Eamon was cooling fast. He should have felt warm and ecstatic, instead of like the *Titanic* on a collision course with an iceberg. He sat on his hands in a bid to calm down and keep them still. 'They have? I guess it's hardly surprising.'

Because they're wankers, the lot of them!

He smiled at the director and concentrated on modulating his voice. 'Most people here think television is a young person's job and I am old enough, probably without exception, to be their grandfather.' He paused for a reaction. None came. 'They see me as behind the times because I don't spend all day wired to a mobile phone, twittering or liking some random social media post.' He pulled an ancient phone out of his pocket. As far as he was concerned, a mobile phone was a device for making or receiving phone calls, not taking endless selfies or playing *Candy Crush*, something his colleagues seemed to devote endless hours to.

'I have been doing this job since before most of them were an itch in their father's underpants. None of them have my knowledge or experience.'

The director general nodded. 'That's true, but these days we live in a very litigious and changing society. We can't afford to get stuck in our ways. We have a legal department and team of researchers for a reason and they feel your go-ahead-at-all-costs attitude may be costly or worse. You have to remember, they're here to protect the company's image. Ignore them or sideline them again at your peril.'

Eamon was about to argue when the man raised his hand.

'The matter is not open for discussion. Do I make myself clear? I need your word that you don't feel this job is too much for you.'

'Absolutely not,' Eamon stuttered, his temperature rising. The veins stood out on the back of his hand. 'I love my job. It is the only thing I have ever wanted to do.' He took a long breath in, like his counsellor told him ... 3 ... 4 ... 5 seconds and breathe out. 'And you said my proposed ideas for the reality series about squatters and cowboy builders had an original twist to them.'

'Indeed.' The director general squeezed the bridge of his nose. 'That sounds exciting, but I can't afford one of my producers to go rogue and start making dangerous decisions. I need your reassurance there's no truth in the rumours about you having counselling for stress.' He looked over his sheath of papers at Eamon.

Somebody has been reading my diary.

Eamon threw back his head and laughed in a bid to mask his anger. 'Stressed – who? Me?' The thought anyone might be discussing him behind his back was something he intended to put in his "bad" book as soon as this meeting finished. He could probably fill an entire book with his thoughts about his co-workers.

The big man opposite raised his head and stared. The drill-like stare was painful. But not as painful as the thought his colleagues had been sticking their knives in.

'I think there may have been a misunderstanding,' Eamon said. 'I have been seeing a counsellor.'

The director general looked up. His eyes widened.

'On a regular basis,' Eamon said, slowly, through clenched teeth. 'As I'm sure my colleagues couldn't wait to tell you.' He could tell from the man's expression, he'd hit the mark. 'What I'm guessing here is that they haven't told you why?'

The director general looked away.

'Is that the real reason you've called me in today? To see if I'm deranged? Some sort of crazy?'

Still no eye contact, but the man looked uncomfortable. Good.

'Let me put you out of your misery. My visits are for research purposes,' he added. 'I am consulting her at the moment to help me understand the personality traits of stalkers.'

That made the big man sit up straighter.

'I could probably have googled stalking, but I like to research my subjects a little more fully than some of my colleagues.' He pulled his hands from under his buttocks and tried to massage some feeling back into them. 'I didn't want to mention this yet, because it is early days, but I am also investigating a new programme idea.' He had the director general's interest now.

'A series I'm thinking of calling *Neighbours or Nutters*.'

The big man's eyes grew bigger and for a second, Eamon thought he was about to choke on the mouthful of water he'd just taken.

'Or maybe "local loonies" has a better ring to it.' Eamon had his full attention now. He returned the director general's stare and cracked his knuckles. 'Does that answer your question?' he asked.

'We might need to take legal advice on the name before we commit,' the director general said.

Chapter Thirty-Three

'Please welcome onto the pitch, our opponents for today's match.' A team wearing a dark blue and black strip ran on and started practising at one end.

'Put your hands together for our own eleven players, Templeton FC.' There was a lot of stamping and clapping hands. Behind Ruby, the beginning of a chant started up.

'We are delighted to have a special guest with us today for our annual charity match against Pottingborough FC. Please welcome to the touchline our mascot for today's match – Adam Finder.'

Ruby, in the directors' box, cheered with everyone else when Adam walked out behind the team and waved. Not an entirely happy bunny.

'Adam is opening a new restaurant in Redford. TOTU is being launched at the beginning of next month, and he's offering you all a free drink with any meal you order, on production of today's programme. Let's hear it for Adam Finder.'

The first half was about to start, when a voice next to Ruby said, 'Move over. Is it okay if I sit next to you?'

'Have they finished with you?'

'They did ask me if I wanted to go to the adventure playground, or for an ice cream, but I said there was someone I wanted to kill in the directors' box.'

'There was nothing on the entry form about age limits. And I said you were thirty-five. It's not my fault.'

'They read it as three and a half. Partly, I guess, because they weren't expecting anyone my age to enter. The competition was on the juniors' page of the paper apparently.'

'It was a very tricky "spot the difference".'

'So they said.'

'I'm not surprised you won. Your average eight-year-old would have struggled.'

'I didn't enter,' Adam said.

Ruby turned and grinned. 'Oh, come on, all you had to do was stand on the pitch and wave. And we get great seats for the match.'

'What were today's competitions? Dare I ask?'

'Usual sort of thing – fill in a questionnaire to describe the character you'd like to be in an erotic novel and come up with an original use for a toy drone.'

'Tell me.'

'Dominatrix. Thigh-length boots, corset, black PVC and spikes.'

'Really?' Adam looked worried.

'Think of it as good PR.'

'Which bit? The boots and corsets or the spikes?'

'No, this. Events 2 Go would have charged you a fortune for ensuring coverage like you've just got. You have my services for nothing.'

'It doesn't look like the stunt has done you too much damage either,' Adam said. 'Was that the chairman I saw you talking to?'

Ruby nodded, happily. 'He wants to discuss a testimonial match and black-tie dinner for their goalkeeper who's played for Templeton for twenty years.'

'And he wants you to organise it because you can't read the rules of a competition?'

'No.' Ruby watched him cautiously, but there was a warmth in his voice, and she thought she saw a smile in his eyes. 'He wants me to do it because he was at an event I arranged a couple of years ago.'

There was a collective sigh from the stands and then a

cheer. To a man, everyone got to their feet. Adam and Ruby found themselves standing, cheering and clapping, too.

'Looks like you've brought them luck, Mascot.' Ruby chuckled and tucked her arm through Adam's. 'They're already a goal ahead.'

'Congratulations are in order, I believe.' Eamon smiled at Emily as they both sat down in the meeting at the studios.

'What makes you say that?' she asked, eyes flashing. 'Who's been talking?'

Shit, she looked wild.

Eamon did his best to appear outwardly unruffled. 'Just about everybody in Redford,' he said. 'Look at all these reviews. And there are hundreds of Facebook comments and emails. The public love you.'

She stared at him for several long moments. 'What do they say?' she asked, eventually.

Eamon selected the pile of emails and read, '"Emily is a lovely girl. I hope she finds true love with Daniel, but if she doesn't, can you give her my telephone number?" Or how about "Emily looks amazing tonight. I thought she was gorgeous three years ago, but she's blown my mind again. Daniel is a lucky man". I could go on, there must be two hundred in a similar vein.' Emily's eyes settled again. Her face was back to looking a picture of calm. 'Could I have those?' she asked.

'I'm putting an album together. I'll make sure you get a copy,' he said.

'Why did you want to see me?' She stroked the top of the pile of papers. 'You want me to do more interviews for my adoring public?' She giggled.

'Sort of. I have an invitation for you and Daniel to the televised launch of Adam Finder's new menu at Bootles, except I believe it has changed its name. All of the *Taking a Chance on Love* guests have been invited. We thought it would make an interesting series finale to get you all together. Take Felicity and Miles, for example. I had a message from them at the weekend. Miles has proposed. Our first *Chance on Love* wedding is scheduled for the end of next year. And some of the rest of you may have other news you want to share. Others hated the experience, but this will give you all the chance to talk about it.'

'At Bootles?' Emily's smile had morphed into a huge grin. 'Adam has asked me to be there?'

'No, Galaxy TV want you there,' Eamon said. 'You and Daniel. Do you think he will be happy to be filmed again?'

'Yes.' *Said without hesitation or deviation.*

'We are going to do interviews beforehand at the TV studios, then arrive together. We want it to look like a group of friends on a night out together.'

'What should I wear?' Emily asked.

Perhaps you could pop into the dry cleaners, see if anyone else has dropped anything off you fancy. 'You'll look lovely in whatever you decide.'

Her nod was so pronounced, Eamon thought she must be secretly listening to Status Quo and head-banging along to a tune he couldn't hear.

'There is one thing. We need you to backtrack on some of the remarks you made on the last show about your best friend.'

'She knows I don't mean it,' Emily said grinning insanely.

'She might do,' Eamon said. 'But our lawyers don't and nor do our viewers.'

'Okay,' she said. 'I'll do it.'

'Good.' Eamon nodded. 'I'll get the legal guys to put together a statement.'

'Will she be there? You know on the launch night?'

'Remind me.' Eamon wished he could take an aspirin. His

head felt about to explode. 'You've probably told me, but what's her name?'

"Congratulations, you are a winner in our Japanese tea competition."

'Yeah right.' Ruby clicked on the email to delete it. She received so many congratulatory emails these days she should be a very wealthy, well-dressed woman. So far, her lucky year seemed to be anything but.

The car outside was the same one she'd had for the last seven years. She'd won a Tartan Army Song Book, but no holiday. She'd won a year's supply of air-freshener and still had another ten boxes of cupcakes to collect from the supermarket. She had a singing fish and a signed photo of Justin Bieber, but no designer luggage.

Something about the email made her look twice. It was addressed to her for a start and not asking for £100,000 to get a sick friend back from some Third World country where someone had run off with their passport, wallet and hotel room key.

In fact, no mention of money at all. No link she was supposed to click. No once in a lifetime opportunity to find out how much pension she needed, or how long she was expected to live. No free pen if she entered a survey to look at her shopping habits. Just a telephone number she had to ring, complete with a proper London code. It didn't look like another marketing number. It even gave a woman's name.

Brutus snuggled into the space between her feet. 'Okay, I'll ring,' she said. 'But if they start asking me if I want double glazing or a conservatory, I will tell them in my finest Anglo-Saxon way what they can do with their prize.'

The woman on the other end of the phone took a while to realise what she was talking about. 'At this stage I just need a phone number and permission to pass it on to our promotions department. Someone will contact you to talk you through the arrangements,' she said, eventually.

It started to feel a lot like a scam, or another carpet tile delivery.

'I'm not sure what the best number would be,' Ruby said. 'I'll have a think and call you back.'

'Why don't I ask them to ring the number you've rung on?' the woman suggested. 'In case promotions are ready to call before you've decided.'

Chapter Thirty-Four

'Don't look like that, it's not magnolia.' Ruby stood, hands on hips and stared at the paint pot in the middle of the restaurant. 'It's a timeless pale colour which will contrast beautifully with your black, grey and pink colour choices. Trust me, it will look stunning.'

'It's magnolia.' Adam laughed.

'It's not magnolia. Malik, is this magnolia?' Malik was fiddling with his phone. His face almost the colour of the paint.

'No, Miss Ruby, it is paint, not a flower. Trick question, right?'

She wanted to tease him, but the look on his face stopped her. 'What's wrong?'

'No.'

'Malik, you can't use "No" to answer a "What" question. I can see something is wrong, please tell me.'

He would've made a decent beagle, everything about his face was droopy. 'My visa is refused. I have been given two weeks' notice. I have to leave the country, or I will be illegal and important.'

'Deported.'

'No. That can't be right.' Adam paused from pouring paint into two trays to give Malik his full attention. 'Can't you appeal?'

Malik shook his head. 'I miss your party and Jamila's father will be angry because he give me money for plane and I can't pay him back.'

Ruby wanted to hug him, but while Malik's English vocabulary might be improving, any form of outward affection had him protesting that he was engaged to be married and looking uncomfortable. 'This is so not fair.'

Adam walked across the restaurant and put an arm on her shoulders. 'We'll do everything we can to help,' he said.

She nodded. He'd said "we" again. Any other time she would have loved the warm feeling the word gave her, but at the moment she was gripped with cold sadness. Empty and cross. 'There must be people we can speak to. I'll look on the internet when we get home, see if we can find a lawyer.'

'No lawyer.' Malik raised his hands. 'If I had money for ticket I would go home.'

'What about your father,' Ruby asked. 'Can he help?'

Malik shook his head. 'He wants me to stay. I can work for him. He say we can move about and visa not important.'

'You can't do that. You'd be illegal.'

'I tell him that, and we argue.'

'If the authorities have you removed, you won't be allowed back.'

'He say they never find us, and Jamila not worth the cost of ticket.'

Indignation raged through Ruby. 'How dare he say that! Love like yours and Jamila's is worth every penny you have.'

'Thank you, Miss Ruby, but I have no penny.'

'Hold that thought,' Ruby said, as an idea started to formulate in her brain. 'I have an idea.'

They spent the morning painting. She was responsible for the white gloss work, but her heart wasn't in it. Malik had been such an important part of her life for the last couple of months. She hated the thought she wouldn't see him again.

'That's three coats done.' Adam stood back and admired his work.

He and Malik had covered all the walls in the pale colour emulsion that was definitely not magnolia and one wall in grey. The walls were patchy where the paint hadn't dried completely, but the restaurant was starting to look bright and modern.

'What do you think?' Ruby asked.

'It's lunchtime, how about I cook some soup for you both?' Adam said.

'I mean about the décor.' Ruby smiled.

'It looks fabulous,' Adam said, looking round the room. 'The lights, linen and decorations should hopefully pick up the colour from the logo. Little splashes of colour rather than anything too overpowering.'

Ruby nodded.

'I always thought cosy and homely would be the way to go, but this feels clean and contemporary, more in keeping with the menu I had in mind. What do you think?' He turned and looked at Ruby and Malik, nervously and bit his bottom lip as he waited for a response.

Ruby kissed his cheek. 'It looks amazing. Seriously amazing,' she said rushing into his arms.

'You're shaking,' Adam said. 'Are you all right?'

'Yes.' She smiled up at him, but then she felt it too. The vibrations. Her phone. She pulled it out of a pocket. A number she didn't recognise flashed up on the screen. She was about to switch it off, let it ring through to voicemail when Adam ran a finger softly over the back of her hand. 'Take it,' he whispered. 'I'll go and sort lunch.'

'I like it too,' Malik said. 'But please don't kiss me. I am intended for Jamila.'

Ruby watched Adam and Malik walk through the swing doors to the kitchen, while the woman on the phone introduced herself and mentioned something about an evening presentation.

'I'm sorry, the signal isn't great. Would you like me to

arrange an evening presentation for you? Do you have a date in mind?'

The woman at the other end of the phone gave a noisy laugh. 'Not organise it, I can do that. You need to be there to collect your prize – the two-week holiday to Japan.'

Japan had been at the top of her bucket list, for as long as Ruby could remember. The one place in the world she really wanted to go to. She'd covered her teenage bedroom walls with cherry blossom and pagoda posters donated by the local travel agent who was having a clear-out, while Ben's bedroom looked like a shrine to Shakira.

Some of her school holidays had been spent at Judo boot camps while Ben played football. She never got further than a yellow belt; he got selected for the county team.

She dreamt of snow monkeys, the bullet train and tea ceremonies. Of Tokyo and Mount Fuji. Still did. Recently she'd even tried sushi. It probably wouldn't be something she'd request for a last meal, but she didn't feign vomit every time someone suggested trying it.

Japan was her ultimate dream. Fourteen days. Tickets for two that included everything: flights, hotels, transfers, meals, entrance fees and spending money. All she had to do was attend an evening presentation at The Ritz, have her photograph taken and recite her slogan on demand. The tickets practically had her name on them. There wasn't any restriction on when she could take the holiday, provided she did it within the next year.

Then the woman told her the date for the presentation.

'I'm sorry,' she said, watching Adam and Malik laughing together in the kitchen. 'I can't make that night.'

There was a silence from the other end of the phone. 'It's not an option. If you're not there, you don't get the prize.'

'I understand that.'

'Let's be clear about this, madam. You'd be turning the prize down. You don't want to go to Japan?'

'I can't make that evening.'

'Presumably you read the terms and conditions?'

'I'm sure I did.'

'The date was there. It's not a moveable feast. Award ceremonies don't just happen. You shouldn't have entered the competition if you had no intention of coming? You've wasted everybody's time. And the judges really liked your slogan.'

They'd have been the only ones who did.

'Have you any idea of the value of this prize? Do you know how much you're turning down?'

'Money isn't everything.' Had that just come out of her mouth? *Jesus, I sound like my mother!*

'Oh please, spare me the clichés. I've had a long day.'

'Look, it might not sound rational.' It wasn't rational. 'Japan is everything I have always wanted, but I have to go with my heart …'

'Hah! So, there's a man involved.'

There was indeed. Ruby smiled and watched the man, through the small window in the swing doors, with his laughing, brown eyes cooking lunch. He was in his element; he looked up, caught her watching him and grinned. His eyes twinkled. Ruby's insides flushed with the intensity of a furnace. She wasn't holding a candle for him, she was carrying an Olympic-sized torch. There was no way in a million years she was going to miss his launch night.'

'A new man, I suppose. Well I hope when your relationship goes tits up, the fact you've given up a dream holiday won't add to your misery.'

'It won't.'

'You say that, but once the passion wears off …'

'Japan will stay on my bucket list. I will go at some time

in the future, hopefully with Adam, but if not, then on my own.'

'You do realise once I put this phone down, there is no going back. You can't ring up in ten minutes' time and say you've changed your mind.'

'I can't change my mind,' Ruby said. 'There's somewhere else I have to be that night.'

Chapter Thirty-Five

Eamon stroked his album of cuttings and smiled. He was at the top of his game.

An envelope was going around the office for another collection. This time for one of the gardening team. Rumour was they'd already gone, so he didn't put any money in. The name wasn't familiar, and he couldn't picture a face. Staff came and went these days so fast he rarely bothered to try and remember their names. That didn't stop him signing the card with his usual sentiment about being successful in whatever they undertook. Probably a job in a garden centre or a *Gardeners' Question Time* audience member.

There was no doubt, the teams were all getting smaller. At the moment, he was pretty sure he was safe, but he collated his best reviews in his happy book, along with copies of social media messages, leaving a handful of pages at the back for the finale. They would make good reading for any future employer if needed.

He'd sat down with the cameraman and they'd gone through all the out-takes from previous episodes. They edited some of the original footage of Emily talking to Daniel when they first met three years ago.

They definitely did meet.

Background noise and music had made it impossible to hear what was actually being said, but subtitles had now been added.

He'd overheard one of the canteen assistants saying she could lip-read. When he'd explained what was happening in the scene, give her her due, she had come up with a plausible conversation, well worth the box of chocolates he'd shelled out for as a bribe. So good, in fact, that Eamon had only needed to tweak the odd bits for artistic purposes. No mean feat when one considered for the most part their backs faced the camera.

He felt a little uncomfortable as he watched the footage again. There was unquestionably something odd about Emily. He wondered whether he should recommend a session with his counsellor.

He'd pulled together sound bites from everyone involved and could use those to fill any gaps. All in all, it looked fabulous.

It was smoking!

The launch party was going to be the icing on top of the cake. Getting them all together was a stroke of pure genius according to the director general. He should have felt a little tinge of guilt passing it all off as his own idea – shouldn't he? Along with Ruby's suggestions for future series.

The lunch he'd had with Ruby Brooks had been worth every penny. He had claimed it on expenses. The director general had practically insisted when he told him he'd single-handedly talked Ruby out of taking legal action. It had been stretching the truth way beyond breaking point but had earned him brownie points.

He owed her. He smiled at the leaflet she'd torn up and written her phone number on. Maybe he should treat her to lunch every month. She could be his advisor, his sounding board before management meetings.

He flicked the paper over. An idea was forming in his head. He dialled the number. It took so long to be answered he thought it would go through to answerphone.

'KKK at your service.'

'What?' Oh God he'd misdialled. Eamon ended the call, glad he'd used his mobile. He'd never hear the last of the fact he'd used the work phone to call a cult. He checked the leaflet and tapped out the numbers again then checked them twice before he hit the green telephone symbol.

'Kevin King's Kitchens, how can I help?'

This was it, twenty-four hours to go. The run through had gone well. Adam stood behind the bar – *his* bar and checked the wine glasses for marks. They'd already been polished to perfection, but one more check wouldn't hurt. Just to make sure.

It was happening. His dream was about to come true. A wave of excitement swept through him.

He was a restaurant owner.

The menus on each table were his menus.

He'd done it. Albeit with a little help from Ruby.

Okay, with a lot of help from Ruby.

She'd been with him every step of the way. Encouraging, persuading and at times downright pushy. The design concept had been his idea, but she'd listened to his ideas, when it all felt too big and impossible, she'd talked him though some of the potential obstacles and helped him make it a reality. He couldn't have done it without her. She'd written his press releases, worked on his social media presence, and sent out the invitations.

He smiled as he watched her across the room, measuring some of the place settings and remembered last week's car boot sale. Ruby's flat looked a lot tidier now that many of her winnings had gone. Ten competitions a day had certainly produced an eclectic mix of junk. 'Not junk,' she'd laughed as they arranged everything on wallpaper pasting tables. 'This is Malik's ticket home.' Adam sort of got the camping equipment, the cat activity centre, even if she didn't have a cat, the steam mop and thermal underwear but he couldn't quite get his head round the ear-cleaning kit.

'Whatever were you thinking of when you entered for this

one?' He held up a complete box set of Poirot's mysteries, in Arabic with subtitles.

'Could I see that?' an elderly man asked – before paying its asking price, to Ruby's delight. She grinned and high-fived Adam.

'Did you ever think it wasn't worth the effort?' he asked when a woman bargained the price of an epilator down to £2.00.

Ruby had looked shocked. 'Never. And I wouldn't have got to know you if I hadn't entered the Valentine's Day competition.'

'I'd have still been your neighbour. You'd have still taken in my parcel.'

'But you wouldn't have had any reason to cook for me and I probably wouldn't have been able to dog-sit for the last few months. Okay, so most of the time it's just been a waste of time, but I have discovered you can't win happiness. Happiness has to come from within. A flat full of prizes doesn't make me feel better about myself. Only I can do that. Oh God, now I've started spouting clichés. How corny is that?'

'Everybody needs dreams,' Adam had said and smiled at her as she handed a bowling ball to a woman in return for a handful of cash. 'Anything else you think I ought to know?'

'Never trust a company that tells you they won't pass your details on to a third party.'

He had wandered round the rest of the field once most of their table had been sold and got talking to a lady from the Redford Art Group about selling their work. He'd spent an afternoon later in the week selecting pictures for the restaurant walls. They were all hanging now, each with a label showing the artist and the picture's name.

He'd got back to the car, just as Ruby and Malik were putting the tables back in the boot. 'Okay, I need you to guarantee you won't be cross.' He took Ruby's hand gently.

'I need more information before I make those sorts of promises.' She grinned. 'Have you done something dreadful?'

'No.'

'Killed someone?'

'No.'

'Voted for Brexit?'

'I've bought you a present.'

'We're supposed to sell things, remember? We're trying to make enough money to send Malik home ...'

Adam held a vintage black lacy dress out in front of her. It was absolutely, breathtakingly beautiful. He'd seen her admiring it earlier in the day. 'I thought, seeing as your favourite dress was missing ...'

'Stolen.'

'You might like to wear this for the restaurant launch.'

She'd stared at the dress open-mouthed and looked like she was welling up.

'I'm a man and I don't know much about these things, but the colour and style look good and I think it's your size.' He hoped they were happy tears. 'If I've got it wrong, I can take it back.'

'You can't,' Ruby breathed. 'I won't let you. It's lovely. I fell in love with it earlier.'

'I know,' Adam said. 'And I want to put it on the record that I'm glad you entered the competition to win the Valentine's meal too. The jury's still out on the mascot fiasco, but I couldn't be more delighted that we met ...'

He looked across the room to where Ruby was now surrounded by men and women dressed in black and white – students from the local catering course who had been drafted in to help with today's rehearsal and tomorrow's launch.

Ruby was explaining how no money would be passing hands, unless the guests wanted to buy artwork or some of the tasting bottles of wine. All staff had a list with all the wines that Adam was going to serve and the characteristics of each that they should make the diners aware of. The list had prices of both wine and artworks on so they could respond if anyone wanted to know how much something cost.

'If you sell a picture,' Ruby said, 'make sure you put a red dot on the bottom corner so that everyone can see it has been sold.'

She handed everybody a small sheet of red dots, then told everyone about the party afterwards and explained they were all invited as soon as the doors were shut.

The afternoon's practice had been fun. They'd run through the timetable with everyone.

Clive had made sure all the students were happy serving from the customers' left using two forks while holding the platter in their other hand and explaining the ingredients of each dish as they served. He'd showed them how to pour drinks from the customers' right, making sure the customer saw the bottle before they started pouring. Some of the waiters hadn't looked entirely comfortable at first, but before long, Ruby and Clive had them relaxed and laughing.

In one corner of the room, out of the way, a group of ladies who used to come into the bistro on a Thursday after their Italian Conversation lesson were putting together goody bags. In the other, a group of waiters now joined by Ruby were sorting out a box of serviettes. They had enlisted the help of the local Chinese restaurant owner to teach serviette-folding techniques.

Adam walked across to join them.

'It's a bird of paradise,' Ruby announced, proudly showing Adam her first try. 'What do you think?' Her eyes sparkled. Her smile was infectious.

'Mine looks like a bloody boat,' Clive grunted, struggling to make his attempt look as professional. 'Can't we wrap them around the cutlery like we used to?'

Ruby raised an eyebrow and pointed her serviette at him. 'You heard what the boss said. We have to raise our game. Just fold.'

Clive mumbled something undistinguishable in return, and Ruby giggled, but three tables were soon covered with "birds of paradise".

This woman gave Adam feelings he never expected to feel again. She made him feel alive. She looked up and smiled. They held the look and he was overwhelmed with happiness.

The door opened diverting their attention. 'Wine order?' a man said. He pushed a sack barrow with four boxes balanced perilously on top of one another into the room.

'Over there,' Ruby said. She nodded towards Adam and the bar.

The man looked at the bar. 'There's another ten boxes in the van,' he said.

'Just stack it there?' She had her notebook in her hands and checked off items. 'We'll sort it later.'

'Whoa, hold on, this isn't ours.' Adam looked at the delivery note. 'We didn't order this much.'

Ruby took the delivery note out of his hand. 'Yes, we did,' she said, glancing at it quickly.

Adam rubbed his chin. 'Are you trying to bankrupt me?' he asked. 'There's twelve bottles of a pretty special South African Cabernet Sauvignon. Did you have any idea how much it costs?'

'Is there a problem?' Ruby frowned. 'You said you wanted to serve it …' She consulted her list. 'With the fish course.'

'In my dreams.' He laughed. 'There are only supposed to be 300 bottles of this in the country. I can't afford one of them, let alone twelve. Nice idea, but they'll have to go back. Sorry mate.'

The delivery man stood between them. He turned his head one way then the other, like the referee in a tennis match.

'They stay.' Ruby held up a hand. 'Galaxy TV is paying,' she said. 'I told you. That was the deal. They film here and in return, they cover the wine bill.'

'Have they any idea how big the bill is?'

'I guess so,' Ruby said. 'They placed the order. The invoice went to them.'

'Sorry, we're not open,' Adam said, looking up from the delivery note, as the door opened again and his neighbour from Flat 7 walked in.

'I know that,' the man said. 'That's why I'm here.'

The man appeared to be brandishing what, on first glance, looked like some sort of small weapon but turned out to be a fountain pen. 'Your girlfriend asked me to write the place cards for the launch.'

'George,' Ruby said, welcoming him with open arms. A gesture that made Adam feel jealous. 'Come and meet our Italian Conversation group. They're filling goody bags but there's plenty of room on their table, unless you need more space. In which case ...'

'This would be perfecto,' George said, smiling at the group. He was clearly bowled over by the women. Adam was sure he would have written place cards on his knee if it meant he could sit with them.

'Could you give George the table plan?' Ruby said as she walked across the room. 'It should be on the bar.'

That was when he saw it.

One name.

Her name.

He felt his blood drain. His muscles went into spasm. He had to get out of there.

Ruby watched him, clearly waiting for him to hand it over. 'Are you all right?' She put down an armful of flowers and walked across.

'Tell me she's not coming,' Adam hissed, jabbing his finger

272

at one name on the plan – Emily Watkins. His chest tightened. His legs felt weak. He needed fresh air.

'She and Daniel are part of the series finale.' Ruby looked surprised. 'Of course they're coming. You and Clive agreed it with Galaxy.' She hesitated, her eyes searching his face.

'I didn't.'

'It'll be all right,' Ruby said. She put up a hand to touch his arm, but he shook her off.

The front door opened. A group of young people walked in; Adam pushed past them and ran.

Chapter Thirty-Six

Adam left Union House at first light. He tiptoed barefoot downstairs and across the car park as silently as a cat burglar, until he stepped in a puddle.

He swore and glanced at Ruby's windows.

Not even a twitch of curtain.

If there had've been, he would've knocked on her door. 'I behaved like a prize pillock,' he would say and pull her into his arms. 'Can you forgive me?'

He watched for a second or two more. Nothing, but it was only five o'clock and it had been gone two by the time she got home.

The keys to the restaurant were on his mat this morning. No note, just keys. The sight of them lying there had made him feel so empty. It was his fault. He only had himself to blame and he needed to apologise, but Jason was due in on the 6.40 a.m. flight from Paris. He had to get going if he was going to make Heathrow.

Adam opened the car and put his shoes on.

She was right, flaming right. Televising the launch was going to be great promotion for the restaurant. He could never afford the sort of coverage that would give him. And she was right, he and Clive had met with Eamon to discuss the show's requirements and agree the schedule. The man said all the couples had agreed to take part. Adam just assumed that because they weren't a couple, and he wouldn't be taking part, neither would Emily. Her name hadn't been mentioned and he hadn't asked. But he could hardly blame Ruby. It was just the shock of seeing Emily's name there on the list in black and white. He'd been so wrapped up in the restaurant launch and Ruby that he hadn't thought about

Emily in weeks. It had been a relief to see the follow-up programme with Daniel. He'd allowed himself to hope that meant she was over him. He no longer worried about her hanging around, following him or getting home-made cards delivered.

He'd argued with Ruby. Except she hadn't argued. He'd shouted at her and then done the grown-up thing and stomped off. It wasn't the first time he'd run out on her at the first sign of trouble and she didn't deserve to be treated like that. He was no better than Daniel.

'Ruby, I'm sorry,' he muttered under his breath as he reversed out of the parking space. He turned out of the car park before he put his lights on.

She'd done such a fantastic job sorting everything out. He hadn't even said "Thank you". The launch was for invited guests only. Seating plans had been worked out. Everything had magically appeared. He had the list of everyone's dietary requirements and where they were sitting.

All he'd had to do was select the menus for the launch night and the autumn menu that the restaurant would run with until the beginning of December, and that had taken him forever. Every other problem, she'd smoothed over.

She'd made him a lapel badge that said: "Do not disturb – Head Chef".

Adam sighed. He loved being with her. Her positivity. She only had to look at him to make his temperature rise and his heart flutter. He couldn't remember the last time he'd laughed as much as he had this year. He was happy, excited about the launch. On top of the bloody world. He shouldn't have reacted so badly.

Think before you open your mouth and put your foot in it had always been his mother's advice. Last night he hadn't. Mouth open, foot inserted. Ruby had never let him down and yet he'd almost accused her of underhand dealings before he'd run off. Implied she was somehow to blame.

He'd made the mistake of picking up the phone as soon as he'd got back to the flat last night and then had to let Clive rant for twenty minutes about his behaviour and shortcomings.

Clive Ford – specialist subject – The Bleeding Obvious.

Thankfully, Adam's phone had bleeped to say the battery was low and he'd cut the call short.

'She's the best thing that's happened to you for years,' Clive said. 'Don't balls it up.'

'I thought I was over Emily. She's with someone new. She can't hurt me any more. I need to put the whole affair behind me, forget her, move on. I thought I had and I could cope,' Adam said, weakly.

'You have and you can. Let's face it. It's not as if you have to do it alone. You're among friends. Every one of us has your back, none more than Ruby.'

Clive was right again.

'And before you throw any more shit around, you knew about the deal that had been reached with the TV company and that it included all couples. Surely, you put two and two together and came up with a figure reasonably close to four.'

Adam leant back against the sofa and closed his eyes.

'A trained monkey would have realised they wouldn't have gone ahead unless Emily was part of the deal. And it's not as if she's coming alone, her latest date is going to be there too. Ruby's only crime as far as I can see is that she screwed the TV company for a sum that even made my eyes water. They've covered the drinks bill for the launch. You're serving Cristal champagne with your flaming canapés. I stipulated the kitchen would be out of bounds, Emily must be accompanied by a member of the television crew at all times and they all had to be out of the restaurant by nine thirty.'

'I know.'

'So, what's your bloody problem?' The noise Clive made suggested he was taking deep breaths while struggling to sound calm. 'Yes, Emily will be there tomorrow night. But seeing as she stole Ruby's dress for her brother's wedding and is now dating her ex, it sounds like Ruby's got reason to be upset with the woman too. But now she's blaming herself for not making sure you were aware Emily would be there. She wasn't even in that meeting.'

Adam didn't need reminding.

'Trust her,' Clive said. 'You owe her that.'

Two words – how hard could that be? There would never be any chance of a relationship if he didn't.

He did trust Ruby, he really did, but broke out in a cold sweat as the pure terror of the last three years rushed up and overwhelmed him. When would that bloody stop?

Even after a lengthy dog walk, Ruby found the prospect of a long day ahead of her, on her own, upsetting. Okay, maybe not ten competitions, but one or two … No point going cold turkey; she could cut down over the next month or so. Who knew, there might even be another holiday. She struggled to make a dual indoor/outdoor thermometer sound exciting – her heart simply wasn't in it. She hit submit anyway and sent off her entry.

The next competition wanted her to find five differences between two pictures. She did, barely registering the prize was a plastic lobster. The sort of thing every girl needs. The next she abandoned. A prize for a day at a spa for two sounded perfect, except she had no one to take and she didn't need an online competition to remind her of that.

She hoped Adam would have popped in. He'd never borne a grudge before. And they hadn't had a row as such. He hadn't given her the chance to say anything.

She wished he would turn up on her doorstep, with or without coffee, pull her into his arms and kiss her. She felt empty. Something was wrong. There was no sound from the flat above. His car wasn't in the car park. Where was he?

Clive had been kind last night, when he'd found her sobbing in the cloakroom. He'd handed her a tissue and sat down beside her while he explained Adam had been in a pretty bad place for the last few years. 'He doesn't always put his brain into gear before he acts or speaks. Give him time. He's nearly there. He's been a different man these last few months and a lot of that is down to you.' He'd taken her arm. 'Walk away if you want to after the launch, but tomorrow he needs you.'

'I get it.' Ruby sniffed. 'Emily caused him pain, but she's with Daniel now. She's building a new life. Why can't he? It's time he faced his devils. He can't spend the rest of his life worried she's going to be outside the restaurant or he's going to bump into her on the street, can he? If he's going to be constantly looking over his shoulder that doesn't give us a chance.'

'There is an "us" then.' Clive had smiled, getting to his feet. 'Just give him tomorrow. Then if he doesn't come to his senses you have my permission to throttle him. Or I will.'

Ruby wanted to knock on Adam's door when she got back last night. She'd sat in the hallway outside his flat for fifteen minutes willing him to open the door.

On balance, she was glad he hadn't.

Whatever would he have thought? Loitering with intent was the sort of thing Emily used to do. Ruby posted his restaurant keys through his letterbox and went back to her flat.

She'd wandered around, too wired to sleep, too upset to sing. The black dress, her outfit for the launch, hung on the wardrobe, taunting her. The dress Adam had bought for her.

The one that made her think he cared for her. Before he'd flounced off and made his true feelings clear.

'Hi-tech walking boots or designer shoes worth £300?' she asked Brutus, still asleep after his morning's exertions. 'What do you think?' But in case he said walking boots, she selected the designer shoe option anyway.

Belinda hugged Ruby. 'You're looking a bit pale,' she said. 'Come on, we've had a cancellation this morning. Let's get you made over, it'll give us a chance to talk and you can tell me all about this evening.'

'There's no need,' Ruby protested. 'I'm not going …'

'You bloody are.' Belinda glowed. Her pregnancy was so obvious now and it suited her. She rested her hands on her stomach and frowned. 'You're his event manager. You put the whole thing together. There's a clue in the job title. You're supposed to manage it.'

'That's what Clive said last night.'

'He's right. But don't worry we're going to make you look amazing.'

Before she could argue, Ruby was spun round and dressed in a hairdresser's gown.

'Sit down.'

Belinda called a junior to wash her hair. Ruby closed her eyes. It was a sensation she loved provided it came with a great massage and the girl didn't mention holidays, the weather, or harangue her about being a horrible person. She could have stayed there all day, except too soon she'd been sat on a chair in front of a mirror; Belinda behind her, staring at the back of her head.

'What happened?' Belinda asked, pulling her trolley closer.

Ruby pouted. 'Adam's not happy about Emily and Daniel being there.'

'Are you surprised? It is his big night. Have you any idea

how stressed he must be about this evening? You do this sort of thing all the time, but I'm guessing it's a first for him. And Emily is a good florist but seriously weird. What happened about your dress by the way?'

'The police are looking into the matter. The dry cleaners want her charged. She tried telling them I asked her to collect it, because I didn't want it any more.'

Ruby's hand was yanked upwards. In the mirror she watched Belinda call one of the girls from reception over and ask her to give Ruby a manicure.

'There's no need,' she said, feebly.

'My treat,' Belinda said, turning her attention back to Ruby's hair. 'Lily's very excited about tonight.'

'She is?'

'It was really sweet of Adam to call in yesterday to invite them personally, wasn't it?'

'Them?' said Ruby. She couldn't have heard right.

He hadn't mentioned adding anybody else to the guest list, but they hadn't really had the time to talk about anything.

'You are okay about Lily and Jeffrey, aren't you?' Belinda said.

'What you mean about my mother having a fling with her yoga teacher? Yes, I guess.'

'I can't believe you didn't suspect.' Belinda laughed. 'You know, sister, sometimes you can be really slow off the mark. Lily thinks Adam is gorgeous by the way. She told me she understood why you kept him secret for so long, and said if she was twenty something years younger, she'd give you a run for your money.'

Ruby frowned. 'I should have told her that Wedding Adam is Malik, not Adam.'

'I got the impression she knew.'

'How can she? And to make things worse, Daniel told her I am seeing a Bryan as well.'

Belinda giggled as she chopped upwards into Ruby's hair. 'Tell me about him,' she said. 'We haven't had much time to talk recently. I want to know all about him. Chef Adam, not Wedding Adam, although he was fun.' She pulled down two lengths of hair on either side of Ruby's face and checked they were level in the mirror. 'Why didn't you tell us who Malik was?'

'Because Emily kept telling everyone Adam was fitting my kitchen. He wasn't and he was delayed in France so he couldn't come to the wedding, but then Lily started making pointed comments about me being dumped, so I asked Malik.' Ruby straightened a little in the chair. 'I should have realised that Emily and Adam weren't and had never been a couple – she had no idea he was working in France and didn't recognise his dog.'

'I'm betting Chef Adam is also Bryan.'

'You guess right.' Ruby sighed. 'Adam knew Daniel had met Malik and thought he was Adam, so when Daniel turned up with the keys he decided it would make things easier to adopt another name.'

'And tell him you were working as an air hostess.'

Ruby grimaced. 'That was a misunderstanding. You know Daniel actually rang my old company?'

'Lily told me.' Belinda continued to cut and check bits of hair. 'Daniel told Ben that Bryan was a bit of a plonker, but from the loved-up way you've been acting lately, it doesn't sound like you'd agree. So, spill the beans. No secrets between sisters. Isn't that what we decided?'

Ruby wiggled her eyebrows – Belinda had hold of her head and she couldn't shake it if she wanted to. But she was sure she'd not agreed to any such thing.

'I thought you liked being alone.'

'I do. Adam wasn't the reason I left Daniel if that's what you're thinking. I didn't want anyone else, then he turned up with a dog and all sorts of problems, but he's as hot as hell, cooks like a god and makes me laugh.' She smiled at the thought of the Zumba lesson and Adam on the touchline at the Templeton FC match. And then she thought about the head-banging sex and the mornings after waking up cuddled in his arms and took a deep breath. The way she felt warm from inside out whenever he looked at her. Kisses that made her dizzy and long for him to kiss her all over. Her lips started to tingle, her nipples started to harden, the most enormous grin crept up her face and she didn't need to look in the mirror to know that her neck had started to colour before she remembered where she was.

Belinda stared at her. 'You're in love.'

'Steady on. I didn't ...'

'You don't have to. It's bloody obvious. Uncross your legs. Even Daniel, Mr Unobservant himself, told us you and Bryan couldn't keep your hands off each other.'

Ruby tried to play it down. 'That was done to get rid of him,' she said dreamily and looked down at her hands, because she was already flushed and didn't want to catch Belinda's eye.

'Whatever and I understand you've passed up the chance to go to Japan because the awards ceremony clashes with the restaurant launch. That made Ben realise Adam must be something special. Japan was your dream destination for as long as he could remember.'

'It still is.' Ruby fiddled with the edge of her gown. Japan had been within touching distance and she'd blown it out of the water, like her dreams of happy ever after with Adam.

For the briefest moment Japan had been in her grasp. All she'd had to do was attend the ceremony, have her picture taken, say how thrilled she was to be going. They were even providing a meal, which according to Adam would be amazing.

'Why did you enter if you didn't want to win?' Belinda asked, still considering Ruby's head.

'I've entered ten competitions a day since January. Not all for things ...' Ruby paused, remembering how delighted Belinda had been with the netball, '... I couldn't live without. I wanted to win the Japanese trip very much. I didn't think I stood much of a chance. My caption was hardly a literary masterpiece, so when I heard nothing, I assumed I hadn't been successful. By the time Adam set the launch date for TOTU, I'd forgotten all about it. Only to make matters worse now, daily reminders about the presentation evening keep popping up on my phone.'

'Ten competitions a day?'

'New Year's Resolution. My stars said I needed to get off my backside and turn my life around.'

'And you have.' Belinda stopped cutting, her eyes were glistening. 'Look what you've achieved this year; new kitchen; new business; new man.'

'For your information, I have also turned down a Mongolian Yurt and a catering-sized, gas-fired barbecue without regrets as well.'

'Ever won anything useful?' Belinda asked, as another tuft of hair hit the ground.

'Lots,' Ruby said defensively. 'We made £263 at the car boot last week selling my competition winnings. And since then, I've won a giant creme egg and a pasta maker.' No need to mention she'd stuffed a purple Morph suit into her underwear drawer that morning or that she'd tried to use the pasta machine a couple of days ago in the hope she'd be able to impress Adam. She watched countless Italian cookery videos in preparation, hunted for pasta recipes on every corner of the internet. It looked easy. Nowhere did it say you needed muscles to use it. He'd found her and her kitchen covered in flour as she'd tried to force a large lump of dough through the rollers. He had pushed up his sleeves and joined in. The secret he'd said, 'is to get the dough the right consistency'.

'Now you bloody tell me,' she'd laughed, but they'd cranked and rolled the dough into thinner and thinner strips, until finally he announced it looked just like tagliatelle. The end result of Pea, Pesto and Ham Pasta an hour later had been delicious, and they ached from laughing so much. But she couldn't imagine using it again any time soon; there were certain things life was just too short for. 'Thought I'd give the machine to Lily for Christmas,' Ruby said.

'Let's hope she likes it better than the family pass to the lawnmower museum,' Belinda said as she contemplated the length of Ruby's fringe. 'See, I told you I'd make you look amazing. Go and see Adam, talk to him, have make-up sex or whatever love birds do, but don't mess up your hair or your nails.'

Chapter Thirty-Seven

Something was weird about the flat. The second she turned the key and opened the door, Ruby noticed it.

There was a smell she couldn't put her finger on. Cheap perfume perhaps, or air-freshener. Chemical, not pleasant. A holdall sat in the hall. She froze, her senses heightened. She closed her eyes, then kicked the bag. It neither moved nor exploded, and she opened her eyes and took a breath. A strange noise came from the kitchen. She pulled off a trainer. Best be prepared. One shoe meant flight would be difficult, but armed and dangerous she could potentially knock out the intruder with foot odour.

Ruby hobbled towards the kitchen. The door was ajar.

Someone was singing. 'Load up, load up with buggered bullies' she heard and even with a broken heart, she smiled as she opened the door. No one she knew could get lines of songs as wrong as Malik.

'I wasn't expecting to see you until this evening,' she said.

Malik's face was pale in a luminescent white and sickly sort of way. He clearly hadn't shaved. His hair was dishevelled, and he was in the same clothes he'd worn to the car boot a week earlier.

'You look like ...' *A zombie.*

'I not sleep.'

She wasn't surprised, pretty certain she'd be in the same boat if she only had two days left before she had to leave the country, or risk becoming an enemy alien facing deportation.

Malik sniffed.

She wanted to give him a hug so much but the physical contact would freak him out and other than that, there wasn't much she could do. He needed money. He could have every penny they'd made at the car boot sale but £263.59 wasn't anywhere close to the price of a ticket to Egypt. Ruby knew it. She'd spent a couple of nights recently on the internet, searching for cheap flights, but even with her firm's letter of apology and their promise that her final month's salary would be in her bank account within the week, all her recent expenses meant she would still have barely enough money to cover the next month's mortgage; she wasn't in a position to chip in the extra.

'You need a rest. Why don't you have a sleep on my bed? On your own,' she added, as Malik's eyebrows shot up and he looked in danger of running away. 'Then you can have a shower. It will make you feel better.' She held up a hand, the international code to stem any argument, and walked ahead of him into the bedroom.

She didn't remember making the bed earlier, but obviously she had. She'd even tidied up the washing basket. She must have lost the plot.

Except she was pretty positive – definitely positive – she'd left Brutus asleep on the bed. Where was the dog-sized dent?

Come to think of it, where was the dog?

He hadn't rushed to greet her when she arrived home. 'Have you seen Brutus?' she asked.

'He's not here,' Malik said. 'No woof. I think you take him.'

'Think about tenses.'

'I am tense. I think either you or Mr Adam take him.'

'Adam hasn't got a key.' She couldn't bring herself to say he'd gone. 'He must be somewhere.'

They scoured every cupboard and opened every drawer in their hunt to find Brutus.

Ruby's sense of unease escalated to one of pure panic. They combed every inch of the flat. Then, when they'd finished, she insisted he search it again while she knocked on every flat door in case he'd slipped out when Malik arrived or Ruby left.

She found papers she hadn't realised she'd lost, a shoe missing since Christmas, but no Border Terrier.

The front door lock hadn't been tampered with which meant she'd either left the door open or Brutus had been kidnapped by someone with a key.

'You speak to Mr Adam.'

'I can't,' Ruby said. *Don't look at me like that.* 'He's busy. He has a lot on his plate. Today means everything to him.' Ruby flopped onto the bed, her head in her hands.

'We go to his restaurant. We say, hey Mr Adam, sorry about dog.'

'It's Daniel. It's got to be. I'll bloody kill him. Come on, we're going to sort him out,' she shouted over her shoulder as she charged down the corridor.

Opening the front door to the flats revealed a short, blonde crocodile wrestler staring at the various bells. In a mini skirt and knee-length black leather boots, Mrs Kevin blocked out all natural light.

'We need to talk,' the woman said, by way of an introduction. 'I've spoken to my husband.'

'This isn't a good time.' Ruby folded her arms. 'But since you are here, you should know you've run out of time and as I warned your husband, I will now do whatever I have to do to get my money back – all of it,' she said, trying to sound calm and business-like.

'I don't blame you.'

'No more excuses or lies, only right now I have something important that needs to be sorted …'

The woman nodded.

Why wasn't she arguing?

'Please. Kevin's told me. All about the granite, everything.'

'And close on two hundred unanswered calls in the last six months?'

The woman's eyes widened. 'That many?'

Clearly, he hadn't told her everything.

'Thirty-two in the last month.'

Mrs Kevin didn't look so sure of herself. 'It's not like him not to answer his phone.'

'Are you accusing me of lying?'

'No,' the woman said as Ruby took another step towards her. 'It's just that he has to, otherwise he doesn't get any work.'

'I'm sure it's only my calls he felt the need to block, unless he's been stealing from other people too.' Ruby fixed her with a stare.

Mrs Kevin blinked slowly. If she'd been about to argue, she evidently thought better of it and nodded. 'You can take us to court and you'll probably win,' she said, her shoulders slumping.

'Definitely win. No question about it.'

'I know.' Mrs Kevin's eyes flickered. 'We have no right to ask you for any favours.'

Ruby inflated her lungs as loudly as she could and puffed out her chest. 'But you're going to anyway.'

'Kevin's been contacted by a television company.'

Ruby let out her breath, before holding it became an issue. 'He has?'

'Galaxy TV want him to design and build a kitchen for a programme they have in mind. The producer said you recommended him. He is going to ask you for a proper reference but wanted to check Kevin's availability first.'

'Tell me, you've not come here because you want me to say there's no finer kitchen fitter in the world.'

'Well,' Mrs Kevin hesitated, 'something along those lines.'

Say no. Put your foot down. Don't let her walk all over you. 'Why?' Ruby stood firm. 'Why should I?'

'Kevin's a professional.'

Professional my arse. I doubt he could even spell the word. 'All his measurements were wrong. His plans even suggested he planned on moving the boiler upstairs.'

'It's quite normal to put the boiler upstairs,' Mrs Kevin said, defensively.

'Not when you live in a ground floor flat,' Ruby snarled.

'Look,' Mrs Kevin said, quickly. 'None of this is your fault and Kevin wants to pay you back everything. We both do, and we will,' she added. 'Only a family he did a lot of work for hasn't paid him since before Christmas. Then he slipped in the snow and put his back out, so he couldn't work for a while and we got into debt.'

'I don't care,' Ruby interrupted and let the silence hang between them.

'We're owed a lot of money for other jobs he's done and as soon as anyone else pays, we'll give you the rest.'

'What do you mean the rest?' Ruby's voice rose.

Mrs Kevin frowned, and scrabbled to regain some dignity. 'I need you to believe'—she held out an envelope—'that's all we can afford.'

Ruby peered inside the envelope; it looked to be full of £20 notes.

'It's money he's put aside for a new van, but if the television programme works out, it will be worth it. Please tell them you're happy.'

'That woman came early,' Malik said. 'I not let her in.'

'We should go,' Ruby said and slipped the envelope into her coat pocket as her mobile announced an unknown caller.

The voice, strangely muffled, asked her to confirm her name and number.

'You rang me. I didn't ring you,' Ruby said. 'I guess you must know who I am, you certainly know my number.' Just her luck to get a sales call when she was in a hurry. 'Have you rung to tell me I've won a prize?' she asked. It is always worth checking before screaming abuse or hanging up.

'Have you lost a dog?'

Brutus! Thank God! And for having had the foresight to have her number engraved on his tag when Adam went to France.

'I found it wandering around in Templeton.'

'Templeton?' Ruby said. 'How did he get there?'

There was a moment's silence. 'He hasn't been forthcoming with that information,' the caller said. 'I will text you the postcode, but you must come straight away.'

'I'll be there,' Ruby said. 'As soon as I can.' The line had already disconnected.

She bundled Malik and his holdall into the car and entered the postcode into her satnav. Ten minutes later they headed into Templeton.

'Turn right in 200 yards,' Satnav Sally instructed.

'There, behind Hosni's Palace.' Malik pointed to an entrance just ahead of them.

'Place,' Ruby corrected automatically. 'This can't be right, we're in a service yard.'

Signs warned of huge fines for parking during weekdays, or taking up more than one space, but on Saturday morning the place was empty. She pulled into a parking space, feeling cold despite the weather.

'No dog,' Malik said.

'I must have got the postcode wrong. I assumed we'd be looking for a house.'

'He is gone.'

'He'll be somewhere safe. They wouldn't hurt him,' Ruby said with less conviction than she felt. Something wasn't right. The number had been withheld. Ringing back wasn't an option. She had to wait for the caller to ring to find out where she was.

She switched off the car engine. The place had started to give her the creeps.

A lot of units backed onto the yard but apart from rows of different sized and coloured recycling bins, the place seemed unnervingly quiet like a bad cowboy movie, in which tumbleweed rolled down the high street. Except the only thing rolling along the ground was a plastic bottle.

A cold sensation washed over her and with it came the dawning realisation of exactly where she was.

The back entrance to April's bloody *Flowers!*

'That's Emily's shop,' Ruby said. It was the only un-shuttered shop in the yard.

'You think she stole the dog?' Malik asked.

'Not think. I know she did.'

'How did she get key?'

Lily said she'd given the key back to Belinda and Belinda had promised repeatedly that she'd keep it safe and never let Daniel near it, ever again.

Ruby pulled out her mobile and stabbed a number into it.

'You've reached Belinda's mobile,' a robotic female voice said. 'Which is probably in the bottom of my handbag right now, still you know what to do.'

'*Arghhh!*' The hairs on the back of Ruby's neck stood to attention. The only unanswered question was whether Emily, or Daniel, was responsible for "Dog Gate" or whether they were in it together.

'Come on, we've got a dog to save.' She opened the passenger door. 'We'll go in, pick up Brutus and be home before you can say Bob's your uncle.'

'Bob is not …'

'It's an expression. It doesn't matter.' Malik sat there staring through the windscreen looking anything but enthusiastic about her idea. Now probably wasn't the right time to mention every fibre in her body wanted to ensure Emily and Daniel both suffered painful and permanent damage.

Malik levered himself out of the small car and they started towards the flower shop back door.

It was locked; she knocked anyway. The top half of the door looked to be double-glazed. There was no answer.

Maybe she'd overreacted.

Then she heard the bark.

No, she hadn't overreacted. That was definitely a Border Terrier bark. Thank God he was okay. Ruby rattled the handle but it didn't move.

'Stay here,' she shouted at Malik. 'I'll go around to the front.' She ran to the main street and hammered on the shop door. The sign in the window read the shop was closed until Tuesday morning. There were no lights on.

'Remember I wouldn't let you sell Kevin's toolbox at the car boot?' Ruby asked, as she returned, out of breath and temper, to the yard. 'Is it still in the car? We need a crowbar or a mallet.'

Malik nodded, took her keys, lifted it out of her boot and wheeled it across the car park. She took a step forward, but he moved it just out of her reach and put up a hand. 'We not damage door,' he said.

'Just give it to me. I'm going to smash the bloody door down.'

'No. We remove the trim and unclip the bottom panel,' he said, looking around shiftily. 'That is easiest and then we call dog through. I do it.' He bent down, but Ruby stopped him.

'Let me,' she said.

He looked wary.

'You can't afford to get into trouble. Just tell me how.'

She followed his instructions to the letter. It wasn't quite as easy as he'd tried to make it sound and smashing the door down would probably have been a lot more satisfying, but twenty minutes later the door panel and trim rested by the wall. Ruby looked through the hole and called.

A dog whined. She couldn't see anything. It had to be Brutus. Wherever he was, Emily must have tied him up, or shut him in a room somewhere.

'I'm going in.'

Malik opened his mouth to object.

'Don't argue. If I get charged with breaking and entering, I'll say I was saving the dog and probably get off with a fine. If you're caught doing something illegal, you'll be deported. Go back to the car. If I'm not back in fifteen minutes with the dog, get help.'

She waited for him to move away and crawled into what appeared to be the back of the shop. 'Emily,' she shouted. 'Are you here?'

No answer.

Behind a door on the right-hand side of the shop came a sound. The key was in the lock. She unlocked it and walked in to find Brutus tethered to the corner of a metal table.

'Thank God you're here.' She bent down and fumbled to untie him, a job made harder because he insisted on licking her face. String had been knotted tightly through the ring on his collar.

'Okay, we have two options – take the table or lose the collar,' she told a frantically excited dog. She unclipped the collar, picked Brutus up and turned ... a millisecond too late. The door slammed in front of her.

Shit.

The room was in complete darkness. She couldn't see a thing. The blackness felt cold and damp. She wished she hadn't talked Malik out of coming in with her.

The illuminated front screen of her mobile read "no

signal", but the torch app showed some sort of stock room. She was surrounded by vases of flowers but managed to locate a light switch. She might not be able to ring for help, but there was no need to sit in the dark. Patience. Fifteen minutes. Malik wouldn't let her down.

'We have to keep each other company for a little while, shall we sing?' she said as she cuddled Brutus tightly.

Chapter Thirty-Eight

Adam put the final touches to his white bean and sage crostini, and the scallop skewers with crème fraîche. He picked up a cocktail stick and stabbed a lamb and salsa verde croute.

Ruby was right, the canapés looked and tasted amazing. There was nothing about the evening he'd felt the need to change. She'd had some great ideas. They'd discussed everything, more often than not, cuddled together after supper on the sofa. He smiled at the thought of her chewing the end of her pencil and making copious notes. And in the folder she'd presented him with at the end of last week, she'd detailed the number of guests, their names and dietary requirements. The back page she'd devoted to Galaxy television. She'd allocated them the two tables closest to the cloakroom, so they wouldn't be in anybody's way. Emily's and Daniel's names were on that list, of course they would have been, he just hadn't read it.

Hell, he needed to apologise. She hadn't been in when he'd brought Jason back from the airport. Her phone went straight through to voicemail. And the text messages he'd sent still said undelivered. Either she'd blocked his number, or she'd switched her phone off.

Adam consulted the two-page to-do list; each item had a time next to it and a box to be ticked as the item was actioned. He looked down the list and checked his watch. He was ahead of target. He wished she was here. A dark cold sensation settled in the pit of his stomach; was he being stood up?

Eamon and his cameraman arrived and set up in the corner reserved for them. Once their initial concerns were ironed out, they seemed happy. They had already been given strict instructions whom they could talk to and who mustn't appear on camera. Ruby had even written notes for the presenter.

Adam should have trusted her. Eamon assured him again Emily wouldn't enter the kitchen or approach him on, or off, camera and besides she was with Daniel now.

Adam wanted to hold Ruby, apologise for being a cretin. As if on cue, his mobile rang, and he smiled. Wiping his hands on his apron, he pulled it from his pocket with two fingers, to find a number he didn't recognise. His smiled deserted him and he let it ring out.

At the police's suggestion he ignored anonymous calls. He turned the ringer off, pushed the phone firmly back in his pocket and busied himself with more canapés.

The swing door squeaked. 'Can I come in?' Eamon said, his face white. 'I know I'm not supposed to be in the kitchen, but I've had a phone call from Emily.'

Adam chopped spring onions for the Peking duck tartlets with plum sauce and tried not to react, even if his heart crashed through his ribcage.

'I couldn't hear properly,' Eamon said. 'The caterwauling in the background made it difficult. She mentioned something about trying to call you about a problem she's having, but it went straight through to voicemail. I told her to ring me back when she had a better signal. It's difficult to concentrate when "Drift Away" is being viciously murdered in the background.'

"Drift Away?" Adam stopped, mid-onion. 'Are you sure?'

Eamon hummed the start of a tune that having lived above Ruby for nearly seven months, Adam recognised immediately.

She must be in trouble. 'Ring her back, find out where she is. We need to get there.'

Eamon stared.

Adam pointed the knife at him. 'Now,' he growled. He

hoped she was local. The clock above the kitchen door showed only five hours until the restaurant opened.

'What's going on, Chef?' Jason asked.

Adam shoved the folder at him, shouted some instructions and picked up his car keys. Eamon met him at the front door, followed by a cameraman carrying a large bag.

'I've spoken to Emily,' Eamon said. 'Something's kicked off at her shop. Ruby's causing problems. Emily said it sounds as if she's been drinking.'

'No way,' Adam said with an adamant shake of the head. 'Car's round the back, I'll drive, you navigate.'

Eamon put a hand on his shoulder. 'You're not going to want to hear this, but Emily says the woman broke into her shop and threatened her.'

'No way,' Adam said, through gritted teeth. 'Get in.' The cameraman threw his equipment onto the back seat and climbed in after it.

Eamon hesitated. 'You say that, but Emily sounded frightened and Ruby has locked herself in the stock room and is refusing to leave. I think ...'

'Either get in or stay here.'

The TV producer climbed into the front passenger seat and made a fuss about doing up his seat belt.

'Where are they?' Adam had the engine running and started to pull away.

Eamon slammed the door and frowned. 'Templeton. She has a flower shop. We filmed some scenes there for the last series. Remind me, what's it called?'

Adam gave him his best "How the fuck should I know" expression. 'Google it.'

'April Flowers,' the cameraman said from the back seat. 'Templeton High Street.'

'It gets worse,' Eamon said. 'Ruby told Emily if she shows up at the launch party tonight with Daniel, she will kill her.'

'Oh please. You can't seriously believe Ruby would threaten that.'

'She wants a guarantee that Ruby won't be here this evening.'

'We need to get there and quickly. Ruby is in trouble.'

'You don't know that. Let's just call the police. Let them sort it out. Probably a case of too much drink and hormones. Handbags at dawn. Give them an hour or two. Ruby will sober up and they'll be best of friends again.

'They won't.' Adam had never been surer of anything in his life. He turned and faced the television producer and the cameraman. 'Ruby is in danger. I'm going to find her and you're either with me or not?'

'We're with you,' the cameraman said. 'It will make a great episode.'

'Okay,' Eamon said, cautiously. 'Are you sure Ruby's in trouble?'

'Absolutely,' Adam said, shooting through the red lights at the bottom of the road and ignoring a driver who was gesturing wildly. 'If she'd threatened murder, she'd be singing "Rubber Bullets" not "Drift Away".'

The world outside might be unkind, but halfway through the second verse, the third time around, Ruby would have gladly swapped an unkind world for the damp, miserable storeroom that was her current prison. She'd told Malik fifteen minutes. She hoped he wasn't going to be much longer.

She heard a sound and stopped singing.

'I'd give it a break if I were you. You're embarrassing yourself,' a disembodied voice said.

'Emily, is that you?' Ruby asked. There was no answer.

'Is Daniel with you?'

'No,' the voice said. 'Just me.'

'Why?'

'That's easy. I hate you.'

'What have I ever done to you?'

'You stole my boyfriend.'

He's not your boyfriend. He never was. Ruby shut her eyes. There was no point arguing. 'So, you thought you'd get revenge by breaking into my flat and stealing my dog?'

'Adam's dog.' Emily made a noise that sounded like a laugh. 'Belinda told me how cross you were when Daniel discovered where you lived. She hid your keys in her salon, she showed me. She thought she was so clever, because Daniel would never think of going into her salon. Actually, I should go and drop them back before she misses them.'

Ruby's head flopped back against the wall. 'You took the dog, because you want to hurt Adam or me, or both of us?'

'No.' Emily shouted through the closed door. 'I'd never hurt Adam. I only want to protect him.'

'By stalking him?'

'I did not.'

'He thinks you did.' Ruby pulled a large white flower from a vase and studied it.

'No, he doesn't. Stalkers are psychotic. I'm not psychotic. He knows that. I don't go around with crazy eyes looking for my next victim.'

Isn't that more zombie than stalker? 'You turned up and drew lipstick hearts all over his car.'

'Once – for a joke. It didn't hurt, and he washed it off.'

'He shouldn't have had to.'

'He blocked me on social media, changed his email address and phone number. He shut down his Facebook and Instagram accounts, how was I supposed to tell him how I felt? It was the only way. Dangerous people don't draw hearts. I'm not dangerous so I can't be a stalker.'

Says the woman who's locked me in a storeroom. Ruby rubbed her forehead. Brutus looked up and licked her hand.

She was glad she wasn't alone. 'There are different types of stalker ...'

'Cut the psychology. You don't know anything about me.'

'I know you're with Daniel now.'

'I love Adam, he is my first love. I like making things for him. Except my bitch friend didn't pass my card on, because she fancied him.'

'I gave him your card,' Ruby said.

'No you didn't. Don't pretend. If you gave it to him, then how come a policewoman ended up with it?'

'Look.' Ruby massaged the bridge of her nose. She could feel a headache coming on. 'I'm sure you didn't mean to upset him. Why don't you let me go? I could explain to him how you are sorry for overstepping the mark.'

'Don't put words into my mouth.' Emily's voice got louder again.

Brutus growled and Ruby held him tighter. 'Mad woman,' she whispered.

'Why did you pretend your kitchen fitter was Adam at Belinda's wedding?'

'Because I found out you were going to be there,' Ruby said. 'I told Adam I didn't want him to come and invited Malik instead.'

'We were together. We were happy.'

'He moved to get away from you. That doesn't sound like happy to me.' The flower she was holding was now just a stem, while she was covered in the small white petals. She took another from the vase. Pulling the petals off at least gave her hands something to do.

'You stole him from me.'

There was no point arguing. They could be there all day, like some bad pantomime sketch. *Oh no I didn't. Oh yes you did.*

'Talking about stealing, what about my dress?'

Emily laughed. 'It suits me, doesn't it? Funny isn't it, that we're the same size?'

A warning voice in Ruby's head cautioned her against saying what she actually thought. 'Do you have any family?' she asked instead and pulled another flower to pieces.

'Just me and my mother. But before you try to dump your psychoanalysis crap on me, I had a happy childhood.'

'What happened to her?'

'My mother?' Emily said. 'Nothing happened. She's a florist. She trained me then retired to Spain. Her name's still above the door – April Watkins, but I run the shop now. She was the one who told me to go out and take what I wanted from life. "Don't sit around waiting for happiness to come to you," she said. "Nothing will stand in your way, unless you let it".'

'Good advice, but don't you think she probably expected you to register on a dating website, swipe a few like-minded individuals, go for a few dates, play the field, not sign up for a flaming televised dating programme.'

Silence.

Had the woman gone? Ruby listened, but heard nothing, certainly not a door being opened. 'Adam didn't sign up, did he?' Ruby said. 'He got roped in at the last minute because your date didn't show. He stood in because he's kind and felt sorry for you.'

'No!' Emily shouted. 'It wasn't like that. He thought I was lovely.'

'He told you that?'

'Yes!' Brutus trembled at the sound of Emily's scream.

When you're locked in a room with your captor outside – possibly the only person who can free you, no survival guide in the world would recommend winding them up any further. Brutus trembling in her arms reminded her of that so Ruby kept quiet.

'I had six weeks of counselling for that programme. They told me what signs to look for. That's how I knew straight away your Daniel fancied me.'

Daniel fancied anything in a skirt. In his case Emily could have ditched the sign-watching and just offered sex or free booze, the result would have been the same. Ruby stayed silent.

'Not that you'd understand. Daniel told me how badly you treated him. We've become very close. He says I'm everything you're not.'

'I am glad the two of you are getting on so well.'

'Are you?'

Bloody delighted if it gets the pair of you off my back. 'Absolutely. So, why don't you open the door? We can have a proper chat about him.'

'I don't think so.' Emily made a noise that could have been a laugh, possibly a snort, but not the sound of a door opening. 'Make yourself comfortable, you're going to be here until at least Tuesday. I don't open Mondays,' she said.

'Don't be ridiculous. You've had your fun. Now let me out.' Ruby banged on the door.

'Can't stop. I have to get ready for a launch party. I'll tell Adam you're otherwise engaged, shall I?'

Chapter Thirty-Nine

'You intend to break into a flower shop?' Eamon asked as Adam braked suddenly, and his car lurched to a stop on Templeton High Street.

'If need be,' Adam grunted. They looked at the large double-fronted shop window. 'You are sure this is where Emily works?'

'She runs it,' Eamon said. 'Used to be her mother's.'

The three men climbed out and stared at the windows.

'"April's Flowers – always delivered promptly, Emily very helpful" according to one review,' the cameraman said from behind. 'The only other one's not so good. "Basket arrangement delivered to funeral parlour, day after the funeral." One unhappy lady.'

'I don't know what we're going to find in there.' Adam inhaled. 'But let's be prepared for the worst.' He was, single-handedly, becoming a pastiche of *The Sweeney*. Not a particularly good one at that.

'It's a flower shop, not an abattoir.' The cameraman swung round and took some footage of the shopfront and the street.

'Flower shops use knives.' Adam narrowed his eyes. 'And scissors.'

'Jeez, I wish you'd told me. I would have worn a body protector and helmet.'

Was the cameraman laughing at him?

Eamon was turning an unbecoming shade of green. 'Just give me your keys,' he said. 'I'll move the car round the back and meet you in the service yard.'

'You're not coming in?' Adam asked.

'You've parked across double yellow lines and a bus stop.

Can't be too careful. This way, if anything goes down, I will call for help.' Eamon's eyes were wide with panic.

'Don't worry Adam, I'll cover your arse. I wouldn't miss this for the world.' The cameraman took another lens out of his shoulder bag, fitted it to the camera, fiddled with a button and hoisted it back on to his other shoulder.

'Thanks,' Adam grunted and then grunted again, nodding at the door and hoping his new partner understood this to mean *I'm going to try the door and see what's occurring*.

The cameraman grunted back.

Sticking his hands in his pockets, Adam walked up to the shop door in a swagger that would have been easier for someone of his age to achieve if they'd spent their life on horseback rather than in a kitchen. He squinted at a sign obscuring one of the door's panels. It told him everything he needed to know about the place. They took Visa, Mastercard and American Express and were closed. *Good start.*

He rattled the front door.

If this was *The Sweeney*, Regan or Carter would have probably kicked it down. It looked solid but would, no doubt, splinter under a barrage of well-aimed kicks from steel toecaps. He'd seen enough old repeats of the programme to know that as it shattered, one of them would roll in, shouting over his shoulder, "Don't shoot any lower than three foot off the ground".

Adam pushed the handle hard. The door flew open and he flew through into the arms of a burly man wearing a dark suit and fiddling with the alarm system.

The sound of sirens filled the air and they all froze.

'Police,' the man said. 'Quick, come in. I reset alarm.'

'Thank you,' Adam said and ducked out of the cameraman's way, gesturing for him to go in first. 'We're looking for a woman.'

'Aren't we all,' muttered the cameraman, circling slowly.

'A pretty lady, chestnut hair and eyes.'

The man kept pressing buttons, which seemed to respond with varying notices of an alarm. To Adam's relief, a number of police cars, lights and sirens flashing, raced past outside.

'Her name is Ruby. She sings when she's upset. She might have been upset today.'

The man said something into his phone that definitely wasn't English and listened, while the cameraman made his way along the shop, deliberately filming everything as he went.

'You need to go.' The man jerked his head towards the back of the shop. 'Police are in the yard.'

'I came here to save Ruby. I'm not going anywhere without her.' Adam pulled himself up to his full six feet.

'The woman that sing about fake slugs has gone.'

'How? Where?' Adam asked, and got a shrug in return.

'I open the door, switch off the alarm,' he said. 'She walk out with the dog and take my cousin. They go to do something urgent.'

'Looks like Edward Scissorhands has attacked the back room. I can't see a single flower stem that hasn't been decapitated, but no one else there,' the cameraman said on his way back down the shop. 'I found this.' He passed Adam a phone. The glass was broken, but he recognised it immediately.

'Ruby's,' he said, gruffly. What on earth had happened that her phone was broken? Had she left it as a signal that something was wrong?

'Come on. We must go.' The man opened the door and keyed a number into the alarm panel. 'Put your hands in air when you walk round corner, in case they think you're armed and shoot.'

'You mean the Armed Response Unit is here?' the

cameraman said. 'This is going to make a cracking episode. BAFTA nominations, here I come.'

The shop alarm beeped as the man shut the door behind them. He locked the door from a large bunch of keys and waited for the sound to stop.

They turned the corner to the service yard where there were four or five police cars with their blue lights still flashing and doors open. They appeared to be in some sort of confrontation with a large group of men who were gesticulating wildly.

'Who are all those people?' Adam said.

'Cousins,' the man said, lifting a hand and waving at a couple of men.

'Your cousins?' Adam asked. 'The one that's gone with Ruby. What's his name?'

'Malik. He phoned his father's brother and said he need help to get Miss Ruby out of shop. We wait until the woman goes and then I open shop with my keys.' He gave a toothy grin and held up a bunch of skeleton keys. 'I install alarms, many alarms. I know the master codes.' He tapped the side of his nose.

'There are so many people here.'

'My father has six wives and many boys.'

'Six?'

He stopped. 'No, you right. He has seven wives and many sons.'

Adam watched the group. 'They dropped everything and came straight away when Malik phoned?'

'We are family. He in trouble, we help. I hope nobody drop anything. We were at dad's palace.' The man jerked his head towards a large white domed building on the edge of the service area.

'Place,' Adam corrected but then read the sign on the opposite side of the car park which advertised Hosni's Palace, "the best Egyptian Restaurant in Templeton". A somewhat exaggerated claim. As far as Adam knew it was the only Egyptian restaurant in the county.

The man bowed, called to someone in the crowd and went to join them.

The cameraman continued to film the group. On its edge, a woman stood watching the proceedings. Adam walked across to join her. 'Inspector Lenham, everything okay?' he asked.

She turned and it seemed to take her a moment to register who it was. 'What on earth are you doing here?'

'Just passing.' He shrugged.

She looked at the cameraman. 'With a camera crew?' She took a step back and her head movement suggested she did not believe him.

A couple of the crowd pointed at them and said something. Others turned and suddenly a large group broke away from the rest, coming across to surround Adam. 'Templeton football,' one of them said.

'You know these people?' Inspector Lenham asked as a number of them started taking photos. 'I've got a good mind to stop and search the whole lot,' she added as she was roughly manhandled out of the way by another group who wanted a selfie with Adam.

They had clearly come to Malik and Ruby's aid. They were there when she needed them. It was just him who hadn't got there in time. He thought of Malik and Ruby somewhere together. Clearly they weren't in danger. He could go back to the restaurant and get ready for the night. He hated the thought they were somewhere together. He shouldn't care what she thought, she obviously didn't give a stuff about him, but he could picture the hurt in her eyes if he didn't help Malik's cousins.

'Except they're not my biggest concern at the moment,'

the inspector said. 'You are. That's Emily's shop, isn't it?' She stood with her hands on her hips and her face seemed to challenge Adam to argue.

'Is it?' He tried for a nonchalant shrug.

'For God's sake, I'm not as green as I'm flaming cabbage-looking. Something's going on and I will get to the bottom of it. Don't move and don't say a word.' She waggled an index finger threateningly and said something to one of her officers that Adam couldn't hear. The man nodded, smiled and moved away, speaking into a walkie-talkie.

Another group of young men crossed the car park and pulled out their mobiles. This time, the inspector stayed out of their way and watched as they took pictures and shook Adam's hand, from a safe distance.

'Four nil, four nil,' they sang.

'Templeton FC mascot? You really are quite the local hero,' she said, once the men had walked back to join the others, comparing pictures. 'I had no idea you did public appearances. Maybe we should book you for our Police Christmas Dinner.'

'To cook it?'

'No.' She laughed. 'After dinner entertainment. There's clearly a hidden side to your character. Could probably find you a costume. I think we have a Green Cross Code man outfit left over from some Stone Age road safety campaign. You could go around and shake hands with everyone, remind them to look right, look left ...'

'Is that the green cross code or the Hokey Cokey ma'am?' An officer grinned.

Another policeman walked back shaking his head. 'Owner said the shop is secure. She closed up about fifteen minutes ago. She's sure the alarm company would have rung her if there had been any security concerns.'

'Did you ask her to come back to check?'

Adam held his breath. The last thing he needed was a confrontation with Emily.

'She said there was no point.'

He tried to exhale his relief quietly.

'There's no money in the till and the flowers would be okay until Monday. She will check then and file a report if necessary.'

The inspector focussed in on Adam. 'What are you doing here? Don't tell me you and Emily made up your differences and are now blissfully happy?'

Adam spluttered. 'Not bloody—'

The cameraman interrupted, moving between Inspector Lenham and Adam. 'He wasn't with her.' Adam could have kissed him. 'I wanted to film the flower shop, give some background. Galaxy TV,' he said. 'We're filming Adam's launch and the series finale to *Another Chance on Love* tonight.'

'Are this lot something to do with you too?'

'No.' He put the camera back up to his eye and the record button turned red. 'Party at the Egyptian restaurant, apparently. Big family affair. The owner's seven wives and sons all came. They came out to perform a lucky dance because there wasn't space in the restaurant.'

Inspector Lenham called her sergeant over. 'A lucky dance,' she said. 'Tell them I want to see it.'

There was a lot of head-scratching as the message was passed to the group who then turned in on themselves in a huddle.

'Cool,' the cameraman said, walking across the service yard, his camera fixed on the group, some of whom had fixed tablecloths to their clothes.

Adam frowned. This wasn't supposed to happen. He had a launch to prepare for. He shifted. 'I really should get going. I'll see you this evening. You are coming to the launch aren't you?'

The inspector put a hand on his arm. 'No need to rush off.'

It was bad enough he'd left Jason to sort things out because he fancied himself as a superhero, the only one who could save Ruby. Except he wasn't and he hadn't. Malik had, and she'd gone off with him. He pulled her phone out of his pocket. It was locked, but a diary reminder flashed across the broken screen. *"Journey time to The Ritz, London, 1h 54 mins."*

The Ritz, London. They'd talked recently about The Ritz. He tried to recall the conversation. The Japanese holiday presentation. He stared at the phone. Did this mean she'd won? She never said.

'How long will the dance take?' he growled under his breath.

'If they're planning on a Tanoura, somewhere between fifteen minutes and a couple of days, I should think,' the inspector said. 'Make yourself comfortable.'

Ruby hadn't planned on a detour to Heathrow. Common sense said she could bundle Malik into a taxi or a train. She needed to be at Adam's restaurant. Except this was Malik.

'Tell him *hza saeidaan*. It means good luck,' Malik's cousin said when he released her from the shop. 'You too, Miss Ruby. You have been a good friend.'

With his words ringing in her ears, she'd persuaded Malik into her car because good friends didn't abandon their pals when they needed them most.

Or shout and run out on them when the chips were down.

She pictured Adam's face and his anger when he realised Emily would be at the launch. It had felt physical. A burning in the pit of her stomach. She wasn't sure there was a way back. She'd hoped he would have got over it and contacted her by now. He hadn't. The look he'd thrown her last night when he'd walked away was pure, undisguised disgust. She'd hurt him, that look had told her as much and more. Their relationship was clearly over. Over before it had really got off the ground. A brief taste of happiness and love snatched away.

Except tonight wasn't about them; even if he wanted nothing more to do with her, she was his event organiser and a professional. She'd written down every last detail in case of an emergency. It was in the folder she'd left on the bar, but if he was a paying client, she would be there to iron out last-minute problems.

The traffic lights turned orange then red and she slowed down, but the car behind her, overtook and shot past. 'Dick head,' she shouted after it.

'You know those people?' Malik asked.

'No.'

'So, why you call them by their name?'

'Good question,' she said. 'My turn. Your cousin said I need to ask you about your letter.'

Malik looked down and concentrated on stroking Brutus.

'You know the one I'm talking about.'

'He good man. I tell him about your flat. He change the locks tomorrow. You ring him as soon as you home.'

'Don't change the subject. Tell me about the letter from the Border Agency.'

'I already have,' Malik said, quietly.

'When did it arrive?' Ruby pulled away, as the traffic lights changed colour, with more aggression than usual and shot him the look that worked so well with Brutus.

He shrugged. 'My English is not so good.'

'Your English is fine. How long have you had it?'

'Two, maybe three weeks.'

'And today is the day they gave you to leave the country by or lodge an appeal. You should've said.'

'You are good woman. You tell police. They put me in a

centre and leave me there. I would not be able to go back to Jamila. I cannot afford appeal. I cannot afford flight. I cannot pay her father; she will hate me forever.' He stared out of the side window. 'My life finished. Stop the car. I get out and you will never see me again.'

'Melodramatic, but not practical.' Ruby turned onto the M4. 'We're going to the airport.' Traffic moved well; she took a deep breath. 'I thought we were friends. I don't understand why you didn't tell me?'

Malik shrugged. 'You have no money. I wanted to finish your kitchen and Mr Adam's restaurant. I didn't want to leave you in river shit without oar.'

'Up shit creek without a paddle.' Ruby corrected and bit her lip. Tears burnt the back of her eyes. She pulled the envelope from her pocket and passed it across to him. 'This is for you,' she said.

Malik's mouth fell open. 'So much money.'

'£5,260.00.' Ruby switched to the fast lane to overtake a driver who seemed to think the middle lane was his, whatever speed he wanted to travel at.

'It is money your wanker owes you.'

'And from the car boot. Have you got your passport in your bag?'

Malik nodded.

'To the airport then.' She turned towards him and smiled. 'There must be planes leaving for Egypt tonight. You're going home.'

She glanced at her watch. It would be tight, but with a favourable wind and decent traffic flow, she could be back at the restaurant to meet the staff before they started their shifts and check everything was in place before the restaurant opened.

A professional, remember that, she told herself. You want to do this for a living. There will be bigger challenges. You can't run away at the first obstacle. He didn't have to see her or talk to her, but she would be there. Full make-up applied!

One night. That was all. Then, they could both get on with their lives apart. She would put on her best brave face, like she used to do when Ben hurt her, stole her toys, or had just been boyish and Lily was too busy to deal with the situation. She could stifle her emotions for one night.

Brutus stretched in Malik's lap, yawned, then settled down again. Ruby stroked his head. The burning in the pit of her stomach intensified. Would he want his dog back? He'd been so busy with all the restaurant preparations, and they'd been spending so much time together recently that he'd been happy to let her continue to look after Brutus.

A big fat tear rolled down her face and hit the steering wheel. She wiped her sleeve across her eyes and sniffed. Losing Adam was one thing but losing the faithful companion who had pulled a broken woman through some pretty bad times was another.

Malik looked up.

'We better let the restaurant know there has been a small change of plan and I'll be a bit late,' she said.

She felt in her pocket. No phone. She glanced at the car's display. It wasn't just not in her pocket; the car didn't show a connected phone at all. Great, she'd dropped it. The find-my-phone app on her computer should be able to track it down providing its battery hadn't run out, or someone switched it off, but there was nothing she could do about it at the moment.

'Can you remember Adam's number?' she asked.

Malik nodded and reeled off a series of numbers. She had no idea whether it was right or not, but his pronunciation was good.

'Ring him,' she said as she pulled into the line of traffic. A large car let her in. A man and a woman. She thanked them and stuck to the speed limit. So far today she'd already broken into a shop, the last thing she needed was a flaming speeding ticket. If she'd been on her own, she'd probably go straight for "Rubber Bullets" about now.

Malik looked at the phone. 'No answer,' he said. 'He must be very busy. I try again later.'

Chapter Forty

'Are you going to answer that or what?' Jason gestured towards the phone Adam was staring at.

'Why can't she bloody well leave me alone?'

'Answer it and ask her?'

The phone stopped and Adam shoved it in his pocket.

'You're quite sure that is Emily?' Jason put his hands up. 'No, don't look at me like that. You said she didn't know your number.'

'Two anonymous calls in one day from the same number. Too much of a coincidence. It has to be. I don't know how she got it and frankly I don't care. Tomorrow I'll change the phone.'

'Could it be Ruby?'

'No.' Adam turned and faced Jason. 'For three reasons. One – she's on her way to London. Two – her phone is broken. And three – I have it here.' He pulled the phone out of his pocket and threw it across the counter.

Jason nodded slowly. 'Your journey time to The Ritz is two hours and five minutes. You should leave now to be there by 7.30.' He looked at his watch. 'Actually, you should have left twenty minutes ago. Is that why you're angry?'

'I'm not angry.'

'You don't know for certain that—'

'She was last seen driving off with Malik to do something urgent in London. Where else would she be going? She's won the Japanese holiday. I don't blame her.' Adam ran his hands through his hair. 'Japan has been somewhere she's longed to visit since childhood. 'What hurts is that she didn't tell me.'

'Is it? Or is it that she's taken Malik.'

'She's planned every detail of this launch. She's left a

folder, everything I need to know. Was that because she never intended coming? And after last night …'

Jason looked at him. 'Last night?'

'I reacted badly. Toys, pram moment.'

Jason leant against the wall, with hands in his pockets. 'Did you tell her you never want to see her again? Or did you just run off? Yes, of course you did. It's what you always do.'

'Okay, cut the concerned friend bit. We have a launch to prepare for. Japan might be her dream, but cooking good food is mine.'

'You're two chips off the same block. You both know exactly what you want from life and are prepared to chase it down.'

'Right.' Adam looked at Jason, sensing a but.'

'But is cooking really your dream? Or is it to cook amazing dishes for people who will taste your food and love every mouthful? For people who appreciate …'

'Enough. Get on with those bloody canapés or get lost.' Adam pushed through the swing doors and left the kitchen before he said something he'd later regret. He could bet his last penny right now Jason would be making a face behind his back, but he wasn't going to give him the satisfaction of turning back and letting him try to make him laugh.

The restaurant looked amazing. Tables had been laid with pristine white tablecloths, printed with the restaurant's new logo. Everything had been arranged with military precision. Place cards in beautiful italic lettering were positioned with a bird of paradise serviette arrangement on each charger plate and the blades of all knives pointed inwards. Three glasses were lined up by each place. The evening's menu and wine list lay on each side plate.

Everything was perfect. Every bit as good as Ruby had said it would be. Adam wished she could see it.

Grey and white balloons decorated the entrance and most of the street. Each printed with the restaurant's new name.

Students' artwork and photographic images hung from the walls. On tables next to the cloakroom were goodie bags containing a press release, prices for the artwork, sample menus, a voucher for a free main course and some artisan chocolates. They were to be handed to everyone as they left.

There were waiting staff everywhere, all dressed in black and white, ready to start their front of house duties.

In a corner furthest from the kitchen, Eamon and his cameraman attended to last-minute details on two tables on which someone had placed signs which read "Reserved for *Another Chance on Love*". Adam guessed there was a hidden microphone in the elaborate flower arrangements.

'Are the TV company happy?' he asked one of the waitresses.

'He'—the woman gestured towards Eamon—'said everything was perfect.'

'Good.'

Through the small window in the swing door, Adam saw Jason's hands involved in the intricate work of arranging smoked salmon cups and onion bread sticks. They were strong hands, yet he worked with a lightness of touch. Something Jason said earlier about knowing what he wanted from life and being prepared to chase it down resonated.

Each canapé was perfectly formed and arranged. Everything was prepared. In an hour's time, the restaurant would be full. The waiters would look after the guests, Jason and the others would keep the food flowing. The bar staff knew what they were doing wine-wise.

'Adam,' a voice from behind him said. He stopped. *Ruby?* He turned to find Lily and Jeffrey standing there. Lily was looking nervous in a blonde wig and turquoise layered dress studded with rhinestones.

'Wow,' he said.

'Will I do?' she asked, her eyes wide. She looked every bit as vulnerable as Ruby did when she was out of her depth. Adam ached from his head to his feet.

'You look amazing. Let me show you to your table then I can give you a hand setting up.' He had added Lily and Jeffrey to Belinda and Ben's table. It had been his only contribution to the seating arrangements. They would have to entertain the head of the local businesswomen's network and her partner, but he thought the table would prefer that to the mayoress and her deputy whom he had squeezed in on an alternative table. The place names had been swapped and the table plans changed to reflect the move. No one, apart from Ruby, would be any the wiser and she wasn't there to object. His ache deepened.

'It's okay.' Lily smiled. 'It's just me and my guitar and you must have lots to do.'

Chapter Forty-One

Ruby looked through the window of TOTU's to find it already a hive of activity. She could have arrived earlier, but after the day she'd had, she took a hot bath, and applied full make-up. She felt almost human and every bit the professional event manager she was supposed to be.

Flat 3 had been more than happy to take Brutus for a couple of hours, not that she planned on being away long, but she should show her face at the launch and make sure everything was going well.

'Don't you worry about us,' the woman had said and waved Brutus' paw at Ruby as she walked away. If Border Terriers could frown, Brutus frowned.

'Right I can do this,' Ruby told herself firmly as she opened the restaurant door to see a woman in a blonde wig belting out, "That Don't Impress Me Much."

She had a nice voice.

Ruby took a second look. *No way. No bloody way.* 'Mum?'

'Hi gorgeous.' Jason appeared by her side. 'You came.' There was something about his expression that suggested he was surprised to see her.

She dropped a kiss on his cheek. 'Of course I did. I am the event planner.' She swerved past a waitress who was so busy concentrating on a round tray with tightly packed glasses that she appeared to have little spatial awareness.

Ruby touched the girl's arm. 'When the glasses are full, no more than six on a tray.' She smiled.

The girl blushed and nodded. Jason and Ruby watched as she approached a table. Ruby moved in before the girl had to make a decision about the tray and handed out the glasses, to the girl's obvious relief. The girl scuttled back to the bar, leaving Ruby to make small talk with some of the guests about the weather and the new look restaurant.

As soon as she could, Ruby returned to Jason. 'Where's the string quartet?' she asked.

'Double-booked,' Jason said. 'But Lily's really good.' He and the guests clapped enthusiastically as Lily finished her song and someone walked across and asked her to play a request.'

Lily nodded and then pushed back her hair and played a few chords on her guitar. The guest smiled and returned to her table behind ... Jeffrey?

Jeffrey waved at Ruby and she waved back. 'What's he doing on the mayoress's table?' she hissed at Jason.

'The mayoress has been moved.' Jason turned her around so she could see the woman deep in conversation with the bank manager's wife. You're looking good by the way.'

She snorted. Trousers, boots, and a loose white shirt wasn't what she thought she'd be wearing.

Her dress had been hanging on the wardrobe door that morning. She hadn't put it away and she hadn't made the bed. And now it was missing. Someone had taken it. And she would bet her last dollar it was the same person who'd kidnapped Brutus earlier.

'Don't change the subject. Why wasn't I consulted?'

'Your phone's broken and ...'

'How do you know my phone's broken?' she asked and then seeing Jason's expression she tilted her head to give him her best tell me or be tortured look. The one historically reserved for her brother.

'Adam found it.'

'And the string quartet weren't double-booked when I spoke to them at the beginning of the week,' Ruby said.

'Okay, okay. He cancelled them. He went to see your mum

a couple of days ago and asked her if she would like to do a regular slot at TOTU and whether she'd sing for the launch.'

No wonder Belinda said she liked him. She watched her mother sing the next number. She certainly had a presence and held the audience in the palm of her hand. Okay, they were invited guests and weren't paying, but when she started singing, the level of talking dropped and they all turned to watch her. She sang with her eyes shut, but she looked relaxed and happy. When a couple joined in with the chorus, she smiled at them and encouraged anyone old enough to know the words to do the same. Everybody did.

'Where's Adam? Is he okay?' Ruby asked as she looked towards the kitchen.

'He's fine.' Jason smiled. 'I'll tell him you're here. He's a tad busy right now and you know how temperamental these top chefs can be.' He disappeared through the swing doors, into the kitchen. Ruby half expected Adam to come straight out, at least look through the window and acknowledge her. He didn't. Sod him. Maybe she had been too hasty turning down the Japanese prize-giving. No maybe about it. It was okay making a heart rather than a head decision, but where had that grand gesture got her?

Inspector Lenham and her sergeant sat at one of the front tables. Ruby checked they had drinks and canapés. She was tempted to mention another dress had gone missing, a dog had been kidnapped and she'd been locked in a room, but the woman looked relaxed and off duty. She'd go into the station tomorrow and talk to them there, as soon as she knew Malik was safely home in Egypt and hadn't become an illegal overstayer.

The canapés were going down a storm. The editor from the local paper wanted more and Ruby popped into the kitchen, returning with another small plate. Adam wasn't anywhere to be seen. 'Popped home to get changed,' Jason said, checking the plate of food before allowing it out of the kitchen.

'That's your lot,' Ruby said, putting the plate down in front of the journalist. 'Only because I'd hate for you to spoil your appetite.' She made sure he had a press pack.

Another Chance on Love participants sat at the two reserved tables. They looked relatively normal. One couple was completely wrapped up in each other and talking animatedly, while another pair pointedly ignored each other. There were just two empty seats – and no sign of Emily or Daniel. They should be here by now. Ruby sighed. *Of course, she wasn't going to come.* She was worrying about nothing. *The woman wouldn't have the nerve to turn up, not after today.*

'Everything all right?' she asked the cameraman, who nodded enthusiastically and gave her a thumbs up.

Belinda and Ben arrived as Lily sang "On a Bus to St. Cloud". Belinda looked blooming. She kissed Ruby and fiddled with a bit of Ruby's hair, positioning it more pleasingly behind her ear. 'The restaurant colours work so well,' she said, enthusiastically as she hopped from one foot to the other.

'Are you okay?' Ruby asked. 'Do you need to sit down?'

Belinda bloomed some more into a beautiful shade of red. 'Ben said I shouldn't ask, only I wondered if I could put hair vouchers in the goodie bags,' she said. Then added that she wished she hadn't said anything.

'Of course.' Ruby laughed, grateful that was all she wanted.

'Weren't you going to wear a dress tonight?' Belinda said. 'I was dying to see it. It sounded amazing. Didn't it fit?'

'Couldn't find it.' Ruby poured Belinda a glass of raspberry lemonade.

'What do you mean?

'Tell you tomorrow,' she said, checking to make sure everyone had everything they needed. She gave Belinda's arm a squeeze before popping into the yard to catch her breath.

She leant against the wall and a tear escaped down her cheek.

Jason appeared and produced a small glass containing something thick and with an orange look about it. 'Drink this.'

She sipped. It was sweet and warming, with a hint of citrus. She closed her eyes and savoured the taste. When she opened them again, Clive was standing in front of her alongside a smaller man Ruby didn't recognise. Both were dressed in chef whites. Clive congratulated Ruby on all the organisation. He bear-hugged Jason by lifting him about twelve inches off the floor.

'I want to hear all about France,' he said.

'We'll have a proper talk later,' Jason squeaked as soon as he'd caught his breath and got his feet back on the floor.

'I don't think you've met Xavier,' Jason said to Ruby.

'*Enchanté, mademoiselle*,' the smaller man said as he took her hand, kissed it and bowed, all in one elegant move.

'Oh my God, he came?' Ruby said.

'Cracking idea. Well done. He flew in this morning with me,' Jason whispered. 'Stayed well out of the way until Adam had picked me up. Clive collected him as soon as the coast was clear. I tell you if ever I decide not to be a chef, I'm going to join MI5. The level of conspiracy involved in getting tonight sorted has me thinking I should have a career as a spook.' He grinned.

'Adam must be thrilled,' Ruby said. 'He didn't think for one minute you'd be able to come.'

'His menu *m'a intrigué*.' Xavier laughed. 'I hear much about it and now I taste it.'

'And what do you think?'

'It is magnificent.' He kissed the tips of his own fingers and patted Ruby on the back. 'And as soon as I see him, I will tell him.'

'You haven't seen him? Where is he?' Ruby spun around to face Jason, who appeared to be rounding up the others and heading them back to the kitchen. 'Jason, what's going on?'

'We need to get going with the starters,' Jason said, over his shoulder. 'Catch you later. After your set.'

'My set?' Ruby frowned. 'Jason …'

'Can you murder "Bat Out of Hell" while the main course is served, and your mother takes a well-earned break?' Jason hummed the opening bars as he held the kitchen doors open for the other two.

Adam sailed past Newbury. His satnav said he was two hours from his destination. He hoped it was a three-course meal and they'd serve it before the presentation. That way there was a reasonable chance he would get there before Ruby had to set off back home. He'd thrown a jacket and tie into the car. How should one dress for a Japanese holiday presentation dinner? He was bound to look out of place, although he couldn't for one minute imagine Malik would be kitted out in a black-tie outfit.

"Unknown caller", his phone warned. Somehow it sounded more threatening coming over the hands-free. He was going to ditch his number tomorrow, so he had nothing to lose by telling Emily where to get off. And according to his satnav he was going to be in the car a while. He could pass time and take the edge off his tension by telling her to go and boil her head.

'What do you want?' he snapped.

'Mr Adam.'

'Not who …' Hang on. The voice at the other end of the phone was male, one he recognised and definitely not Emily.

'Malik? Is that you?'

'Yes, Mr Adam.'

'Are you okay?'

'Very okay thank you. I have a plane at 10.30. Jamila is so happy. She will meet me at Cairo airport.'

Ahead of him, Adam could see brake lights. 'Ruby is not with you?'

'No. She couldn't stay. Traffic was bad and she had to get back for your party.'

'She's not gone to London?'

'Why would she go to London?' Malik asked, cautiously. 'Your party is in Redford.'

'I thought she'd gone to collect the Japanese holiday prize.'

'She couldn't. She turn that down,' Malik said. 'Miss Ruby said it was a heart decision, but you couldn't win happiness.'

'You mean hard decision.'

'No, she said her heart tells her she would be happier with you. She will go to Japan one day, but not on teabags. You will take her perhaps.'

The significance of Malik's words hit him so forcibly that Adam felt his eyes water. 'You rang earlier?' he said, his voice gruff with emotion.

'Miss Ruby lost her phone. I tell you she would be late. And now you tell her about plane and Jamila.'

'What about this afternoon? Did you ring me then?'

'To tell you Fuck-off Emily had shut dog and Ruby in shop. You were busy and no answer, so I called my cousin.'

'I met your cousins. You have a lot.'

'Hosni has seven wives and many sons.'

'Thank you,' Adam said, weakly, 'for rescuing her. I am glad you were there.'

'Ruby is good friend and kind person. I like her and I like that you like her too.'

I like that I like her too. Several cars in front of Adam

appeared to have come to a complete standstill despite the motorway warning sign optimistically telling drivers to stick to 40. *Shit*. According to the overhead sign, it was going to take twenty minutes to get to the next junction.

'You both come to my wedding and you be best man,' Malik said.

'What?' Adam swerved between lorries back into the slow lane. Usually with his luck, whichever lane he chose would go slower than the others, but today that seemed to be moving fastest.

'It's okay, I teach you to dance.'

'You haven't seen me in Zumba classes.' He undercut another couple of cars and pulled as close to the truck in front as he dared in case someone was tempted to squeeze into the space between them.

'Miss Ruby say your feet don't know right from left.'

'She did, did she?' Adam smiled. Fine talk from someone who couldn't tell her merengue from her reggaeton pump. When the teacher had said "Show me your attitude, I know you've got it in you", it was unlikely she meant take out the row behind you. He smiled at the thought and felt a warmth sweep through him. The ache in his chest lifted. 'Aren't you being a bit premature though? You can't be sure Jamila will say yes or that her father will let her marry you. In England, we have to ask the father's permission before we can make it public knowledge.'

'Ruby's father has been gone a long time.' Malik said. 'You have to ask her mother?'

Adam's phone pinged as a WhatsApp message from Jason flashed up on his screen. He squinted at the two words, "She's here" and smiled.

Chapter Forty-Two

'Have you got a minute?' the police inspector asked as Ruby passed her table.

'Is something wrong? Can I get you anything?'

Inspector Lenham shook her head. 'Everything's fine. More than fine,' she said smiling. 'We're being really spoilt. I understand that Emily Watkins is coming tonight and just wanted to check you're all right?'

The woman's words sounded genuine. The way her forehead creased with concern made Ruby stop.

'I've just spoken to the TV producer. I know you were involved in the trouble this afternoon at Templeton.'

'I guess you want to interview me about the break-in.' *It would do her good to get it off her chest.* 'Am I in trouble?'

'I know nothing about a break-in, so no, not as far as I know.' It could be a clever ploy, but the inspector seemed momentarily to look confused. Then she squeezed her hand. 'But we really do need to talk to both you and Adam.'

Ruby wanted to tell the truth, but if she coughed now, they still had time to get to the airport and arrest Malik, if he hadn't managed to get a seat on the Egyptair flight. 'Could we do it tomorrow?'

The inspector nodded as Lily started a new song and the door opened. Emily, in a black dress, walked in on Daniel's arm. Not any black dress. Ruby's dress.

'No bloody way.' Ruby's mouth dropped open. She clamped it shut, hoping the camera wasn't pointing in her direction. 'That's my dress. She's gone too far this time.'

The inspector stood up.

Two older waiters arrived by Emily's side in less time than

it would have taken Superman to analyse and sort a world-threatening situation.

'This way, madam,' they said and steered her between the tables.

Emily spotted Belinda and Ben and tried to make a detour, but her bouncers weren't having it.

Don't make a scene, Ruby's inner voice screamed out. She hoped it was inner and she hadn't said anything aloud. A number of people were staring at her.

'She's got a nerve,' Inspector Lenham said.

'Tell me about it. That's my dress.'

'I thought your dress was green?'

'Another one. She stole it when she kidnapped my dog, well Adam's dog. We haven't ironed out the custody arrangement thingy yet.'

'That's why you were at April Flowers in Templeton?'

Ruby nodded. 'I didn't break into the shop to get the dress. I only did that to get Brutus back.'

'You broke in? You didn't set the alarm off.'

'It wasn't on. I suppose I should've realised that meant someone must be in the shop.'

'Emily? Are you sure?'

'Quite sure. She locked me in the storeroom and talked to me through the door.'

'So how did you get out? On second thoughts don't tell me. I'm not on duty tonight.'

Ruby sighed. 'I will come and hand myself in tomorrow and tell you everything, I promise.'

The inspector nodded. 'I understand Emily has been invited tonight.'

'She was part of the deal, in exchange for Galaxy TV filming Adam's launch.'

'Yes, which is why they're here.' The inspector pointed towards some of the waiters. 'Undercover police,' she said, under her breath. 'They'll move in, at the first sign of trouble.'

The woman had a kind face, but there was an edge to her voice. It was probably a warning not to take Emily out with a steak knife.

'I ought to say hello.' Ruby picked up a bottle of fizzy water. She wove her way around the room, smiling and joking with other guests until she got to the television table.

'I'll take care of this table,' she said to a waitress who peered over the tray of champagne glasses at the new arrivals. 'Emily and Daniel, so lovely of you both to come.'

The relief she'd felt earlier at Emily's no-show exploded. And the professionalism she'd maintained so far was in danger of shattering too. The only saving grace was that Emily didn't look happy either. Her right eye and bottom lip twitched. Not a good look for a television star. Actually, not a good look for anybody.

'What are you doing here?' Emily growled.

'Where else would I be?' Ruby's face ached from the smile she'd forced her face to wear. She held up the bottle. 'I guess you'd both prefer water to champagne. Fizzy or still?'

'No,' Emily and Daniel said together.

'Surely, in your condition, water would be best?' Ruby continued to smile as she filled Emily's glass. 'Please don't worry about the food. I've asked Adam to make sure none of the sauces contain raw egg or soft cheese. Anything else I need to be aware of? Obviously, I've never been in your condition, so you'll have to excuse my ignorance.' She went to pour some water for Daniel, but he put his hand over the top of his glass.

'I thought champagne was on offer.'

Emily stood up, leant across the table and glared at Ruby. 'You shouldn't be here.'

'Why's that?' Ruby said and stared straight back at her. 'Where should I be?' *Stay professional.* 'Nice dress by the way.' She wanted to lean on the table, her legs trembled, her stomach fluttered with fear. 'Adam is right though, black can be such a draining colour. Thank goodness I decided against it. Some people can wear it and some people should stick to floral patterns. Don't you agree, Daniel?'

Do not let her upset you.

'Oh and Brutus is safe, thank you for asking,' Ruby said. 'Sorry about the mess in your storeroom. He couldn't help it. He was upset. Not the bravest bunny in the world.'

They continued to eye each other up. Neither moved. They were being filmed. Ruby was acutely aware of the camera at her shoulder and that Eamon Dixon was nowhere to be seen. Great.

'Where is your Adam tonight?' Emily sneered. 'Has he left you or has he been deported?'

Don't react.

Don't say anything to fan the flames.

Be charming.

Keep smiling … Oh damn it. 'My Adam is in the kitchen, cooking tonight's meal,' Ruby said, aware of her heart beating a tattoo in her chest as she fought to stay calm.

'Actually, he's not.'

Ruby felt Adam's breath against her neck as he slipped an arm around her waist.

'Hello Emily.'

The closeness of his body comforted her. If they hadn't been standing in front of a hundred people, she'd have snogged him. He'd left the sanctuary of his kitchen to save her. At that moment she couldn't love anyone more.

'Are you all right?'

Ruby checked to make sure he was talking to her before she made a complete fool of herself. The concern etched on his face made her want to kiss his worry lines away. 'Uh-huh,' she murmured, overcome with emotion.

'I'm fine thank you.' Emily straightened, fluttered her eyelashes and pouted.

'Oh please,' Ruby groaned.

'Good.' Adam flashed Emily a tight smile. It stretched across his lips but didn't meet his eyes. 'And let me tell you, I'm so pleased you've found Daniel and love too. I realised what a difference love could make when this woman entered my life. I was in a bad place at the time, but she gave me a reason to be happy, showed me how to laugh again and reminded me life was out there to be lived.'

Ruby's eyes stung with tears. Her mouth was dry.

'Thanks to you, Emily, I've spent three years doing my best to withdraw completely from everything because I'm not great at dealing with conflict and couldn't cope with my emotions. Then she walked into my life and I realised emotions are good and I don't want to live without them, or her. Ever. I've always run away from problems, but with her by my side, I can face anything. I'd never have had the confidence to think about any of this without her support.'

A tear trickled down Ruby's cheek and she turned to look at him. 'I didn't know you were here,' she murmured then lifted her face and kissed him. His arms tightened round her waist and he kissed her back. It felt good, really good. She felt warm and safe in his arms and didn't care they were stood in the middle of a restaurant full of diners who were probably all watching.

Behind her she heard a chair being scraped back, then another and another. Someone started clapping. The whole restaurant was on their feet and clapping. She looked at Adam and smiled.

'I thought you were in danger earlier, I was so worried,' he said.

'Oh please, pass me a bucket,' Daniel said.

'Everything's okay.' Ruby held a finger against Adam's lips. 'Malik and his cousin rescued me.'

'He told me.' Adam laughed.

'You spoke to him?'

'He's got a flight. Jamila's going to meet him at the airport and he wants us to go to his wedding. I'm going to be his best man and he's promised to teach me to dance properly.' He stroked her face and brushed a tear away with his thumb. 'What's wrong?'

Ruby shook her head, too choked up to speak.

'Tell me you're not about to sing.'

'No.'

Adam turned to Emily and Daniel. 'We hope you can find a way to be as happy as we are but once tonight's over, could you leave us alone forever?'

'Nice speech.' Daniel clapped his hands together slowly. 'You're being a bit premature though Bryan. I hardly know this woman. We haven't even got around to talking about another date.' He said it in a sort of "wink wink say no more, all blokes together" way. It might have been funny if he was in the pub but made Ruby shudder. He clicked his fingers at one of the waiters. 'Can we get some champagne on this table?'

'Don't be ridiculous.' Emily grabbed Daniel's arm in a vice-like grip that made him wince. She smiled at the camera. 'We're in love. We were three years ago and if anything this time round it's stronger. 'What is it they say about absence making the heart grow fonder? I'd never have looked at you, if Daniel hadn't been held up,' she added, pointing at Adam.

'What does a bloke have to do to get a drink round here?' Daniel said.

'Allow me,' Ruby said, when it looked like he might end up wearing the waiter's tray of drinks. She set a glass in front of him.

'Cheers.' He tasted it and then took another swig, without taking his eyes off Ruby. 'What did you mean – no raw eggs or cream cheese?' He turned to Emily. 'Don't tell me you are some weird kind of vegetarian, doll.'

Emily turned an angry shade of red that managed to clash with the restaurant's logo, but annoyingly set off the dress rather well.

'She must be pregnant,' one half of another couple whispered.

'No way,' Daniel said, looking Emily up and down, in a not very attractive way. 'You can't be. And if you are, it's not mine. I took precautions.'

'Shut up,' Emily hissed and puffed up her chest. 'It's time we were going.'

Ruby hoped she wasn't going to do an incredible hulk impression. That was her dress, the one she should be wearing, and she wanted it back in one piece.

'We haven't had our meal!' Daniel said as Emily pushed back her chair and marched across the restaurant.

'Go after her,' Ruby said as Emily slammed the door.

'I was promised a meal.' Daniel necked the rest of his champagne. 'Look here …' He pointed a finger at Ruby, as he had so often before. Any minute, a torrent of insults would spill out of his mouth and he'd probably break something. She felt as if she'd run a marathon, her heart beat so fast, but her legs didn't move.

Inspector Lenham appeared by her arm. 'Everything okay here?'

Ruby inhaled. 'More than okay. Daniel is leaving.'

At first, he looked as if he might argue, but then pushed back his chair and got up. The waiter he'd insulted earlier held the door open while Lily sang "Bye Bye Blackbird" with feeling.

'I've asked one of my officers to pull her in,' Inspector

Lenham said as they watched the door close. 'I was going to leave it until tomorrow, but I wouldn't like to say how she's going to react.'

'Don't let her damage that dress,' Ruby said. 'I will get them back won't I?'

'We have to hold on to them for the time being. At least until a decision is taken as to whether to prosecute or not. They are evidence, but I'll do my best.' Inspector Lenham smiled. 'Enjoy the rest of your evening. I intend to. But you both need to come to the station tomorrow to give statements.'

'We'll be there,' Adam said.

One of the older waiters came forward. 'And I will be asking you a few questions about Brutus.'

'You will?' Ruby said.

'Sorry, he's newly promoted,' the inspector whispered. 'Just arrived from London, eager to make his mark.'

'Is he here tonight?'

'Brutus? No.'

'Why would that be, madam?' The faint inflection at the end of his question added a sense of menace to his words. If they'd been alone, Ruby would have expected him to continue with the "and anything you say" caution she'd heard them say so many times on police television programmes. She guessed it took a great deal of restraint for him not to.

'Health and Safety regulations,' she said, cautiously. The inspector next to her smothered her face with a napkin and her shoulders were shaking. Clearly she was doing her damnedest to stifle a giggle.

'So, where is he?'

'Number 3 is looking after him.'

'Bring him tomorrow,' the waiter said.

'Who – number 3?'

'No madam. Brutus.'

'What's he done this time?' Adam asked, his lips curved in a smile.

'We don't need to talk about this now,' the waiter said, touching the side of his nose. 'Let's just say there are some questions I'd like him to answer.'

'Not much point, unless they or you can teach him to speak, and frankly I imagine these two have better things to do tonight.' Inspector Lenham laughed. She held a hand up when it looked like the man might argue. 'Brutus is a dog.'

Chapter Forty-Three

Eamon smiled at his happy book. It bulged in comparison to his sad one. It had been sometime since he'd written anything in that. His counsellor should be impressed. Hopefully, this afternoon, she would tell him he could cancel the rest of their appointments. Clearly, he didn't need her any more. He was doing okay on his own.

For the first time since the director general's arrival at the company, he had walked down the corridor to see Eamon. His visit had been unexpected so when the door flew open, revealing the big man himself, Eamon had jumped and promptly swept his books into the top drawer of his desk. The DG planted himself in the chair opposite.

'Okay, the networks have agreed an hour-long slot for the series finale. Are you sure you have enough to fill it?'

Eamon sat back in his chair and smiled. 'More than enough.'

'I understand the police have asked to see our footage.' The director general stared at him as he rubbed his chin. 'Anything likely to cause us any problems?'

'No, we've co-operated with their enquiries and made arrangements for them to come in and view it in the screening room. The cameraman will copy anything they need to take away. The legal team said the worst they can do is ask us to blur a few faces, that sort of thing, but they don't envisage there should be any problem showing it.'

'What about this Emily? She apologised for the remarks she made last time?'

'In a manner of speaking.'

'What do you mean?'

'I'm no psychologist ...'

'No, you're not Dixon. I understand the researchers had concerns about her relationship with the chef and you shrugged off their worries as a "joke that had gone too far".'

'All's well that ends well.'

'Says whom?'

'The chef has found love.' In Eamon's top drawer, his sad book sat, taunting him. 'Emily announced on camera that Danny boy is, and always was, her Mr Right. Her first choice three years ago and the chef never quite matched up. I can show you the footage.'

The director general waved a hand dismissively. 'Anything else I should know?'

Eamon pursed his lips and pretended to be considering the statement. 'You remember the Scottish couple,' he said at last. 'They announced their engagement. We're going to see what we can do with some careful editing. It got a bit lost by Emily's pregnancy announcement.'

The director general's eyes widened.

'It's okay, she's not. Just another lie she told. But the Scottish couple have asked us to film the wedding. It's going to be set in a castle. Lots of kilts. Probably June next year. I'm thinking of running the wedding as a prequel to the next series.'

'You are?'

'Uh-huh and there's a couple of other ideas I'd like to run past you when we've both got more time. Only ...' Eamon shuffled some unimportant papers and made a great show of checking his watch. He had a three o'clock appointment with his counsellor he had no intention of missing.

As mornings went, Ruby's had been productive. A conversation with the editor of the local paper had gone well, and he'd said barring life-changing catastrophes, the restaurant launch would feature prominently in this week's edition. She spoke to Eamon who confirmed he had everything he needed for a fantastic finale. 'I don't like to blow my own trumpet,' he said laughing and then had proceeded to do exactly that for the next ten minutes in-between talking about the next series of *Taking a Chance on Love* and the Scottish wedding and his idea for a series about rogue builders. 'Your kitchen fitter is already keen,' he said. 'I'm looking at putting together a team to find a run-down property that they then have to renovate and sell. If they make a profit, that gets split between them instead of paying a fee. If they make a loss, they get nothing. Did you get your money back by the way?'

'Half of it and I'll deduct the cost of the units the kitchen company sent, but not a penny more. I'm keeping his toolbox hostage until the balance arrives,' Ruby said, booting up her computer while Eamon ran through the potential awards, he considered he was on track to be nominated for.

'Let me know, if he doesn't cough up the balance,' he said. 'I can always threaten not to use him.'

Out of habit Ruby entered an ultimate hiking competition, another for a designer organiser, a bucket of carp food, a kettle, fifty-two bars of soap, a leather handbag, and a smartphone.

She'd been about to submit an entry for a box of lemon and goat's cheese flavoured chocolate when it occurred to her the reason for making the competition resolution in the first place had been to turn her life around and she'd done that.

She was her own boss, had a dream job, a state-of-the-art kitchen, a new boyfriend and a dog. She hated goat's cheese and already had a hot water tap; she didn't need a kettle or a thousand emails telling her how much it would cost to buy one if she didn't win. She'd won a trip to Japan and turned it down. She smiled and cuddled herself. A good call. Adam had a great launch night and afterwards had been

338

pretty special too. Life had definitely got more interesting. Happiness wasn't something you could buy or win and her happy-ever-after felt like it had already started even without a car or expensive handbag. The Japanese holiday had been a dream since childhood. Adam had said last night he would take her to Japan once TOTU was up and running. They might not have the luxury of an all-expenses paid trip, but they'd be able to explore the country together.

Two new emails popped into her inbox. Her finger was poised over the delete key when she noticed one was from a former client, a local funeral director. *Subject: "Team-building day"*. She read through his ideas and sighed. It was going to be hard work getting that one to fly, but then she saw the fee he was offering. 'Lesson one of event management,' she told Brutus. 'If the client wants it and they can afford to pay, they get it. And it's not the most unusual request I've ever had to deal with. I'll give it some thought and reply later.'

The oven buzzed, so she switched off the computer. The penultimate batch of cupcakes had finished cooking. Every inch of her new kitchen working surface was covered with cupcakes, cooling at various temperatures. Two were already eaten; three hundred and forty-six to decorate. She heard a key turn in the lock and the front door open. She smiled.

Malik's cousin had changed the locks; there was only one other person who had a key.

'What on earth?' Adam asked, poking his head around the kitchen door. He looked at the worktops, she liked to think in awe but probably surprise. She had another box of twelve to bake today, unless she treated the best before date on the packets as an idea rather than a given.

'I'm baking. I thought we could take the cakes down to the police station when we go to say "Thank you". Don't just stand there, they need icing.'

'You appear to be wearing most of the ingredients.' His

lips curved up into a smile. 'Interesting look.' He made the whole room light up. His smile was contagious. 'But you are still gorgeous.' He crossed the small room and folded her into his arms. 'Did I tell you I fell in love with you the moment I first saw you.' He kissed her forehead. 'Even when I thought you had an alcohol problem. I loved you even when I thought you were dating your half-witted kitchen fitter.'

'Not half-witted.' Ruby did her best to look offended. 'No-witted. Completely wit-free.' She wrapped her arms around his neck and smiled up at him. 'Sorry, carry on.'

'I loved you,' Adam said, 'when I thought you were Emily's friend. I still love you, even though you seem hell-bent on killing most of Redford police force with a serious sugar overdose and worse ...' He looked over at the box she'd put the icing sachets in. 'You expect me to help? Are you for real?'

Ruby laughed as Nickelback started singing.

'Ruby Brooks, mass murderer,' she said accepting the call on her phone. 'And who would you like my help killing today? Hello ... Lily ... No, no one's dead ... It was a joke ... Really, it's okay ... No, mother, I haven't touched Ben's action man.'

Thank You

Thank you, dear reader, for choosing *Recipe for Mr Right*. You have no idea how excited I am to be sharing this story with you. I hope you enjoy reading this as much as I enjoyed writing it.

While the town of Redford and all the characters are entirely fictional, ten competitions a day and problems with a kitchen weren't entirely made up!

If you've enjoyed *Recipe for Mr Right* please leave a review for the book on Goodreads or the retail site where you bought the book. You can also follow me on Twitter for news on my next books (details of my Twitter account can be found on the next page). Looking forward to hearing from you.

Anni x

About the Author

Anni lives in Wiltshire with her husband, her sister, two dogs, a cat and a grey speckled hen. She has had a number of short stories published in various magazines and her work also appears in a number of anthologies.

She has wanted to write for as long as she can remember. As a child, she produced reams of stories. Thankfully most of them have been lost over the years, although the 'Attack of the Killer Tomatoes' did resurface recently! And when not writing, she reads voraciously.

Work might have got in the way for a while, but writing was a love that never died and she loves it as much now as she did back then.

These days, she writes modern day romances with – spoiler alert – a happy ending and a healthy dollop of humour thrown in. Away from writing, Anni can usually be found behind a camera, walking her dogs, enjoying her husband's curries or one of her sister's bakery treats.

For more information on Anni visit:
Twitter: @AnniRoseAuthor
Facebook: www.facebook.com/anniroseauthor
Website: www.anniroseauthor.co.uk

More Choc Lit

From Anni Rose

Recipe for Mr Perfect

How do you know if you've found Mr Perfect or Mr Perfectly Useless?

Jess Willersey realised things with Martin weren't perfect, but it's still a shock when he leaves. Is she destined to a singleton lifestyle with only her cat for company, or could a certain hat-astrophic encounter with a handsome stranger at a rather unusual wedding signal a turning point?

At the same time, Jess's best friends and work colleagues, Maggie and Sarah, are going through their own personal disasters – from shocking family revelations to dodgy dating app-related drama.

To top it all off, it seems that the handsome stranger won't remain a stranger – and when Neil Jackson turns up at the friends' offices with yet another bombshell, how long will he stay 'Mr Perfect' in Jess's eyes?

Visit www.choc-lit.com for details.

More from Choc Lit

Why not try something else from the Choc Lit selection?

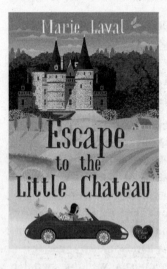

Escape to the Little Chateau
Marie Laval

Will Amy's dreams of a Provençal escape come true?

There are many reasons Amy Carter is determined to make Bellefontaine, her farmhouse hotel in the French countryside, a success. Of course, there's the time and money she's put in to making it beautiful, but she also has something to prove – particularly to people like Fabien Coste.

Fabien is the owner of the nearby château, and he might just be the most arrogant, patronising man Amy has ever met … unfortunately, he's also the most handsome.

But as rumours circulate in the local community and secrets about the old farmhouse begin to reveal themselves, Amy quickly sees the less idyllic side of life at Bellefontaine. Could Fabien be the man to help prevent her Provençal dream from turning into a nightmare?

Visit www.choc-lit.com for details.

Lily's Secret
Kirsty Ferry

Book 2 in the Cornish Secrets series

'There's nothing logical about Pencradoc!'

Aspiring actress Cordelia Beaumont is fed up of spending summer in the city. So, when the opportunity presents itself, she jumps straight on a train to pay a visit to Pencradoc – the beautiful Cornish estate where her friend Merryn works.

But far from the relaxing break Cordy imagined, she soon finds herself immersed in the glamorous yet mysterious world of Victorian theatre sensation, Lily Valentine. Lily was once a guest at Pencradoc and, with the help of visiting artist Matt Harker, Cordy comes to discover that the actress left far more than memories at the old house. She also left a scandalous secret …

Visit www.choc-lit.com for details.

Introducing Choc Lit

We're an independent publisher creating
a delicious selection of fiction.
Where heroes are like chocolate – irresistible!
Quality stories with a romance at the heart.

See our selection here:
www.choc-lit.com

We'd love to hear how you enjoyed *Recipe for Mr Right*.
Please visit **www.choc-lit.com** and give your feedback
or leave a review where you purchased this novel.

Choc Lit novels are selected by genuine readers like yourself.
We only publish stories our Choc Lit Tasting Panel want to
see in print. Our reviews and awards speak for themselves.

Could you be a Star Selector and join our Tasting Panel?
Would you like to play a role in choosing which novels
we decide to publish? Do you enjoy reading women's
fiction? Then you could be perfect for our Tasting Panel.

Visit here for more details…
www.choc-lit.com/join-the-choc-lit-tasting-panel

Keep in touch:
Sign up for our monthly newsletter Spread for all the latest
news and offers: www.spread.choc-lit.com. Follow us
on Twitter: @ChocLituk and Facebook: Choc Lit.

Where heroes are like chocolate – irresistible!